Amazing Grace

Clare DOWLING

POOLBEG

Published 2003
by Poolbeg Press Ltd
123 Grange Hill, Baldoyle
Dublin 13, Ireland
E-mail: poolbeg@poolbeg.com

A catalogue record for this book is available from
the British Library.

ISBN 1-84223-121-9

Typeset by Magpie Designs in Palatino 11.5/15.8
Printed by Creative Print and Design (Wales)

www.poolbeg.com

About the Author

Clare Dowling began her
writing career as a playwright with the
independent theatre company, Glasshouse
Productions, of which she was a founder member.
She has written short films, children's books,
drama for teenagers and is currently a
scriptwriter with RTE's *Fair City*.
She lives in Dublin.

ACKNOWLEDGEMENTS

Thanks to:

All at Poolbeg, especially Paula Campbell, Sarah
Conroy and Brona Looby.

Gaye Shortland for her continued editorial guidance,
and for working overtime.

Clare Foss of Headline UK for all her editorial input,
and to Sherise Hobbs.

Darley Anderson, my agent, and Elizabeth, Julia and all
at the agency.

Friends and fellow-writers Ho Wei Sim, Sian Quill,
Caroline Williams, Marie Therese Duggan, Bernie
Downes and Brian Gallagher.

All the wonderful Irish girls: Sarah Webb, Tina Reilly,
Marisa Mackle, Cauvery Madhaven, Martina Devlin,
Jacinta McDevitt, Dawn Cairns, Catherine Dunne, Anne
Marie Forrester, Mary Ryan and others whom I have
yet to meet over a Chinese takeaway.

Margaret, for always pitching in and giving a hand
whenever deadlines loom.

My family in Kilkenny, as always.

Stewart for the ice pops and unwavering support, and
Sean for the reality checks.

And a special thanks to Ella, who arrived in the middle
of this book. An inspiration!

FOR ELLA

ONE

It was a warm bright morning at the end of July when Grace Tynan consulted her map of County Meath. Its shape reminded her of France, and she involuntarily thought of vineyards now, and little street cafés full of locals. And baguettes, brown and warm from the oven. And crêpes, perhaps with clotted cream and a little sugar . . . oh, she wished she'd made time for breakfast this morning.

"Anyhow!" she said. She talked to herself quite a bit in the car. Some days they were the only decent conversations she had.

There was a packet of cheesy crisps in the glove compartment and she opened them now. It was a free sample that Ewan had brought home. Free samples were one of the perks of his job. If you could call it a perk – they still had a whole case of Mega Curry Beans to finish up.

Thank God – here came an elderly man on a bike. She rolled down her window and beeped her horn enthusiastically. "Hello there!"

He hadn't expected this, and his bike wobbled dangerously.

"Sorry," she said. "It's just that I'm lost – would you be able to point me in the direction of Hackettstown?"

He looked at her rather peculiarly, she thought. Perhaps it was

1

a mistake to have flagged down a strange man on a deserted country road. Especially in a flash car with her leather handbag lying on the front seat. She might as well beg to be car-jacked! Really, this was the very last time she would swap with Lisa – if she really was getting a wisdom tooth out, the fifth now by Grace's calculations.

But the man just said, "If you're *sure* you want to go there, drive on about two miles, take a left at the crossroads and then the next right." He added heavily, "Good luck," before wobbling on.

"Thank you!" She quickly scribbled down what he'd said on the back of an envelope. She had learned over the years never to trust her own memory when it came to directions. It was already burdened enough with the school-run rota, essential items she must buy in the supermarket and nine different pin numbers. Oh, and the damned passports! She must ring Ewan as soon as she could, because he wouldn't remember them either. Head like a sieve, Ewan. It hadn't always been that way. His memory seemed have got worse over the years as hers had improved, a development that hadn't escaped her in its convenience.

Hackettstown. Twinned with Wart-Hausen. Grace slowly drove past the road sign and up a narrow mean main street, which boasted outlets such as Go West Fashions and Brenda's Unisex Salon (20% off dry-cuts on a Monday). But there was a brightly lit Spar farther up, and quite a pretty little square with some roses in it – mind you, a group of the town's teenagers seemed to be tearing the heads off them, and threatening each other with what looked to be penknives. They turned dull envious eyes on her silver BMW as it went past.

"Hello there!" She waved a bit nervously at them and drove on.

Bridge Road was out in the suburbs. The driveway of Number 17 was empty and the house looked deserted. Grace parked acceptably and turned off the ignition. The radio, set on some station the boys favoured, was cut off mid boom-boom. She had only been listening to it at all because one of the other mothers had told her at the school gates that the whole class was tuning in to explicit songs about sex and drugs. But after weeks of monitoring, Grace had yet to make out a single word in any of the songs. Except perhaps 'yours was yum', once, but she was too embarrassed to report this to the others. Also she wasn't quite sure what it meant. Well, she had her *suspicions*. Then she found that she couldn't get it out of her head: yours was yum, yours was yum! And she a married woman, a mother, and therefore not expected to think about sex. (Why then did she find herself wanting to rush out and buy the entire album?)

Ten to nine. Good. She was early. She closed her eyes and lay back in her seat.

The car was a good place to think – or not to think. Grace could spend the whole day in the car, dreaming, and indeed once had.

Mind you, that had been open to a slight misinterpretation.

"Oh my God, Harry, she's after killing herself!"

"Quick – can you see the hosepipe? There must be a hosepipe from the exhaust!"

"Still, would you blame her? Would you blame anyone?"

"Shut up! We need to pull out the hosepipe!"

She'd opened her eyes to find Hilda and Harry Brennan from next door pressed against the windscreen, handkerchiefs clamped over their mouths. At least they'd cared enough to investigate. The boys would have come eventually, she was sure. Hunger would have brought them if nothing else. Would Ewan? Probably. It would depend on how engrossed he was. Well, he did work from home. He couldn't always come running every time a member of the family decided to disappear for ten minutes, as he had said mildly at the time. He had a point, of course – but at the same time, how long *would* she have to be gone before he'd come running? Three days? A week, perhaps? She was being most unfair now, he felt – he would certainly notice if she disappeared for a week. At that juncture the Brennans had made their excuses and left.

3

Grace had continued to enjoy stolen moments in her car. It wasn't that she was anti-social or unfriendly, but honestly, didn't you get heartily sick of people sometimes?

"Hello there, Grace! Found the place okay?"

A red-faced man of around forty propelled himself out the front door of number seventeen and towards her car. He had a tape measure in his hand, extending out to about ten inches, and he waved it at her excitedly. "I've got something to show you."

Grace got out of the car, doing a swift trawl through her short-term memory banks – Fergus? No, Fergus was yesterday. This one must be Frank. After ten years, clients were beginning to look the same she was ashamed to admit.

"Frank – nice to meet you again." He'd been in the office last week.

But he ignored her outstretched hand now and brandished the measuring tape with a loud snap. "That fellow from your office measured up the place wrong," he announced. "The bathroom is nearly a whole foot wider than what you've put down on the brochure."

"Is it?"

"Eleven and a quarter inches, to be exact. Look!"

"I'm sorry about that. I don't think it'll make much difference, though."

She was taking this altogether too calmly for his liking, she could see.

"Some people," he said, "bathrooms are their *thing*. Sandy spends about four hours on average in the bathroom every day. That's why she never picks up the phone if you ring – she can't hear it, you see, what with taps running and water gurgling and the ballcock hissing." He must have seen Grace's startled expression, because he added, "She's a Pisces. She loves all that."

"And Sandy is . . . ?"

"My fiancée."

"Oh! I didn't know you were engaged."

"There's no need to look so surprised," he said.

"I wasn't – "

"You think nobody would want to marry me? You think I'm not relationship material or something?"

"Not at all," Grace said, trying desperately not to look at the small pimple on the end of his nose. The more she tried not to look, the more she *looked*, until all she could see was one enormous pimple. Dear God, had it started to throb?

"Anyhow!" she said, whirling around to look at the house. "You have a very nice place here, Frank."

More lies. It was a horrible low brown bungalow with nasty net curtains and fake oil lamps over the front door. A small notice had been propped in the glass panel: *No Jehovah's Witnesses Please.*

She retrieved her clipboard from the car and consulted it efficiently. "I have three couples booked in to view your house this morning. Now, the first pair is due in about ten minutes, so you should really . . . "

He just stood there.

"You might have a little shopping to do . . . ?"

He still stood there.

She said gently, "Or you could just drive around if you don't have anywhere to go."

His chin jutted up. "Of course I have somewhere to go! I have any number of places I can go. In fact, I've been invited over by a very good friend of mine – Mrs Carr. That's her house across the road."

Grace looked over. The house was like something from a fairy tale – all turrets, and bits added over the years, higgledy-piggledy. An ancient sign hung over the pink door saying *Lodging House.*

Grace thought it was a shame she wasn't trying to sell it, rather than Frank's brown bungalow. They didn't sell houses outside Dublin as a rule. They had only agreed to take on Frank's house at all because he was related to one of the partners' wives – an accident of marriage, she had been at pains to point out.

Frank was looking across the road in discontent. "Look at that grass verge out the front!"

Grace did. "What's wrong with it?"

"Nothing! That's the whole point! Because I had to take out my own lawnmower this morning and mow it. She couldn't be bothered. She never can. But I didn't want people arriving here to view my house thinking that this was some kind of lower class neighbourhood, some shabby do-what-you-like kind of place to live."

"Well, people do tend to notice their surroundings," Grace offered, patting his arm. Over the years, she had come to realise that her job wasn't just about selling houses. Depending on the situation, she was often required to provide moral support, relationship counselling, intervention in community disputes, and sometimes just to jolly people along. Lay people didn't realise how multi-layered a career in property was! They thought, rather harshly, that it was all about location and greed and pitting cash-strapped purchasers against each other like it was some kind of blood sport.

"Still, we mustn't lose sight of the bottom line, Grace," as a young male manager from Head Office had explained to her at a 'training meeting' last month. "Sales, sales, sales!"

Apparently, she was taking too much time with clients. Gathering unnecessary detail about a property, such as the fact that Paul McCartney's second cousin had once owned it. Or encouraging clients to stay in touch once their properties had been sold, that kind of thing.

"All that might have been fine when you started as a trainee a decade ago, Grace." He made it sound like a century. "But with competition what it is, we just can't expect to deliver the same kind of personal service we used to."

She had looked across at him and, with all the weight of her experience and the maturity of her thirty-four years, had slowly explained to him that these were people's homes they were talking about: places where they had laughed and cried and fought and lived and, in a couple of cases, died (although, she assured him, that this was not something she generally pointed out). Moving house was for some people like ripping a heart from its chest! Surely he could see that it was part of their job to support their clients as well as take their money?

"Absolutely," he had said, smiling and nodding, before informing her that they would be setting time limits on call-out visits to assess or show clients' homes.

In pure defiance now, Grace gave Frank an encouraging smile. "Go on."

"Well, in the end she said I could mow the verge but I wasn't to touch the garden gnomes."

Grace saw the gnomes now. There were three of them, all grinning widely, their hands wrapped firmly around fishing-rods. Someone had broken off the rods halfway down. The result was unseemly.

"Vandals," Frank said, his complexion turning a darker hue.

"There's no point in falling out over a garden gnome, is there?" she said soothingly, trying to usher him towards the gate.

"It wasn't the gnomes we fell out over. It was the rose bushes."

"Pardon?" she said.

"I just gave them a little trim. Well, more than a trim. But honestly, people like her, they let down the whole tone of the place. And I ended up telling her that too. Been wanting to for eleven years!" he finished up stoutly.

Grace had heard of plenty of people who had feuded with the neighbours soon after moving in, but never upon moving out. And after eleven years too! It was a tragedy. Mrs Carr seemed such an interesting person as well; apart from the gnomes, she had two wooden deckchairs parked on the uneven front lawn, and a rickety plastic table, as though she might decide at any moment to flop down with a bottle of wine and say to hell with the world.

"Frank," she said, with the calmness and authority born of years of family mediation, "why don't you go over to her and just apologise?"

"She says that she'll never open her door to me again."

"She would if you bring her a replacement rosebush."

"She says she's got her husband's shotgun."

"I'd imagine she was pulling your leg."

"She showed it to me."

Grace looked over at the house. "Are you sure?"

"What, you think I dreamed it all up or something? You think I'm hallucinating?"

"No, I just meant that it might have been a toy or something. My sons have water guns and they look very real – "

"She says she's so mad at me over the rose bushes that she's going to come out and stand on her front lawn and wave the shotgun around when people come to view the house. She says she might even fire a round or two into the sky if the mood takes her. She says that nobody will buy my house when they see they'll have a raving lunatic right opposite." He paused for breath. "I wasn't going to tell you, but I suppose you should know."

"Thank you," Grace said, faintly.

"So," he said, "what do you think we should do?"

The first thing that came into her head was that she did not have time for this. She was booked on a three o'clock flight from Dublin airport to Heathrow, and from there she was flying to Orlando. She was going to Disneyland today – hurrah! Well, tomorrow at any rate. The first night they were staying in a motel somewhere on the outskirts of Florida. She had never stayed in a motel before. The very word conjured up seediness and sex and debauchery, and she found herself strangely excited by it. Perhaps that's what happened when you went to the Isle of Man three summers in a row. Or listened to too many obscene lyrics on the radio.

"Let's call the police," she declared. This was their area, surely.

Frank's eyes popped behind his thick glasses. "We're going to have people arriving to view the house at any minute! We can't have police cars parked outside!"

"Maybe we could ask for an unmarked one or something?" Grace wondered aloud, reaching for her mobile phone. Should she dial 999 or just ring the local Garda station directly? But she didn't know the number of the local Garda station and so she'd have all the rigmarole of ringing directory enquiries. If she rang 999 it seemed to be making such a big deal of it. Then again, a gun *was* a big deal in this country. She would dial 999.

"Look, I know her," Frank pleaded. "She likes to huff and puff. It's not as though she'd actually go through with it."

"We can't just ignore it."

"Why not?"

"Because she might shoot one of the potential purchasers!" Not to mention her. But Grace was professional above all else.

"Not if we get them to park as near to the house as possible," Frank said. "Then kind of encourage them to run to the front door keeping their heads low. Once they're inside, they're safe, and you can show them the house. Then we get them back out to their cars the same way, and tell them to drive off fast."

"Maybe we could get a booking deposit off them as well before they're shot dead?" Grace enquired coolly.

"Oh, come on! The woman's a nutter! How many nutters have you come across in your profession?" He stared at her rather psychotically. "If you were to pander to them all, you'd never sell a property! Nobody would ever move house!"

Grace's hand wavered on her phone. It was tempting . . . and, really, he was probably right about Mrs Carr saying that just to frighten him.

"Why don't you just ring your office? They'll know what to do," Frank suggested.

Grace felt rather patronised. "We don't actually have a set of guidelines lying around on what to do in the event of threatened shootings, Frank."

Anyhow, it was nine o'clock; right now all senior staff would be in the meeting that was held on the last Friday of every month to assess performance and set targets. The rest of the crew would be on the road, like herself. Some of them had been showing houses since seven this morning (to facilitate people on their way to work) and would still be showing them at seven tonight (to accommodate people on their way home from work). Grace sometimes thought it was only a matter of time before they went twenty-four hours. And opened a branch in Hackettstown.

And even if she did phone the office, she would most likely be referred to herself. She had a reputation as being 'a safe pair of hands' (which always managed to sound vaguely insulting). If anyone could deal with shoot-outs, Grace could, they would declare. She didn't know why. It wasn't as though she encountered violence on a daily basis in the drawing-rooms of the middle classes. This was hardly what you'd call a high-risk job. Not physically, anyway – certainly there were huge risks financially, as she had often explained to Ewan. Look at the asking price for Frank's house, for example! People having to mortgage themselves into old age to pay for it! It was only worth half the money, in her opinion. Three-quarters at most. But you couldn't say that to people, of course; increasingly, selling houses made her feel very dishonest.

"Try selling people a chocolate bar that claims to aid weight loss," Ewan had said gloomily.

"You got the account then?" It would be nice if just once they finished off a conversation about her job before they moved on to his. But apparently selling second-hand houses was not as exciting as dreaming up television advertisement campaigns, and there was no use pretending that it was. At least, nobody in Grace's house pretended, and hadn't for years.

"By a whisker," Ewan had said. "Right now I'm playing with,

10

'Slimchoc – the Chocolate Bar with Lots of Taste that Sheds your Weight!'"

"And does it?"

"Does it what?"

"Shed weight?"

"Oh, I don't know, I doubt it. We have to talk to the legal people yet. We might have to add, 'as part of a calorie controlled diet'."

His gloominess had all but disappeared. It was an act he put on periodically to pretend that he belonged to that greater part of the human race who generally hated and loathed their jobs. But it was no use. The man would literally hop and skip up the stairs to his study on a Monday morning with indecent haste, humming little jingles under his breath, or trying to find a three-syllable word to rhyme with 'bubblegum'. There wasn't one, he'd informed her cheerily, at least nothing that wasn't obscene.

"So, what do you think?" He'd waited keenly for her opinion on his slogan. She had once been very flattered by this, until he had told her that she was a living example of most advertisers' demographic ideal: a white middle-class female in her mid-thirties with a couple of product-hungry children and a successful career to fund luxury goods and impulse-buys. She had taken umbrage; he had said, you're at the top of the food chain, what the hell are you complaining about? She didn't know really. It made her sound so smug, or something.

He added, "I brought a box of samples home, by the way. Jamie's already had one. He says they taste like washing-up liquid."

So they would join all the other samples that were piling up in the garage. Despite her nagging, Ewan wouldn't throw them out. In some ways he reminded her of a small boy, hoarding things up. When she emptied out his trousers pockets to take them to the dry-cleaners she didn't find mysterious phone numbers or credit card receipts for lingerie shops, but elastic bands and half-eaten chocolate products and pencil sharpeners. And a foam cup from the inside of a ladies' padded bra once. That had aroused her interest, until he'd explained that when it was matched with a second bra cup, which his colleague Mick had in *his* trouser pocket, it formed exactly the right spherical profile for the new Easter Egg campaign they were working on. They couldn't use the Easter Egg itself, of course, which was entirely the wrong shape to sell itself.

She had believed him. Nobody could make that up. Besides, Ewan would have neither the interest nor the organisational capability to have an affair. It wouldn't be because he was so dedicated to Grace, so desperately in love with her. He did love her, she knew that. But sometimes she suspected that he would love any woman who had ended up agreeing to marry him – so long as he was left largely to his own devices, of course, and wasn't interfered with too much. He mightn't like her so much then.

"Oh my God," Frank squeaked beside her. "Take cover!"

"What?"

"She's pointing the gun at us!"

Grace swung around towards Mrs Carr's house. One of the side panels of the front bay window was open. Something long and shiny was poking out under the net curtain and directly out across the front lawn at them.

"Are you sure it's a gun?" she asked, trying to buy time.

"What else do you think it is?"

"I don't know . . . "

"Her hoover maybe?"

"I'm just saying – "

"Don't just stand there chattering, for heaven's sake! Take cover!"

Heedless of chivalry, he elbowed past her and dived down behind her car, commandeering the safest spot by the driver's wheel.

Grace stood alone and exposed in the middle of his cobbled

drive, staring across at the double barrel poking out Mrs Carr's front window. Net curtains had never struck her as menacing before now.

"Hello there!" she tried, giving a friendly wave across. She had read somewhere that sometimes it worked if you established a personal relationship with the aggressor. "Lovely morning!"

The gun malevolently reared out another inch.

Really, when you thought about it, the whole thing was rather cowardly on Mrs Carr's part, Grace decided. If she wasn't going to declare herself openly, then why should Grace demean herself by galloping hysterically to her car? On the other hand, she did have two children at home who needed her (sometimes), and a husband who loved her (he had said so two Christmases ago), and she should give some thought to her own safety. She would, she decided, take cover, but she would do it her way.

So, very casually, very unconcerned, she turned and started to walk away. Not wanting to appear to be making for the car too obviously, she did a little circuit of Frank's front yard, her hands clasped at the small of her back as though she were out enjoying a Sunday afternoon stroll. When a robin chirped nearby, she raised her head towards it and allowed a faint smile to play about her lips.

"What are you doing?" Frank barked. "Do you want to get your head blown off?"

She quickened her step after that, and approached the car at what she hoped was an oblique angle. Then she looked down and pretended that her shoelace had come undone (she was wearing sandals). She tsk-ed loudly before bending down as if to tie it. Then she made a crafty and dramatic lunge sideways for the protection of the car, landing on top of Frank.

"Watch it!"

"Sorry."

She wasn't really. Her heart was pumping fast with unaccustomed adrenaline and her face was strangely hot. She felt like she was in a western, or at least *Hawaii Five-O* – although, on the telly the aggressor tended to be a sinister attractive man rather than a dotty pensioner. She couldn't wait to tell the boys about this. Her, dodging shotguns! Surely they couldn't fail to be impressed?

Although you wouldn't know. Since they'd been about eight she'd had the feeling that they considered her to be mostly background noise. Well, that was probably unfair to them – it was just that she had been hurt about it and still was. In the space of about six months they had changed from her soft-faced twin babies into these semi-grown ups who wanted replica Uzi machine guns for their birthdays, and who spent most of their time beating each other to a pulp. What they did not want any more was her undivided attention and love – she would always remember that heartbreaking moment when Jamie had wriggled out of a kiss, a look of near contempt on his face. It was Ewan they followed around now, Ewan they implored to 'Watch this!' and 'Will you come outside with us? Pleeease?'. Grace would be left waving them off at the doorstep like some kind of benign and detached housekeeper whose sole function was to provide clean socks and hot meals.

Disney had been her idea of getting them all together as a family again, properly. So she'd booked the whole month off work and bought the tickets, cleverly hiding them in homemade fortune cookies which she'd presented one night after dinner.

"A whole month? We'll go mad," Ewan had declared, looking worried.

"Would this be during school term?" Neil had asked, the youngest twin by twenty-two minutes but by far the craftiest.

"My ticket is burnt," Jamie, the other one, had said.

Grace had looked around at them all. They could have changed the car with what this trip would cost. They could have gone to the Maldives, and lain on the peaceful sand for a month, which was what she would have liked, instead of traipsing around the Enchanted bloody Tiki Room in the scorching sun in Florida.

So instead of cajoling and pleading and talking them around, she had dumped the Disney brochures on the coffee table, and let them do what they wanted! They had opened them, of course, and seen the fantastic water rides and the jungle cruises, and they were dying to go then.

A loud, high-pitched call cut through the morning air. "Frank Gorman! You stay away from my house now, do you hear me?"

Frank visibly shook. "Jesus Christ. She's going to shoot me."

"Don't be ridiculous," Grace said. Lifting her mobile, she rang 999, and inched up a little to peer through the car window and across the road. Someone had stuck a piece of chewing-gum to the inside of the window. Neil probably. She would murder him.

"Don't provoke her," Frank warned.

Across the way, the net curtain was pulled back a bit from Mrs Carr's front window. Grace caught a glimpse of lots of white-grey hair piled atop some kind of ruffled dress, or bathrobe. She was reminded of one of the witches from *Macbeth*. The gun was now halfway out the window. It jerked unsteadily before being cocked haphazardly towards the sky.

"Does she drink at all?" Grace asked.

"Like a fish," Frank confirmed.

Then the net curtain fell back into place, as though Mrs Carr were tired of holding it. Or possibly she had gone to get another drink. The shotgun stayed.

Grace's feet started to ache. Her sandals had three-inch heels which always hurt after about an hour, but what could she do? A certain image had to be presented when selling houses, especially houses in the better parts of town. This accounted for the racks of sophisticated, neutral-coloured suits hanging in her wardrobe at home. The general idea was to complement a property's décor scheme; to blend in, as such. Once she had blended in so well that a client had lost track of her in the same room. There she'd been, standing right by the wall the whole time, while he had turned around in circles muttering, "Where's that blasted woman gone?"

15

"Emergency services." The 999 operator's voice burst out of her mobile phone.

"Police, please," Grace said.

A pause, then a man from the police switchboard was on the line, asking her what he could do for her.

"I'm at Number 17, Bridge Road," she said efficiently. "And there's a woman across the way who's threatening us with a gun."

A gun? He sounded alert.

"Yes. A shotgun."

Was she sure?

"A double-barrel shotgun," she said for good measure.

She heard the man saying something to another person in the background, and she looked at Frank importantly. This was probably the most exciting thing that had happened to them all month. It certainly was to her.

The man was back on the phone. Was this woman threatening them right now?

"Yes. There was a dispute over a rosebush, you see."

A rosebush?

"That's correct. Frank mowed down her rose bushes and she got mad."

Who was Frank?

"Mrs Carr's neighbour."

Okay, who was Mrs Carr?

"The woman with the gun . . ." Grace could sense she was diluting his interest with unnecessary detail. "Look, it's all a bit complicated. The fact is that she has a gun and she says she's going to fire a few shots into the air if the mood takes her. She might even do it right now."

That got his attention again. Was the woman pointing the gun at them at this moment, he wanted to know?

"Yes," Grace said decisively.

She could actually see the gun?

"Yes, I can actually see the – "

Across the road, the gun abruptly withdrew and the window slammed closed.

After a little pause, she said, "Would you believe it – it's gone now!"

The policeman paused too. And the woman, he wanted to know?

"She's actually gone too . . . but she was there a second ago. With the gun. I saw it with my own eyes!"

She could feel herself being ticked off at the other end of the phone as a crackpot to be checked out whenever a patrol car had a quiet ten minutes.

"Aren't you going to come down to the scene?" she asked.

He told her he would send a car.

"When?"

Soon. In the meantime, she was to stay exactly where she was. Under no circumstances was she to approach the woman or in any way attempt to communicate with her. That went for that guy Frank too.

"Okay. Thanks for your time!" Grace said. She always ended her phone calls like that. It was a work habit. Even when people took up *her* time, she ended up thanking them.

Frank was fretting. "I hope this doesn't affect the sale."

"I'm sure it won't." To take his mind off it, she said, "So, where are you moving to?" She expected him to say Navan, or Dunboyne maybe.

"New York," he said.

"Oh!"

"Sandy is American, did I not mention that? Yankee Doodle, I call her! She loves that – cracks up every time. She says I've got a great sense of humour. Anyway, she lives in Brooklyn. She works as a nursery nurse, but just until she has her own kids, she says, then she's going to give up work and be a stay-at-home mom. But at the moment she's just happy doing her job, and taking out her disabled kids' group at the weekends and doing the soup kitchen for the homeless on Tuesday and Thursday nights."

It was a wonder Sandy got to spend a minute in the bathroom at all, never mind the four hours daily that Frank gave her credit for. But Grace just said, "Wow! A busy woman."

"Too busy," Frank with a frown. "I tell her, you know. I say, Sandy, you have to think about yourself sometimes. But she doesn't listen. It's no wonder she's been feeling tired lately."

"When are you moving over?"

"Two weeks' time," he said. "I'd have gone sooner only I'm finding it kind of hard to fix up a job over there."

"What do you do?"

"Birds," he said.

"Pardon?"

"I'm an ornithologist. I do work with wildlife foundations, zoos, that kind of thing. And I'm compiling a book, *An Introduction to Birds For Beginners*. Sandy thinks it's a great idea, she says she had no idea until I came along that it was a complete myth that cuckoos went around dropping eggs in other birds' nests the minute their backs were turned. Well, they *do*, of course, but it's much more complicated than that. Sandy says she could listen to me going on about birds all day," he added.

Grace said, "I suppose New York . . . well, there would be pigeons, wouldn't there?"

Frank didn't seem too worried about his slim job prospects. "Sandy says she'll support me for a while." How she would do this on a nursery nurse's salary, he didn't say. His big red face was all dreamy. "She's just amazing, do you know that?"

Well, she seemed to like Frank, Grace thought, and that was surely a feat in itself.

TWO

Julia Carr was making beans on toast in her kitchen, the shotgun on the worktop beside her. She wasn't in the slightest bit hungry but it was best for the stomach not to be entirely empty. There was a danger of vomiting then, apparently. It had taken three months to store up thirty-six prescription sleeping pills, cajoling and hoodwinking Dr Noonan, and she was not about to waste them.

She was having a little trouble with the tin of beans. It was one of those ones with a ring attached to the lid, which you were supposed to pull to open the tin. She eventually got her finger through and pulled hard. The ring snapped off and came clean away in her hand.

"Bugger."

This had never happened to her before, wouldn't you know it. Anyhow. A quick inspection of her cupboards revealed that there were no beans left. There was very little of anything, really. Well, it had seemed pointless to stock up on food that would only get thrown out in the end. Besides, pension day wasn't until Tuesday.

So, for her final meal on this earth, she was faced with the choice of a tin of prunes or chickpeas, both of which were out of date. She had decided on the chickpeas (she actually was getting a little peckish now) when she suddenly remembered that they

19

would do a post-mortem on her. She knew this from reading forensic detective novels. What would they think when they discovered a can of out-of-date chickpeas in her stomach, mixed up with the pills? There might be some confusion over what had actually killed her. Possibly they might have to resort to all kinds of costly tests. No, she would already be causing enough trouble to everyone. She would eat nothing.

Now she couldn't stop thinking about food. The image of a fresh white loaf and a nice bit of cheese popped into her head. It was most inappropriate given the circumstances, and she guiltily decided she would leave the kitchen altogether. First she checked that the windows were closed and the taps turned securely off. She had scoured the cooker an hour ago and it gleamed. She'd meant to get around to the kitchen floor – that milk she'd spilled last week was starting to smell – but she was out of mop-heads and a trip to the supermarket would have put the whole thing back by several hours. In the end she'd just had to prioritise, as you do.

And at least the bathroom was clean. Michael would be poking around upstairs, and Gillian, their noses upturned probably. Julia had put out on her bedside locker several copies of *Hustler* magazine left behind by one of her lodgers as a little surprise for them.

The plastic jar of red and yellow pills was laid out on the coffee table. And a jug of water with ice in it, along with a glass. And a photocopy of her will, for everybody's convenience. It didn't look like much now; in fact, it looked a bit thoughtless and mean, as though it had been organised by the public health service.

Maybe she should add a vase of flowers? Or at least put a couple of doilies down on the table to hide the coffee stains. But she didn't know how these things were usually done, except that people sometimes played a piece of music that meant a lot to them. She didn't have any special piece of music like that, except maybe the song playing on the transistor radio the day she and JJ had gone out on the lake with a picnic to celebrate their fortieth wedding anniversary, and he had kissed her to the strains of 'Boogie Wonderland', which didn't seem all that fitting right now.

She sat down for the last time in JJ's big old red chair. It all seemed very unreal, and she half-expected someone to walk through the door and ask her what on earth she thought she was doing, and she would laugh and say, 'You know, I have no idea! I was just being silly for a moment – will we have a cup of tea?' But nobody would come. She had been on her own in this house, save for a few sporadic lodgers, since JJ had died two years ago. Even the cat had run away.

She had continued to function, of course: to eat, to sleep, to open her mouth and have words come out. But there was nothing happening inside. She often thought of herself as one of those accident victims in intensive care units who kept breathing long after what made them human had died.

So, on this rather dramatic note, she slowly placed two pills on her tongue and reached for the glass of water.

Hail Mary, full of grace, The Lord is with –

The phone rang. Bugger and blast anyway. She would just ignore it.

The Lord is with thee, blessed art thou amongst –

But it just kept ringing and ringing until she could bear it no longer and she spat the sleeping pills out into her hand and snatched the phone up.

"Hello!"

"Mammy?"

"Michael?"

He sounded a bit hurt. "Of course it's Michael."

She tried not to sound irritated. "It's just that you usually don't phone at this time."

"I know, but I'm in the car on my way to a meeting – just thought I'd check on you."

"There's really no need." Since JJ died Michael had become a constant fixture on the end of the phone. She had to take it off the hook in the evenings just to watch *Fair City*.

"Well, you're on your own now, Mammy," he pointed out, tactlessly. "And you know that sometimes you forget to eat."

"I do not forget to eat." Sometimes she forgot to wash, certainly, but she didn't mind about that. Old people were expected to be smelly. "So," she said, trying to think of something to say. She seemed to have been trying to find things to say to Michael since he'd been a child. "How's Gillian?"

"Great! She thinks it's not a chest infection now at all."

"Good."

"She thinks it might be bronchitis."

"Wouldn't she be in hospital if it were bronchitis?" Julia enquired. "Or in bed, at the very least?"

"Apparently with some strains of bronchitis you hardly know you have it at all. She was reading it in her medical books."

"Well, tell her I hope she gets over it soon. And Susan?"

He sounded gloomy. "She's not talking to me again."

"What have you done to her this time?"

"That's just it. I don't know."

Julia clucked. "She's thirteen, Michael. It's just the age."

"Was I like that at thirteen?" he asked eagerly.

"The very same," she declared, guiltily. Michael hadn't been all that memorable at thirteen. Or at any other age, really. Except that he ate a lot, even back then. "Anyway, if that's all, Michael, I have a few things to do . . ."

"Right, sure – so we'll see you on Thursday?"

"What?" They'd been over only last weekend. It usually took her a fortnight to recover.

"Your birthday, Mammy."

Her heart sank. Blast anyway.

"Ha!" he said. "You thought we'd forgotten, hadn't you?"

"Yes," she said weakly.

"Not a chance! We're all coming over for the whole day, have a big party. We have it all planned – Gillian's going to make a cake and everything. Bronchitis permitting, of course," he added.

"Michael, I really don't want you to go to any trouble – "

"No, no, we insist." Her lack of enthusiasm must have conveyed itself to him because he said, awkwardly, "Look, I know you didn't want a fuss for your birthday last year, what with Daddy dying and everything. But he wouldn't have wanted you to go on mourning forever, Mammy."

The glibness of this, the presumption that her grief could be simply shrugged off once an appropriate time had passed, annoyed her. "You have no idea what JJ would have wanted."

"Well, no, of course not, all I'm saying is – "

"JJ liked a party as much as the next person. He threw some wonderful birthday parties for me. He flew me to Paris three years ago, for God's sake!"

There was a hurt silence on the other end of the phone.

"It's . . . I just don't feel ready, Michael." She suddenly remembered that she would be dead anyway, and that it was immaterial. "Look, come over if you want," she said generously.

"Okay," he said, cheerful again. "We'll bring masks if Gillian's still infectious."

She realised now that this was the very last time she would be speaking to him. Her only child. It seemed very important that she say something memorable to him. "Michael?"

"Yes, Mammy?"

"Just . . . thanks for everything. You've been a very good son." It sounded stiff and cold, not what she really meant at all. But maybe he was touched because he was silent for a minute. "Michael?"

"Sorry, Mammy, I just went through a tunnel there – what did you say?"

"Oh, never mind. Go to your meeting."

She hung up. Now, where had she been? Oh yes, *Hail Mary*.

And now she was down two pills as well. Still, hopefully she had enough left to do the trick.

"Oh!" Her hands had started to shake. Look at them, wobbling away! She tried to stop them. But the more she tried, the more they shook, until they were bouncing up and down on her knees as though they were playing an imaginary piano with gusto.

A few deep breaths and everything would fine. There was no point in getting in a heap about something that she had made a perfectly sound decision on weeks ago. Months ago! Well, she hadn't actually made a decision as such. She wasn't a person who made decisions – they always seemed to be accompanied by such a lot of unnecessary angst and weighing up of pros and cons. Instead she had notions and ideas and impulses, and once in the grip of one, nothing would do her but to pursue it with all her energy and vigour until its conclusion. Take the rockery out the back, for instance; she had been doing the dishes at the sink one morning, staring out the back window, when she observed how little she had to look at. She had not rested until she had placed the very last stone on the top of a wonderful rockery (which was rather lopsided in truth) with her bare hands. JJ had watched, amused and impressed by her single-mindedness. She'd promptly forgotten about it then, of course, and taken up a home-brewing course.

A couple of months ago – she couldn't remember exactly when – she had woken up one morning and lain there in the bed for an age trying to muster up the energy to present herself to the world for yet another day: to find a dress that was clean, maybe smear a bit of colour onto her lips, rattle around an empty house until it was time to go to bed again. And she just didn't want to do it any more.

Once the thought was there, it was a natural progression to cultivate an insomnia problem, to procure a variety of sleeping pills from Dr Noonan, to update her will and tie up other bits and pieces. That one thought had led her right here to this room, to this table, today. She just had to bring the sequence to its conclusion.

"Stop it!" Her hands would not stop shaking, and she was getting angry with them. Her body was always letting her down, with its litany of aches and pains, its increasing unpredictability; little things designed to irritate her, it seemed, but not serious enough to kill her and save her all this trouble. If it had had any decency, any loyalty to her, it would have died naturally in the weeks after JJ was buried. She had not eaten or slept, she had not even drunk water; she'd downed enough sleeping tablets to fell an ox, and her body just kept on going. Living, even though every fibre of her being had wanted to die. It was a snivelling, cowardly, stupid thing and she would be glad to be rid of it. To be rid of everything.

She managed to tip out more pills onto the table but couldn't hold the glass of water. Her hands were shaking too much. She would just have to go into the kitchen and find a bendy straw with which to kill herself. The indignity of it! She was raging now.

The minute she opened the kitchen door, the smoke hit her. The cooker grill was on fire.

"*Bugger.*"

She'd put two slices of bread on for the beans on toast and had forgotten all about them. Now flames were bursting up through the rings of her immaculately scoured cooker, and threatening to set the curtains alight.

She put the jar of pills down beside the cooker and ran to wet some tea towels. By the time she got back, the jar and her precious pills had melted and were oozing across her worktop in a glorious multicoloured puddle.

The answering machine was on at home.

"Ewan, it's me – can you pick up? Ewan, sorry to disturb you, but can you pick up the phone? It's important."

Ewan screened calls; otherwise he said he'd get no work done.

25

She'd offered to get a second phone line in, so that he would have his own work number and he wouldn't be bothered by domestic calls. But he had fretted that he would have no excuse for avoiding people if they knew he had his own work line. Sometimes she felt like pointing out that he was inventing advertising slogans, not some ground-breaking vaccine. Oh, when had she become so mean? More to the point, when had he started screening his own wife?

"Ewan, I know you're there. Pick up the fucking phone."

"Grace?" He was on the other end, startled.

It just showed how rarely Grace used bad language. She wasn't in favour of it as a rule – not with children around.

"Not tearing you away from Chocslim, I hope?" she said.

"Slimchoc. And I'm not working – we *are* supposed to be going on holidays today." He was semi-cool in response to her sarcasm, and she was sorry now.

"Are you on your way home?" he asked.

"Not exactly." She was stretched out on the back seat of her car, out of Frank's earshot and Mrs Carr's line of fire. The leather was getting warm from the sun. If she drew her knees up, she was just about able to curl up like she had as a child on long car journeys, her cheek pressed into the seat and the motion of the car eventually lulling her to sleep. She always liked the part when she woke up and she would look out the window to find herself in a completely different place – a bustling town, or a quiet country road, or even the seaside, if it was summer. That's when her love affair with cars, and sitting in them, had started.

"Grace? Are you still there?"

"Yes – listen, there's been a slight change of plan. Depending on what happens, I may have to meet you at the airport."

"What? But what about the packing?"

"Do you even want to know why I'm going to be late, Ewan?"

He must have sensed the chill down the phone line because he said hurriedly, "Yes, of course – why?"

26

"I'm caught up in a shoot-out," she told him.

"Okay," he said.

Grace counted to three.

Then he said, "Did you just say a shoot-out?"

"There's been a dispute with a neighbour. She has a shotgun aimed at us," she said airily. "We're waiting for the police."

"That's quite a bit of drama," he said, sounding marginally more interested. Or at least fully present. Sometimes when she talked to him he would give every indication that he was absorbed by her words: he would nod and smile and respond at all the right moments. Then she would bring up the topic again a couple of days later and he would look at her blankly and she would know that his mind had been somewhere else the entire time. It wasn't always on work, to his credit. Once he had mentally planned an entire motor route through Germany during a lengthy description of her mother's run-in with a stomach virus.

It had been loveable once, this trait.

"Yes," she agreed.

"Are you in danger?" He was concerned now, and she felt a little warm glow inside. It was like when she'd burnt her arm quite badly last year and he had spent ages pressing damp face-cloths on it before bandaging it all up.

"I don't think so. I'd say her aim isn't too hot. And she's been drinking."

"All the same – don't do anything to antagonise her," he ordered. The glow grew warmer. Not that she could ever admit it in front of her girlfriends, but it was so nice to be looked after by a man sometimes. To be fussed over. Bossed. Protected, even.

"I suppose you'd better not tell the boys. In case it might upset them," she said doubtfully, playing up to him a bit. She even let out a kind of a nervous, jittery breath.

"Do you think?" he said. His macho phase was disappointingly brief, as always.

"I don't know, Ewan – what do *you* think?"

She desperately wanted him to round up the boys with an urgent bellow, and have them gather around the phone while their mother relayed the whole tale in gory detail. She wanted to hear them clamber to ask questions and to express worry about her safety. Then they would all pile in the car and race to the scene.

"You're probably right. I won't say anything to them," Ewan decided.

Here, Grace thought, was a man who worked in advertising. Here was an expert in consumer psychology, a master at manipulating a highly sophisticated and jaded audience. But in his own house he couldn't pick up a lousy hint?

She knew that it was a childish impulse on her part anyhow. But she'd been like that recently, saving up jokes or funny stories she'd heard on the radio to tell the twins over dinner, and beaming with disproportionate pleasure if she made them laugh. Or pulling minor stunts to impress them, such as showing them on Shrove Tuesday how she could flip pancakes just like that chef on the TV (and had the consistency been a little less runny, she might not have burnt her arm so badly).

She was like some pathetic new kid in the schoolyard, trying to get in with the cool gang. Being children, they could smell a fake a mile off, of course, and the more she tried the less interested they were. It was a vicious circle, with her attempts getting more outlandish. A mere shotgun would probably not be enough now. She might actually have to get herself shot before they'd be sufficiently impressed.

"What do you do when you go off with them?" she asked now.
"What?"

"You and the boys. When you disappear for hours on end?"

"It's hardly 'hours', Grace." He added, "You didn't happen to tick things off a list, did you? When you were packing?"

She could hear him faffing about in the background with bits of paper.

"Take last night, Ewan," she said loudly. "After dinner, you said you were going to take the boys to the park for half an hour. You didn't come home until it was dark."

"Didn't we?"

She could just see his face, puzzled that she would even have noticed such a thing – such a trivial thing as to where her husband and children had disappeared!

"We were just horsing around, like usual."

"What does 'horsing around' mean, exactly?" She tried not to sound too curious and pathetic. It's just that he never told her. They would all traipse home, red-faced and panting like young bulls, and nobody would think to tell her what they had been doing, or where they had been. She never lowered herself to ask; in fact, she would barely look up as they stormed past to the fridge in case they thought she might be in any way interested.

"We play football, mostly," Ewan said. "A bit of basketball. Catch various living creatures down at the river, that kind of thing. Boy scouts' stuff." He added, "You'd think as they got older they'd start playing by themselves a bit more."

"Um," Grace said. So it wasn't like the three of them spent their time trading secrets or anything. It wasn't as if Jamie and Neil were confiding things in him, revealing bits of their precious selves that they used to whisper to her in the dark, and still did sometimes, when she tucked them into bed at night.

"Why do you want to know?" Ewan said.

"Just wondering."

A part of them was still hers. They had not taken that from her, and her heart grew less pinched.

The car rocked now as the bonnet suddenly sprang up. Frank. Grace peered out through the front seats. What on earth was he was up to?

"This is about that disused mine, isn't it?" Ewan suddenly blurted hotly down the phone.

"What?" Grace said, trying to keep up.

"I didn't know it was a disused mine, okay? It's not like it had a sign on it saying *Disused Mine* or anything! Actually, it might have, but it was very unclear, ask the boys. But anyway, your mother can say what she likes, Grace, but I would not willingly walk my children into danger for the hell of it!"

"Ewan, I know, okay? Nobody is accusing you of anything."

Years before the disused-mine incident, Ewan had once taken the twins up to the top of the Papal Cross in the Phoenix Park on a particularly windy day and parked them in their double-buggy without remembering to put the brake on. Only for some quick-footed Japanese tourist, there would have been carnage. If Ewan had thought about it, he would have seen the wisdom in keeping this incident to himself. But he wasn't devious like that, and he was too young to know the way marital arguments and resentments can resonate a decade on. And so he'd confessed when he'd got home and, from that day on, he'd acquired the label of being 'lightweight', as Grace's mother had put it upon hearing the tale. It was a label he had fought against for many years (although fought was perhaps too strong a word. Complained would be a more accurate description. Strongly, at times, to his credit).

Eventually he stopped complaining and accepted it; embraced it even, and made it his own. His reputation amongst friends and family now was that of an amusing scatterbrain – very intelligent though, very creative, which seemed to excuse him somewhat. He'd added other bits and pieces to this myth as time went on: absent-mindedness, for example. A poor memory. A pre-occupation with career. But he was *marvellous* with the boys, which excused him entirely.

When Grace thought about it, the whole thing suited him down to the ground.

For her part, having lumped him into a box in the first place, she was forced to compensate by going in the other direction. Now she was the organiser in the family, the head bottle-washer as such. If anybody wanted to know where to find something, they asked Grace. Need a dental appointment? Grace will make it. She, who on her very first date with Ewan had been so nervous that she'd mixed up the venue! There she'd sat for an hour in Bewley's café in Westmoreland Street while Ewan was sitting down the road in Bewley's in Grafton Street. It was Ewan who'd eventually had the presence of mind to walk up and check, lest there had been some mistake.

Wasn't it funny how you could grow into the kind of person that you'd never started out as, Grace thought? She remembered again that excited, dreamy girl sitting over a cooling coffee, wearing a black and white striped scarf that Ewan had said made her look like Dennis the Menace. She'd had two tickets in her pocket to a talk by Neil Jordan in the Irish Film Centre on the state of Irish film, and afterwards she and Ewan had sat cross-legged on the floor of his bedsit, passionately arguing back and forth until four in the morning.

And here she was, fifteen years on: a woman who made dental appointments and who blended seamlessly into wallpaper.

"Grace?" On the phone Ewan sounded anxious. "What's happened, has she started shooting?"

"No, no."

Frank's head poked out from the side of the bonnet. He waved frantically. He had an oil filter in his hand.

"I have to go," she said to Ewan. "You're going to have to finish the packing."

"Right . . ." he said, mournfully.

"There are some things you might like to remember, such as the passports and stuff." She desperately wanted to mention the travellers' cheques and the health insurance documents but wouldn't let herself. Perhaps he would mention them. But he didn't, of course. It would never occur to him. Now she would be fretting about the blasted things all morning. Really, weren't there some days when you just did not like yourself?

"Ring me when you know what's happening," he said.

31

She hung up, pushed open the car door with her foot, and slid back out onto the cobblestones, anticipating that her oil needed changing or something.

"The first one is here," Frank hissed instead.

Grace saw a red hatchback drive at a leisurely pace up the road. Her first viewers. What was she supposed to do?

"Get them to drive up as far as they can to the house," she urged Frank. There was no sense in leaving them down there by the gate like sitting ducks.

"Good idea," Frank said, a thin sheen of sweat visible on his forehead. Plucking a white handkerchief from his pocket, he draped it over the top of the oil filter. Then he stuck the makeshift flag out from behind the bonnet and waved it around erratically in the direction of the red hatchback.

Nothing happened for a moment as the car occupants obviously conferred. Then the hatchback crawled cautiously up the driveway. Another burst of flag-waving from Frank brought up them right up behind Grace's own car, where they stopped.

"Well done," Grace said to Frank admiringly, and he pinkened a bit.

She scuttled down to the hatchback on her hands and knees and popped up at the driver's side window.

"Hi!" she said.

The occupants jumped. They hadn't seen her until now. Her clipboard was still in her hand and she consulted it.

"Aidan and Amy, isn't it?" It was strange how often prospective buyers' names began with the same letter, Grace had noted. Pat and Pauline. Lisa and Liam. She'd once had a Frances and a Francis. Stranger again was how often people moved to roads that sounded similar to the ones they had just left: from Emmet Road to Elmer Road, for example. Sometimes the house number was even the same. Why was everyone so afraid of change? Increasingly Grace was beginning to think that there was little comfort in the familiar.

"I'm Grace Tynan," she told them. "I'll be showing you Frank's house today." She reached in through the window to shake hands with them. The angle was awkward and she ended up sort of patting them instead.

"I'm sure you're wondering what's going on," she said.

"Well, yes," the woman said.

"Anyway!" Grace said – no sense in alarming them – "why don't you have a look at these and if you have any questions, I'd be delighted to answer them for you."

She handed in two glossy brochures, surreptitiously taking note of the seat headrests. They were nice big leather ones, plump enough to shield the passengers from Mrs Carr's view. They should be safe enough. "Back in a minute – oh, and try not to make any sudden movements, okay?"

She scuttled back to her own car where Frank was waiting anxiously.

"Did you mention about the bathroom?"

"No, I did not."

"Sandy said you should. That's what they do in the States when the brochure is incorrect."

"Well, we're not in the States now." She stood up straight and took stock of herself. Her linen skirt was a mess of lines and creases, and her tights were snagged. She brushed herself down as best she could and wondered if she'd remembered to put a lipstick in her handbag.

"What are you doing?" Frank was alarmed.

The front window in the house across the way remained shut tight. There was no other sign of activity. Mrs Carr had probably passed out with drink. And Grace had to get to the airport.

"Back in a minute," she told Frank, and set off across the cobblestones, her high heels hitting the ground with a sharp click each time. Honestly, she thought, if you wanted something done, you had to do it yourself. If you wanted *anything* done.

Well, maybe one day she just wouldn't bother. She would

ignore what had to be done. She would say, hang it, let somebody else do it for a change! And if they didn't do it, she would say hang that too! Who cares! Not her. Because maybe deep down, once you stripped away all the appointment-making and the efficient neutral-coloured suits, maybe she was in fact a sloth.

"Hello? Mrs Carr? Sorry to disturb you, but I wonder could I pop in for a moment to talk to you?"

In the kitchen, Julia swung around, heart hammering. She looked through the open kitchen door and down the gloomy hall. She hadn't heard the doorbell. It must have rung several times, because there was a person pressed up against the frosted glass panels of the front door, hands cupping their eyes as they tried to see in. The cheek of them.

"Who is it?" she called.

"My name is Grace Tynan – I'm Frank's estate agent – Frank Gorman from across the road?"

Why was she speaking like that, as though Julia should really have known these things in the first place? Julia had a vague recollection of a thin woman in a big car and carrying a clipboard. She had reminded her of those career women you see on American television programmes – shiny and kind of brittle, not real at all.

"I'm afraid I'm busy right now!" she answered cheerily. She had just managed to put the cooker flames out, and the kitchen was filled with rancid steam and smoke. The two pieces of bread were charred black lumps when she extracted them with a serving fork and hurled them into the sink, and she realised she would have to clean the cooker all over again, and probably wash the curtains, and she was crying now – furious hot tears at her own incompetence. Far from this being the brave and sensible thing to do (a part of her had even thought it noble), the whole episode had descended into the plot of one of those cheap melo-dramas JJ used to take her to in the cinema in the fifties, the two of them giggling in the dark at the sheer idiocy of the heroine.

"Mrs Carr?" That blasted woman again, at the front door. "About the gun . . ."

"Yes, sorry about that. I'll put it away now. You're quite safe."

"Well, yes, but . . ."

"Goodbye now! Cheerio!"

She shut the kitchen door on the woman. Armed with rubber gloves and a Brillo pad, she threw open the back door to let the smoke out. She found an old wine bottle and made up a solution of bleach and detergent, then went to work on the cooker.

In retrospect perhaps the shotgun had been unnecessary. But those rose bushes had been planted in the spot where JJ used to put a chair out on summer evenings to read his engineering reports. Not that Frank had known this, in fairness. But he had this knack of rubbing her up the wrong way. Had been doing it for eleven long years. Let him sell his house and move to New York to his fancy woman. She for one wouldn't miss him.

When she straightened from the cooker, Grace Tynan was looking in through the back kitchen door.

"Oh, hello again! I hope you don't mind me coming around the back. It's just that you wouldn't open the front door."

Julia didn't say anything. For the second time that day, the woman had frightened the life out of her.

"Frank is very sorry, Mrs Carr."

"I doubt that. I've never met a more insensitive man in my life."

"It's just that he's a little anxious about his house. And then the pressure of getting married . . ."

"Yes, well, I wouldn't be surprised if that fell through. No woman in her right mind would marry that little arse of a man."

She watched as the estate agent woman's eyes darted involuntarily down to take in the rubber gloves, the smouldering cooker, and the shotgun on the worktop. Half of Julia's long white hair had escaped its clip too, and hung around her face in straggles. She must look like a mad woman. Normally it was not a tag she'd have minded in the slightest. But today it felt just a little close to the bone.

"I burnt some toast," she said very defensively.

Grace Tynan just nodded sympathetically, and said, "I'm always doing that. Will I make you some coffee or something?"

Julia was taken aback. Nobody had offered to make her coffee in a long time.

"I only have instant," she said. Why hadn't she said no?

"Instant is fine! And have you had something to eat?"

"No. The ring-pull broke off the tin of beans," she said. Honestly – any second now, she would be blubbering!

"Never mind. If you've got a tin opener, I bet I can get this lid off in a jiffy. Now, which drawer do you keep your utensils in?"

And she was off, opening drawers and hunting for tin openers and coffee jars. Julia knew she should get rid of her, like she had Frank that morning. Instead she stood there like a small child, thinking how nice it was to have someone else take responsibility for a change. How comforting it was not to have to cope on your own, even for five minutes.

"And leave that cooker – I'll have a go at it in a minute," the woman said cheerfully.

Julia found herself nodding in agreement. Wasn't this Grace person marvellous? She'd found a big mug now and Julia watched as she spooned in the coffee.

"Where do you keep the sugar?" she asked Julia.

Julia turned to point to a cabinet. She was turning back to say that she didn't actually take sugar when she saw the woman quickly add another spoon of coffee to the mug. With her other hand, she deftly confiscated the wine bottle of detergent.

It dawned on Julia. "You think I'm drunk."

"What? Oh now, I never – "

"Please leave my house," said Julia.

"Mrs Carr – "

"Now."

"All right, fine. If I could just take that gun . . ."

She reached for it. But Julia was faster. How dare she try and make off with her property?

"Mrs Carr. I'm not going until you give me the gun."

"No." Julia gripped the gun tighter between her rubber-gloved fingers. "I won't disturb your precious house viewings again, if that's what you're worried about."

The woman stood her ground. "I'm afraid you might hurt yourself."

"That's highly unlikely. It hasn't been loaded since 1974."

"All the same, I'd be worried."

"Your concern has been noted. Now, if you do not leave my house right now I'm going to call the police."

They both jumped as the telephone extension on the kitchen wall rang. It rang seven times before Julia eventually reached over and picked it up.

"Hello?"

It was the police. Sergeant Daly, actually. He was wondering whether she would come out and talk to him. And could she please bring the gun?

Baffled, she looked over at Grace Tynan, who didn't seem a bit surprised.

Cornered, Julia put the phone down and turned to look at Grace with chilly contempt. "Take the gun if it will make you happy."

She wouldn't please the woman by going over to her; instead she held out the gun, barrel correctly facing the ground, and made her come and get it.

Grace Tynan put out her hand and said, "Thank you – "

Afterwards there were various theories and explanations as to what exactly happened next. Grace Tynan confessed to the police that it was entirely possible that she had accidentally knocked against the trigger in the handover, even though she didn't think it was all that likely. Sergeant Daly was inclined to blame the rubber gloves – he tried on five different brands during the course of his investigation and he could confirm categorically that they had impeded his sensitivity. Julia Carr argued fiercely that she had never gone anywhere near the trigger, rubber gloves or not. And forensics marvelled that a bullet that had unwittingly sat in the barrel of a rusty shotgun for nearly thirty years could still deliver such a punch.

THREE

"Where did you shoot her?"

"I didn't shoot her! Well, it might have been me, we don't know yet – "

"Where?"

"In the foot, okay? I shot her in the foot!"

"Oh my God," Ewan moaned on the phone.

Finally she had managed to surprise her own family. Unfortunately it wasn't an occasion to be particularly proud. There wasn't even a peep from the boys. She could sense them in the background, hanging over Ewan's shoulder.

"Where are you now?" he asked.

"Accident & Emergency. They've taken her off to look at her. You know, to see what the damage is." She didn't go into details. The boys could watch any number of sadistic cartoons but they might not be able to handle the idea of toes hanging by bloodied threads. Well, it was only one toe, and it was more a deep cut than anything else. And it was her little toe as well, as Frank had helpfully pointed out: in fact, she would hardly miss it.

"And, like, is she okay?" Ewan asked.

"No, she's not okay! Would you be okay if you got shot?"

Several people in the crowded waiting-room turned around to

39

have a look. They were all there with sprained ankles, or accompanying toddlers who had swallowed small ornaments – nothing as glamorous as being shot. Was it possible that Grace was some kind of gangster's moll? Despite the oatmeal-coloured suit?

As for Grace, she huddled farther down in her grey plastic chair, the mobile phone pressed to her ear. She had that sick shivery feeling that accompanies accidents. And who would have thought that burnt flesh had such a smell? Like that shoulder of pork they'd overcooked until the blackened skin had curled skywards. At the memory of it, her throat made an odd choking sound.

"Are you all right?" Ewan asked.

"It's the fright of it," she said. "I mean, I could have killed her."

"Come on, Grace."

"She's an elderly woman, Ewan! Supposing she'd had a heart attack?"

"She didn't."

"But supposing! Stress can bring it on! Look at Harry."

Harry Brennan from next door had suffered severe chest pains just after watching the National Lottery programme on television and discovering that he'd won (in the event he'd actually mistaken a nine for a six and hadn't won at all, but the surgeons said it was just as well because they'd found enough fat in his arteries to open a chip shop).

"Why don't you come on home?" Ewan said, and she had that nice warm glow again, that sense of mattering. Wasn't it a pity she couldn't keep on shooting people?

"I can't," she said. "I might have to give a statement to the police."

"Tell them you're going on holidays."

"I already did, but I got the impression that they thought I was trying to leave the jurisdiction or something."

For a while back there, she had thought that Sergeant Daly was actually going to accompany her to the hospital and stand beside her the whole time lest she try and pull a fast one. But he had only followed her back over to Frank's house after the ambulance had left to see if she could give him a quick tour of the house while she was there.

"You want a tour?" She wasn't sure she'd heard him right. The blast from the shotgun had left her temporarily deafened, and the last thing she wanted to do was show a property and pretend to be perky. But her professionalism had got the better of her and she had ended up following him around Frank's dark, airless rooms.

"For yourself, is it?" she'd shouted, the buzzing in her ears not letting up.

"No, no, my son Tom has just got engaged . . . whirlwind romance . . ."

"That's nice," Grace had said, shaking her head a little. But the buzzing wouldn't stop.

"Yes, met in Birmingham . . . name is Charlie, apparently . . . they want to come back and settle in Ireland . . ."

"Oh! Well, ah, good luck to them!" It was the first gay marriage she'd heard of in this country.

"Tom says Charlie's keen to start a family pretty much straight-away," Sergeant Daly finished up.

"Kids?"

"Yes. Do you think the study would be suitable for conversion into a playroom?"

"I think it'd be perfect," Grace had said. Possibly Tom and Charlie were considering surrogacy or something. "Well, I hope everything goes well for them. And you'll make a great grand-father!"

"I hope so," he'd said, nearly bursting with pride. "I'm going to pick them up at the airport now. None of us has met Charlie before – but to honest, I'm just glad that Tom has found someone."

Wasn't it marvellous to be so open-minded, so supportive of your children, Grace thought now. It was a lesson to her: to all parents.

"Can you put the boys on the phone? Just for a minute?" she asked Ewan, feeling a sudden rush of tears to the back of her eyes. This whole shooting business was more upsetting than she'd thought. Right now she just wanted to be at home with her children – to wrap her arms around their hard little bodies, to plant kisses on the side of their necks while they squealed, 'Aw, Mum!' and tried to get away.

Neil came on the line first. "Did you shoot someone?"

"I did," she said, resisting that schoolyard urge to sound boastful. She could feel his respect down the phone line.

"Who? A murderer?" he said breathlessly.

"Well, not exactly."

"What, a robber then?"

"Not as such . . . Anyway!" she said, hoping he would drop it.

But he went on doggedly, "What weapon did he have?"

"Um, he didn't actually have a weapon . . ."

She could sense a hole developing in his admiration. More a crater, actually. "You shot an unarmed man?" he said eventually.

Oh, for heaven's sake! "It was an old lady, okay? I shot a defenceless little old lady!" More people turned to have a look. "But it's not too serious," she added loudly. "The bullet hardly got her at all." Or so she hoped. Still, there hadn't been any great commotion so far. The ambulance hadn't even put its siren on as it had driven off.

"Oh." Neil's interest had now evaporated entirely. "Can I have the window seat on the plane?"

She was glad of the change of subject. "You can have anything you want," she said indulgently.

"Anything?"

"Within reason." You constantly had to be on your guard with Neil.

"So I can have the window seat on the plane?"

"You can have the window seat."

She had thought this was a selfless act on her part (she was a claustrophobic flyer and usually got the window seat) until the phone went muffled at the other end and she heard Neil shouting tauntingly, "I've got the window seat! I've got the window seat! Mum said so!"

"You little shit!" Jamie.

Grace was powerless as she heard several blows exchanged in the background, along with howls of hurt and outrage. Then Ewan intervening, and a door slamming down the hall. Then the phone being picked up again.

"Hello?"

"Neil! That was very unfair of you!"

"This is Jamie."

She didn't miss a beat. "How dare you use language like that!"

"He hit me in the eye," Jamie protested.

She softened, gave a little cluck. "Is it bad?"

She extended a good deal of secret sympathy to Jamie. He was the smaller of the twins and had always approached the world with more caution. He'd been slower to smile, to talk, to be toilet-trained. He was afraid of heights and bruised easily, which made him a natural target for other children. Over the years she felt that he had always needed her protection and intervention more, and the two of them would sometimes sneak off from a game of rough and tumble to read a book about mystical fantastical creatures from long ago, or to cook something exotic and colourful in the kitchen, and they would giggle together like they were playing truant from the real world.

"It's not too bad," he conceded now.

"Tell you what. Neil can have the window seat on the flight out," she said. "And you can have it on the flight back. Okay?" She would make do with an aisle seat.

"I suppose. They have an Astro-Orbiter in Disney," he added.

"Do they?"

"See you later."

"Okay – and Jamie?"

43

She was about to tell him that she loved him; that he was her baby, and that she would see him soon.

"I have to go," Jamie said. "One of Dad's ads is on the telly. The cola one – it's brilliant."

The phone went dead.

"Bye! Thanks for your time!" Grace said loudly, not wanting the other occupants of the waiting-room to know that she had been hung up on by a ten-year-old.

Ewan would ring back in a minute. Well, she didn't know if she would answer the phone! Wouldn't you think that today, of all days, he wouldn't go upstaging her? Wouldn't you think he'd have turned off the television and said, 'Now, lads, this thing is bigger than cola', or something like that? He just didn't think. He never did.

And he wasn't even going to ring back! Her phone lay silently in her hand, and she felt like some teenage girl who had been left waiting all evening for a call from a thoughtless stupid lump of a boy.

Whatever else you do, don't marry him, she found herself imploring the teenage girl. Or, if you insist on marrying him, don't do it at the age of twenty-three, when you have your whole life ahead of you! No, steel yourself against his good looks, his Kawasaki ZR motorbike, the little poems he writes you that always seem to rhyme – even the ones about your first day as a rookie estate agent when you sold a house that wasn't actually up for sale. Oh, he might be great fun, but fun is a poor companion in the supermarket on a Saturday morning with screaming twins trying to vault out of the shopping trolley while he peruses the slogans on tubs of butter (even if he uses quirky accents and ends up making the babies smile). But he'll never phone. He'll never phone you when you want him to.

Her phone rang. It was Ewan. "Grace? I'm sorry about that. I've just turned off the television."

There was a little pause, like he was waiting to be patted on the back or something, and she felt even more annoyed. "Don't do me any favours!"

"I beg your pardon?"

"I said don't turn off the TV on my account."

"I just have. I told you."

"Only because you felt you had to. Really, you'd much rather be watching your own ads than listening to me on the phone!"

"That's a terrible thing to say!"

She wasn't going to let him off the hook this time. "Oh? Any other man would have got into the car and come out to be with me! Any man with feelings!"

There was a little silence, and then he retaliated, "The packing isn't finished. If I were to come out to you, we'd either miss our flight or have to go with no clothes!"

His rationale, his *excuses*, made her even crosser. "You didn't even offer! That's the real insult!"

Now he sounded a bit cross too at being on the end of what he obviously saw as an unprovoked attack. "You want me to make you an offer I have no hope of keeping? You want an empty gesture or two? Why, I had no idea, you should have said!"

Oh! Just when you thought he was as docile as a lamb!

"You have no feelings," she informed him loftily. "Except what you could fit onto the back of a tub of butter."

"What?" he snapped. "What's butter got to do with anything?"

"I'm going to hang up now," she said, haughtily.

"Grace," he said slowly, "I know you've had a shock, so I'm putting this down to your nerves, okay?"

Well, he would have to put it down to *something*, wouldn't he? Explain it away. Because surely there couldn't be anything seriously wrong with her, with them. That would be too inconvenient, just when he'd landed the Slimchoc account (apparently Slimchoc biscuits, mini rolls and Wicked Slimchoc Cake were in development). Then he might actually have to do something, to get involved, to dirty his hands. It was much easier to horse around and pretend he was one of the boys, leaving her to deal with the grown-up world of responsibility and emotions.

"Goodbye," she said.

"Goodbye," he said back, sounding very annoyed. Well, let him! She was sick of being treated with the kind of benevolent tolerance one would show to the family mutt. She who, single-handed, coordinated the complicated and frequently tiresome operation that was the family unit!

But Disneyland lay ahead. Home of the Astro-Orbiter and the free-spirited holidaymaker! Grace found that she was looking forward to it fiercely. They would be different people out there, she told herself; they would be adventurers, challenging the coyotes in Critter Country, or rafting down the rapids in The Great Outback. She would wear shorts and skimpy tops, and a pair of white strappy sandals that fashion magazines would describe as 'amusing'. She had never bought footwear on the basis of its entertainment value before, and she had walked out of the shop with the kind of giggly, confident feeling that comes after two gin and tonics. She didn't know if she'd have the nerve to wear them, though. It would depend on how the holiday went. It would depend on how liberated she was feeling.

Deep down she knew she was fooling herself. Ewan and the boys and herself would not step off a plane and suddenly turn into people who were more interesting, and nicer and kinder to each other. Worse again: instead of them all being somebody else, they might just be themselves but in a more concentrated form. She could just imagine it: Ewan speaking in rhyming couplets and watching the shopping channels on the TV; the boys clawing lumps out of each other and cursing. And her – what would she be doing? Fussing around the place like some kind of demented mother hen and falling over in her new white sandals. It was enough to make her weep. In fact, she did weep, squeezing out two little tears and allowing herself a sniffle.

"Don't worry. She'll pull through," the man next to her said, startling her.

"Sorry?"

"That poor woman you shot."

"Oh, yes. I, ah, certainly hope so," Grace said with a watery smile.

There was a picture in the Disney brochure of a family on one of the water rides – a couple and their two children in a plastic-looking log canoe, coming off a bend. The man was all testosterone and bravado, his brown face split in a cheesy grin. The two kids in front were laughing and displaying thousands of dollars worth of orthodontics.

But it was the woman Grace looked at the most.

She was perfect. She had that indefinable aura that only very confident people had. Oh, she sickened Grace. You just knew by looking at her that she had never experienced a moment of self-doubt in her life! She had turned out exactly the way she had wanted to all along; everything about her was rounded and complete and full. She just . . . *was*.

In the photo she ignored the man entirely. And the two brats in front. Not for her the desperation of bribing her family with a trip to Disney. No, she was looking straight ahead, her blue eyes frozen on some rosy future that would no doubt be rewarding and comfortable and where nobody would ever dare to take her for granted, while women like Grace struggled and juggled and usually ended up making a balls of things.

Frank bustled up. "You'd nearly want to have your leg hanging off in here before they'd treat you."

And, actually, there *was* a man with his leg nearly hanging off over there, but he didn't seem to be getting treated any quicker than the rest of them.

"Well?" Grace asked. "Did you find her?"

"They said she was in a treatment room and that I was to wait out here."

"Maybe they're waiting for a special doctor to come. A foot doctor." She wondered was there such a thing. Guiltily, she stole a glance at her watch: she had to leave in precisely one hour if she was going to make it to the long-term carpark in the airport on time. Surely Mrs Carr would be discharged by then?

But Frank announced, "They asked me for details of next of kin."

Grace's throat closed over. "Next of kin?"

"It's standard procedure," Frank said, and she relaxed a bit. "To be honest," he confided, "it didn't take very long. Everyone belonging to her is dead, or nearly dead. Between you and me, she doesn't even have that many friends."

"So there's nobody?"

Frank waved a hand. "Well, except for Michael, of course. That's her son. And Gillian, her daughter-in-law. I gave them their phone number at reception."

He consulted his watch now too. "I suppose I should let Sandy know what's happened. She'll be very disappointed if this holds up the sale. She said to me, 'You get your tush over here right now before I find myself another man!'" He added quickly, "She was only joking. I mean, she's not . . . loose or anything."

"I didn't think for a moment – "

"She goes to church every Sunday. Sings in the choir and all. That's if she's not doing a reading."

Sandy seemed to be putting in an early pitch for canonisation. But Grace just put this thought down to jealousy on her part.

"I suppose this gun business has held up the sale?" Frank said gloomily.

"Well, obviously we had to send the three couples away . . ."

"But you'll reschedule them, right?"

"Of course," Grace lied. The sight of Mrs Carr being carried out on a stretcher from the house across the road, followed by various members of the elite police force in bullet-proof gear and packing heavy-duty firearms, had very likely terminated their interest in Frank's house.

"Mrs Carr. Mrs Julia Carr?" A medical person in green scrubs was standing by the swing doors holding a chart and looking around expectantly.

Grace stood quickly. "That's us. Frank, you mind the seats."

She picked her way across outstretched legs and sleeping children. The medical person was gruff and busy and she hadn't seen him around Casualty earlier. She hoped that he didn't know that she was involved in the shooting.

But he said, straight off, "You're responsible for Mrs Carr?"

Was nothing going to go her way today? "We don't know that for certain yet," she said strongly, trying to resist the urge to look shiftily at the floor. But really, whatever had happened to innocent until proven guilty?

The man looked at her impatiently. "You accompanied her here, though?"

"Well, yes."

"She's just being prepared for surgery now."

"What?" She was shocked. It was the word 'surgery'. It always had such an ominous ring.

"There are some pellets quite deeply embedded. And then there are the bones."

"What bones?"

"The metatarsals. Two of them are going to have to be reconstructed. Or what's left of them anyway." He gave her another accusing look. Grace squirmed.

"So it's quite serious?" she said.

"An injury is always more serious in someone her age," he said, the implication being that she should at least have picked on someone younger.

"Thank you for telling me," she said. "Maybe I should talk to her surgeon or something?"

"You are," he said.

"Oh!" Now she had offended the surgeon. This sort of thing would never have happened to the woman in the Disney

49

brochure. The woman in the Disney brochure wouldn't have been here in the first place; the very idea of landing in such a mess would have brought a wry sweet smile to her perfect face.

"How long will she be kept in?" Grace enquired.

"That depends on her recovery, but she seems fairly robust. She should be out in a few days."

A few days would not make any difference, Grace decided quickly. She would simply arrange to meet Ewan and the boys in Florida. She'd have to forego the motel, but that was a small price to pay for her actions. She owed it to Mrs Carr.

"Okay," she said.

"She'll be in a wheelchair or on crutches for several weeks, of course – at least until we see how the bones are knitting. And you'll need to bring her up for regular physio and the rest." Unaware that her face was losing what bloom it still had, he efficiently consulted the chart again. "You might want to talk to your husband and see what you can work out in terms of support for her at home."

Ewan? She wasn't sure what he had to do with anything. "Well, yes, I suppose I could discuss it with him . . ."

"Good," he said.

There was no doubt now that he knew she had pulled the trigger (allegedly). He was more or less telling her to face up to her responsibilities. And he was right. She would do no more wriggling or squirming to try and get out of it.

"And don't be afraid to rope in other members of the family as well," he added.

Grace blinked. Her parents mightn't be that easily persuaded from retirement in County Mayo to look after a complete stranger. And her brother Nick was house-sitting for her and Ewan while they were in Disney, to write his new album, and driving thirty miles to bring Julia Carr bowls of chicken soup would probably not be compatible with his brand of heavy rock.

"Yes," she said, because she didn't know what else to say.

The surgeon had his hand on the swing doors now. "You can phone later on to see how your mother-in-law is doing."

"What? My mother-in-law? She's not – "

But he leaned in, quite friendly now. "A lot of the elderly people we get in here don't have any family at all, you know. Then we have to send them home alone, weak and in pain. Tragic." His face hardened. "If I could get my hands on the person who did this to her . . ."

Her mouth, which had opened in readiness to protest further, slowly closed.

"Anyhow," he said. "Goodbye, uh . . ." He checked the chart. "Gillian."

And he walked off through the swing doors, taking a good portion of her immediate hopes, dreams and wildest expectations with him.

This is a Public Service Announcement. Please do not leave your baggage unattended at any time in the terminal building or we may have to blow it up.

They didn't actually say they would blow it up, of course, but that's what they meant, Grace knew. Security was tight that day. It was a bonus to have got past the airport police at all, with her snagged tights and reeking of gunpowder.

"Hurry up, Neil! And Jamie – give me that bag, for goodness' sake, or they'll blow it up."

She snatched up his hand luggage and continued her march down the hall towards Departures. The flight had been called three times already.

Beside her, Ewan gave another low moan and said, "I just can't believe it." For almost an hour now he hadn't been able to believe it. "I mean, why didn't you just *explain*?"

"I tried to! But everything happened so fast! And besides, I didn't want them thinking I was trying to dump the woman or something."

"So instead you let them think that you were her daughter-in-law?"

"Yes. Which would make you Michael."

"This isn't funny, Grace."

"Nobody's laughing." As if Ewan would have done any better in the situation! He couldn't even bring himself to correct a mistake in a restaurant (once he'd eaten his way through a stuffed calf's heart rather than point out that he'd actually ordered a pizza. Possibly he had been waiting for her to do it for him).

"Neil! Jamie! Stop that *now*." They had hijacked a luggage trolley. When they got up enough speed, they both jumped onto it and careered wildly down the tiled floor as though they were tobogganing down the Cresta run.

"Maybe we could ring the hospital from here," Ewan fretted. "Explain the situation or something. Damn – where did I put the boarding passes . . .?"

"You gave them to me to mind. And what exactly am I going to say to the hospital on the phone, Ewan? That I'm very sorry I shot her but that I'm buggering off to Disneyland for a month?"

"Well, I don't know, do I!" Ewan said. The boys careered into a row of seats now. He winced. "When do you think you'll be able to fly out?" he asked anxiously.

"I don't know."

"I mean, a foot thing – it couldn't take that long to get better, could it?"

"She's still in the operating theatre, Ewan." She didn't mention the physio and the rest. Ewan wasn't someone who dealt very well with large chunks of reality at any one time. Best to split things up and give them to him gradually. Suddenly she was reminded of when she used to sit the twins up in their high chairs and spoon-feed them vegetables she had painstakingly blended to a mush, a little at a time.

Ewan added, "She has relatives. I don't see why they can't look after her."

His baleful tone, his lack of sympathy for Mrs Carr, made her so cross that she said loudly, "Maybe they can! I don't know yet! All I *do* know right now is that three hours ago I shot an old woman, Ewan! An old woman who's having two metatarsals reconstructed in an operating theatre right now because of me!"

Ewan sighed. "Don't be so dramatic, Grace – "

"So I'm sorry if this disrupts all our plans! I'm sorry if it's all very inconvenient, but if I can't find a bit of compassion in my soul at a time like this – well, then, I'm not much of a person, am I!"

Ewan and the boys exchanged a look, as though she were half-cracked, or pre-menstrual or something. Right now, for two pins, she would walk out of the airport and leave them there! (But she was in charge of the boarding passes, and the drinks for the flight, and two travel board games for the boys, and Ewan's book.)

This is the final call for Flight EI 102 to London Heathrow. The gates will close in five minutes.

"Jesus," fussed Ewan. "After all this, we're going to miss our flight."

This seemed to Grace to be further recrimination for spoiling everybody's day, and she grimly quickened her pace down the terminal building, bags swinging out of her and boarding passes held aloft, like some kind of manic air hostess. Ewan and the boys had to run to keep up.

"Grace. Wait." He obviously saw that he had upset her in some way (he was quite good at that, even though he usually had no idea how) because he puffed, "You never know. She could be discharged from the hospital in no time and you'll be on your way out."

It was the first reference any of them had made to what Grace was missing out on: to her own disappointment. The boys might be excused on the grounds of excitement, but Ewan?

"Maybe," she said.

They were at the Departures gates now, and she reached into

her bag for all the bits and pieces that she had spared everybody else the worry of until now.

"Be good now," she said automatically to Neil and Jamie. "And I'll talk to you on the phone, okay?"

"I need a drink," Jamie said in response.

She handed over a bottle of water. And as she looked at his excited little face – at both her children's faces – she was suddenly overcome with emotion: they were going off without her, on a great journey, and she was being left behind!

Impulsively she hunkered down and threw her arms around them both. "Goodbye! I'll miss you!"

They squirmed and wriggled and looked around to see was anyone watching the embarrassing display. "You'll probably see us in a few days," Neil complained.

Well, yes. The moment had somehow gone, and she let go of them quickly and stood.

Now she handed over all Ewan's things. He blinked and frowned as he tried to find pockets for everything.

"Well, have a good flight," she said.

"It's the next leg I'm worried about – all the way to America!" he grumbled. "Did you pack those games for the boys?"

"You just put them in your coat pocket, Ewan."

"Oh, yes."

"So! Goodbye then!" She waited for his hug.

This is an announcement for flight EI 102 to London Heathrow. The gates are now closed –

"Oh my God!" Ewan grabbed a twin in each hand, and they trampled past Grace towards the gates.

She regained her balance, to see them ducking under ropes and trying to get to the top of the queue.

"Ask those people if you can squeeze in before them, that you're late," she urged.

They did, and the airport official manning the gates scrutinised the three boarding passes, and quickly waved them through. Thank God.

Grace shifted over a bit so that she could see through the gates to wave goodbye to them. But Ewan and the boys were preparing to empty their pockets at the security scanners. She hoped Neil had remembered to leave the penknife at home that he routinely carried around.

Now the three of them waited in line to go through the metal-detector. And, looking at them, Grace was suddenly shocked to notice that Jamie and Neil reached to Ewan's shoulder. How had she not noticed how tall they'd grown? She must have been looking the other way too when Neil decided that the nice pair of jeans she'd bought him last week would actually be much better as surfer-style shorts, with the help of a pair of scissors. His legs, thin and hairless still, poked out from the fraying ends, but he walked with his feet planted far apart in a good imitation of a macho strut. As for Jamie – her little boy! – was that his *underwear* deliberately pulled up over the waistband of his jeans?

They were growing up. Shedding their childish loveliness and turning into big, hairy, brutes of men. All underarm sweat and willies. She didn't know if she could bear it.

She saw Ewan turning around.

"Goodbye!" she said, waving.

But he had turned to say something to the boys. The three of them laughed, all buddy-buddy and boys together. The depth of her resentment towards him shook Grace. Perhaps it was because she had done the dogsbody work all these years: the disciplining, the runs to basketball and football and dance classes (which had only lasted two weeks, in fairness). That's not to say Ewan had ignored them – no, he had descended from his perch every evening at six o'clock on the dot, just when she had finished bullying them into doing their homework, and they would run to him like he was their saviour, casting dark looks back at their tormentor.

They got through the metal-detector successfully, and they

were now putting everything back into their pockets and collecting their hand luggage. In a minute, they would go through that frosted glass partition and they would be out of sight.

"Ewan!". She gave another little wave.

But he didn't look back.

"Jamie? Jamie!" He had the best hearing. But no. She dropped her hand, a bit embarrassed. Honestly – they knew she would have waited. Wouldn't you think they'd at least have looked back?

They didn't. Not once. They filled their pockets with all the things she had carefully looked after for them – and they went right on! Through that frosted-glass partition without one of them turning to wave goodbye.

Gone. Without Ewan even saying he would miss her desperately!

Or that he would miss her at all.

The realisation was so upsetting that she stood there, in the middle of the vast tiled floor, long after the flight had closed.

"Are you all right? Do you need help with anything?"

Some nice airport attendant had stopped. Grace felt herself being assessed from her scraggly hair right down to her scuffed shoes as a possible security concern.

"No, thank you, I'm fine," she said, smiling brightly.

She kept smiling brightly as she retraced her steps all the way back through the terminal building, down the rickety elevator, and into the short-term car park.

FOUR

"At least your lot are away in Disney," her brother Nick said. He was standing in her kitchen. "Mine are only down the road in Drumcondra – fat chance they'll stay away from me for a whole month. Was I telling you that Janis got on a bus all by herself last week and ended up in Newbridge?"

"You were."

"The amazing thing is that the bus didn't even go to Newbridge, the police said, so she must have got off and changed connections at some point. I couldn't even tie my own shoelaces at five." Nick pondered this with amused wonder. "Have you any more tea bags, Grace?"

"Second press over."

She'd forgotten how much tea he drank. He didn't seem to have brought any tea bags of his own, despite the mountain of luggage he'd deposited in the hall. No food either, unless you counted a Toffee Crisp. But maybe you had to provide food when you asked people to housesit. Not that they had actually asked him – he'd more or less offered his services. Insisted, in fact, only two days ago, when they'd got all their arrangements in place. Said it would be a mutually beneficial arrangement – he would get to finish his new album and at the same time keep vicious and

57

unscrupulous thieves away. Ewan hadn't been that keen (it was to do with the fact that he worked with advertising jingles as opposed to 'real music', as Nick had once said over a Christmas dinner at which too much wine had been consumed). Still, as Grace had said, Nick was her brother and they should be glad to be able to help him out. And it would be a change from that tiny flat he'd moved into since he and Didi had separated last year.

She just hadn't expected to be in the house when he arrived, that was all. And, watching as he dripped tea all over her lovely clean kitchen floor, she wished she wasn't.

"So! How are Dusty and Lennon?" she asked.

Nick and Didi had named their children after rock legends, which had seemed a great idea when they were babies. Dusty was fourteen now and wanted to change her name by deed poll to Jane.

"Great. Lennon wants to stop going to school," Nick said, spooning sugar into his tea. Half of it missed the cup and went on the worktop.

"Does he?"

"Can't say I blame him. State propaganda, the lot of it."

"And what does Didi think?" Grace enquired.

"Didi! She says he has to go, of course. Says that if he drops out now, he'll have no qualifications, no chance of a proper job, his whole future will be ruined, blah-bloody-blah!"

"Well, he is only nine," Grace offered. You had to be careful on the subject of Didi. Nick could be a bit sensitive.

"Anyway," he said. "Didi says she'll probably drop by here with Lennon to discuss it at some point – is that okay, Grace?"

"Fine by me. I just hope you get some work done on your album, that's all."

"Yeh," he said, adding milk to his tea. Some of that missed, too.

"How's it coming along, anyway?" she asked.

"What?"

"The new album."

"We haven't really started," he said.

"Oh. Okay." She had thought they were under pressure. "And look, I don't want to nag, but tell Derek and Vinnie that they're not to block anyone's driveway with their vans, okay?"

Derek and Vinnie were the two other members of Steel Warriors.

"They probably won't be around much anyway." He didn't quite meet her eyes.

"Why not?" They played lead guitar and drums, for heaven's sake.

"We've decided to change direction," he announced. "To be honest, I've been moving away from all that heavy rock stuff for a couple of years now. It's just too immature and loud. You can hardly hear my lyrics."

"Oh." Grace always felt backward when Nick started talking about music. It went back to their teenage years when he had roundly scorned her for listening to Duran Duran while he played The Ramones in his bedroom.

Then Nick gave a sigh that seemed to shake the whole kitchen. "I suppose you're going to find out anyway. Steel Warriors have broken up, okay?"

"What?"

"The record company dropped us last month. So there's no band, no new album, no money, nothing. And Didi says she's sick of scrimping and scrounging and sticking the kids in second-hand clothes. She says that unless I pay six months' arrears in maintenance she's going to take me to court. Isn't that lovely!" He said all this very fast. "Would you have anything to eat around the place at all? I didn't get a chance to have lunch before I left."

"I think there's a pizza in the freezer," Grace said, kind of numb. Steel Warriors, broken up! "What are you going to do, Nick?"

"A computer course in Clonliffe Road."

She was more shocked. He bent to rummage in the freezer, his big awkward body hunched over clumsily. He looked like he had been grown specially to jump around an open-air stage in tight leather. He did not look like a computer operator.

"What about the rest of the, uh, warriors?" she ventured.

"Derek's just got a promotion in Dublin Bus – he's in charge of ninety-six double-deckers now. And Vinnie's going to stick with insurance."

"What a cop-out!" she cried.

"He's got another kid on the way, Grace."

"Oh. But all the same! A band can't succeed if everybody isn't giving it a hundred per cent – like you, Nick!"

"Yeh, and maybe I've been the stupid one."

Grace was appalled "Don't ever say that."

"No? I'm thirty-five years old, Grace! And look at me! A failed band, a failed marriage, three kids who have never even listened to one of my records – they like hip-hop, for God's sake! I've no money, no qualifications, no flat – "

"No flat?"

"Did I not tell you? I kind of fell behind in the rent – is it okay if I stay here until I find something else?"

"Ah . . ."

"Thanks. So you see, it's over, Grace," he declared solemnly. "I sold my guitar yesterday and bought computer course books with the money. I'm starting a new life." There was a little silence. "You might at least wish me luck."

"Sorry. It's just hard to take it in, that's all."

He looked glum too. "I know."

"Do you remember the very first gig you played?" she said, after a bit. "As support in the SFX?" She had been sixteen and she remembered being sick with excitement when her parents had said she could go along.

"God, yeh," Nick said. "Derek out of his head on cider. And

60

Vinnie so nervous he couldn't remember how to tune his guitar."

"But you? You were magnificent!" Grace cried. "Standing up on the stage like you owned the place! Pointing out the fire exits to the crowd and telling them you'd hurl them out head first if they didn't stop throwing things at you."

"And they did," Nick said, excited too. "We managed to play three whole songs and they loved it! And your friend – what was her name – Fidelma?"

"Philomena."

"Fainting! Having to be carted up on the stage at the very end in that little white vest! God, that was beautiful."

"Wasn't it?" Grace said, giving a little clap. They had all walked the streets of Dublin afterwards for hours, too young to get into pubs, too high to go home. Grace had just assumed that this was the start of a global career for Steel Warriors and that she would be a small part of it by virtue of her relationship with Nick – even if she thought their music was, well, awful.

But she hadn't said that, of course. Instead she'd had her hair cut in a kind of rock-chick bob, which had lasted until the release of the Warriors' first single, *Dead Dingo*. It did moderately well. The next single bombed. But she had continued to believe in the cause, in Nick.

"How can you bear to give it up?" she blurted. Steel Warriors was so much a part of him – the very fibre of his being. No matter how hard things got, he was always so sure what he was doing was right. People like that tended to inspire a higher purpose in others. And now he was caving in at the prospect of a job in IT?

"Give what up?" he asked. "The gigs playing to five people?"

"Stop it. You've played to more than five people."

"Our record company has dumped us, Grace."

"So what! Find a new one!"

Why was he being like this? Cynical and hard and washed-up?

"I know it's tough," she pleaded. "But surely you should give it one last shot? Don't you owe it to yourself and the guys?"

"What, you mean muster enough energy to record another album so that you can buy fifteen copies of it?"

Grace flushed.

"I saw them in the garage when I was putting in my car. Are you trying to offload them on all your dinner-party friends?"

She met his eyes. "As a matter of fact, I do give them to some of my friends. I tell them how great you are. How fortunate you are to . . . to have followed your dreams!"

She regretted the ebullience of this statement the minute it was out of her mouth.

Nick laughed again, loudly. "Anybody can follow their dream if they don't mind being on the dole. But then you wouldn't know about that, would you?"

The nasty little silence was broken by a knock on the back door. Hilda Brennan from next door stuck her head in stiffly.

"I heard voices and I just wanted to check that there weren't wild parties going on or anything. Not that I'm sticking my nose in where it's not wanted." Her voice was full of hurt and self-righteousness.

"No, it's only me," Grace said. "I didn't fly out with the boys after all."

"What?"

"Her and Ewan have broken up," Nick explained. This was his type of humour. But Hilda, who was short on humour of any type, took a step forward fiercely.

"What are you talking about?" she barked.

Grace intervened quickly. "Hilda, this is my brother Nick. Nick, meet my next-door neighbour."

"Uh, hello," said Nick.

Hilda just favoured him with a long, distasteful look, and then kind of shook her head at Grace as though to say, '*This* is what you've chosen over us!' Oh no, it hadn't blown over yet, by any means, the rift that Nick had unwittingly caused between the Tynans and their good friends the Brennans next-door two days ago. Harry and Hilda had been most upset when told that they needn't keep an eye on the house while the family was away, as they had done every year for the past decade. Harry had asked Ewan whether they didn't trust them any more around the silver. Hilda had not popped around for coffee yesterday as usual and didn't hang her washing out until after dark. The whole thing had nearly got ugly until Grace had sent Ewan around last night with a bottle of whiskey and a big bunch of flowers.

Right now, Hilda wasn't going anywhere. Nick took a step closer to Grace.

But Grace was through baby-sitting men today, and so she picked up her car keys. "I have a cooker to clean."

"What?" said Nick.

"See you later," she said, and walked out.

"Look at her. She seems so . . . old. And tiny!"

"Now don't go upsetting yourself, Gillian. She's just after coming through an operation. Anybody would look a bit rough."

"That could have been me lying there, you know, Michael. With my bronchitis."

"Yes, well, thank God it was only a too-tight bra-strap in the end."

"That's still only a theory. The results of the tests haven't come back yet."

Julia heard the hushed voices from somewhere far away. But she lay very still anyhow. She wasn't quite sure where she was for starters. She could hear a steady *bip bip bip* noise near her ear and thought that perhaps she might be in a spaceship. Or an amusement arcade. But to play the fruit machines surely she should be standing upright?

A different voice now. Childish. Spoilt. "Dad, can I turn on the television?"

"I told you already. No."

"But Buffy is on!"

"Susan, your grandmother has just been shot!"

"Yeh, but she's not going to die, is she?"

There was no need to sound so hopeful, Julia thought. The events of the morning came back to her in a rush. Which meant that she was on her side in a hospital bed recovering from a shotgun blast, and not on a spaceship on her way to pill-induced eternity. She tried to open her eyes but her eyelids felt glued together, and there was a nasty, antiseptic taste in her mouth, which was gaping wide open. So was the back of her blue hospital gown, leaving her bloomers on show for the whole world to see. Terrific. She tried to roll over, but she hadn't the energy. In fact, she felt like she would break up into tiny little pieces at any moment – *ping* – which would float off into space, leaving a pleasant nothingness behind.

Hang on – maybe she *was* dying! Maybe this was it. The big exit. Very possibly a sombre phone call had been made to the family: 'I'm afraid the operation on your mother's toe didn't go as well as we'd hoped. Maybe you'd better come in.'

And now they were all gathered around her bed to witness the momentous event, faces grave and handkerchiefs at the ready. The hospital chaplain might even appear towards the end – he had for JJ, surely he'd show up for her? Then they would all go to a warm pub somewhere and tell stories about how great she'd been.

For a brief moment Julia was overcome. Her time had finally arrived. She was *dying*.

"Mammy! Can you hear me? Mammy, it's Michael."

He couldn't let her die in peace, of course. She was reminded of when he'd been a child – always demanding her attention, always pleading with her to 'see what I can do!' And when she would turn he wouldn't be doing anything at all; he had just wanted her to look at him. Funny little Michael.

"Mammy?" Then he said, "Here, Gillian, you have a go."

Chairs scraped back. Then a charm bracelet jangled loudly near

Julia's ear and a finger poked in her upper arm. Oh, it was maddening – nobody could die in these circumstances!

"Julia? It's Gillian here." An expectant pause. Julia lay defiantly still. "Julia, we're going home for our tea now, but we'll come back in the morning, okay?"

Their tea? She was hardly dying if they were going home to scoff ham sandwiches. She mustn't even be on the critical list!

Failure, twice in one day. She lay there on the bed in dank dark misery, letting the rustle of their departure wash over her: Gillian's handbag snapping, Susan zipping up her coat, car keys jangling.

"Susan, say goodbye to your grandmother."

"But she can't hear me, Dad."

"It would still be a nice thing to do."

Julia was almost touched, but then Gillian chimed in, "You know, I was reading in one of my medical books that lots of coma victims respond to the voices of their families – imagine!"

"Really," Michael said, sounding impatient. Well, anybody would, after fifteen years of marriage to a hypochondriac.

"There was this case study of a man who had been in a coma for twelve years – a total vegetable, the poor man. And the very day they were going to switch off the life-support machine, he heard his young grandson's voice, and he woke up just like that and recited the alphabet!"

"I want to say goodbye to her!" Susan squealed now.

How Julia longed to spring up in the bed and give them all an almighty fright. But unfortunately she hadn't the energy and was forced to lie helpless as Susan leaned in over her ear.

"Granny? It's Susan here." Pause. "Your granddaughter." Then, peeved, "She didn't do anything!"

"We'll try her again in the morning," Gillian said indulgently.

Everything was quiet for a moment, and Julia thought they had gone.

But then: "We're going to have to sort something out, Michael."

"I know."

"I mean, the Emergency Response Unit was on the way, for heaven's sake!"

"I know, Gillian."

"And two units of the fire brigade. We'll probably get billed for that."

"Never mind about that. I just hope they're going to charge that woman who shot her."

"It was an accident, Michael. It wouldn't have happened at all if your mother hadn't gone bats and started waving a shotgun about."

"Please don't talk about her like that."

"I'm just saying. We're going to have to sort something out."

Then they were gone, and Julia was almost sorry (what could they have meant, 'sort something out'?) and then she drifted off again somewhere that was neither pleasant nor unpleasant.

Rachel, I'm going on my break now. Those two files are for Dr Ryan. Will I bring you back a chocolate muffin?

She surfaced again. She had been dreaming about JJ. He was holding a baby in his arms – Michael, about six months old. And JJ was looking down at him with such love, holding him with such pride.

She tried to hold onto the image of JJ's beloved face, but it grew muzzy and distorted. And why was he wearing lipstick?

"Awake at last!" A nurse was bending over her. There was a chocolate crumb on her uniform.

"Was my family in?" Julia enquired. She wanted to be sure she had not dreamt that too.

"They certainly were! Very concerned about you too," the nurse said. "He looks very like you, doesn't he? Your son."

Julia was a bit taken aback. "Well, maybe a little around the mouth . . ."

It had never occurred to her that she and Michael were similar in any way, even appearance.

66

"He's the absolute spit of you," the nurse declared emphatically.

"Yes, is there any way you can limit their visits?"

"Sorry?"

"You could tell them I need my rest and can't be disturbed," Julia suggested brightly.

"Um, I'd have to talk to your Ward Sister . . ."

"I'd appreciate it if you would."

"I'm enquiring about Mrs Carr? Mrs Julia Carr?"

At the other end of the phone the hospital receptionist sang efficiently, "What ward is she in, please?"

"I don't know. She was going for an operation. Has she had it?"

"Are you a relative?"

Grace hesitated. "More a concerned bystander." Well, there was no point in getting into the whole thing on the phone.

"We can only give out information to relatives." The voice was firm now.

"Can you at least tell me if I can go in and visit her?"

"If she was due to have an operation then a visit today isn't advisable. Especially if you're not a relative."

For heaven's sake. "But all her relatives are dead," she protested. "Or nearly dead."

The person on the other end of the phone wasn't to be swayed. Grace hung up and looked at Frank, shaking her head a little.

"I'll give you Michael's number," he advised. "Her son. He'll be able to tell you."

He bent to rummage in a drawer. Grace had called in to get a spare set of keys to Mrs Carr's house. She was going to spend the evening scouring the blackened cooker and washing the smoke-damaged curtains – it was the very least she could do in the circumstances, she felt. Hopefully Nick and Hilda had struck up a friendship back at the house.

Frank held out the number on a scrap of paper to her, and then said, rather shyly, "Would you like to see a photo of Sandy?"

"I'd love to," she said.

She already had a mental image of a plainish woman, large maybe (well, all right, fat), with uneven teeth. And a bleached moustache. Oh, she knew she was being unfair – but, honestly, what else would you picture for Frank? Cindy Crawford?

And so she was quite unprepared for the vision that stared out at her from a silver photo-frame that Frank handed her.

"That's . . . Sandy?"

"Yes."

Sandy was blonde, tanned, toned and thin. She had two adorable big bouncy breasts, and a skinny waist, and all her own teeth, and wasn't a day over thirty.

Grace knew now why Sandy took up to four hours in the bathroom. Every strand of her hair was teased and sprayed into submission, her make-up was lavish, and her nails were little round ovals of perfection. Just looking at her made Grace feel tired.

Oddly enough, her right hand was chopped off in the photo, right at the wrist.

"She hasn't . . . the hand thing is a mistake, right?" Best to be up front about any amputations straight away.

"Oh, yes. The photo was taken with an ex-boyfriend, you see. She's resting her hand on his shoulder. She didn't want to upset me, so she just chopped him out."

It occurred to Grace that the ex must have been quite short – about three foot four, at her estimate – but possibly he had been kneeling at her feet or something. After all, she *was* lovely. And if she could get men to kneel before her, then you had to say fair play to her.

"She's beautiful, Frank."

"Yes," Frank said, taking the photo back protectively. "That's the only photo I have. I keep asking her for more, but she says she gets shy around cameras."

Sandy appeared to be modest too; if Grace were that nice-looking, she would have her photo taken all the time, she thought. Not that she was bad-looking. But she just looked ordinary, which surely must be the worst thing to look.

"I know what you're thinking," Frank said belligerently.

Grace was startled. "What?"

"I'm aware that I'm no oil painting, okay?"

"Frank – "

"I was voted Student Most Likely to Stay Single at boarding school. Twice. But Sandy says looks don't matter to her. She says she's sick of the kind of guys who try to hit on her all the time. She doesn't go to clubs or bars or the gym any more because of all these muscly, good-looking guys trying to have sex with her."

It sounded like heaven to Grace, but she just murmured sympathetically, "Awful." Frank continued fervently, "She says she's never found a meaningful relationship with anyone until she met me, that I am the light in her darkest days, and that we should get down on our knees and thank God that we found each other!"

Grace was a bit taken aback. Sandy sounded a bit, well, over the top. She was obviously very much in love with Frank.

Which was terrific, of course. God knows the romance would wear off soon enough – usually a couple of years into marriage, and was more or less extinct by the arrival of the first child. By the second, it was a prehistoric relic that reared its ancient head only briefly on St Valentine's Day and maybe during a sun holiday in Crete or somewhere, after too much wine in a bar and a walk back along the beach to the Bella Vista family apartments.

She left Frank gazing fervently at his framed photo of Sandy, and went across the road to Mrs Carr's house. She was used to letting herself in to other people's houses when they weren't there, and in no time at all she had familiarised herself with the light switches, and the loose floorboards in the living-room that could trip you up if you weren't careful. Not that she had gone into the room to snoop – that guilty curiosity in seeing how other people lived had passed years ago – just to close the bay window properly. She'd seen from the street that it was open a crack. She pulled up the net curtain energetically and closed the window with a sound bang.

A man was approaching the garden gate from the road, and the window slamming gave him a bit of a start. Reflexively, he jerked away. He was carrying a big heavy backpack, and what seemed to be a bundle of placards, which, in his fright, he swung upwards, knocking the side mirror off her BMW.

They looked at each other through the closed window. Eventually Grace reached forward and opened it again.

"Sorry," he began, trying to piece the mirror back together again.

"No, *I'm* sorry. Leave that."

"Your car . . ."

"Banging the window at you like that . . ."

"I didn't mean to . . .the mirror is clean off . . ."

"Don't worry about that, I can get it repaired."

And they kind of smiled at each other.

"Can I help you?" she asked at last.

"Is this Park View House?" he said. He sounded Australian, or possibly he was from New Zealand. The surfer shorts could have come from either country. And he was more a boy than a man. In his early twenties maybe. Not that Grace was a great judge of these things – the older she got, the less accurate she was about the ages of those younger than herself. Which was fair enough, given the way teenagers callously and wildly overestimated the age of anybody over twenty-five.

"I'm not sure," Grace was forced to admit. There was no park in evidence. Not that that had ever stopped anybody. She could go on for a whole day about the silly names people gave their houses (La Maison Rouge – for an ex-council house in Crumlin!) Instead, she opened the window a crack more and leaned out to see the number over the front door. "It's Number 28 anyway. What number are you looking for?"

He consulted a grubby bit of paper. He had very blue eyes. Or possibly they looked bluer because his face was so tanned. "I don't have a number. Just Park View House. Mrs Julia Carr?"

"Oh! Yes."

"Nice to meet you."

"No, no, I'm not actually Mrs Carr. I'm . . ." It was all too complicated, so she just said, "This is her house."

He seemed satisfied with this. "Great. I've just walked all the way from the train station and I thought I was lost." He smiled at her easily. "I don't usually get lost."

She could believe that. Now that he was sure he was in the right place, he opened the garden gate and walked right in. He wore the biggest boots she had ever seen on anybody. Walking boots. He rocked back and forth on them now, confidently, cockily. His blondish hair was in dreadlocks that bobbed about his ears like fat little puppy tails, and an earring glinted in one ear.

"So," he said. "Are you going to let me in?"

"I beg your pardon?"

"Into the house."

Grace kept smiling even as her mind raced to process the implications of this. "You want to come in?" she clarified.

"Well, yes." He consulted his bit of paper again. "Do you want to be paid upfront or something, is that it?"

"No, no, not at all!" she said happily, her confusion turning to a ridiculous determination to battle this thing out. "Did Mrs Carr say anything about being paid upfront?" Best to throw it back at him.

"She said I could pay when I left."

"I see," she said, even though she didn't.

"I did book, you know," he said. "I got the number from the local tourist office and I rang her last week."

Of course! The woman ran some kind of Bed & Breakfast. Grace made sure her expression didn't alter.

"I'm afraid there's a bit of a problem," she told him. "Mrs Carr is actually in hospital."

"Oh."

"She won't be home for a couple of days."

"Nothing serious, I hope?" He looked like he meant it.

"A foot thing," Grace said vaguely. "The thing is, she won't be in any fit state to look after lodgers. So, obviously . . ."

His face fell. "Yes. Of course."

"I'm very sorry about this," she said. "Maybe you could try somewhere else?"

"Sure." He hoisted his backpack further up on his broad shoulders, and shifted the placards from one arm to the other, wincing slightly at the weight. "I don't suppose there's any chance I could use your phone?"

Grace hesitated. She didn't want to go inviting strangers into a house that wasn't hers.

"My mobile is out of credit, so I'd have to walk all the way back into town to find a pay phone. And to be honest, I'm beat."

He did look tired. And besides, this thing was partially her fault in the first place.

"Come in," she said. "I'm sure we can find a phone directory somewhere."

Inside the front door he took off his boots without any invitation. Grace waited as he lined them up neatly on the mat beside the backpack and the placards, and turned to face her in his stockinged feet. Slightly different social customs obviously prevailed in Australia. Or maybe he belonged to one of those religions that frowned upon footwear indoors.

She kept her own shoes resolutely on and led the way to the living-room. She settled him in the tatty red armchair and presented him with Mrs Carr's cordless phone and a copy of the local directory.

"I really appreciate this," he told her.

His manners were lovely though. And he had very nice teeth too, even if she longed to take a brush to that hair. Still, the main thing was that he didn't look as though he might make off with Mrs Carr's valuables the minute her back was turned.

She left the kitchen door open all the same when she went back in to attack the cooker with a box of cleaning agents she'd brought from home. It wasn't much use.

The top she feared was blackened forever, but at least the rings still worked. She might even cook her dinner on them this evening, given that Nick seemed to have taken over her entire kitchen. It had taken a great many utensils to prepare a cup of tea at any rate. Already he was irritating her, the way he'd done all through their childhood. How was she going to live with him until she would fly out to Florida? However long that would be. If at all?

It struck her then, all that she was missing: the seedy motel, Critter Country, hot dogs and buttery popcorn – she wouldn't experience any of it. Her new strappy white sandals would remain unpacked, along with the chance to shake off this weird fake person she had somehow become. Instead she was stuck in the Midlands looking after a cranky old bag. Happy holidays!

"Excuse me?"

The boy was at the kitchen door. It was an effort to smile. "Yes?" she said.

"I'm out of luck."

"They're all booked out?"

"There are only four other B&Bs listed in the town," he told her. "Three of them are full and Dairy Cottage burned down last month."

"Good Lord."

"Some lodger was smoking in bed. Anyhow, thanks for letting me use your phone."

He had his boots on, she saw. And his backpack was over his

shoulders again, and the placards under his arm. They were covered in some kind of protective plastic and she couldn't see what was on them.

"Where are you going to go?" she asked.

He shrugged. "I'll find somewhere."

Of course he wouldn't – what was he going to do, bed down in the ashes of Dairy Cottage?

She told herself that he was not her responsibility, but it sounded very weak, given that she had shot his landlady. But what was she supposed to do with him? Take him back to Dublin with her? Nick would have a fit. Ewan too.

And what if Mrs Carr had been counting on the money? Judging by the condition of the house, cash could well be in short supply. Grace felt even guiltier; not only had she put the woman in hospital, but she was jeopardising her meagre source of income too.

She looked at her watch. It was almost six o'clock. "Would you be able to find somewhere in the morning, do you think?" she asked.

He looked hopeful. "I'm sure I could."

She made a decision rapidly. "All right. One night so. You'll have to fend for yourself for dinner though."

"All right," he said. "And what about breakfast?"

"What about it?"

"Well, if I'm paying for Bed & Breakfast, then I guess I should get breakfast – right?"

He had a point.

"You'll get breakfast," she said grandly.

"And towels are provided, right? And hot water?"

"Absolutely," she said. "I'll sort it out now."

She set off for the stairs in her new capacity as lodging-house proprietor. She found that she wasn't even surprised, given the way her carefully planned day had turned so spectacularly upside down. In fact, she didn't think she would bat an eyelid if

74

the roof fell in on top of her at that very moment.

"Go right ahead and make yourself at home!" she called back, suddenly inexplicably happy.

He bent down and took his boots off again.

FIVE

"No, really, you've done the whole thing right," Natalie declared.

They were eating take-away Chinese in Mrs Carr's kitchen that night. Grace had not wanted to stay in the house all evening on her own with a strange man (his name was Adam). She could have phoned Nick, of course, but that would have entailed all kinds of explanations. And she couldn't very well go home and leave Adam to fend for himself. No, she would stay the night and leave first thing in the morning. Nick wouldn't even miss her and, in the meantime, Natalie had been very willing to come over. Her second baby was due in eight weeks and, as she said herself, it was probably the last time she would get out for a couple of years.

"What exactly have I done right?" Grace enquired.

"Timing," Natalie said. "You married young so you didn't have to take the leftovers the rest of us were faced with at thirty."

"No offence to your Paul," Grace said.

Natalie was mortified. "God, no! Paul is great. But you know what I mean. You got in early. Did the whole marriage bit, bought the house, had the babies while you still had the energy. And now they're all grown up leaving you to concentrate on yourself. We were only saying it in the office today, you make us all sick."

Natalie had a desk opposite Grace, only she was in Rentals and

Lettings and she dealt mostly with apartments in the city centre where rents were high and turnover higher. This meant that she always seemed to be renting the same properties over and over again, a situation she often darkly predicted would drive her over the edge.

Grace laughed. "I never thought of myself as being in such an elevated position before."

Natalie stuffed a forkful of noodles into her mouth. She had started this pregnancy hopelessly overweight from the last one, but had remained very cheerful about it, to her credit. "I often think the rest of us were daft," she said. "Devoting most of our twenties to that damned company, only to watch the really big promotions go by because we're either off having babies or thinking about it." She leaned in. "Imagine – they guessed in Head Office that Orla was pregnant before she knew it herself!"

"That was because Mark went around bragging after the Christmas party," Grace said.

"The point is that they mentally write us off," Natalie insisted. "Look at me! Stuck in Rentals and Lettings for the past four years. The soft job. And you, with your children practically reared and your whole life ahead of you! Oh, it's too much to bear!"

She took the last spring roll without asking.

"Yeh – like I had it all planned or something!" Grace scoffed bravely. "You think I sat down in my early twenties with a list of Things To Do and ticked them off one by one?"

"Did you?" Natalie cried enviously. "And there was me getting pissed and backpacking around Europe!"

"Exactly!" Grace said. "*I* envied *you*!"

"You didn't even know me then."

"I knew people like you! Hundreds of them!" This sounded a bit insulting so she hurried on, "I was stuck at home rearing twins while you were up to all sorts!"

She had meant travelling and drinking too much, but Natalie's face turned rather dark. "They're very transitory, you know. The pleasures of your twenties. They don't last. Or at least you hope they don't," she added.

"It's just the way things worked out," Grace said, lamely.

The minute the final exams were over, her friends had nearly all scattered to the four winds. They had gone to seek adventure and careers in London, New York, Australia – anywhere but the city where they had spent four years in dingy flats on student grants. And who could blame them? She had been left behind, through her own choice. Things were very serious with Ewan. (Why hadn't she realised that, if they were that serious, he would have waited for her to come back? Had she been worried that distance would cool their ardour? Or that experience would shape them into different people?)

Things were different back then, of course. Jobs were scarce and Ewan was one of the lucky ones: a junior copywriter with an advertising agency! A dream job in the dreary late eighties. How could she have demanded that he give it up and go on the dole with her in London, or Los Angeles (where they didn't even have the dole)?

It wasn't that she regretted marrying him, as such. Certainly she did not regret her two beautiful boys. And who was to say she would be any happier if she had waited, like Natalie, and was facing into it all now?

But whatever had happened to that elusive girl in the black and white striped scarf that had made her look a bit dangerous? Was she gone forever, buried under obligations and commitments?

"Maybe I have regrets," she said loudly, changing her mind. "Maybe I wish I hadn't married young! Maybe I wish I'd had my twenties to myself!"

"You wouldn't." Natalie was quite definite about this. "People are too silly in their twenties, they haven't a jot of sense. This way, you've got the grunt work done and now you can sit back and enjoy it all."

"Enjoy what?" Grace enquired.

"Having time to yourself."

"To do what?"

Natalie shrugged: if Grace didn't know that . . .

"Well, obviously, there's my career," Grace said hastily. She didn't want Natalie to think life was wasted on her altogether.

"Word is they're considering opening a branch out here," Natalie confided. "If I were you, I'd signal my interest now."

Grace smiled weakly. The mere thought of managing a property branch filled her with doom. The only reason she stayed in the job at all was that she liked meeting people.

"Or you could do some courses," Natalie added. "I'd love to have the time to do stuff like that. Drama. Or maybe art."

"Maybe," Grace said, slowly.

"Look into it anyway," Natalie advised. "Now that you've all this time on your hands."

"Yes," Grace said. Doing art courses at her age had a kind of an ominous feel to it: anything to take your mind off yourself. Or impending death.

She heard the front door open and close quietly. Adam. He had gone down the town ages ago.

"I'd better go," Natalie said with a sigh. "Rosie won't go to sleep unless I'm in the house – remember I was telling you Paul pretended to be a monster the last time I went out for the night? And I have an appointment in the hospital first thing tomorrow. They think the baby might be breach. They're going to try to turn it around or else I'll have to have a section."

An art course sounded like bliss in comparison, and Grace wondered whether she was being altogether too picky. All things considered, she had a perfectly satisfactory life by any standards. It was ridiculous to suddenly be obsessing about a stripy scarf and a café mix-up that took place nearly fifteen years ago.

"Here, hold the fort for a minute, will you?" she asked Natalie.

She'd left her bag upstairs in one of the spare rooms (she hadn't wanted to tempt anyone – well, all right, Adam – by leaving it lying around). She took her mobile phone out of it and the scrap of paper with Michael Carr's number on it, and dialled.

She had her little speech all rehearsed; how sorry she was to be the cause of his mother's injury, how she would be prepared to foot any hospital bills – she must remember not to use the word 'foot' – and how she was ringing to enquire after Mrs Carr's health. She hoped this would lead to some kind of discussion about plans for her convalescence, and who would be looking after her. (Well, Grace had her own life to consider too, and the boys would want to know when she might be expected to join them.)

"Hello?" A girl's voice answered, sullen.

"Hello, is that Michael Carr's house?"

"Yeh. I'm Susan. Dad can't come to the phone right now," she added. "Mum is having palpitations."

"Oh!" Grace said, thrown. "Maybe I should get off the line . . . you might want to ring the emergency services . . .?"

"No, she's coming around now. She thinks the coleslaw might have been cross-contaminated with shellfish or something." She raised her voice. "Dad! *Phone!*"

Grace's entire speech had gone out of her head now and so she said quickly, "Look, I just wanted to know how Mrs Carr is? And her foot?"

"She's not going to die," Susan said.

"Great!" Grace said. She felt more confident now. "You're probably wondering who I am. You see – "

"Dad says if he gets his hands on the person who did this to her, he'll murder them," Susan confided in her. "With his bare hands. But Mum says it was a blessing in disguise, because only for that shotgun today we wouldn't have known how crazy Granny really was until it was too late. My friend Kate's Granny lost her marbles and started eating grass and stuff."

"Really," Grace managed. "Anyhow, you see, the gun thing, it was an accident – "

"Dad says he might try and sue or something. He's hopping

mad." Then she shouted, "*Dad!* Are you going to take this call or not?"

Grace said, quickly, "Actually, there's no need to bother him. I'll just visit Mrs Carr in hospital tomorrow."

"All right," Susan said. "The hours are between two and four in the afternoon. Dad says he might monitor visitors. He doesn't want her getting too tired, you see. Mum says he's carrying on as if Granny's foot had been amputated or something. Dad went *totally* ballistic at that!"

He sounded rather over-protective and the last of Grace's intentions to declare herself died a swift death. She had also wanted to tell Michael Carr about her presence in his mother's house, and that she was putting up a lodger. But he sounded like the type who might not take it in the spirit in which it was intended, and march over straightaway and eject her.

So she held her tongue; and now she really was illegally in a stranger's house.

"When is she coming out, do you know?" she asked. "Your grandmother?"

"Friday, we think," Susan said.

Three days, then. She and Adam would be long gone from the house. Guiltily, she thought that if she left the place exactly as she had found it – apart from the cleaned-up kitchen, that is – then there might be no need to get into explanations at all. She could slip the B&B money into a drawer or something, as a pleasant little discovery for Mrs Carr somewhere down the line.

"Who did you say you were again?" Susan enquired.

"Oh, nobody," Grace said, and hung up. She would send a big bunch of flowers to Mrs Carr in hospital tomorrow. She couldn't risk a visit; a conflagration with Michael Carr across his mother's bed might upset the poor woman further. But when would they discuss Mrs Carr's convalescence? And Grace's part in it, if any? Oh Lord. It was getting more complicated by the minute.

There was laughter coming from the kitchen below. She could

hear it through the ceiling. Natalie said something in animated tones. More laughter. Curious, she went back downstairs.

Natalie and Adam were eating chips from a wad of newspaper on the middle of the kitchen table, the whole room filled with the delicious smell of grease and vinegar. He was perched on the edge of the table, one brown leg swinging casually back and forth. Grace found that she was a little irritated; she would never walk into a stranger's house and get up on the furniture. But they had such confidence these days, young people. They had been brought up never to experience a moment of self-doubt.

"You're just saying that!" Natalie was round-eyed. Giggly.

"I am not. Scouts' honour," Adam said. "Oh, hi, Grace."

Natalie gave her a look as though she were spoiling the party (in her condition!). Grace wanted to say something witty and unusual, just to show that she could, or else ask to be let in on the topic of conversation, but ended up saying gaily, "I suppose we'd better organise sheets and towels for you!"

That finished any more light-hearted banter. Natalie and Adam ate up their chips rather sullenly, she thought, while she hovered at the door like some kind of over-zealous dormitory mistress. Natalie made her goodbyes, smiled coyly at Adam, and lumbered off out the door.

"She's very nice, your friend," Adam said. He would be the sort of man (or boy, Grace couldn't make up her mind which) who would notice attractive women. It wasn't that he was sleazy or lascivious or anything like that; but to him, women were firstly women, whereas to Ewan, women were just other people. If he noticed them at all.

"She is," she agreed vigorously. She couldn't think of anything else to say, so she just kind of looked towards the door, and Adam, taking what he obviously thought to be a heavy hint, set off for the stairs in front of her, making no more attempts at diversionary conversation.

Well, she just wasn't used to this! Having to make strangers at home in a house that wasn't even hers! In fact, technically both of them were trespassers. And what on earth was she going to cook him for breakfast in the morning?

"You're not a vegetarian or anything, are you?" she asked Adam's back as they ascended the stairs. Although what difference it made, she wasn't sure. Mrs Carr's cupboards were not promising for meat-eaters or any other kind of eaters.

"No," he said.

She had picked out the largest of the three guests rooms for him. She threw open the door with another cheery, 'Here we go!" He loitered by the bed as she hunted in the chest of drawers. If this were like her room across the hall, there would be sheets and towels in the bottom two drawers.

"They're not fitted, I'm afraid – the sheets. And are two towels enough?"

"Plenty," he said.

"Great! I've put the immersion on if you want a shower or a bath. And there are spare pillows in that cupboard over there, okay?"

"Yup." He was looking around, not really paying attention.

She raised her voice. "There's a fire exit at the bottom of the hall, and I would remind you not to smoke in bed. Look what happened to Dairy Cottage."

He was sitting on the bed now with his back to her, taking off his socks, not even listening.

She flushed. Really, the day had been long enough without some hippy guy refusing to take proper note of the fire exits! And she was doing him a favour by letting him stay at all!

She flung the sheets, towels and pillowslips onto the floor at his feet. Now he was paying attention all right.

"You can make the bed up yourself."

"I hope you're going to bill him for it."

"It wasn't his fault. Well, not entirely."

"He broke your side-mirror off. It's a good thing I know a decent garage."

Frank had officiously appointed himself in charge of her damaged car. She wouldn't be getting it back from the garage until tomorrow. Hence he was giving her a lift down to the Spar to get provisions for breakfast in the morning.

"Who is he anyway?"

"He's Australian."

"That's it? You let a stranger into my neighbour's house – if Michael got wind of it he'd have a fit – and all you know about him is that he's Australian?"

"And he likes chips," she added lamely.

"My God! He could be anybody! How do you know he's not got a string of criminal convictions behind him?"

Grace refused to give in to his brand of cynicism. "Because I just got a feeling off him, okay? Generally, you get a feeling off people. You can sense whether they're good or not."

"Bah," Frank said rudely.

"Well, what was your feeling the first time you met Sandy?" she asked.

"What?"

"You must have felt something."

"I don't think that's any of your business."

"It is if you're going to criticise my choices in people."

"I can't remember."

"You can't remember?"

"No."

Grace thought about the beautiful Sandy. No man would forget his first glimpse of such perfection. "Well, did she smile at you? Do you go over and say hello to her? Was it in Ireland? America? Did your eyes meet across a crowded room?"

Frank was getting more hassled. "You're making fun of me now."

"Frank! I'm not making fun of you. I'm just curious about the first time you met, that's all."

"We haven't met, okay? We've never met!"

Grace didn't immediately know what to say.

"I suppose you think that's peculiar. Odd. That's why I don't tell people, you see. People just love to curl their lip knowingly when you say that you've met someone on the Internet. They go, oh, he's a sad loser who can't make any real friends, he has to go on the Internet and exchange meaningless facts with other sad losers. Or else they think you're a weirdo. They hear the words 'chat room' and they think you must be a pervert who only wants to have conversations with other perverts about bondage and fetishes and . . . and animals! Well, Sandy doesn't get off on animals and I don't either!"

Grace still didn't know what to say.

"Sandy says she doesn't care what people think," Frank said defiantly. "She says that we must follow our hearts and believe in destiny. We must not let the aura of our love be tarnished by negativity."

Sandy was beginning to lose the run of herself in terms of purple prose. But Frank seemed to be lapping it up.

He looked at her now, blinking a bit fast. "Just because you write it down on a computer screen instead of saying it doesn't make it any less real, you know. And sometimes you can say a lot more in a few words that you can in a whole conversation."

He had a point. God knows she and Ewan had plenty of conversations where there wasn't a thing said.

By the time they pulled up outside the Spar, Grace was feeling rather melancholy. If they sold wine, she would buy a bottle, she decided. Or any liquor, really. She felt like it tonight.

The Spar was cool and empty. Fluorescent lighting bounced off shiny products that promised to satisfy hunger, thirst, and shift stubborn stains. At the counter a girl with greasy hair looked up. With callous speed she registered, assessed and dismissed Grace as non-threatening, and went back to her teen magazine. How

Grace longed to tell her that she had pulled the trigger on a shotgun this morning – a real shotgun!

The girl wouldn't care. Grace was almost old enough to be her mother, she realised. In her designer track bottoms and white runners, she looked like a typical middle-class suburban woman out to get a pint of milk for the kids' breakfast in the morning, and a sneaky bottle of wine for herself. No threat in the world.

She picked up a basket, and put in a pot of strawberry jam and some bread. Then to the cooler section, where she got milk and juice and butter. And would eight sausages be enough?

She was perusing a packet of smoked rashers when another customer came in and went to the counter – a man, good-looking. The girl looked up, said hello, and blushed. He said something back; she laughed, went smartly to get his cigarettes. Oh, she was very pleasant now. Grace smiled too, benign and forgotten in the background, and she lifted the waistband of her expensive track bottoms and slipped the packet of smoked rashers down the front of her knickers.

The shock of cold plastic hitting her skin was almost pleasant. Out of her peripheral vision she watched the man hand over money. She snapped her tracksuit waistband back into place over the top of the rashers and pulled her t-shirt down securely. She moved up the aisle a bit and picked up a pot of sour cream as though she had all the time in the world.

"Excuse me," said the man, stepping past her on his way out.

"Sorry!" Grace said carelessly. He left. The shop girl turned to look down at her. Had she seen something suspicious? For the first time, Grace realised fully what she was doing. Shoplifting. *Stealing*. She was going to try to walk out of here with a packet of cured meat down her knickers: her, Grace Tynan, devoted mother of two and respectable estate agent! Had she gone quite mad?

There was a kind of a humming in her ears now, and everything suddenly seemed brighter, slower, louder – like in a movie. The rashers began to drip.

At the counter, the shop girl closed her teen magazine. Ominously? Grace pretended to dither over the sour cream, buying time. Two hundred and eighty calories per pot! She put it down quickly and bent to pick up some Greek yoghurt instead. Almost as fattening. But the movement had dislodged the rashers. They slipped wetly down an inch, and she clamped her thighs together hard. Mother of God. What was she going to do now?

"Do you need any help?" the shop girl asked. She had a flat, unattractive voice.

"Me? No!" *Divert, divert,* some part of Grace's brain commanded. "Well, yes, actually. Do you have any low-fat yoghurt?"

That was the kind of thing a thin, middle-class woman like herself would eat. The girl seemed to relax a little. "We're out. We're waiting for supplies to come in."

"When?"

The girl frowned. "Thursday. Maybe Friday."

"Right! Great! Well, I'll take the Greek yoghurt until then. And the sour cream."

She smiled brilliantly and chucked in a couple of pots of each. Frank would be in after her in a minute, wondering what was keeping her. But what if further movement dislodged the rashers altogether and they slid down the leg of her pants?

On the other hand, she couldn't remain at the cooler section all night. At some point it would start to look suspicious. She berated herself for not stealing the sausages instead. They were far more compact. Or some biscuits or something. This was what happened when you were an amateur.

Right. Clutching the basket very close at pelvic region to stop any more slippages, and under the watchful stare of the shop girl, she did a kind of sideways shuffle up to the nibbles & dips section. She snatched up a bag of nachos and added it to the basket. Then she pretended that a tin of shoe polish had caught her eye on the next shelf. That got her up another couple of feet. Gradually she worked her way up shelf by shelf to the counter, acquiring some nappies, indigestion remedy, bottled chillies and a tin of dog food on the way. But no wine, dammit. She'd never make it all the way over to the drinks section: it was too risky.

Now came the dangerous bit: getting the basket on the counter without incurring disaster.

"If you could just give me a hand . . . thank you!" She dumped the basket down on the counter, and clamped her hands together fiercely over the rashers.

The shop girl looked at her curiously. "There's a customer toilet if you want to use it."

"Oh! No, thanks. I'll, uh, hang on." Immediately she regretted this. She could have moved the goods to a safer position in the toilet cubicle.

The girl gave her another penetrating stare, and began to take items from the basket and scan them with remarkable speed. Grace looked around casually, pretending to wrack her brain in case she'd forgotten something. She felt a thin trickle of condensation from the packet of rashers slide down her thigh. And another one. Oh God. She was leaking.

Beep. Beep. Beep. The girl packed items into bags as she scanned them. Now she had the sausages in her hand. Was this the point where she would mention the rashers? Grace's heart jolted so hard in her chest that it hurt, and she looked blindly past the girl in the hopes of finding some distraction.

Our Policy is to Prosecute Shoplifters. It was there in bright red letters on a big sign – just beside a CCTV camera, actually, which seemed to be angled right now at Grace's crotch. She thought she would vomit.

Then the girl pounced, her voice deliberate and accusing. "Was there anything else?"

"What do you mean?" Grace said weakly.

"I mean, is this everything that you want to buy?"

Apart from those rashers down your pants, she might as well have said. Grace just stood there, thighs frozen, mouth open but with nothing coming out. Was this what people risked everything for? This feeling of utter panic and fear? She never would have guessed that shoplifting was so stressful. Or so damp.

She couldn't even claim that the rashers were to feed her starving children – not with a fat purse in her hand. No, in court they would brand her as a wealthy bored housewife, out to get her thrills. The shame of it! Although she wasn't sure which charge was worse – bored housewife, or shoplifter. Ewan would die. They could never go to a dinner party again. And as for the kids! They would be outcasts at basketball, pariahs at school (although she would bet that there were other light-fingered mothers at those staid parents' evenings. Would they seek each other out?) Everyone would try and blame it on stress, of course. The strain of modern living. They would murmur kindly that she was on medication. Why else would she go stealing rashers from rural Spars? Her, with not a single thing in the world to complain about!

"Is this everything?" the girl repeated, her hand dipping stealthily under the counter; reaching for that little red alarm button Grace knew they always had just beside the till.

She couldn't breathe. She felt everything closing in on her like a vice. The rashers slipped another inch, leaving a trail of frozen flesh in their wake. She bared her teeth at the girl, shook her head, kept shaking it like a dog just out of the sea. The girl's hand moved slowly, inexorably, towards that red button, the hotline direct to Sergeant Daly's desk –

"Yes! Yes! I have everything I need!" Grace rasped desperately at the very last moment.

Beat.

"Okay," the girl said, and her hand came back into view, holding a roll of stickers. "Are you collecting the coupons?"

Suddenly everything snapped back into normal time. The

lights seemed to dim and Grace's hearing returned. "I beg your pardon?"

"For the gift catalogue."

"No," Grace said. Was the girl toying with her?

"You're due two coupons," the girl insisted. "You can get an electric kettle for fifty. Or a turbo sunbed, but you need five thousand for that."

Grace allowed herself a cautious breath. "I'm not collecting them."

"Do you, um, mind if I have them then?"

"Sure. Go ahead," Grace said.

"Wow – thanks!" The girl smiled – a big, warm, guileless smile and it transformed her. She couldn't be more helpful now – neatly folding and packing Grace's receipt, and handing over the bags, handles first.

"Thank you," Grace said.

"No problem. See you again!"

And that was it. Grace made her way to the door, unimpeded by security guards or CCTV cameras. Sergeant Daly's squad car did not roar into the carpark as she stepped out through the glass doors into the cool night air.

"You were ages. I was about to go and look for you," Frank complained, standing by his car.

"Sorry," she said.

He took the two bulging plastic bags from her. "Nappies?"

"Don't ask."

He went around to the boot of the car, fussing and grumbling. Grace reached down and extracted the rashers. They were streaky bacon, she saw. With two rashers free, ironically.

She wasn't proud of herself. Absolutely not! It was totally the wrong thing to have done. It was mere luck that it hadn't all ended in shame and disaster. The whole thing was a moment of madness that would never, ever happen again.

But she hitched her pants back up with a bit of a swagger, and expertly flicked the packet of rashers through the air and into the car boot. Frank looked up, startled. She jerked a thumb at him and spoke out of the side of her mouth.

"Let's go, cowboy."

Adam must have gone to bed because the house was in darkness when she made her way up Mrs Carr's uneven front path. It was a lovely warm night, hardly a breeze. She looked up at the sky. Ewan and Jamie and Neil were up there somewhere, half-way to America now. Maybe they were asleep – it was a long flight and they would be tired out from all the excitement.

The seat next to Ewan would be empty. *Her* seat. Was he looking at it right now, missing her and thinking that the holiday wouldn't be the same without her? She liked to believe that maybe he was, and not hunched over a scrap of paper and pencil trying to find words to rhyme with 'weight loss'.

"Grace?"

The word came out of the darkness. She swung around, the shopping bags clashing painfully against her knees.

"Sorry," Adam said. "I didn't mean to give you a fright."

He was sitting on one of Mrs Carr's wooden deckchairs on the lawn, his bare feet up on the rickety plastic table (he really was taking great liberties with the furniture). He had a bottle of beer in his hand.

"Well, you did," she said, sounding a bit sharper than she'd intended. But she was tired. She had not expected to arrive back to find her lodger whooping it up on the front lawn. What if the neighbours complained to Mrs Carr when she got out of hospital? Mrs Carr, who knew nothing about Grace entertaining lodgers in her absence? "Beautiful night, isn't it?" he said.

"Lovely," she said in a voice that wasn't encouraging.

But he didn't notice. He rocked back in the wooden deckchair, looking at the sky. "It's winter back home now, but it'd be as warm as this. Kind of makes me homesick."

"Which part of Australia are you from?" she asked, because she felt she ought to.

"Nowhere," he said. "I'm from Tasmania."

Tasmania. Grace tried to find a point of reference. Dracula country? No, that was Transylvania. But it was famous for something, she knew that.

"Oh, yes – criminals!" she cried.

Adam looked startled.

"Isn't Tasmania where they used to send all the, uh, prisoners in the last century?" she added more sedately.

"That's right." He smiled nicely. "Mostly from Ireland, actually. Export the problem, as usual."

Well! And she only trying to make a little polite conversation! "If you find Ireland so disagreeable, what are you doing here at all?"

"I came to find my roots," he replied.

Not another one. Ireland was in severe danger of being strangled by the roots of a hundred million third-generation Irish across the globe.

"That was a joke, by the way," he said, with a smile that was dazzling. He seemed to have about five rows of perfectly white, even teeth. She was just admiring them when he said suddenly, "Was he your boyfriend?"

"Sorry?"

"That guy who just dropped you off just now?"

"Frank? Jesus, no!"

"I thought he was a bit square for you, all right," he said, and Grace found the observation oddly disconcerting.

"He's just . . . just a neighbour." It was too complicated to go into the whole business at this hour of the night.

"He's got a telescope trained on the house," he added casually.

"Pardon?"

"Well, not on this house specifically. He kind of rotates it a bit – sometimes he watches the neighbouring houses, especially if someone comes or goes. Sometimes he'll just monitor the traffic. It's behind a net curtain in one of the upstairs rooms, but I can just about make it out. I just thought you should know."

"He's a bird-watcher," Grace told him.

Adam took another swig of beer, said bluntly, "I think he's watching more than birds. If I were you, I'd put black-out curtains on the bathroom window."

Grace didn't like it: the arrogant dismissal of Frank as some kind of predator. And worse, the portrayal of herself as a sexual victim who had to resort to hiding behind black-out curtains.

"I'll give your suggestion due consideration," she told him.

He said, "I can see I've offended you."

"How could you have offended me? You don't even know me. Or Frank."

"But I'd like to."

"Pardon?"

"Get to know you." He gave another blinding smile. "Not Frank though." He swung his feet down from the table, brushed the surface off with his hand. "Have a beer with me."

"No, thanks," she said.

He seemed mildly surprised. "You don't drink?"

"Oh, I'm always drinking," she assured him. "It's just that it's late, I've had a hell of a day, and it's not in my job description to entertain lodgers." But he didn't look as put out as she had hoped. So she added, for good measure, "And you probably shouldn't stay out here too late. It can get quite chilly in Ireland at night."

"Yes, ma'am," he said, touching two fingers to his forehead in a little salute.

Grace looked across the lawn at him. "You seem to find me hugely amusing in some way."

"It's just a while since I've been mothered, that's all."

She was glad it was dark now; glad that he couldn't see the way her face bloomed bright red. But her years of dealing with all kinds of uncomfortable situations stood to her now, and she gave one of her professional laughs – light and totally unaffected.

"Just making sure you're comfortable, that's all. As Mrs Carr's guest."

Before he could reply, she contented herself with an extra-cheery, 'Goodnight!" and set off up the path to the house.

It was only after she had put away the groceries and climbed the stairs and got tucked up in the musty single bed across the hall from his room that she remembered that he had not actually said what he was in Ireland for. And she might have denied that Frank was her boyfriend, but she had failed to mention the fact that she was married.

SIX

That night Grace dreamed she was making love with a black man.

Well, it wasn't so much 'making love' – so boring – as having wild, dirty, delicious sex. He looked like one of the characters from *EastEnders*, which she found terribly erotic because she'd never met a soap star before, let alone had sex with one.

"I fancy you something rotten, luv," he told her as they rolled about on the bed. The East End accent was a bit of a turn-off, but she ignored it because he really was very beautiful. And they were doing all the things that she had always wanted to do but hadn't known whether they were legal or not. And his certainly was yum.

Then, without warning, he stood up and started to pull his clothes back on.

"Got to go, pet, I'm due back on the set at three. But will I send in Dirty Den?"

"Ooh, yes, please."

Grace woke up, and she was in a strange bed, and there was no black man from *EastEnders*. No Dirty Den either; just Mrs Carr's scratchy white sheets and dubious sense of décor.

She flopped over in the bed and looked at the ceiling,

wondering about this recent preoccupation of hers with seediness and sex – and how one automatically suggested the other in her head. She hoped she wouldn't want to start buying pornography or something. Ewan would be appalled. Or maybe not. But it was not something he would expect her to add to the *To Buy* list pinned to the fridge. He had boasted once that he had seen such things, though. But that was back when they were young and were expected to watch films like *Working Girls 2*. (The very title sent a small frisson down Grace's spine now – what was *wrong* with her?)

And it wasn't as though her and Ewan's sex life was all that bad. Well, perhaps it lacked a little adventure. Over the years they had settled into the same patterns as every other married couple, apart from the oddballs who were into swinging and all that (and it was debatable whether they were that odd at all, Grace some-times thought. Maybe they alone understood that monogamy was both unnatural and a waste). Occasionally, on a Saturday night, one or other of them would get drunk and attempt to take things into the realms of the unknown, but the sober one would usually be vaguely embarrassed, and besides, they always seemed to lack some basic food ingredient or piece of equipment, the reminder of which would induce greater embarrassment the next morning.

No, they generally stuck to the tried and tested. Ewan seemed reasonably happy with this – or at least he never complained. She was too, she supposed, although she couldn't imagine another forty years of the same or fifty years, maybe, if medicine con-tinued to progress at the same rate.

Sometimes when she thought in terms of the years and decades stretching out in front of her, she was seized with a kind of panic, an urgency that she couldn't quite explain; it was to do with the decades already behind her, and the feeling that she hadn't done much with them at all.

There was a smell of frying bacon. She hoisted herself up on one elbow and sniffed the air. Sausages too. She was starving.

She found an old dressing gown in one of Mrs Carr's closets and put it on – she was too impatient to dress. The cerise pink colour wasn't all that flattering and the nylon material scratched, but it buttoned up securely from her ankles to the very base of her neck and that seemed quite important. It was one thing to fantasise about being an extra in *Working Girls 2* but at the same time she was in a strange house with a man who had more or less said he didn't want to be mothered. She was still trying to figure out what that meant.

He was at the cooker when she entered the kitchen, his dreadlocks tied in a ponytail. It looked terrific, all streaky from the sun. He threw a casual look at her, jerked a thumb towards the table.

"Sit down. I'll get you a cup of coffee."

"Thanks."

He turned his back to fill the kettle. The silence stretched, broken only by the hiss of sausages in the frying pan. Grace, with ten years of conversation-making under her belt, couldn't think of a single thing to say. Adam didn't seem bothered; he just moved easily between cooker and sink, not a tense muscle in his body. Grace vaguely resented him and everyone like him – people who could share a room with others and not be bothered by silence. It was always the ones like her who wilted with embarrassment and who eventually felt obliged to say something, *anything*. She could just imagine herself at seventy, twittering on in dental surgeries and other public places, while the other occupants gave her murderous looks.

Well, today she just wouldn't twitter! She sat and watched as he deftly flipped over a rasher, and he had no idea that it had nestled in her underwear last night, and she gave a little snicker.

He looked up. "What?"

"Nothing," she said sunnily. "So – what's the plan for today?"

He shrugged, gave a wide smile. He smiled a lot, she noted,

suggesting an easy-going nature. Somehow she didn't entirely buy it. "Hang out. Maybe mow the grass for the old lady – Mrs Carr. She probably won't be up to much when she gets out of hospital."

Grace was taken aback. "Well, no, but – "

"And something needs to be done about all the loose floor-boards in the living-room. They're dangerous, especially for someone who might not be great on her feet."

"Adam, I thought you were moving on today."

He shrugged earnestly. "I've already tried. I phoned around all the guesthouses again this morning. There's nothing."

"Mrs Carr is back on Friday. The day after tomorrow," she stressed.

"And I will absolutely be gone by then," Adam assured her.

"Adam . . ."

"Just one more night. Come on, you're not going to throw me out on the street, are you?"

And he gave her such a winning look that she felt all shivery. And even though she knew she should refuse – it wasn't even her house! – something perverse and probably lustful made her murmur, "One more night then."

"Thanks."

Belatedly she wondered how she was going to explain away a freshly mown lawn and some DIY jobs to Mrs Carr. She could blame them on Frank, she supposed, even though he looked like he wouldn't know one end of a hammer from the other.

Adam laid two plates piled high with greasy fried food on the table. Toast followed, and coffee. It all looked divine. She hadn't had a fry in ages; and certainly not one she hadn't cooked herself.

"Eat up," he said. "You need to put some meat on those bones."

When had he been assessing her bone structure? Before or after he had asked about her boyfriends?

"What age are you?" she asked.

"Why?"

"Just wondering."

"What age do you think I am?"

"I don't like guessing games."

"Why not?"

"I just don't. They're silly."

"And you're too old for them, right? Too mature."

"We're not talking about my age," she said, regretting ever starting this.

"Just give one guess," he said.

Oh, for God's sake. "Twenty-three," she snapped.

"Wrong."

"You know something? I don't think I care anymore. Pass the butter, please."

"You're supposed to say, up or down?"

"Butter, please."

"It's down. I'm less than twenty-three."

"Right now I would guess you're about *three*."

He laughed. "I'm twenty. And I would guess you're about . . . oh, thirty-nine."

"What?"

"Up or down?"

"Down! Down-down-down!" She was smiling now too.

"I was only joking," he said. He looked at her seriously, this way and that, and she felt acutely consciously of her shiny, just-out-of-bed face. "I'd say you're about thirty-three. Maybe thirty-four."

"And you're right. I'm thirty-four," she said, still smiling, but a little disappointed that he had not thought that she was younger. Thirty, maybe.

He just reached for more toast, pleased with himself. (He might be confident but he had a lot of work to do on his sensitivity.)

"What are you doing in Ireland anyway?" she asked.

He looked surprised, as though she should have known. "*Full Blast.*"

"*Full Blast?*"

"The music festival?"

"Oh. Right." It was like Glastonbury – but with the emphasis on rock music. Nick had gone two years ago, and hadn't been seen for nearly a week.

"That's near here, isn't it?" she said.

"Four miles," Adam confirmed, and Grace immediately wondered whether Frank knew about this. But he must. The festival was in its fifth or sixth year now. Last summer, tens of thousands of people had descended with tents and camper vans and taken over the whole countryside.

"You're a music fan then?" she said, trying not to sound like a maiden aunt. But he had that effect on her: of making her act much older than she was. She wondered whether it was some kind of defence mechanism on her part – he was quite attractive, after all, if you liked that macho sort of thing. And she was a woman whose husband and children were away . . .

She stopped, amused at the train of her thoughts. As if she'd ever have the nerve! (She had once been propositioned by a senior partner at the staff Christmas party years ago. He was sixty if he was a day, and he had been drunk, and he had put his hand on her arm and told her that she was lovely. She had made fun of him to the girls afterwards, of course, and they had all laughed their heads off. But she remembered that word, 'lovely'. It was a digni-fied word, not like 'gorgeous' or 'sexy', and it was quite the most flattering thing anybody had said to her in years, and she would remember it whenever she and Ewan had a row).

" . . . not that I particularly like indie music. But I could listen to it," Adam finished up. "How about you?"

How about her, what? "Sorry, I didn't catch that," she said, hoping to fudge it.

"It doesn't matter," he said. He didn't like it, the fact that she had not been hanging on his every word. Look at him! He was positively sulking.

Grace didn't dare smile. He was not a boy – man? – used to being ignored by anybody, she guessed, especially not a woman.

He finished up his breakfast rather abruptly and stood. "Do you know where she keeps her lawnmower?"

"You could try the garden shed."

"Right."

And he was gone, his shoulders held a bit stiffly. Grace chewed slowly on a rasher, thinking how much more delicious something was when it was stolen.

Julia was woken from a nap by the snoring. She glared across the ward – that old biddy Ivy from Cork who had bored everyone senseless last night with her daft ramblings about her youth. As though none of the rest of them had ever been young: they just knew better than to go on about it all the time.

"Julia? Are you all right?"

You only had to stir in this place and there was a nurse down on top of you. So much for cuts in the health service.

"Yes, yes, I'm just going to the toilet if that's okay."

"I'll get you a bedpan."

"I don't want a bedpan."

"Now, now." The nurse clucked in that irritating way they all did, as though they were dealing with overgrown five-year-olds. "You've had an operation, Julia. You shouldn't be out of bed at all."

Julia knew she would have to humour her. So she smiled in a kind of half-doddery way and put a hand confidentially on the nurse's arm. "I know. But I'm too embarrassed to use a bedpan. If you could just help me as far as the toilet . . . you're ever so good . . ."

"You'll need your crutches," the nurse said indulgently. She got them, tucked a stern hand into Julia's armpit and more or less bore her aloft to the toilet. Once there, the nurse whipped up her nightdress – "Now!" – deposited her on the toilet bowl –

"Comfy?" – stuffed a lump of toilet paper into her hand – "There!" – and issued her with instructions to ring for help when she was finished up.

"Certainly," Julia said, with what dignity she had been left.

"Oh, and some flowers arrived for you," the nurse said as she left. "From someone called Grace."

Grace? Julia turned the name over in her head. She didn't know anybody called Grace. Could it be someone from JJ's side? They always tended to crawl out of the woodwork when there was some misfortune or other.

Sitting up on the toilet like that gave her an opportunity to see her mangled foot for the first time. Not that there was much on view – rolls of white bandages swathed the top half of her foot. A yellowish substance had leaked out in the region of the small toe, but other than that it all looked very innocuous. She couldn't even feel anything. Of course, she was pumped full of morphine. It was starting to wear off a bit now though. She was glad. It made everything very vague and unclear. She had been shot though, she was sure about that. Or was she?

Sitting there on the cold toilet bowl, her bony white knees poking out from under the soiled hospital gown, she suddenly felt weak and small and she wanted to call the nurse, the big bovine nurse who made everything better with a single reassuring 'Now!'

She wanted JJ. Sometimes at night when she woke in the dark the silence was so still and so thick that she could hear her own eyes blink. It was the loneliest sound in the world.

The crutches were stiff and unfamiliar and it took her two attempts to get her forearms through the grey plastic rings properly. But she did. And she managed to open the toilet door without falling over. Hurrah! It was quite cruel really, the way age blasted standards out of the water: now merely staying upright was a cause for celebration.

Michael and Gillian were lying in wait back at the ward. They had obviously got past the ward sister.

"Hello!" Julia said, hoping she sounded welcoming. "Bit early for visiting, isn't it?"

"Naturally we wanted to know how you are, Mammy," Michael said.

"We brought you some grapes," Gillian said, wafting past to the locker. Where other women wore perfume, Gillian always smelled of Deep Heat. Already she was looking around surreptitiously for an air-conditioning system, or anything at all that would suggest germ control.

"How's the bronchitis?" Julia enquired. "Did those test results come back yet?"

Gillian looked at her a bit suspiciously. "No. But I'm feeling much better." Her voice was squeaky and breathless. "More to the point, how are you?"

"Great," Julia confided. "I just had a bowel movement and everything."

Nobody said anything for a moment; then they busied themselves finding chairs and settling down. Michael spilled out over the edges of his. Gillian perched on the seat of hers like an anorexic bird. Julia sometimes imagined the two of them in the conjugal bed together. How did he not crush her to death? Mind you, she was the sort of woman who detested physical activity of any kind so it was highly likely that the risk was minimal. About twice a year, at a generous guess. Poor Michael.

She must stop this. They were her family. The only people left who belonged to her in the whole world. It was nobody's fault that they hadn't a damned thing in common.

"The doctor was around this morning," she offered conversationally.

"Oh?" Gillian squeaked. Julia wanted to oil her.

"He was one of the doctors who saw JJ when he was brought in."

"Was he?" Michael said.

"Remembered JJ the minute I mentioned him. Said he had never seen anybody sitting up in the bed like that after a major stroke."

"Imagine," Gillian said.

"JJ was even able to tell him the results of the football – can you believe it? But he was always very mentally strong. He broke his leg climbing in the Alps once, Gillian, that's when he was working on that bridge in Switzerland. The pain must have been immense but he never let on to any of them who were bringing him back down."

"I know. You've told me before," Gillian murmured.

Julia couldn't remember doing so. But there were so many stories about JJ.

"Listen, Mammy, Gillian and I were talking about it and we'd like to pay for private care for you," Michael said. He hadn't listened to a word she'd said.

"Why?"

"You'd have your own room, and there's a consultant here, Dr Murphy – "

She was still stung. "The doctor I have is fine."

"We just want the best for you, Mammy."

They had never bothered with health insurance, her and JJ. In fact, JJ hadn't been great with money at all. Spend while you have it had been his motto. And they had, until there wasn't anything left.

Loyally, she said, "If the public service was good enough for JJ, then it's good enough for me."

Gillian said, "But he died."

"Gillian!" Michael was appalled.

"What? I'm just stating a fact – "

"Well, don't! It's upsetting Mammy."

Gillian gave an impatient laugh. "The man was mortal, believe it or not."

"Gillian!" He turned to Julia. "Mammy, I'm very sorry about

Gillian's . . . lack of tact."

Gillian reddened, then said, stiffly. "Yes. That *was* tactless of me. Sorry, Julia."

Ivy across the way loudly broke wind. It added to the pressure-cooker atmosphere, and Michael pitched forward in his chair, cleared his throat, and blurted, "Look, we've arranged for someone to come around and visit you, Mammy."

"Who?"

"A kind of a social worker-type person," Gillian said brightly, although it was obviously an effort.

Julia looked mildly interested. "But not actually a social worker?"

"No," said Michael. "He's more a . . . well, a kind of a . . ."

"A what?"

"A psychiatrist."

"A *shrink*?"

Gillian gave a little laugh. "They don't call them shrinks any more, Julia. They're more like friends. In fact, Dr Brady is a friend. He's my own psychiatrist."

"So he should be able to recognise madness when he sees it then," Julia said.

Gillian's eyes grew cold.

"Look, I am not bonkers," Julia added. "So you can forget about trying to lock me away in a home somewhere."

Michael looked shocked. "Mammy! What on earth are you talking about?"

"I heard you yesterday. 'Sort something out'. I won't be put away."

"Putting you away in a home is the last thing we'd ever want! Isn't it, Gillian?"

"Yes," she said, with just the right dollop of doubt.

Michael said, "Mammy, about Dr Brady. We just want you to have a chat with him, that's all. Maybe there are some things you've been bottling up that you might like to talk about."

"Like what?"

"I don't know. Maybe there are some issues surrounding Dad's death – "

"I do not have issues surrounding JJ's death." She was angry now. "Am I not to be allowed to grieve?"

"Of course you are."

"Is grieving somehow wrong?"

"No. I'm just saying – "

"Michael." Gillian turned to Julia and said, very measured, "Julia, you're in trouble with the guards. It's very serious. You threatened somebody with a shotgun you had no license to hold."

"For heaven's sake. It was only Frank. I wouldn't waste a bullet on him."

"It's not funny. Michael spoke with the police this morning. He thinks he might have convinced them not to press charges. He said we would get you help. Psychiatric help."

"Psychiatric help!"

"Yes. It might not sound very nice, but I'm sure you'd rather make smart comments to a psychiatrist than to be hauled up before a court. Am I right?"

She might look as if a gust of wind would carry her away, but she knew where to hit where it hurt all right.

"Fine," Julia said, dignified. "Send in the goons."

Sandy had sent a new photo of herself. It had been scanned in and e-mailed to Frank's computer just that morning and he had printed out five copies immediately.

"What's that on her chest?" Grace enquired.

Frank leaned in to have a look. "Oh, that's a printer error on my part. I think it was supposed to run across the bottom."

It was a line of smudged text. *To Frank. With all my love – Kitten.*

"That's a pet name," he added, boyishly. "She has one for me too, but I don't think I should tell you. It's a bit rude!"

"In that case, better not," Grace said hastily. Her breakfast hadn't settled sufficiently.

She studied the photo. Sandy looked as magnificent as ever. Her make-up was perfect and her hair was styled to within an inch of its life. She was wearing a tiny bikini and she smiled out blandly from a beach.

"She took her disabled kids swimming last weekend," Frank explained. "She says that's where it was taken."

There were no disabled kids in the background. Just a couple of blonde, All-American children building a sandcastle. A very good-looking man helped them. In fact, everyone on the beach seemed to be good-looking. Grace couldn't see any fat people, or men with big hairy chests, or women with cellulite.

Then she noticed something else.

"What's that in her hand?"

Frank peered at the photo. "A towel. Obviously she's thinking of taking a dip."

"Frank, it's a tea towel."

"Is it?"

They both looked at the photo again. It was most definitely a tea towel. It was stripy and with a picture of carrots on the front.

"Maybe she made a mistake," Frank said. "It's very easy to pick up the wrong thing from the airing cupboard, especially when you're in a hurry."

"But she's not actually holding it. It's like it's draped over her hand or something . . ."

There was definitely something odd about it. As if it had been added to the photo afterwards or something. It was her left hand too, Grace realised – the same hand that had been chopped off in the last photo.

"You should ask her about it."

Frank was dismissive. "Ask her about a tea towel? Like we have nothing better to talk about!"

There was something in his voice that made her look up from

107

the photo. "Is something wrong?"

"No, no . . . well, I won't be going over in two weeks' time as planned after all."

"Oh, Frank!"

He looked very deflated. "Her sister has just split up from her husband."

"That's a shame. But, um, what has that got to do with your travel plans?"

"Sandy's flying up to Utah, you see, to be with her sister. But that's Sandy all over. Too kind for her own good, I tell her. But she's already booked time off work and she's going to be flying out the exact day I was due to go over."

"That's a bit of a coincidence."

"I know, isn't it? But Sandy says that we'll fix a new date just as soon as her sister is back on track. *Que serà serà*, she says. What will be, will be – that's one of her favourite expressions. She's very philosophical that way."

He shook his head in admiration.

"Couldn't you go to Utah with her?"

He looked mildly alarmed at being around all that female angst. "I don't think that would be a very good idea. Anyhow, Sandy has everything all booked. I don't want to go changing arrangements. Especially when she's feeling so tired."

"She's still feeling tired?" She didn't look tired in the photo. She looked as healthy as a horse.

"She really should go and see a doctor," he said. "In fact, I'm going to e-mail her this very minute and suggest it." He gathered up his precious photo. "By the way, Sergeant Daly rang."

On reflex Grace froze. Blast those rashers anyway: would the guilt never leave her?

"Tom and Charlie are over from Birmingham, they want to come and see the house."

She relaxed. "Great! I'll ring the office and get someone to come out."

"You wouldn't be showing it to them yourself?" Frank was disappointed.

"You see, I'm actually on holidays . . . "

"It's only across the road."

"Yes, I know, but Natalie is covering for me. "

"They could call around tomorrow morning. You'll still be here, won't you? Now that you've allowed that Adam fellow to stay another night – not that Mrs Carr knows anything about *that*."

He *had* to point it out, of course.

"Anyway, Sandy says it's always better if just one person sells your property. That way the focus doesn't get diluted." He seemed to take it as a given that Grace would be showing his property, because he moved right on to another subject: "By the way, Sergeant Daly says to keep an eye out for any agitators."

"What?"

"Apparently they're coming for the festival. Activist types. They might try and book into accommodation, he said."

"What activist types?"

"Don't know." Frank left, anxious no doubt to get back to his computer to compose a turgid email. Grace wondered what pet name Sandy had for him. He'd said it was rude. Mr Stiffy, perhaps. But she remembered that they hadn't actually consummated the relationship yet. Then even thinking about Sandy and Frank doing it kind of put her off, and she went upstairs to shower and change.

She got dressed in her clothes from yesterday. She'd washed her underwear out the night before but her socks weren't dry and so when she wandered out into the garden an hour later with two coffees she was barefoot. Adam had finished mowing and the smell was wonderful. It was years since she'd felt grass between her toes (the back garden at home was set in patio, with a barbecue area) and she wandered about amongst overgrown shrubs and a most peculiar-looking pile of stones that resembled a grave, or a lopsided mausoleum. Maybe a beloved pet was buried there – although it would have to have been a very large dog, or possibly a young elephant.

Adam was cutting the hedge at the end of the garden with a pair of clippers.

"I brought you a coffee," she said.

"Great. I'll just finish this bit."

She sat down on the lawn and watched him for a while. Well, it was hard not to. He wore a very white T-shirt which rode up every time he clipped at the hedge. Sitting there, drinking coffee and ogling him, she felt a bit like a builder, and had to resist the urge to let out a wolf-whistle.

"So! What do you do in college?" she asked in what she hoped was an interested but detached voice. If he reached over a bit more she might just see his belly button . . .

"How do you know I go to college?"

"Hmm? There's a university sticker on your wallet."

"Prying?"

"I most certainly was not. It's sitting there on the hall table for anybody to see."

"Why are you always so defensive?" he asked.

"I am not defensive!" she said, defensively. "I just don't like people accusing me of being nosy, that's all."

He wiped an arm across his eyes. The underside of his ponytail was damp. "If you must know, I dropped out of college."

"Oh."

"But the course title was 'Business Studies'."

"Was it not a good course?"

"It was a great course. Churned out sixty-four proper little capitalists last year. Just what the world needs, don't you think?"

This somehow seemed to be a dig at her. She felt all defensive again. "Why did you apply for it then?"

"It was the only course I was offered." He gave a little laugh, and hacked at a particularly tenuous lump of hedge with the shears. "I thought college would be interesting," he mused. "I thought I'd meet like-minded people. People with opinions and convictions and ideals. Instead I ended up with a bunch of self-centred, label-obsessed assholes who just drank their heads off." He sounded hurt, nearly. "What was it like in your day?"

"What, way back thirty years ago?" she said tartly. He smiled. She was getting better at this. "Probably not much different. We did a lot of drinking, that much I do remember."

"But did you have any opinions?" he asked.

"On what?"

"On Beirut. World peace. Communism versus capitalism."

"Maybe . . . I can't really remember," she said, guiltily thinking about all those nights in the pub spent discussing sex and clothes and the possibility of getting a date with Damien from Applied Physics.

Adam seemed a bit disappointed in her. He turned back to his hedge at any rate. But, honestly, he was so idealistic! She wondered should she tell him that she had been a vegetarian when she was sixteen. That might impress him. He needn't know that it had only lasted three weeks and that she had caved in sobbing at the feet of a roast chicken one Sunday lunch-time. Oh, when would she grow up and stop trying to impress young boys? Her own, and other people's?

She was so cross with herself that when he said to her, "What are you doing here anyway, in the middle of nowhere?" in a kind of judgemental tone, she snapped back, "What business is it of yours?"

"None – "

"None. Exactly."

He wasn't deterred. "I just didn't think the countryside would be your thing."

"What, you think I'm the type who shrivels up and dies once I'm outside a three-mile radius of a shopping centre?"

He looked startled. "I was just asking a simple question – "

But she was on a roll now. "You were not! There was an innuendo there! A snideness! Just because you're nineteen – "

"Twenty."

"Twenty!" A pipsqueak! "Just because you're twenty you think you know everything. Well, you don't. And you don't know me either so stop acting as if you do!"

He put down his shears slowly, and looked at her. "Feel better now that you have that off your chest?"

She looked right back. "It's just that I was prepared to be nice and civil to you, but you just keep niggling away at me and I'm wondering why, that's all."

He took a gulp of his coffee thoughtfully. "I don't know, to be honest," he said. "I'm inclined to think it's because I want to corrupt you."

Grace had to bite back a nervous laugh. "Corrupt me?"

Those very blue eyes of his fixed on her as if across a hot dark nightclub. "Yeh. I just have this urge. Silly, isn't it? Childish." He smiled at her. "But there you go. I can't help myself." And he took off his white T-shirt altogether. Just like that! He stood there half-naked before her while she picked up the severed head of a daisy and twirled it around in her fingers nonchalantly, as though threats to corrupt her were everyday occurrences.

"Oh, I'm pretty incorruptible," she said, lightly. Had that come out as a challenge? Dear God.

"So you say." His hand was resting on the waistband of his shorts now and for a wild moment she thought he was going to take those off too.

"I don't know what you mean," she said, wondering was he wearing any underwear. But he didn't undress any further. He said, "Well, you're here on your own in the countryside in a house that doesn't belong to you, and without a change of clothes even. You drive a big swish city car, you left a wedding ring on the washhand basin upstairs, and you don't know Mrs Carr any better than I do, do you?"

When he laid it all out like that, it looked terribly incriminating. It must suggest to him that she was running from some dark and dangerous secret at home, or else that she was a flake who periodically broke into other people's houses and started operating B&Bs out of them. No wonder he thought that she might be ripe and ready for a little challenge.

She got to her feet quickly. Things were getting dangerous. "I assure you my reasons for being here are perfectly legitimate," she said haughtily, adding for good measure, "At least I don't have Sergeant Daly after me." Not unless they examined the CCTV footage in the Spar at any rate.

"Who?"

"The local fuzz – is the term known in Tasmania?"

He looked at her a little cagily, she thought. Interesting.

"It is," he said.

"Apparently there are some activists around the town of Hackettstown. Agitator types with very little else to do." She let that sink in for a moment, and added dramatically, "I was told to keep an eye out for them."

"And are you? Keeping an eye out?"

"It depends on what these agitators are up to. I don't want to get myself into hot water. If you know what I mean."

He took a step closer. It was a very long time since a half-naked stranger had made any kind of advance on her, and her temperature jumped up a little.

"Risk it," he said. "You might like it."

The air seemed to shimmer over the lawn between them, and Grace could feel her considerable reason and intelligence turn to dust. Then, the ring of a mobile phone in his shorts pocket.

"Hello?"

She watched his whole face crease into the kind of smile she had not seen before. "Babe. How are you?"

She bent down and picked up the two coffee mugs, smiling a

bit. "Excuse me," she murmured in his direction, and she went back inside.

SEVEN

"What do you think I should give Paul for his birthday?" Natalie asked on the phone that afternoon.

"Sex," Grace said.

"I beg your pardon?"

"Sorry, sorry, that just slipped out – how about a nice pair of slippers?"

There was a suspicious silence. "Are you all right, Grace?"

"Fine! Perfect! Here, do you know what the difference is between a lodging house and a B&B? Because I've rung the tourist board and they don't seem to know."

"I didn't know there *were* lodging houses any more," Natalie said.

"There are. I'm in one. And I'm confused as to whether I'm supposed to be providing Adam with – " She almost said sex again, but pulled herself up just in time. " – with dinner or not."

Natalie pondered this. "Have you asked him if he wants dinner?"

"No." For some reason she hadn't wanted to go back out to Adam in the garden again.

"Ask him," Natalie said authoritatively. Then she giggled

lasciviously. "I'll ask him for you if you want."

"Stop it, Natalie."

"What? He's a bit of a ride – "

Grace said coldly, "He's my lodger. You shouldn't be talking about him like that."

Natalie was surprised. "For God's sake, Grace. I was only joking – I don't know what you're getting in such a huff about."

Neither did Grace. It was just that those kinds of sentiments sounded vaguely ludicrous when coming from a woman of Natalie's age and circumstances. And Grace was a year older. It would have been different had they been men. Wasn't bloody everything? Still?

She had no more time to ponder inequality because there was so much to do when it came to running a lodging house. There was the laundry for starters. All those towels, and sheets, the duvet covers and the pillowslips – you could spend your whole day washing if you weren't careful! Not to mention all the dusting and hoovering and cleaning. Mrs Carr wasn't too hot on that aspect of things. Grace had opened a couple of presses in the bathroom and closed them again very quickly.

She went upstairs with two clean towels, and went into Adam's room, sure that this feeling of guilty pleasure wasn't normal for a landlady. He had made the bed himself, she was glad to see, and had put away any dirty clothes into his rucksack. The placards were stacked neatly under the bed and she cast a curious look at them as she picked up two used towels from the floor. Then she left, pulling the door quickly closed behind her and running lightly down the stairs, the towels pressed against her chest. She dipped her head and had a quick sniff. They smelled of soap and shampoo, and she felt a bit like a thief.

There was an old radio on the kitchen window and she put it on to a station she liked – *Lite FM*, but she wasn't ashamed – and she loaded the washing machine, turned the oven on, and started to make dough in one of Mrs Carr's wonderful big mixing bowls.

She was elbow-deep in sticky bliss and singing lustily along to 'Wake Me Up Before You Go-Go' when her mobile phone rang.

"Hello!"

"Grace? Is that you?" Ewan sounded a bit taken aback by her ebullience, or maybe it was just the distance.

"Of course it's me – is everything all right?" She could never enjoy a conversation until she had ruled out the possibility of accident or injury to either of the boys.

"I suppose – how are you?"

"Great! Well, all right," she added hastily. Best not to sound too cheerful. "Wishing I was there, obviously."

"You sound like you're at a concert." He sounded a bit peeved.

She hurried to turn down the radio. "Sorry about that. Where are you?"

"The motel."

"What's it like?"

She had an image of a grubby double bed with sheets that smelled of sex, and street signs blinking redly through the dirty window: *Adults Only! XXXcitement!!*

"It's got a double power-shower and you can make your own tea and coffee," he said.

"Oh." How disappointing. Was every last thing in this world to become standardised? Sanitised? She was suddenly glad she was here in Mrs Carr's shabby, run-down house.

"Did the boys enjoy the flight?"

"I think so, yeh." He was never one for giving a satisfying blow-by-blow account of things. Didn't he understand that when it came to her children, she would like to know what seats they had, whether he had remembered to give them sweets to suck during take-off, whether they had had the chicken or the fish for their in-flight meal?

"Where are you?" he asked instead.

"Me? In Ireland, Ewan."

"Yes, but where in Ireland exactly? I just rang home and Nick told me you'd gone missing."

Damn. She had meant to let her brother know the change in arrangements.

"He's sick with worry," Ewan added.

Now, that was a bit of an exaggeration. Nick had probably wondered about her once or twice and gone back to his computer books, via the fridge.

"I'm in Mrs Carr's house."

"What are you doing there?"

"Just tidying up for her and the rest." She tried to sound very casual. He wouldn't understand at all if she said that she was in fact entertaining a lodger behind Mrs Carr's back.

"How is she anyway? When is she coming home?" he asked.

"Friday."

"So you've spoken to him then? The son? What's his name – Michael?"

"Well, not exactly . . . I mean, I've rung his house . . ."

"And?"

"And what?"

"And are they going to look after Mrs Carr, Grace?"

"Look, it's all a bit complicated."

She was trying to think of the best way to explain it but Ewan jumped right in again, rather belligerently. "What, he's happy for you to look after her? Does he even know that you should be in Disneyland with us right now?"

"I didn't mention it, given that I've put his mother in hospital," she said coolly.

"It was an accident. Surely he can see that? For God's sake, you have two kids, Grace!"

She thought of the airport again, and her hurt. "So it's not out of concern for me, then, this . . . inquisition? It's for the benefit of the boys? And then maybe you?"

There was a little silence on the phone, then Ewan blustered, "Don't be ridiculous! I mean, when Nick said you hadn't come home – I was worried. You shouldn't be spending your holidays cleaning a stranger's home, Grace. You should be relaxing."

She wanted to believe in his concern and so she said, more muted, "I know. But I feel it's my duty, Ewan. I mean, there's nothing organised for her yet."

Ewan backed down even more. "Well, I suppose in that case . . . we can do without you for another day or two." He even gave a little laugh now. "Nick was trying to wind me up on the phone – you know, saying when the cat's away and all that."

"That's just his sense of humour."

"I know. I said to him, '*Grace*, of all people'." And he laughed again.

"What do you mean, 'of all people'?" she enquired after a moment.

"What?"

"Just wondering. It sounds a bit derogatory or something."

"It wasn't meant as derogatory – "

"What did you mean then?"

"I just meant you're too nice, too good – oh, you know what I mean. Just that you wouldn't do something like that, that's all."

"Sure about that, are you?"

There was another empty little pause now. Then she laughed, and Ewan laughed again too, heartily – great, relieved guffaws rolling across the Atlantic Ocean.

"What's the weather like?" she asked. It was a wifely question and he was further reassured.

"Fabulous. We've already been out to get breakfast – a real America-style breakfast, grits and everything, can you imagine?"

She smiled. "Did the boys eat them?"

"Every bit. They're really determined to make the most of this holiday. Even if you can't be here," he added swiftly.

"I know."

"We *are* missing you, you know, Grace. It's not the same without you."

Wasn't it interesting the effect the tiniest bit of uncertainty can sometimes have on people, she reflected? Just the smallest insinuation that things were not entirely as he had left them?

"I miss you too," she said, wondering if she did.

"Grace, the coach is here – hang on." His voice grew muffled as he turned away to issue orders. "Neil – turn off that TV. Jamie? Come out of the bathroom now! What are you doing in there all this time anyway?"

She listened to the background scuffle as they were propelled onwards in their journey and she was suddenly awash with longing to run out of this dirty old house and jump on a plane to shiny, plastic Florida and eat grits. She didn't belong here, pretending to be in charge of a lodging house and playing word games with a cocky young man just out of his teens.

"I have to go," Ewan said. There was no time to talk to the kids, just a hurried 'ring you later' from Ewan and then the phone went dead.

Ivy from Cork was crying and carrying on again about people dead so long that only she remembered them any more.

"Poor Ronald!"

"Ronald who, Mammy?" her daughter enquired. You could see her impatience. She had two children climbing up on the end of the bed and probably a car boot full of chilled groceries.

"Ronald Wainwright," Ivy sobbed.

"From Clonmel? Amy, get down!"

"From Waterford. With the stables."

"Oh, yes, the show jumper."

"No! No! He wasn't a show jumper. He never rode a horse in his life!" Ivy was raging, her chalky white fingers shredding a tissue while the children bounced up and down on her bony legs. And the daughter looking at her, bewildered, wondering who was this stranger in the bed.

Julia tried to close her ears to them. She had never felt old until the last two days. She had never even felt elderly. She had, she believed, stopped ageing somewhere around fifty-six. It was such a nice mature age, past those difficult forties, and not afraid any more of anybody or anything.

But here in St Catherine's ward she felt ancient. It was in the very air, which was always too warm, and smelled of old people. She found herself ridiculously upset by the sets of false teeth that sat in glasses on lockers, the pink prosthetic leg lying over there on a chair – all bits and pieces of broken bodies that had to be gathered up and re-attached before the simplest of human tasks could be carried out.

More visitors arrived into the ward. Elizabeth across the way was the victim this time.

"What did you have for tea, Granny?"

"Shepherd's pie."

"That was nice. Did you have a yoghurt or ice cream afterwards?"

"Ice cream."

"Oh good, you like ice cream. What flavour?"

"What? I can't remember."

"Was it vanilla? Or maybe strawberry?"

"I don't know! It doesn't matter – why the hell does it matter!"

"All right, Granny, calm down." To the husband: "I told you her memory was going."

For the first time Julia was glad that JJ had gone the way he had. She was grateful now for the suddenness of it, which had been so profoundly shocking at the time: no chance to say goodbye, no chance to say anything at all. She couldn't even remember her last words to him, but they would have been mundane because they had just come in from a walk in the rain and had gone upstairs to change into dry clothes. When he hadn't come down she'd gone back up and had found him on the bedroom floor. He had regained consciousness in the ambulance on the way to the hospital and had spoken to doctors. But she'd stayed behind to get him some clothes and things, not realising the seriousness of it, and Frank had driven her in an hour later. JJ had had the second stroke by then, of course, and was gone.

Which was a blessing really, when you thought about how it could have ended up: bedridden, and at the mercy of your family.

Happy birthday to you, Happy birthday to you, Happy birthday, dear Mammy, Happy birthday to you!

Here they came, Michael bearing a cake aloft, and Gillian and Susan bringing up the rear. The whole ward, of course, turned to have a look, clucking benignly at the spectacle. Several of the nurses clapped. Julia wanted to pull the bedcovers up over her head but instead managed a few gasps of surprise and delight.

"You shouldn't have," she said, meaning it.

"Speech, speech!" Michael said, as excited as a young boy.

"I'm not one for speeches," she said, flapping a hand at him.

"Make a wish then," Susan said.

Julia smiled fondly at her only grandchild. "And what do you think I should wish for?"

"A battery-powered scooter that every single person in your whole class has," Susan said, throwing a filthy look at Michael.

"I've told you. They're too expensive," he said.

"That's a crock of shit," Susan sighed. "You're on a hundred grand a year."

"Susan!" Gillian hissed.

"Anyway!" Julia said, in a very jolly voice. "Here goes!" She closed her eyes tight, and leaned forward to blow out the candles on the birthday cake. Not that they were lit – it was against hospital fire regulations, Michael explained. But the cake was lovely: a big white frosted affair, with her age marked out by seven pink candles and three blue ones, and a pink ribbon around the whole lot. You had to hand it to Gillian, who had remained in good health long enough to bake it.

She sat down at the end of the bed now, delicate-looking in peach and dabbing occasionally at herself with a tissue that smelled of antiseptic. "Happy birthday, Julia."

"Thank you, Gillian," Julia returned, equally civil. "And to you, Michael, and Susan. You've made it a very special birthday."

"You haven't had your presents yet," Michael said, presenting her with several gift-wrapped parcels. Julia made appreciative noises as she opened perfume, a silk scarf, a box of handmade chocolates. Then a silver photo-frame, face cream that one of those supermodels advertised, and a really beautiful gold bracelet.

"This is far too much . . ."

But Michael just beamed at her happily. "Nonsense. It's your birthday."

Susan had been getting herself more and more worked up. "How come she gets all that stuff and you won't buy me a lousy scooter!"

Michael looked embarrassed. "It's not your birthday, Susan."

"I didn't get *half* that for my birthday! Did I, Mum?"

"For heaven's sake!" he exploded. "This is your grand-mother's day! Can you not stop thinking about yourself for five minutes?"

Susan's lip was actually quivering. She looked at Michael, very hurt. "I'm just saying it's not fair."

"That's enough now," Gillian murmured. But she too was looking at Michael in a hurt kind of way.

Julia, the cause of this family rift, put on her best dotty-Granny smile, and said, "You know, I hardly ever wear jewellery – why don't you borrow the bracelet, Susan? On a long-term basis? And take those chocolates too, I only get indigestion. And when are we going to get around to tasting some of Gillian's delicious-looking cake?"

Susan was somewhat appeased. Gillian recognised a sap when she saw it, but was gracious enough to swallow it. Michael, largely oblivious to the politics, jumped to hand around card-board plates with Winnie-The-Pooh on them – it was all they had in the supermarket, he said – and Barbie drinking cups, and he dished out cake and poured coke for Susan, and non-alcoholic wine for the adults – again, due to hospital regulations.

"To Mammy!" he said, and they all raised their Barbie cups, and Julia smiled under the watchful eyes of Gillian, and thought that she had never missed JJ more than at that moment. But she couldn't say that, because Michael and Gillian and Susan didn't want to hear it. Not now, not two years later, when she really should have bucked up and got on with things and stopped boring everybody with her grief.

So she blinked back her tears and spooned some of Gillian's dry, fat-free, low-sugar frosted cake into her mouth, and said, "This is absolutely delicious, Gillian."

Tactless as ever, Michael failed to echo the praise, saying instead, "Mammy, we have one last present for you."

She was embarrassed now by his attentions. Surely he had never been this fawning before? Or had she just not noticed? "I've already had lots of presents."

"They were just stocking-fillers." He looked at Gillian, and she gave a tight little smile of acquiescence, and from his pocket he took a small, gift-wrapped box and handed it over, and said very intensely, "Go on, Mammy. Open it."

Julia was suddenly aware that there was an 'atmosphere'. Three sets of eyes followed her every move: Michael's, giddy with antic-ipation; Susan's, unenthusiastic; and Gillian's . . .? She was still smiling but there was something else too. A hint of martyrdom, Julia thought.

She opened the present. "It's a key," she said, surprised.

"Yes," said Michael. He was nearly bursting now.

"You haven't . . . bought me a car?" Julia said, wilting. Please God they weren't going to try and force her to drive – not at her age.

Michael laughed. "Not a car, Mammy. It's too small to be a car key anyway."

Julia turned it over in her hands. It was a simple stainless steel key, the kind you would find on any key ring.

"Don't look so worried, Julia," Gillian said with a little laugh. "It's not for the front door of a mental institution."

Oooh. The gloves were coming off.

"Dr Brady declared me sane then?" Julia said. She'd had a session with him yesterday afternoon. He was a very nice man, as it turned out, and a bridge fan. He had a dog called Mopp, and four grandchildren, and he'd been to Crete on his holidays last year. Julia had found out more about him in ten minutes than he'd managed to extract from her over the course of two hours.

"He didn't say a thing about you. Client confidentiality," Michael assured her. "But at least we've got the police off your back."

Julia just snorted.

"Do you not want to know what the key is for?" he asked.

Actually, the whole thing had lost its appeal by now, and she just wanted to go for her afternoon sleep.

"Tell me then."

"It's a front door key," Michael said, determined to extract more drama out of it, damn him.

"Whose front door?" she asked.

"Yours. Well, to your new house."

Her patience ran out and she snapped, "For heaven's sake, Michael, what are you talking about?"

Michael looked at Gillian, who looked at Susan, and then they all looked back at her.

"We're converting the garage into a granny flat, Mammy," Michael announced. "We'd like you to come and live with us!"

"I'm just ringing to enquire about Mrs Carr?"

"Are you a relative?" came the standard reply.

"No, I'm not. And I know you can't give out information to

people who aren't relatives, but I only want to know whether she'll be out on Friday?"

"I'm sorry. We can only give out information to relatives."

"Yes, I know that, but . . . Look, can I speak to her directly on the phone?"

"Her son is in with her right now. Would you like to speak to him?"

"Ah, no, thanks."

Stymied, Grace hung up and went back to preparing dinner. That's if Adam showed up for it at all. He had disappeared for the whole afternoon. Not that she was keeping *tabs* or anything. Well, all right, she was. She had already been up to his room to check that his belongings were still there. They were, and she was relieved for a number of reasons.

At eight o'clock she stood in the dining-room and looked around. It had seemed a bit too cosy to feed him in the kitchen, so she had dusted off the big dining-table and put on a white linen tablecloth. She had found Mrs Carr's silver cutlery and laid two places opposite each other – well, she was hardly going to eat afterwards, like the hired help. It seemed natural to add a candlestick and a vase of fresh flowers she had picked from the garden.

But now the candlestick looked a bit inappropriate or something. Intimate. It looked like they were on a *date*. She whipped off the candlestick, already regretting the wild mushroom and asparagus risotto simmering away in the kitchen. Didn't asparagus have a reputation as a food of seduction? And what would he make of her dessert meringues, with their stiff white peaks topped by juicy red strawberries? Oh Lord. She should have stuck to spaghetti bolognese. And they would eat in the kitchen.

Too late. She heard the front door opening and closing, followed by a clunk-clunk as he deposited his two big walking boots on the hall tiles.

He entered the dining-room, looked around, stopped in his tracks.

126

"Hi!" She looked up very casually, hoping to convey to him that she for one dined in splendour every evening of the week, and that he would betray his own lack of class if he mentioned it.

"Why are we eating in here?" he asked immediately.

"Mrs Carr left instructions to serve formal evening meals. She's old-fashioned that way," she lied. She hoped her tongue wouldn't curl up and turn black, like she often warned the boys would happen.

"Fine by me." He looked different. Keyed up or something. Excited. She wondered had his afternoon sojourn involved the person he had called 'Babe'. She had a brief vision of slim pale thighs wrapping themselves around him like a pair of frisky boa constrictors.

The thought automatically sent her into motherly mode. "I hope you're hungry!" she chirped. Raging, she escaped to the kitchen before she started patting him on the head or something.

She would tell him tonight that he must leave in the morning. Mrs Carr would be coming home in any case. She wouldn't even ask him for money. Somehow it would be crass and wrong to charge him for what had seemed like a little holiday. Well, for her anyway. She would go back to Dublin tomorrow with the smell of fresh-cut grass still on her clothes, and flour under her fingernails.

"Can I help?"

"Oh!"

He had come into the kitchen without her noticing. He seemed to be standing very close. But it was only to look over her shoulder at her French onion soup (nothing sexual could be read into French onion soup, could it? Maybe it meant something very suggestive in France. Maybe it was seen as a direct invitation to foreplay over there or something. Sweet Jesus).

"No, thanks," she said briskly. "I have everything under control."

Apart from her hands, which had suddenly become very

clumsy. She piled far too much cheese onto the bread floating on top of the soup, but then decided that she didn't care about the calories. She was starving. Everything seemed to taste better in the country; it was like her taste buds had suddenly awoken after a number of years in a perpetual slumber.

"A good cook as well," Adam said.

"As well as what?" she asked, wondering whether he was flirting with her. It was difficult to tell, given that nobody had flirted with her in years.

He shrugged, the picture of innocence. "Nothing. Just a figure of speech."

Back in the dining-room they ate their soup and slices of her homemade bread and watched each other across the table. He had got the sun today. His forehead and forearms seemed even browner. So had she; her own face was sprinkled with freckles. She had examined them in fascination in the bathroom mirror earlier, unable to decide whether they made her look sexy or homely. On balance, she liked them.

"Delicious," he declared.

"Thank you," she said demurely

"The soup too."

Oh! She felt a bit warm, then decided she had misheard. She asked casually, "Nice afternoon?"

"Yes, thank you," he said. Whether he had spent it shagging Babe, he wasn't going to say. Instead he put down his spoon with a satisfied sigh, got up from the table and left the room. Just like that! Did he think dinner was over? How could he call her delicious in one breath and then walk off on her the next? So fickle!

She was wondering what to do when he reappeared, holding a bottle of wine.

"For you."

"Me?"

"Well, us. Thought you might fancy a glass."

She watched as he opened it and poured two glasses before sitting down opposite her again.

"Let's have a toast," he said.

"To what?"

"Maybe to Mrs Carr? Seeing as she can't be here in person?" he suggested.

"Yes, of course," Grace said, guiltily lifting her glass to the woman she had shot and whose house she was merrily entertaining in. Still, she and Adam would be gone tomorrow. When Mrs Carr got back on Friday, she wouldn't know a thing. They still had the matter of her convalescence to discuss, but that would have to wait now until the woman was home.

"And to you," Adam added.

"Me?" She tried a breathy little laugh. It came out as a kind of nasty smoker's cough.

"For a wonderful meal," he elaborated.

"You haven't eaten the main course yet, it might be horrible."

"Don't put yourself down like that – why do you do that?"

She had only been joking; but everything with him was so intense! She tried to imagine a conversation between him and his friends; it would all be terribly serious and earnest and nobody would ever be allowed to crack a joke.

"It's gone a bit dark in here," he said now.

"I'll turn on a lamp – "

"Why don't we just light that candle up there on the mantelpiece?"

"We could," she said slowly, trying not to let the situation get away on her. He was pushing it now. After all his 'Babe' talk on the phone, too! What she needed to do was briskly stand, clap her hands and say, 'Now! Dinner! Have you washed your hands?'

But she didn't. She stayed sitting there. She was just curious, she told herself. It would be interesting to see how far he would go. How far she would *let* him. Which wouldn't be very far at all, of course. She was a married woman after all.

Still, she had to remind herself of this when he looked at her over the romantic glow of the candle and said, "I was thinking earlier. I don't know anything at all about you."

"What do you want to know?"

"Anything. Everything."

He fancied her. Most definitely. She might be out of the dating game but she could tell that much.

"I'm not sure I want to tell you," she said coyly. She was flirting right back! It mightn't be the best flirting in the world, it might lack finesse, but it was still flirting. There wasn't any harm in it. Was there?

Then he said, "Where do you go to in your head, Grace?"

"Pardon?"

"When you're on your own. When you sit in your car and you think nobody is watching you."

Oh! He had seen her! And she had only got into the car at all this morning to check that the garage guys hadn't left grease all over her seats. (Somehow, here in the country, she didn't feel the same urgent need to lock herself in the car as she did at home – which was a terrible indictment of Ewan and the boys, when she thought about it. She did love them really. She was just sick of them.)

"That's an interesting question," she said. For someone who just wanted to get into her pants.

"You look like a dreamer, that's all."

"I think about lots of things," she told him coolly.

And she would. Mostly she would have detective fantasies, where she would be a cop, modelled exactly on Clarice Starling in *Silence of the Lambs* – the type of heroine who was serious and unsmiling and self-reliant, and who still solved the crime (Grace was quite particular about her role models. The descriptions 'feisty' or 'sexy' would never apply to her heroines, for example). She never told anybody about these, obviously – she knew it would look odd for a woman her age to be having far-fetched fantasies which other people had left behind as children.

But why did it all have to end when you became grown-up? It was as though you had to accept your life the way it was and never dream again of being hand-picked by the CIA in the cereal section of the supermarket and whisked away on a secret mission. Anyhow, her fantasies had matured as she had grown older, she felt – at least now they tended to centre on action/adventure, and not meeting a very attractive rich man who wanted to marry her and have children with her. When she daydreamed about romance at all, it tended to veer off very quickly into those lurid porn fantasies again.

Other times, when she sat in the car, she didn't fantasise at all. She thought about the credit-card bill and where they would go on holidays next year. Then it would probably be time to get out of the car and go make the tea.

"I think about private things," she qualified to Adam, lest he think he could dissect her that easily with his schoolboy questions about what went on in her head. "Excuse me."

She left him at the table and went into the kitchen again.

The risotto was done to perfection. She added a pile of parmesan shavings, and took a few deep breaths. She felt all hot and bothered. Not that she couldn't handle the situation or anything. No, no, she was well able for him. The problem was that she shouldn't be enjoying it so much.

But all the same she touched up her hair a bit and made a rather dramatic entrance into the dining-room, the risotto held aloft. Round two!

Adam was gone again. Blast. Deflating rapidly, she was about to go in search of him when she saw him crouched down in the far corner and fiddling with what seemed to be an old gramophone. She hadn't noticed it until now, nor the records piled in a dusty heap on the floor beside it.

"Dinner!" she said.

But he was enthralled. "Look at this – old 45s." He examined a couple of records. "The Everley Brothers – 'Bye Bye Love'. Pretty good nick too."

He obviously knew his 50s music. Grace didn't. She needed to get back the mood, so she said, hopefully, "Risotto?"

"And Buddy Holly! 'Peggy Sue'," Adam said. He didn't even look at her.

"With wild mushrooms!" She waved the risotto around a bit, hoping the aroma would reach him. Maybe the way to a man's heart really was through his stomach.

"Will we put it on?" he said, holding up the record.

"Oh, I don't think so."

"Why not?"

"It belongs to Mrs Carr. She mightn't like us poking through her things."

"We're not poking. We're just playing some music. I don't see how she can object."

"Maybe after dinner."

He was putting the record on anyway. "Come on, Grace. Don't get all stuffy on me again. You were doing so well."

"I beg your pardon?"

"Do you not have music-making equipment in your leafy Dublin suburb?"

"I don't live in a leafy Dublin suburb," she said, even though she did. How did he know she lived in Dublin anyway? From her car registration plate, probably.

'Peggy Sue' erupted tinnily from the record player. She gave up and sat down at the table, and nodded her head once or twice to the beat, but felt middle-aged and silly and stopped. She wanted her dinner, she realised.

"Let's dance," he said.

She started. "Sorry?"

"Dance. It's when you kind of jiggle about to music."

"I know what dance is. It's just . . . I don't dance, okay?"

"Why, is there something wrong with your legs?"

She didn't like him any more. "No – "

"They look pretty good to me."

With a heavy-lidded look, he grabbed her hand, dragging her up from her cosy, safe chair.

"Please me let me go, Adam."

"That's the first time you've used my name. And I've never heard it sound better, to tell you the truth."

There was no time to respond: he was flinging her around the place, twisting her arm and twirling her like around a spinning top. There was no time even to feel foolish – one lapse of concentration and she could end up disabled for life.

"I don't know how you listen to this stuff," she said, as 'Peggy Sue' went into a cheesy second verse. "Would you not prefer something from your own generation?"

Somehow it was important to keep talking, to poke fun at him. He just gave her a look, and pulled her up very close.

"I have very particular tastes," he said, looking at her lips. She felt her colour rising, like she was seventeen again and dancing with the best-looking boy in the class at the school disco.

"Can we stop now?" she asked.

"Sorry, is your arthritis playing up?" he enquired, and twirled her away before she had time to reply. She hated him now. She twirled back a little harder than he expected and caught him squarely in the chest, winding him.

"Sorry," she said insincerely. "Can we sit down now?"

He let her go immediately. "Fine. You're obviously not enjoying yourself."

He had given up. She had played too hard to get. Which was exactly what she had wanted, of course. Absolutely!

They ate dinner and talked about travel, and books, and he declined second helpings of her breast-shaped meringues, and when she went to blow out the candle he didn't stop her, and she felt very flat somehow. Which was ridiculous! She'd had her bit of fun, and he'd had his and it was best just to leave it at that (when had it occurred to her that it might turn into something more?).

He offered to help wash up but she wouldn't let him. She told him that paying guests did not wash their own dishes (she'd changed her mind about making him pay). He offered to make coffee but she wouldn't let him do that either. Eventually he gave up and took the remains of his wine outside to the back garden.

She went upstairs and rang Ewan from Mrs Carr's cordless phone, making a mental note to leave money on the hall table for the call.

"Grace? Is something the matter?" He sounded a bit hassled and very far away.

"No, no. Is something the matter with *you*?"

"No."

"It's just that you said you'd ring later and you never did."

"We've just arrived in the park this minute."

"The park? You mean Disney?"

"Yes. It's unbelievable. We've just seen a huge . . ."

He was drowned out by a roar in the background, like something large passing at speed. She could only imagine what – a giant grinning electronic Mickey Mouse or something.

"Are the boys all right?" she asked, when she could hear him again.

"Having a ball. Do you want to speak to them? Neil, come over here! Neil – Mum's on the phone. She wants to talk to you. *Neil!*"

She moved quickly to smooth over the dawning embarrassment that Neil did not actually want to speak to her on the phone. "You know, Ewan – why don't I ring when it's evening over there your time? We can all have a proper chat then."

"All right," he said. He added, confidentially, "He can be a bit difficult, you know – Neil. I think it's something we should keep an eye on."

134

"Yes," Grace agreed. She had been keeping an eye on it for years.

"How is she anyway?" he asked. "Mrs Carr? Is there any news?"

"Well, she's not home yet," Grace said lamely, unwilling to recount her fruitless conversations with the hospital.

"But what about Michael? Surely you've spoken to him at this point?"

"Um, we're working something out," she said, hoping to fudge things.

"All right, great – Neil! So when do you think you'll be flying out? I mean, I'm just asking," he said quickly, obviously not wanting a repeat of their previous phone conversation. "I don't want to put you under any pressure or anything – Neil! Excuse me for a moment, Grace." He was gone, and there were rapid-fire muffled voices in the background, and then Ewan was back. He sounded a little under strain. "Anyway. Hopefully you'll make it out soon. After all, you're missing your holiday too."

"Well, it's hardly exciting stuck here," she agreed. "I'm just about to go to bed in fact. Curl up with a good book or something."

She was making it out to be worse than it actually was. She didn't know why. It wasn't as though she had anything to hide.

"Good idea," he said. "You know, I was thinking – you should really make the most of these few days. Take time for yourself. Relax, put your feet up. I can just about manage the boys by myself."

"Good," she said. He needn't sound so martyred – she did it all year round.

"I mean it. I don't want you thinking they're pining away without you," he said, and then added insult to injury: "In fact, it'll probably do you all the world of good to get away from each other."

"What's that supposed to mean?"

"What? Just that you could do with the break from them."

"That is not what you said."

"Grace – "

"Are you hinting that I'm smothering them?"

"Now you're twisting things." He said this with another little martyred sigh.

"Oh, go back to Mickey Mouse, Ewan."

There was a little silence, and then he said, "Why are we arguing like this, Grace? We never do normally."

"Maybe we should!" she said loudly. "Maybe it'd be a healthy thing to have a good row every now and again! Shake things up a little before we both die of boredom!" This was a little extreme. But she felt it was called for.

There was a pause. Then he said, "Can we talk about this later? I'm trying to keep tabs on the boys here."

Typical man, she thought viciously. Can't do two things at the same time, whereas women routinely did fifteen – and with a jolly smile on their faces.

"Fine," she said.

"When – tomorrow?" He sounded anxious.

"Soon," she said again, enigmatically.

If he was not going to stick to definite arrangements about times to phone, then she wouldn't either. She mightn't ring for two whole days! But that would be as long as she would last without word about the boys.

Adam was sitting on an old rug on the grass when she went out to say good night. She shouldn't have gone out at all. It was a silly thing to have done in the mood she was in, and she would reflect on the folly of it afterwards.

He looked up at her as she hovered. "Everything all right?"

"Fine. Why wouldn't it be?"

He just shrugged. "Want to sit down?" He moved over on the rug to make room for her.

"I should really go to bed . . ."

He didn't try to dissuade her. She sat anyway. Her shoulder glanced off his and she shifted over quickly.

He was smoking something that he had rolled himself, something pungent. He caught her looking at it.

"You don't mind, do you?"

"Mind? Not at all!" she said, hoping that she sounded blasé and sophisticated. She hadn't smoked weed since her college days. It had been the most rebellious and depraved thing she had ever done and the memory of it now, combined with the two glasses of wine she'd had at dinner, made her reckless.

"Can I have some?"

He looked mildly surprised. "I didn't know you smoked."

"Like you said, there are a lot of things you don't know about me," she said grandly.

"I can roll you one of your own," he offered.

"No, no, I only want a few . . . puffs." Was that the right word? Or was it hits? Although she thought 'hits' might be something to do with heroin. She hoped Adam wouldn't realise how hopelessly out of touch she was when it came to drugs. But he just handed over the joint to her. She held it languidly, a bored expression on her face, and tried not to burn her fingers. Finally, when he stopped looking at her, she lifted it quickly. The filter was damp from his mouth. Her own lips seemed to stick fast to the thin cigarette paper and for a moment she thought she would have to ask him to go get a tweezers or a knife or something. But she managed to inhale and extract the thing, choking back a cough. So far so good.

Adam was looking at the sky reflectively. "It makes you feel very small and insignificant, doesn't it? That great big expanse of sky. We're just pin-pricks down here on earth, of no consequence in the greater scheme of things."

"Hmmm," Grace said, her mouth full of smoke. There was a nasty burning sensation in her throat. Probably the drug doing its thing.

"Yet look at us all, scurrying around, busy-busy-busy," he continued ponderously. "But what's it all for at the end of the day? What do we all want?"

The joint had obviously worked its magic on him. Grace herself was nowhere near discussing the meaning of life yet, despite two more big drags.

"I couldn't tell you," she admitted. "Happiness, maybe?"

"Happiness!" His scorn rang out across the lawn.

"What's wrong with that?"

"The way I see it, you've only got one life and if you can't make a difference to the world in that time, then you might as well forget it."

"That's aiming rather high, isn't it?"

"When really it's much easier just to get a nice job and a nice car and marry a nice man and to hell with the starving masses?" He looked at her pointedly. She kept her gaze on the sky, took a last big drag of the joint and handed it back.

"That stuff is useless," she said haughtily.

"What?"

"It just tasted of tobacco."

"It is tobacco."

"Whatever stuff you mixed in with it, then. You'd want to change your dealer. I've had a better hit off a cigarette." To show her sophistication she was going to offer to give him the number of her own drug dealer, but thought this might be going too far. (Besides, he would be very surprised when he got Nick on the end of the phone. Nick would be more surprised at being asked for recreational drugs.)

"This *is* a cigarette," he said. Then he smiled. "What did you think it was, cannabis?"

"Cannabis? Ha! Don't be ridiculous!" she said. Oh God.

He put his arm around her and gave her an affectionate little squeeze, which was nearly more insulting. "Poor Grace. You're trying so hard, aren't you?"

"What?"

"To break the rules. To be a little crazy. And I'm not helping at all."

"Don't flatter yourself." She shrugged his arm off, furious. Was she really so transparent? She felt ridiculous, like some kind of teenage upstart determined to prove her coolness by smoking a joint. "I think I'll go to bed," she said.

"Don't," he said. "I'll be all lonely on my own."

She couldn't imagine Adam ever being lonely. He was too self-sufficient, too sure of his purpose in life. She, on the other hand, seemed to have spent most of her adult life just bobbing along in a sea of other people's expectations.

"I'm sure you know more interesting people than me who you could hang out with," she said.

"I don't know anybody like you," he said. "No, no, don't get all puffed up and defensive. I meant it as a compliment."

"What?" The word wasn't all that familiar to Grace.

"All the girls my age are cynical and hard-boiled, nothing in their heads but the gym and the latest Gucci bag," he said dismissively. "But you – you're so . . . you're so . . ."

She waited rather belligerently. Look at him – he couldn't think of a compliment now!

"Kind," he said eventually. "Thoughtful. Funny. Beautiful."

"Beautiful!" She gave a little laugh. She thought that she might be falling in love with him, a little bit.

"You are." His voice dropped a bit. "You're amazing."

The extravagance of this would have been amusing coming from anybody else. But from him, it sounded perfectly natural. Authoritative. Indisputable, even. She was amazing.

Her mouth felt a little dry; she felt his hand drop from her shoulder to rest casually around her waist.

"Why are you so tense? All bunched up," he murmured.

"Sorry," she said.

"There's no need to apologise."

Their ages seemed to have somehow reversed; he was now the worldly, mature one who was complimenting and reassuring her at the end of a dinner date. She was all huddled up on the rug like a nervous virgin, overwhelmed by his attentions and not knowing what to expect next.

She was soon enlightened when he leaned over and kissed her hair. It wasn't her lips, granted. But it was still enough of a shock for her to shy away from him.

"What's wrong, Grace?"

"I'm married," she said. But her voice carried no great conviction.

"Yes," he mused. He wasn't taking her marriage seriously either, and that somehow annoyed her. It mightn't be perfect but she had invested eleven years of her life in it, and it was the only one she had.

"And you have a girlfriend," she pointed out.

"Yes," he said, not seeming to take this very seriously either.

"She wouldn't mind you canoodling on a lawn with another woman?"

He considered this for a moment, then said, rather coldly she thought, "My girlfriend is not an issue."

So, that only left the husband. *Her* husband, she reminded herself. Ewan, for heaven's sake – the father of her two sons! He was probably canoeing down a creek in Critter Country right now, blissfully ignorant of the fact that a Tasmanian devil was kissing his wife's hair.

"All that, it's the real world," Adam elaborated. "They're not here. Not now. It's only you and me, Grace."

"And that's supposed to make it all right?" she asked.

He shrugged, seeming to think she was creating problems where there were none. "Won't we be back to it all tomorrow?" he said.

And that was it. They didn't attempt to legitimise it any further: there was no more discussion of partners or life in the real world.

There was only Mrs Carr's dark garden and the fresh cut lawn and the smell of tobacco on Adam's breath as he kissed her. It was a curiously unpushy kiss, chaste nearly, and it reminded her of when she'd first started dating at seventeen and eighteen, when the kiss at the end of the night was the highlight of the evening in those innocent days. The teenage magazines at the time would devote pages to this kiss; whether to French kiss or not, whether this could lead to pregnancy, how to stop him nicely if the good night kiss made him want to 'take things further'.

It did, obviously. Adam was trying to push her back on the rug now. To get into any kind of horizontal position was dangerous; she knew that from experience as well as from magazines. Best to signal in plenty of time that she was putting the brakes on.

"Adam," she murmured.

"Sorry. Do you not want to . . .?"

"No! I mean yes! I'm sure it would be very . . ." She was glad that he could not see inside her head then; every pornographic fantasy she'd ever had was playing in Technicolor, with him in a starring role. " . . . nice," she finished chastely. "It's just that we hardly know each other."

"I know enough about you," he said.

She felt the generation gap very strongly. It wasn't that she had been all that prudish at his age. But she suspected attitudes to casual sex were very different now. And she was married, after all.

"I might know you a bit better in the morning," she said. There was no harm in hedging her bets, was there? And, after all, they would never see each other again after tomorrow . . .

"Till the morning then," he said, making it sound like a promise.

"Yes," she said, wondering whether he intended infiltrating her bedroom at dawn. There was no lock on the door either. She could put a chair up against it, she supposed. But she knew that she wouldn't.

She sat on the lawn for ages after he had gone to bed, hugging her knees and looking up at the sky and the stars and what was beyond, and she thought that Adam was wrong about how humbling the enormity of it was, because tonight she didn't feel insignificant at all.

EIGHT

"You look different," Frank said rather accusingly the next morning as he stood in the middle of the kitchen.

"How?" she said guiltily.

"I don't know, just . . . different."

"Probably because I'm wearing Mrs Carr's clothes." Her own wouldn't stand up to another day's wear and were now spinning around in Mrs Carr's washing machine. If she hung them on the line outside they would be dry in time for her to go back to Dublin this afternoon. In the meantime she had found a kind of shapeless robe-like red garment in the wardrobe that could only be Mrs Carr's from some other era, and had put it on.

"Where's Adam?" Frank enquired now.

"In bed." His own bed, that was. He had not gatecrashed hers that morning after all. Possibly she had read him wrong. She had lain there naked for an hour just in case, her teeth brushed and her hair fanned out on the pillow becomingly, as though she always woke up like that. She had even rehearsed a token speech about how they ought not to do anything they might regret. In the end she had gone to the bathroom noisily, just in case he was a heavy sleeper. But still he hadn't come. Could it be that he was playing hard to get?

143

Frank said, "Could I borrow a cup of flour?"

"Sorry?"

"I'm baking some bread. Sandy says the smell of baking bread is very persuasive. You know, for when you're showing the house to Tom and Charlie."

"Sandy has worked in real estate, has she?" Grace enquired.

"What?

"It's just that she seems to be quite the expert when it comes to selling houses."

Frank sensed criticism. "Obviously she's interested in how things go for me. We *are* going to be married, you know."

Grace backed down. "Yes, of course. And how are preparations coming along? For the big day?"

"Well, she can't decide on a dress." Frank gave a little sigh, but anyone could see he was delighted. "She's torn between the Grace Kelly strapless ivory, or the Little Bo-Peep style – that comes with a staff, by the way."

"And what about sheep?"

"Pardon?"

"Look, never mind about the dress. Have you set a date yet?"

"I'm keen on October. But Sandy thinks the weather will be too bad. And I can see her point – if she's going to shell out all that money on a wedding dress, she doesn't want it to get wet, does she?"

"Golly, no."

Frank said, "You don't like Sandy much, do you?"

"I don't know Sandy. "

"Exactly. You don't know her. So please spare me the innuendo."

"I just hope that she's as committed to this relationship as you are, that's all."

"Do you know how many times she mailed me last night?"

"Frank – "

"Do you?"

144

"Of course I don't."

"Eleven times! And the last time was just to tell me that there was a moth in her bedroom with the most beautiful silky wings, and she asked me to look it up in one of my books to see what it was, and when I mailed back, she was sitting in the dark because she had turned all her apartment lights off in case the moth burned itself! *That's* the kind of person she is – the most decent, honourable, sweet, generous person I've ever met in my life!"

"But you haven't actually met her, Frank."

Frank's face went even redder. "I knew you'd bring that up!"

"Did you ask her about the tea towel?"

"As a matter of fact I did." He was triumphant now. "She brought along a barbecue to the beach that day for the disabled kids, because some of them don't eat as often as they should, and she bought the food out of her own pocket and she stood over that barbecue for three hours in the heat and the smell while everybody else had a great time dipping in the sea."

Grace said humbly, "Oh. I – "

"Then she burnt her hand quite badly but didn't say anything to anybody, just covered it with that tea towel, and smiled for that photo which little Tommy was taking. He's a paraplegic, by the way."

"Sorry." Grace wanted to crawl on the floor now. "She's an example to us all."

"I won't even mention this to her," Frank said loftily. "Not when she's feeling so tired and everything."

"Has she been to the doctor yet?" Grace tried to sound very concerned to make up for things.

"She's made an appointment. Between you and me, I think she's probably a bit low in iron. She doesn't eat meat, you see. She thinks that animals have as much right to live as we do. Even rats! She has a place in her heart for everything." He had gone all dreamy-eyed again.

"Incredible," Grace murmured. "Any news on her sister?"

145

"Sandy thinks she's managed to talk her into going to counselling with her husband. So I should soon be able to book my flight."

"That's great, Frank," Grace said with feeling. "I bet you two can't wait to get your hands on each other!"

Frank looked a bit startled. "Ah . . . uh . . ."

"Unless Sandy wants to . . . wait until you're married?" She probably did too, the sanctimonious little cow.

"You know, I haven't asked her."

Grace felt bad now. "Look, Frank, it's none of my business."

But he went off with his cup of flour, looking rather preoccupied. Grace took her tea to the kitchen window and looked out at the lawn. Something glinting on the grass caught her eye: Adam's forgotten wine glass from last night. She felt reassured: she hadn't imagined the whole thing. He *had* kissed her. He *had* told her she was amazing. It wasn't some lurid daydream she'd cooked up involving risotto, Peggy Sue and Mrs Carr's young lodger.

"Why are you in such a good mood?" Natalie demanded when she rang Grace's mobile phone a few minutes later.

"Because I'm thoughtful and funny and lovely," Grace said airily. Adam had said so: she remembered it all, every word.

"Oh, you got it too!" Natalie cried.

"What?"

"*Learning To Love The Real You*. Lisa was on about it in the office." Lisa was a self-help junkie.

"A man told me, actually," Grace boasted.

Natalie sucked in her breath. "A real man?"

"Very real," she said, thinking of Adam's chest. She bet it felt as smooth as a baby's bottom.

"For God's sake, who?" Then she sucked in her breath. "Not Adam?"

Grace gave such a light, incredulous little laugh that she nearly convinced herself. "Hardly."

"Who, then?"

"Just somebody." She had forgotten how persistent Natalie could be and was beginning to regret saying anything at all.

"What else did he say?" Natalie said excitedly.

"That I was beautiful."

There was a chortle. "Beautiful!" Then Natalie hurried on, "I mean, of course you're *attractive*. And you've a very good figure, even after twins."

"But I'm not beautiful?"

Natalie tried to stop digging. "You are! You're gorgeous! I just meant that it seems a rather . . . elaborate thing to say, that's all."

"Yes, isn't it great?" Grace said cheerily, refusing to let the good be taken out of it. Anyway, she didn't care about the beautiful thing (she knew she wasn't really beautiful, but then most people weren't). No, the bit she remembered most of all, the bit that replayed over and over in her head, was him saying that she wasn't like anybody else he knew.

He thought she was different. Special. Unique, even. And she hadn't even had to resort to bragging about the shotgun, or retelling bad jokes she'd heard on the radio. He had not been fooled by the whole public persona of Grace Tynan. She felt that he had seen something in her that nobody had seen for a long time – even herself. And he had liked it – at least enough to try and get her to lie down on the lawn with him.

Right now he was lying in his bed upstairs.

"I think I might be on the verge of doing something silly," she blurted to Natalie now.

Natalie immediately pounced. "How silly?"

"I don't know." If he had come to her room this morning, she might not even be having this conversation. The silliness might be in full swing.

"On a scale of one to ten," Natalie said, egging her on.

"A nine."

"A nine!" Natalie was shocked. "I've only ever done a seven.

147

Remember, when I took off my top at that party?"

"That's a seven? Mine is a ten then," Grace said.

"Bloody hell," Natalie whispered.

"I know. What should I do?"

"How do I know? You haven't even told me what the silliness is!"

"I can't, Natalie."

There was a very heavy pause, then Natalie said solemnly, "If this silliness should happen to involve a man who has been telling you you're beautiful, then I would have to strongly advise you against such a course of action, Grace."

"Yes, I thought you might," Grace said. It was immaterial anyway. He had not come to her room and tried to make love to her. Not that they were in love. It would be more a question of having sex. Which would be very cold and tawdry (well, morally anyway. In every other way she found it desperately exciting). No, it was just as well it had ended where it had. She could hug his words to her all day – or for the rest of her life if she felt like it – with the assurance that she hadn't really done anything, well, foolish.

"You *are* married, Grace," Natalie finished up. She made it sound like a government health warning.

"So are you," Grace said, adding a bit spitefully, "and up the pole." She hung up, ran her fingers through her hair and her tongue over her lips, and went upstairs. She knocked on his bedroom door.

"Adam? Breakfast is ready."

She must say something – just very casually – about being up since dawn. She didn't want him thinking that she had lain in bed for hours waiting for him.

"Adam?"

Possibly he was a very heavy sleeper. Eventually she opened the door just a crack, half-hoping to catch a glimpse of his brown body spread across the sheets. Did he sleep naked?

He wasn't there. The bed was empty and neatly made. Far from planning an assault on her bedroom, he had been up and about before she'd even woken up!

She felt a bit foolish now. Imagine having taken a bit of flirting so seriously! And the kiss – had she taken that too seriously too? For all she knew, he might do this kind of thing all the time – seduce landladies on lawns in every port in the world, after first telling them they were amazing. *And* he had a girlfriend! (She had a husband, of course, which was worse – but it didn't stop her feeling slightly bruised and used.)

She wondered where he had gone. To meet the woman otherwise known as Babe? Grace wanted to tear her limb from limb and boil her head in a pressure cooker.

The thoughts of pressure cookers immediately set her mouth watering. And no wonder – she had given over so much time to unrequited romance this morning that she had neglected her stomach entirely! Gathering the red robe around herself in the manner of a Greek goddess, she set off down the stairs in search of breakfast.

Half an hour later she found herself back at the scene of one of her previous crimes: the cooler section of the local Spar. She popped on her dark sunglasses just in case she was recognised, and was trying to decide between a pack of plump sausages and some juicy gammon steaks (would it be too greedy to have both?) when someone said, "Grace!"

She swung around to find herself face to face with Sergeant Daly.

"I was going to pay for these," she blurted, wondering whether this was some kind of sting operation.

But Sergeant Daly just chuckled heartily. "Only the innocent ever look guilty, Grace. I've learned that much in thirty years of law enforcement if nothing else."

She didn't want to tell him that his thirty years were completely wasted in that case and so she just chuckled back.

"Is this about my statement?" she said. She had gone down to the station yesterday afternoon in between washing towels and putting on the risotto. She'd never had to make a police statement before. It wasn't half as exciting as she'd imagined it would be – they'd even made her tone down the phrases 'pumped a shot' and 'the victim collapsed to the floor, the colour of putty.' "Just stick to the facts," they'd said. Honestly, by the time they'd finished with it, it had all read rather like a boring school essay.

"No, no, your statement is perfect," he said. He leaned in. "It was actually the house I wanted to have a word with you about."

God. You could keep no secrets in a small town. "I'm leaving today, okay?" she blustered. Could he have her up for breaking and entering? "And Adam too. And I'll come clean to Mrs Carr. Really, it was all an accident of circumstance."

Sergeant Daly looked confused. "I'm talking about Frank's house. You're supposed to be showing it to Tom and Charlie later."

"Oh! That's right!"

He looked a bit pinched or something, so she said, "There's no problem, is there? They arrived from Birmingham okay?"

"Yes," he said.

"Great! And did you meet Charlie?"

"I did," he said, very heavily. Then he pitched forward over the cooler section and said, very low, "Do you remember I was asking you about conversions?"

"Yes – turning the study into a playroom. It's simple enough, they wouldn't need planning permission or anything."

"How about something more radical? Supposing they wanted to convert the whole house into something else?"

"You mean like a crèche, for example?"

He looked over his shoulder furtively, and said out of the side of his mouth, "A club."

She was a bit taken aback. "Eh . . . what kind of a club? I mean, would there be alcohol served?"

"Buckets of it," he said grimly.

"It's a residential area. I don't think they could," she said. "But all this stuff – isn't it more your area?"

"I wasn't sure, you see," he whispered. "And I didn't want to bring it up down at the station. Not in front of the other lads, you know? I'd never live it down."

"I know," she said, none the wiser. She felt a great need to put some distance between herself and the law at this point, and so she said, "Actually, I'd better get going if I'm going to keep my appointment with your Tom. Let's hope they like the house, eh?"

"Um," he said, very unenthusiastically.

Grace escaped from the Spar, with neither sausages nor gammon steaks, and she was almost light-headed with hunger. So when a shop door opened up the street and the smell of hot coffee and sticky buns wafted out, she elbowed past a couple of pensioners in her haste to catch the door before it closed.

Inside, she went to the counter. "Coffee, please!" she said to an assistant. "And one of those scones."

Now that food was definitely on its way, she could relax enough to look around. The café was full of mid-morning shoppers. She was just looking for an empty table when her eye fell on a red T-shirt with the slogan *Save The World* on it. The wearer was Adam.

She whirled back to the counter, hoping he wouldn't recognise her in the red robe and sunglasses. What if he thought she was following him?

Then she was annoyed with herself. It was a free country, wasn't it? She was as entitled as anybody else to walk into a café and order a coffee! She had nothing to feel guilty about.

So she slowly turned back and had a peek. He was sitting at a window table, drinking a coffee and talking earnestly to someone. Grace was ridiculously relieved that it was not some delicious young hippy girl but another young man wearing scruffy denims and a couple of friendship bracelets, although he didn't look all that friendly to Grace. His mouth barely moved as he spoke.

"The special is cream of carrot soup."

Grace swung back to the counter. "Sorry?"

The café assistant held out her coffee. "The soup."

"Thanks anyway, but I don't think . . ."

She only wanted cake. But the assistant seemed to take umbrage. "It's home-made if that's what you're worried about. Minnie made it first thing."

"Oh! Well, in that case . . . I'd love a bowl."

The assistant sniffed a bit, knowing a blow-in when she saw one, and went to get a bowl of the soup. Grace snuck another look over her shoulder. Adam and his companion were joined now by a third person: a chunky young woman with long hair pulled into a careless ponytail. She was not Babe either, Grace just instinctively knew. It was in her body language when she squeezed past Adam to take the third stool. Far from displaying any affection or intimacy, she muscled in roughly until she had sufficient room and he had to move over, and Grace admired her for it.

"The main course special is Irish Stew." The café assistant was back, holding out a steaming bowl of soup. Grace put it onto her tray.

"To be honest, I'm not a stew fan," she said regretfully. Stew was a food from her childhood; she couldn't remember the last time she'd eaten it. Anyway, it was only eleven o'clock in the morning.

The assistant gave a suit-yourself shrug. "I'm not either. But that was before I tasted Minnie's."

"Good, is it?"

"Good?" the assistant barked. "Do you like meat?"

"Yes, I suppose."

"Minnie back there doesn't scrimp on meat. Big chunks of the best Irish beef! And carrots from her own back garden – onions too, and those tiny new potatoes. She makes her own stock from scratch from the best bones they save for her over in Morrissey's. Then she marinades the whole lot in a big pot for two days in the yard out the back before cooking it all up."

Grace suspected that this went against all health regulations, but her mouth was watering like crazy. And she'd had no breakfast after all.

"I suppose it's very fattening?" she said regretfully.

"Lethal," the assistant said. "She doesn't even trim the meat."

"Does she skim the fat off the top?"

"Nope. Says that's what gives it all its flavour."

"I'll have a bowl," Grace decided.

"You won't regret it."

"Not too big though!"

"How about a medium-sized portion?"

"Perfect. And maybe some of that home-made bread?"

"I'll fix you up with two big chunks, and a couple of pats of butter."

The assistant nodded in satisfaction and went off to get the stew. Grace looked around again at Adam's table. There seemed to be some kind of intense discussion going on. The three of them had their heads so close that Adam's dreadlocks were brushing against the girl's face. She flicked them away – so roughly! – and said something else that seemed to greatly antagonise him. He whispered back fiercely in any case. But she overrode him. She was in charge, Grace guessed. Of what, she didn't know – some kind of clandestine coffee-drinking group? Sergeant Daly was fretting about nothing.

The assistant was back with the stew and Grace eagerly added it to her tray. By the time she reached the checkout, she had been easily persuaded into trying the dessert special of apple crumble with clotted cream, a glass of pressed apple juice and a slice of banana bread, all made fresh this morning by the miraculous Minnie. Grace strained to get a glimpse of her in the back kitchen, but couldn't. Possibly she had collapsed from exhaustion.

"Excuse me . . ." She made her way discreetly towards the nearest empty table, kind of moving backwards. With any luck, Adam wouldn't see her at all and she could eat her lunch in peace and go. But she had forgotten that she was still wearing her black sunglasses, which gave rise to a minor understanding.

"Noel, help that woman – she's blind."

"No, no, I'm not actually . . ."

"Noel, she's going backwards, turn her around."

Apparently she was also deaf, and without a sense of direction.

"Really, I'm fine."

But Noel had been dispatched and he stood in front of her now and firmly took her tray from her.

"Now, let's get you a seat," he said.

Please God, let Adam not notice. But a swift glance his way confirmed that the argument was ongoing. "That table is fine," she instructed Noel, pointing to the nearest empty one.

Noel wasn't thrown by her ability to spot an empty table despite her blindness. In any case he ignored her and set off towards the back of the café – and an empty table right next to Adam.

"Noel . . ." she said.

"Let the lady through please," he told the other diners officiously.

Grace had no choice but to follow him. Everyone drew in their legs sharply and scraped up any handbags that might lie in her way like booby traps. Chairs were hastily pulled in.

"Thank you, thank you," she murmured, quite enjoying the attention now. Then she guiltily thought that real blind people probably didn't enjoy it at all.

"I can take it from here," she murmured, choosing the chair with its back to Adam and sliding in discreetly. He didn't even turn his head her way, and she didn't know whether she was insulted or not.

"Okay," Noel said, patting her on the shoulder. But he was

kind. People generally were very kind, she thought, as Noel went back to his table, his back a little less stooped.

She took a surreptitious look over her shoulder. Adam was close enough for her to reach back and touch. She would very much like to touch him too; the more she thought about it, the more it became a compulsion, until her fingers were positively itching to lunge over and fondle his bottom. She could always claim to the other diners that she was blind and that she'd thought he was a milk jug or something.

Guiltily, she turned her attention to her lunch. The soup was delicious (Minnie wasn't sparing when it came to double cream either). She polished it off quickly – at this rate she would have her lunch eaten and would be gone before she was spotted at all. Then the occupants of a large table close by upped and left the café, and all of a sudden she could hear what Adam and his friends were whispering about.

"I am not selling baked potatoes," Adam said, low but very definite.

Interesting, she thought.

"It is just a suggestion," the girl said. She pronounced 'is' like 'iz'. French, Grace thought. "We could hand out leaflets with every purchase. What do you think, Joey?"

Grace expected Joey must be Italian, or in some way Mediterranean.

"I don't give a balls," he said.

Irish, then.

She wondered should she mention to Adam later that the Spar had a sign up looking for staff. She remembered seeing it the other night. That way he and his friends wouldn't have to resort to selling fast food if they were running a little short of cash.

But then Adam said, "You can mess around with baked-potato stands if you want, Martine. They tried that at Oasis last year, and Robbie Williams the year before. And you know what? People were too busy stuffing their faces to listen to the message!"

What message? Grace took a little bite of her stew. It was fantastic.

"All right, cool it," Joey muttered. But it was obvious whose side he was on. "We need to come up with something, and fast. We have less than four weeks to go."

"I say we need to make a big impact," Adam said. "Do something a little less conservative. I'm sure Martine would agree with me. If you're not too busy perfecting your culinary skills, that is. Comrade."

Grace glanced over her shoulder to see Martine give Adam a filthy look. Then she grabbed his packet of tobacco to roll herself a cigarette but, in her belligerence, sent it flying to the floor instead.

It landed at Grace's feet.

"Grace?" Adam had turned around in his seat.

"Mmm? Oh, Adam! Hi." He was looking a bit shocked. "Just popped in for an early lunch." And she went right on eating her stew – she might as well brazen it out at this point. There was a little silence at the table now. Grace turned round again. Martine and Joey were looking rather accusingly at Adam. Grace offered them her most harmless smile. "Hello there! I'd recommend the stew. It's delicious."

At this point, Adam was compelled to explain her. "This is Grace, my, uh, landlady."

They said nothing, just looked at her. Grace had another spoon of stew and re-crossed her legs under the red robe. She wondered should she take her sunglasses off but decided against it.

"You don't look like a landlady," Martine said at last, her tongue rolling contemptuously around the vowels.

"I'm just starting out," Grace confessed. "In fact, Adam is my very first lodger. We've been muddling along quite nicely, haven't we, Adam?"

Adam looked alarmed, as though she were going to reveal that they had been snogging in the garden last night. She just gave him

156

a rather pointed look, before turning to Martine and Joey.

"I didn't know Adam had friends in Hackettstown?" She deserved an explanation too.

"We're not friends," Martine spat. Grace wondered where she got the energy to be so aggressive all the time. Then Martine hastily corrected herself. "I mean, we are, kind of. We hooked up to go to the music festival together."

Joey wasn't going to explain himself at all, that much was obvious.

"I've seen the posters for it around town. It looks great," Grace said chattily. "But aren't you a little early for it?"

By nearly a month, actually. There was another tense silence. Martine glared at Adam for bringing this inquisition down upon them. Joey cleaned under his nails with a penknife.

"I have relatives here," Martine said finally. "I'm visiting them before going on to the festival. And Adam is going to see some of the country first."

"Is he?" Grace said, with great interest. Adam looked at her rather imploringly but she didn't let him off the hook. "You never mentioned anything at dinner last night."

He eventually said, "Didn't I?"

"Maybe you're feeding him too well," Joey said. His eyes were flat and knowing as he looked at her. "Or something."

"Maybe," she said, with a little laugh.

Martine was oblivious. "My landlady is the tightest bitch in the whole of Europe," she complained loudly, uncaring who heard her. "I haven't had a decent meal in two days."

"Perhaps she's worried about overheads," Grace murmured, feeling she should defend one of her own.

"Overheads!" Martine sniffed. "The shower is set on a timer – you only get five minutes of hot water and then it goes cold!"

"Oh, well, that's not right," Grace said. There were overheads, and then there was just plain meanness. "Maybe you should say something to her?"

"Maybe," Martine said doubtfully. "I'd move only I can't find anywhere else."

"Maybe your relatives . . . ?" Grace prompted.

She watched as Martine thought furiously for a moment. "Unfortunately they live in a caravan," she declared at last.

"Yes, most Irish people do," Grace murmured into her stew, earning another suspicious look

"I don't suppose there's a free place in your house?" Martine asked.

Adam didn't like this. "Grace only has one guest room."

That wasn't true. There were three guest rooms in total. But it was immaterial anyway. Grace was leaving today. And so was Adam – so what was he angling for?

"I could sleep on the floor," Martine said. "I could go back with Adam later and see the place."

"It's not Grace's house," Adam argued, looking to Grace for back-up. For some reason he didn't want Martine going back to the house with him.

She didn't look at him. "He's right. The owner, Mrs Carr, will be back tomorrow and you can ring her then if you want. Her number's in the book. But she's convalescing and I doubt she'll be up to taking on lodgers."

She took two large bites of her apple crumble – delicious – and slipped the bit of banana bread into a napkin, which she deftly pocketed. Then she stood and nodded at Martine and Joey. "Nice to meet you."

Adam caught up with her at the door. "Sorry I left without saying goodbye this morning."

"You don't have to check in with me."

He looked hurt. The power of it was almost dizzying.

"I didn't think you were the type of woman to play games."

"Adam, I have to go and show a house. And then I'm leaving for Dublin."

"Can I see you back at Mrs Carr's before then? Just the two of us?" he said, looking very intense.

"I suppose I can spare a few minutes," she said rather grandly. She pushed her sunglasses back up on her nose and made an exit.

NINE

"Ivy's dead," Elizabeth said later that morning.

"Stop that," Julia snapped. Ivy might have kept them awake half the night again but there was no need for that kind of talk.

"No, I mean she's really dead. A heart attack," Elizabeth said, her voice quivering. They all looked over at Ivy's empty bed. She'd been scheduled for an early morning x-ray, and they thought that she'd just been held up. "The nurses say she died about four o'clock. Just like that, they said. Hardly made a sound in the end, for her." And she started to cry. Julia reached over and covered Elizabeth's bony hand with her own, but it was scant comfort to either of them.

Ivy's bed was stripped and remade by twelve, and a new occupant installed by lunch-time. The speed and efficiency and sheer mundanity of it all was profoundly shocking, and Julia returned her lukewarm fish pie and trifle to the hospital kitchen untouched. She had a brief conversation with the Ward Sister, then she pulled her bag out from her locker and began to pack.

It was a slow process on crutches and she was still at it when Michael arrived half an hour later.

"Oh, hello, Michael. I'm sorry to drag you away from work. Did the Ward Sister explain?"

He didn't waste any time on pleasantries. "What, that you've decided to discharge yourself on a whim?"

"I'm sure she didn't say that."

"You're not due to leave until tomorrow, Mammy!"

"Yes, but I've decided to leave today instead. I just have to sign a form at the desk on the way out. Nobody can keep me here."

"The Ward Sister has told me it's very unwise. She's not a bit happy – "

"I know, she's already told me. Look, are you going to drive me home or do I have to ring Frank?"

Michael stopped blustering and looked at her with concern. "Are you all right, Mammy? You look a bit pale."

"I'm fine."

"At least let me finish that." He took the bag from her to finish the packing.

Julia watched from the chair, huddled in a cardigan. For some reason she couldn't seem to get warm and thought that perhaps she had caught a chill.

"Do you want to put your painkillers into your handbag?" he asked.

"No, you keep them for me," she found herself saying. She, who had hoarded up any pills she could get her hands on in order to kill herself! She could hardly believe it now.

She didn't know what had changed. Perhaps it was her foot, freshly bandaged and resting between her crutches. She had never known disability before, had no idea what it was like to be dependent upon others for even the smallest thing. It tended to make you inclined to hang on to those parts of you which worked properly, and not poison them with pharmaceuticals.

She had also realised that there wasn't a lot of glamour in pain. Even less in dying. Look at poor Ivy.

Or maybe it was this place. In a few short days it had leached away her courage and confidence, bit by bit, like one of its intravenous drips. It was dangerous.

"Hurry, Michael," she urged.

He insisted on bringing the car around to the front of the hospital. She let herself be installed in the front seat. Before she could stop him, he had put her crutches in the boot. Her feelings of helplessness, of foreboding, grew, and she sat there clutching the straps of her handbag fiercely like you see very old women do.

When she eventually took note of her surroundings half an hour later she saw that they were driving into Michael's housing estate. Big white mock-Tudor houses passed them by.

"I thought we might stop by for a bite of lunch," Michael said. "The Ward Sister said you haven't touched a thing today. You have to build up your strength, Mammy."

"Michael, I just want to go home," she said. To have normality, or what passed for normality, again.

"I rang ahead. Gillian is cooking a roast for us."

"Oh."

"And I thought we might take a look at the garage afterwards."

Julia turned to him. "Michael, this is all very sudden. This Granny-flat thing."

"I know. But like we said, there is absolutely no pressure on you."

"In that case, don't you think we should talk about it before you go taking measurements?"

"We're not going to be taking measurements. We just wanted you to see the place now that it's all cleared out."

"You've it all cleared out?"

"We've just thrown out all the junk. It's no big deal."

She tried to make him see. "But it is, Michael. Me moving in is a very big change for us all. I mean, what does Gillian think?"

He waved his hand. "If it was her mother, we'd do the same."

"Her mother is dead, Michael." He didn't say anything, so she pressed on, "And what about Susan?"

"What about her?"

"She's thirteen. It mightn't suit her to have a geriatric granny

162

cramping her style."

"She'll come around in the end. Mammy, I'm just asking you to have a look at the place, okay?"

He seemed intent on railroading everybody with this ridiculous idea of his; Michael, who could never say boo to a goose.

At the house Gillian waved to them from the kitchen window. She was wearing what appeared to be a gas mask.

"Does she wear that to cook?" Julia asked. Possibly she was allergic to vegetable oil or something. She already had nut, garlic, yeast, fish and dairy allergies. At one point her diet had been right down to dry crackers and olives, until she discovered she was allergic to olives too.

"No, no, she's just been fumigating the garage. After she's finished with the place, you can be sure you'll be the only living creature in it."

"*If* I move in, Michael. There's been no decision made yet."

"Oh, I know," he said.

Gillian came out of the house. Thankfully she had removed the gas mask. "Julia! Welcome home."

"This is not my home," Julia said sharply. Why had people suddenly stopped listening to her?

"I meant it in a general sense," Gillian said evenly. "Anyway! I hope you're hungry; lunch is ready."

But Michael was already setting off eagerly for the garage. "Come on, Mammy."

He had forgotten she was on crutches, and she was left to hobble slowly across the grass after him with Gillian at her elbow in case she might trip.

"I was never on crutches," Gillian said, sounding envious.

"Do you want a go?" Julia offered.

"Lord no!" But you could see she was tempted.

Michael waited in front of the double-garage. "Ta-da!" he said.

A dense fog of insect spray hung over the place – which didn't resemble a garage in any sense of the word any more. Already partitions had been put in place to divide it into rooms. Fresh wiring hung in clumps from the wall, and a new front door, which presumably her key fitted, rested against a wall waiting to be built in.

"I thought you said you were just at the clearing-out stage?"

"We managed to get a builder at short notice. We didn't want to say anything in case he fell through," Michael said, his double chin quivering with excitement.

Gillian added, "Michael sanded down everything yesterday, all ready for the plasterer as soon as they get the front finished. We didn't expect you home today, or we'd have had the front door up and waiting for you!"

The idea that she would want to come and live with them seemed to have become a fully-fledged presumption, and she was angry. "I didn't ask for this," she said loudly.

There was a little silence.

"Maybe you just need to think about it for a while," Gillian suggested.

"I have thought about it. And thank you for the offer, but no. It wouldn't work out."

Michael and Gillian exchanged a look over her head.

"Mammy, we just don't feel comfortable with you living on your own any more," Michael began. "After . . . what happened with the gun."

"And you'd feel more comfortable with me living in the same house as you? Would you not be afraid that I might come in and mow you all down with an Ouzi?"

Gillian gave a nervous little start.

"We're just trying to do the best here for you, Mammy," Michael said.

"But did I ask you, Michael? To do anything for me?" Suddenly she felt on the edge of tears. Her own son, patronising and talking down to her. Treating her as though she had no mind of her own any more: or at least no mind worth taking any notice of.

Her outrage was as great as her new insignificance.

"Please drive me home now."

"But lunch – "

"I'm not hungry."

Now he looked upset. "Mammy, I can see we've gone about this the wrong way. We just wanted to surprise you, that's all. How about we go inside and sit down and talk about this thing properly?"

"No. I've made up my mind."

Gillian threw up her hands, said to Michael, "Oh, let her go if she wants."

"Gillian – "

"No, Michael! We've bent over backwards for her! Stayed up the whole night working on that place! And she hasn't even bothered to say thank you!"

"Sorry to throw your great act of self-sacrifice back in your face," Julia said. "But nobody asked you."

Gillian was furious now. She looked at Julia, and saw her vulnerabilities immediately; knew exactly what to say to pierce her most. "Fine. Go back to Hackettstown. Hobble about in that big old house on crutches. I just hope you don't fall down in the middle of the night, that's all, with nobody to help you."

"Gillian!" Michael said, his face white.

"I have neighbours, you know," Julia retaliated. She hoped her voice wasn't shaking. "And friends. Plenty of them! I don't need you and Michael. You've never bothered with me before anyway so I don't know why you're starting now!"

Gillian cut a look at Michael. "Beats me. I'm not trying to fill the shoes of a dead man."

"What?"

"Gillian! Enough!"

Michael took a step forward and for a horrible moment Julia thought the whole thing was going to come to blows, but Gillian just turned to her and said, almost triumphantly, "You'll be back yet."

She turned on one emaciated heel and walked off.

There was going to be a heat wave. The weatherman had said so on the local radio news at noon. Not that you could believe a word out of the mouths of them usually, but today Grace was inclined to believe they were right. She felt almost giddy as she sat on Frank's manicured grass verge on the side of the road, her bare feet tucked up under her, and her face turned to the midday sun.

A passing car hooted at her. She waved boldly back at it. She had always been brought up to know that waving at cars or trucks or building sites was a cheap thing to do. But it seemed finicky to worry about that now, after kissing a backpacker on the lawn last night.

Her mobile phone beeped. A text message, from Ewan.

Missing you
It's true
Disney is blue
Without You

It wasn't one of his better ones. But it was enough to make her throat tighten with guilt.

Still, Adam was leaving this afternoon. It was just as well. There was no telling what she might do in bare feet and a heat wave (what had he meant, about having a few minutes alone with her before they parted?).

As though to banish any temptation, she read Ewan's poem again, slowly. It was quite sweet, really. And there was another bit at the end; she hadn't scrolled down far enough.

PS Did you pack mosquito repellent?

If that wasn't just typical of him! He'd only wanted to know about the mosquito repellent all along! The love poem was just to soften her up!

Once, when he had forgotten her birthday, to her great hurt and consternation, he had sent a funny poem in the post to her every day for seventeen days until she had eventually caved in, wet-eyed with laughter.

"You see – you love me really," he had said. Well, yes. But somehow that didn't excuse him any more.

Maybe there were some people who should never have got married at all. She wasn't talking about *herself* – look at her organisational abilities, for heaven's sake! Her sensitivity to the needs of others! Her willingness – her blind eagerness – to mother a whole group of males, whether they were her offspring or not. She was perfect marriage material, she thought gloomily, and she had no one to blame for that except herself. (She could also whip up the lightest batch of scones in the country when the mood took her.)

No, she had meant Ewan. There was a man who, left to his own devices, could actually do very well. There would be no female around to whinge about his absent-mindedness, which would grow and mature over the years until it achieved mythical status: 'Oh, Ewan Tynan? Gas man! For the birds!' People in the advertising industry would swap amusing stories about him in the pub. He would win lucrative jobs purely on the strength of having lost his car in an underground car park two years ago – for surely somebody that kooky must be a genius?

She could see it now: his hair would grow long and he would wear handy non-crease T-shirts with clever slogans on the front. After about two years he would look exactly like Bob Geldof, and he would live in a city-centre apartment that he would never clean and he would develop a short list of easy-to-prepare dishes, such as macaroni cheese and omelettes. Every six months or so he would go on a date with someone from the advertising world: a slim, blonde woman as clever as him, and they would eat Japanese food and then sleep together. But, from what Grace had seen of them, most women in the advertising world were too busy to take on 'challenges', and so would be unavailable when

Ewan rang for a second date, and he would be saddened (but only briefly) and he would pour the experience into whatever project he was working on, which would go on to win numerous prestigious awards and he would be happy.

He might miss not having children though. But he could always father a few without ever having to marry anybody, like Picasso or one of those, and he would have the best of all worlds. Wouldn't that just be like him?

She was being very harsh. Deep down she knew that he would be lost without her, aimless and adrift without the anchorage of marriage.

But the point was there was a part of Ewan that would always remain unmarried. Perhaps it was the same with all men. They seemed to have a small, hard core inside themselves that was independent and theirs alone, and that they protected fiercely against emotional demands.

Had Grace been as sensible? Had she heck! The day she'd walked up the aisle, she had willingly let herself be devoured body and soul by the twin institutions of marriage and motherhood. Women had been doing it for centuries, of course. She thought of her predecessors now: all the Beryls and Anastasias and Desdemonas – had they, like Grace, woken up some morning in their mud huts or castles, surrounded by crabby children while their husbands were off inventing wheels or practising with their bows and arrows, and thought, sod this? Had they too lustily eyed up some nubile young stable boy or farmhand with a view to taking something for themselves for a change?

A rental car screeched past her into Frank's driveway, kicking up dust into her face.

"Hello!" a man shouted at her from the driver's side. Tom or Charlie, no doubt. Annoyed, she didn't return the greeting. (Company policy was not to antagonise potential purchasers at least until the booking deposit had been paid. But she wasn't on company time today.)

The man getting out of the driver's seat looked like Sergeant Daly around the chin and the mouth but everything about him was slicker, edgier.

"You must be Tom," Grace said, going over.

"I was the last time I looked," he said, and she laughed politely. He jerked a thumb over to the passenger side. "And this is Charlie. Charlie?" He peered into the car. "For Pete's sake! There's no need to powder your nose. We're just viewing a house."

He shook his head in despair for the benefit of Grace.

She smiled politely, anticipating that Charlie must be quite a character. Did he wear full make-up or just the trimmings?

The passenger door was thrown open and a pair of long, tanned legs swung sexily out into the road. A bejewelled hand shot forward to grip Grace's.

"Hello there! I'm Charlie."

Charlie was a woman, of course. Grace wondered how she had got it so wrong; there was nothing masculine about Charlie from the tip of her unlikely platinum-blonde hair right down to her painted toenails peeking boldly from a pair of stiletto sandals. Her top was tight and low-cut, and when Charlie hiked up her bag, the top rode up to reveal a black lace G-string and a diamond belly-button stud. Grace began to understand the peculiar expression on Sergeant Daly's face earlier.

"The heat!" Charlie said dramatically, fanning her heavily made-up face with a copy of the house brochure. "Tom, where are you going?"

He had wandered off up the driveway, putting his weight down hard every third step or so. Grace wondered whether he had a limp, or a war injury of some kind, and then she realised that he was testing the cobblestones.

"Laid down long, are they?" he asked.

"About five years."

"Men!" Charlie said to Grace, patting her arm familiarly. "He likes to know he's getting his money's-worth. Us women tend to go more for the feel of a place, don't we?"

The back door of the rental car opened. Grace hadn't noticed a third occupant.

"This is Gavin," Charlie announced. "I had him when I was seventeen – didn't I, love?"

Gavin had big brown eyes and a cow's lick. "She did," he told Grace.

"He's thirteen now. Thirteen! I'll have to get him to lie about his age soon – won't I, love?" Charlie put an arm around him and squeezed him. He endured it, expressionless.

Grace's arms ached emptily. "I have two ten-year-olds," she said.

Charlie nodded and said 'Ah!'

"Are they here?" Gavin looked around warily.

"No, no, they're in Florida with their dad."

"Oh."

"This guy's got a weather dial!" Tom called, seeming to find this very amusing. "Come and have a look, Gav."

Gavin trailed over to Tom, his sneakers not quite lifting off the ground.

Charlie looked at Grace sympathetically. "You must miss them. Your boys."

"Yes." Grace blinked a bit.

"It's hard. God knows it's hard," Charlie sighed. The timbre of her voice was slightly husky and coarse. She had probably spent a lot of money trying to sound more feminine and less like she had spent her youth in a smoky pub, which she probably had. "But if there's one thing I've learned, it's to try and get on with him. No matter what you think of him, hide it. Bury it. Even if you hate his guts. Even if you want to stab the bastard in the eye!"

"Stab who?"

"Your hubby, of course. Are you still married to him?"

"I think so, yes."

Charlie clucked. "Have you considered flying out to Florida?"

"What?"

"I know, I know, maybe everything's too raw yet. But you have to think of those two boys. So you need to talk to him. Establish priorities. Promise each other that no matter how filthy the divorce might get, the boys are kept out of it." She jerked a thumb towards Gavin. "I drove over his dad with a Jeep."

"Tom?" Grace was shocked.

"No, no, Tom's not Gavin's dad – I meant Jimmy, my first husband. Well, we never actually got married, it's a long story. But anyway, I had the opportunity one day: there I was, in a four-wheel drive with reinforced fenders, not another sinner around. He was right there in front of me like a sitting duck – it would have looked just like an accident." She shrugged. "But he survived, and I got a suspended sentence. Gavin was very upset about it all. And that's when I realised that he needs his father. They'll always need their father. No matter what kind of a slimy shit he is," she added venomously.

"Well, me and my husband, we're not actually . . ." For some reason she stopped. A simple clarification was all that was needed to put Charlie on the right track. But that would mean claiming Ewan – Ewan who had cunningly wriggled out of the kind of hard work and commitment she had invested in their family unit over the years. If he could do it, so could she.

"We're trying to get through the separation as best we can," she murmured discreetly instead. She thought of Ewan, maybe on a ghost train or a Big Dipper at that very moment, ignorant of the fact that he had just been dumped by his wife. Maybe he was even composing another love poem to her on his mobile phone . . . Oh Lord. She must stop the lie at once. But Charlie was patting her on the arm again.

"Good on you. And it'll only get better, you know. Once you get rid of him you'll be a different person! I felt that way after all five of mine."

Grace suddenly found herself a separated mother-of-two with

divorce proceedings pending. Still, she would never see Charlie again after today, she reasoned guiltily. And it was only pretend, like her daydreams.

She felt better now. And really, it was quite invigorating to have shrugged off your entire family in one fell swoop. No more nagging or festering resentments! No more endless list-making and people taking her for granted! And she would have the bathroom all to herself in the mornings – unless it was her week to have the boys, of course.

She was getting carried away now. But the white lie somehow added to the sunshine of the day, making her feel bolder. After eleven years, she was a free woman.

"Let's start the viewing!" she cried joyously, producing a set of spare keys and sweeping forward to Frank's front door. Charlie, Tom and Gavin trailed behind her, slightly taken aback. She said, "If you'd just bear with me while I turn the alarm off . . . not that we get many burglaries around here."

And she was off, slipping easily into a stream of polished chatter. Had Charlie and Gavin been to Ireland before? They had, but only to Dublin and then it had rained. And what did they think of Hackettstown so far? Not much, judging by the little look they exchanged.

"Thanks so much for showing us the house at such short notice," Charlie told Grace.

Tom said, "It's her job, Charlie." He smiled at Grace to take the sting out of his words.

"I know that, honey, I'm just saying thanks. Don't forget I know what it's like to have to deal with the public."

Tom shot an embarrassed look at Grace. "Yes, well, that's all behind you now," he said.

"I know," Charlie said with a pensive little sigh. "I'm a dancer," she told Grace.

"Oh?"

"I don't know if you'd classify it as 'dancing'," Tom muttered.

"It was dancing. I trained and everything," Charlie said. She said to Grace, "His Dad doesn't approve."

"I thought we had agreed we weren't going to tell him," Tom said to her accusingly.

"I have nothing to be ashamed of, Tom Daly," Charlie said, flapping a hand at him. But Grace thought her face went a little pink under the heavy powder. She hoped this wouldn't degenerate into a domestic. It happened sometimes.

She ushered them all through the front door. Frank had forgotten to put the lights on, and the place was gloomy and uninviting.

"Here we go!" she said brightly, to compensate. "This is a very big entrance hall for this type of house – I'm sure you'll agree." She gestured around in a practised flourish, drawing the eye away from the mud-coloured carpet and towards the nice high ceiling. "There are tons of things you could do with this space – maybe put in some tall leafy plants, or a telephone unit, or just paint it a nice bright colour and go completely minimal. The good news with minimal is, it hardly costs anything." It took a moment, as always, but then Tom gave an appreciative little chuckle.

"Minimal," he explained to Charlie. "As in nothing – "

"I know what it means, I'm not stupid," Charlie said.

Grace breezed on. "What do you think, Gavin?"

"I think it's dark," he said.

"I agree," said Charlie.

"We'll paint it a nice bright colour, like she says," Tom interjected, jerking his head towards Grace.

"My name is Grace," she said clearly. She didn't feel like blending into the wallpaper today. She was a single mother who had just come through a break-up, after all. She was a survivor! "Let's move on to the kitchen, will we?"

She threw open the door to Frank's cold, small, bare kitchen. The smell of burnt bread hung in the air. Her smile began to feel brazen and pinned on. "This is one of the best rooms in the house!" she declared falsely, crossing her fingers behind her back.

Tom inspected the place. "Look — there's a door out to the back garden so you can put the rubbish out. That's handy, isn't it?"

"Yes," Charlie said, smiling very courageously indeed for a woman who judged a place by the feel of it.

"The cooker, is it built in?" Tom wanted to know.

"Yes, it comes with the kitchen." Grace couldn't bear the look on Charlie's face, so she added, "Unless you wanted to buy a nice new one, of course. That might jizz the place up a bit."

"No need," Tom said. "Charlie doesn't cook anyway. Or at least I'm trying to persuade her not to, eh?"

He winked at Charlie. Her smile looked a bit tight over the cheekbones.

"You don't cook either," she said.

Go on, girl, Grace thought.

"You know," Tom finally declared, "I didn't think much of the place from the outside, but I'm starting to think it has a lot of potential."

Charlie murmured something incoherent. Gavin was silent.

Grace felt it was her duty to say, "Absolutely! It just takes imagination, that's all. And a good eye. With a small investment, you could turn this place into a . . ." She was going to say 'palace', but that would have been laughable. Then she was going to downgrade to 'gem' or 'cosy bolthole', but even those would be gross exaggerations. But hadn't nearly every word out of her mouth so far been a half-truth, or an overstatement, or a downright lie?

She stood there in Frank's grim kitchen and, not for the first time recently, she felt so compromised that she had to look at her shoes – her grubby runners, actually, poking out incongruously from under the hem of Mrs Carr's red robe. And they offered her a reprieve: she was not standing here as Grace Tynan MIAVI today, but purely and honestly as herself (if you overlooked the whopping great lie that she and Ewan were separated).

A great wave of righteousness overcame her. There was absolutely no reason why she could not present the facts and let them make up their own minds. Why not? They were adults, weren't they? They didn't need to be patronised or lied to! No, she would no longer be a mere pawn in the great property game; she would stand up for her principles and tell it like it was. Adam would approve utterly.

"Well, let's face it, the place is a total dump," she said cheerily. "I wouldn't pay one red penny for it myself. Now – the living-room!"

She swept off down the hall. She heard them whispering behind her.

"Did she say dump?"

"She did not say dump. She said it was . . . divine."

"Divine? You'd have to be blind to think the place was divine!"

"Are you calling me blind?"

"Yes, well, you're calling me deaf!"

"I really think you're being very negative. We could do this place up, sell it on, make a fortune."

"I thought we were looking for a 'family home'?"

"Jesus Christ! There's no pleasing you, do you know that?"

There was more muffled conversation, then they arrived into the living-room, smiles back in place.

"So!" said Grace.

They waited expectantly for her sales spiel, but she was feeling so full of integrity now that she decided to say nothing. Not a word! She stood there benignly and let them see for themselves the brown patterned carpet, the nasty fake chandelier, the armchair with the sheen of grease on the headrest. Even Tom grew fairly quiet.

"Any questions?" she asked brightly.

"What does that side window look out onto?" Tom asked eventually.

"A brick wall," she said.

They all laughed and the tension eased.

"No, it really does look on to a brick wall." She kindly whipped back the heavy net curtain that she had warned Frank on pain of death to keep pulled over. Solid grey concrete looked back at them.

"It's a wall all right," Tom said eventually.

They all considered it for another moment.

"We'll knock it down," he added strongly. "Plant a row of trees instead. Poplars."

"You could try," Grace said. "It's a boundary wall. You'd have a hell of a job with planning permission."

Well, there was no point in raising false hope. She thought she saw Gavin grin.

Charlie had been getting more and more worked up. "I don't want my living-room to look out on to a boundary wall."

"It's only the side window. The main window faces out to the road," Tom said.

But Charlie wasn't going to back down this time. "So I get a brick wall on one side and traffic on the other?"

Tom turned to Grace for support. "Yeh, but the traffic is light here, isn't it? It's the middle of the country, for God's sake!"

"Not for much longer," Grace said sympathetically. "They're building a new motorway to Dublin."

"You're joking."

"I'm not. The M3. Or is it M4?"

"Yes, well, it couldn't be that near . . ."

"All the same, if I were you I'd check out the plans." She would too.

"Thank you!" Charlie exploded. "I'm sorry, Tom. I know how much you were hoping this place would be right. But it's just not."

Tom threw up his hands. "What's the matter – too basic for you? Well, don't forget I'm paying."

Charlie's colour began to rise again. "I don't mind basic. I do mind bringing up my child beside the M4!"

"As opposed to what? The M11 when you were living with Jimmy? Or the M6 when you shacked up with Phil? I get so confused sometimes."

Grace stepped forward quickly. She hadn't meant to start any rows with her plain speaking. "Perhaps the motorway might not be that near. I could check the plans for you myself – "

"It's not just the M4!" Charlie snarled at Tom. "It's everything! The brown carpet and the poky rooms and the smell! And have you seen the bathroom? That suite is from the 60's!" To Grace: "You're right – it is a dump!"

"Perhaps I've been a bit too honest," Grace said desperately. "It has a certain charm, if you were looking for a modest country residence . . ."

"No, no, I appreciate your honesty! Your honesty has saved me!" Charlie cried.

"Here we go," Tom sighed. To Grace: "Too much confessional TV in the afternoons. Watch TV is about all she's done since she stopped flashing her fanny in bars."

Charlie shot him another murderous look. "They were licensed dancing clubs! That's where we met, I'll remind you!" Then, to Grace: "Only for you, I'd have let myself be talked into buying this kip! Into burying myself down here with a man like that! A man who only feels good when he puts other people down."

"Oh, really?" Tom said back. "Why didn't you say so when I was buying that great big rock for your finger last month? In fact, why don't you just give it back?"

It was like the air had been sucked out of the room. Grace watched in horrified fascination as Charlie's face took on the look of a street fighter. Gavin edged closer to Grace as Charlie's impressive bosom swelled further and she planted her balled fists on her hips. She was not a woman to be trifled with in any sense of the word.

"You know something? I'd be glad to," she said to Tom in slow, measured words. "I'd be delighted to! Because I'm sick of spending my life living for men. Going from one to the other. Thinking I was nothing unless I had a man on my arm, no matter how pathetic and small-minded and insecure he was! Stupidly letting myself be used and abused and put down by bullies like you!"

She spat this last bit and Tom jerked away. "Calm down, Charlie."

She went right on as though he hadn't opened his mouth. "And I would have gone on doing it! Never getting up the courage to step out on my own, never learning my lesson – until I met a woman like Grace here."

"Pardon?" Grace said.

Charlie gave her a fervent look. "A woman who's just broken up with her husband. A woman whose kids are all the way in Florida!"

"Actually, that's not strictly true – "

"A woman who was entitled to stay at home this morning and cry in her bed but she came here to show us a house instead!"

"If I could just clarify one or two points – "

"Look at that woman!" Charlie commanded Tom. He did, meekly. "A woman who should have been trying to shove this house down our throats! But she didn't! And God knows she could do with the commission – heading for divorce and left without even a decent set of clothes!" All eyes fell on Grace's red robe, and the scuffed runners poking out incriminatingly. "Does she run mewling to a man to look after her? No!" Charlie was almost weeping now in admiration. "She stands there, true to herself – which is more than I've ever done. She's an example to us all!"

The only thing missing was a trumpet fanfare to finish it all off. Everyone stood looking at Grace. She felt the weight of expectation and wondered whether she should make a little speech. Or do a cartwheel or something. Eventually she cleared her throat and said, "Would anyone like to see the hot press?"

Tom looked to Charlie, pleading. "Will we?"

"No," she said.

"You know you like hot presses."

"It's over, Tom. Take your ring and go back to Birmingham."

He wrung his hands in agony as she twisted off the tasteless diamond engagement ring and thrust it out.

"Goodbye."

"Charlie . . ."

"Beat it, buster!"

He seemed to realise the futility of further argument. He dug car keys from his pocket and without looking at anybody, walked out, leaving a little frozen tableau behind him. To underline it, Grace could hear a clock ticking somewhere.

"Whew!" Charlie said at last. Her voice was shaky. "Come here, sweetheart."

She held out her arms for Gavin who walked into them obediently. He didn't seem all that perturbed by the drama. Possibly he was no stranger to it.

"I'm very sorry," Grace said. She felt terribly responsible.

"No, no," Charlie said. "It's been coming a long time. Lately, we just haven't been getting on. So what do I do? I agree to marry him! Isn't that just so . . . clever." She was crying now, great black mascara tears into Gavin's hair. "Sorry, honey, sorry."

"It's all right. I didn't like him anyway," Gavin said stoutly. "Or any of the others," he added.

Charlie eventually lifted her head and dabbed at her swollen eyes with a tissue. "You wouldn't have the number of a taxi firm, would you?" she asked Grace. "I think there's a train leaving the station for Dublin at three. Maybe they'll let us bring forward our flights back to Birmingham."

"I can drive you to the station. It's no trouble." Grace was desperate to make amends in any small way she could.

"Thanks. That would be great." Charlie gave a watery smile. "I thought Tom was my saviour, you know. Finally I could stop working my ass off in cheap clubs! Finally, I wouldn't have to pay over half my earnings to that shit who owned the place. I thought this was it, no man would ever exploit me again. But Tom just put a different gloss on it."

"What are you going to do now?" Grace ventured. "Go back to the club?"

Charlie threw back her great mane of white hair. "No way! I'm through with that scene. Why should the guys behind the scenes make all the money while we get groped by some fat jerk out front?"

Grace wondered should Gavin be hearing all this. But Charlie was oblivious.

"No, I'm going into management. If you can do it, Grace, I can too!"

The logic of this escaped Grace, but she didn't say anything, because Charlie had started to cry again.

"I really loved him too! The bollocks."

Grace couldn't send her on her way in that state. "How about we all go across the road and have a nice cup of tea?"

"I'm sure you've things to do . . ." Charlie protested.

Well, yes, but how could she possibly enjoy a romantic interlude with Adam while a devastated woman cried, watched by her young son? When Grace herself had contributed to the upset? It would take a heart of stone! (Anyhow, they might finish up their tea quickly and be gone.)

"Come on," she said.

TEN

Nick was sitting on the front doorstep when they walked up Mrs Carr's garden path. "Gracie!"

She was immediately suspicious. She was only ever 'Gracie' when he needed to borrow something, or when a small loan was required.

"I don't have any money on me, Nick," she said.

He shot an embarrassed look at Charlie and Gavin. "I'm not looking for any."

She was filled with a sudden dread. "Nick – have you done something to my house? Please tell me there hasn't been a fire or something!"

"Of course there hasn't!" He was in a proper huff now. "You haven't been home in a couple of days – I came to check on you, that's all!"

She wanted to believe him, even though there was no possibility at all that this was the truth. He might have *intended* to check on her at some point but, like most other things, would never have got around to it unless something else drove him to it. Something more Nick-centred.

Beside her, Charlie loudly hissed, "Is that him? Your husband?"

"No, no."

181

"Her husband's in Florida," Nick supplied helpfully.

"Yes, it's a shame, isn't it?" Charlie sighed. Nick looked baffled.

"Anyway!" Grace said.

"I've been trying to tell her to keep things amicable," Charlie told Nick. "It's hard when they're complete bastards though."

Nick said, "What – "

"When all you want to do is stick a ten-inch knife into his gut and twist it until he squeals like a pig. Or rip off his privates with your bare hands and chuck them into a vat of acid!"

Nick reared away in alarm. Charlie started sobbing loudly again.

Grace's remaining hopes of a final rendezvous with Adam were rapidly vanishing, so she said to Nick, "As you can see, I'm all right. Never better! In fact I'll be home later this afternoon. "So . . ." How to put this politely? "I guess you can go on back to the house and get on with your computer studies. How are they going anyway?"

He shuffled evasively. "Aren't you going to invite me in for a cup of tea at least?"

"No."

"No?"

"I can't, Nick. It's not my house."

Charlie was quick to interject, "Oh, you should have said. We won't stay either."

"*You* were invited in for tea?" Nick said to Charlie, wounded.

Grace threw up her hands. "Right! Fine! Tea for everybody! Why not!"

Oblivious to the look exchanged between Charlie, Nick and Gavin, she led the way into Mrs Carr's house. The three of them sat in silence at the kitchen table looking at the row of porcelain ducks on the wall while she made big cups of tea and found an out-of-date can of Coke for Gavin.

"Just the trick," Charlie said with a sigh.

"Absolutely," Nick said, adding, "I haven't had a cup of

tea in two days."

Grace looked at him. "Why not? I bought more tea bags before I left."

He looked shifty again. "I've been trying to cut down, that's all. Apparently too much caffeine – "

"Nick!"

"All right! There, ah, seems to be some kind of problem with the electricity."

"Oh God."

"It wasn't my fault! It just went off! And the electricity people said they'd be around but they haven't come yet."

"Wonderful!" Now she was going home to a house with no power.

Charlie took a packet of Silk Cut from her bag, the extra long ones. "Want one?" she asked Nick.

"I shouldn't really," he said, taking one. "I'm a singer. Well, I was."

As always, that had an impact. Grace gave up any hopes of hurrying them out the door as Charlie and Gavin sat up. Nobody had ever looked at Grace like that. Except Adam.

"I knew it!" Charlie cried. "Well, not that you were a singer – but I knew your face."

Nick sat up eagerly. "Did you?"

"The minute I saw you, I said to myself, there's someone dead famous!"

"She knows all the famous faces from the magazines," Gavin said proudly. "She recognised Adam Ant in a petrol station once, didn't you, Mum? Even without his make-up."

"I wouldn't be that famous," Nick admitted, adding hurriedly, "Not in the UK anyway. Although we were quite big over there in the 90s. Well, more 1991 really. When did 'Dead Dingos' enter the British charts, Grace?"

"The first week in September," she said, tempted to add that it had exited the British charts the second week in September.

"I don't think I've heard of it . . ." Charlie ventured.

"It was from our album, *Hell and Back*. Kind of along the lines of the Stones. Only more original, if I say so myself."

The mention of the Stones did the trick. Any lingering doubts as to his rock-legend status were put to rest.

"Do you know Mick Jagger?" Gavin enquired, excited.

"Not that well in person," Nick said with admirable under-statement. "But I met him at a party once. Lovely guy. Sound."

"Charlie didn't really like the house. Frank's house," Grace said quite loudly. Perhaps Charlie would tell Nick about Grace's bravery, and how she was an example to women everywhere. Perhaps Adam would come in just in time to hear it.

"Oh, let's not go there again!" Charlie said with a little laugh. She turned back to Nick eagerly. "Have you ever played at Wembley?"

Standing by the sink holding the teapot, Grace felt herself fade. Even the silk of her robe seemed to lose some of its shimmer. She was thrown back to their teenage years, where she would hang around in the background while Nick and his friends would jam together, occasionally conferring with her about the base levels or the possibility of light refreshments.

Nick leaned back in his chair, taking a thoughtful drag of his cigarette. "Wembley, let me think . . ."

"You haven't played Wembley," she said clearly. "You've never even been to Wembley. And Mick Jagger had left that party before you'd even arrived."

She walked out, leaving Nick to bluster about how he'd met Mick at a different party; that it was hard to keep up.

Upstairs, she stripped her bed in the guest room and neatly folded the blankets away. She gathered up the sheets and towels. She would put a wash on downstairs. Then she changed out of Mrs Carr's red silky robe and back into her sensible track bottoms and T-shirt, dry from the washing line outside. In the bathroom she ran her fingers under the cold tap and ruthlessly smoothed down her hair, and found some powder to take the shine off her nose. When she was finished patting and pulling and readjusting in front of the mirror, that feverish look was gone. A neat, tidy woman looked back at her blandly. She could have been anyone.

"Who were you trying to fool anyway?" she asked her reflection. She was a thirty-four-year-old mother with the first sign of wrinkles, and a job in residential property. She could run around in bare feet in a country town for all she was worth, pretending that she was an FBI agent without a tie in the world, but at the end of the day she had a carefully constructed life to go back to: a life that involved too many other people, with too many commitments and too much emotional investment already made, and to stray from it now would surely only lead to heartache. Anyway, it wasn't as though she had anything better lined up.

Adam was waiting outside the bathroom when she emerged.

"There's a whole bunch of strangers sitting in the kitchen," he complained.

"Yes."

"Smoking and laughing and drinking beer."

"I didn't give them any beer." Nick must have found some. He was like a ferret that way.

Adam looked her up and down. "Why have you changed back into those clothes?" It was obvious from his face that he didn't like them.

"Because this is the way I dress," she said evenly.

His eyes were on her face now. Belligerent, nearly. "Your freckles. They're gone. What's that stuff you have on your cheeks?"

"Make-up. Adam, I was wondering whether you would mind leaving now?"

"What?" He was taken aback.

"I need to tidy up the house before Mrs Carr gets back tomorrow," she said blandly. "Most B&Bs require people to be out by eleven. You're way over."

"Cut the crap, Grace. I thought we had an arrangement".

"Did we?" Her expression didn't change. "Well, unfortunately I can't keep it. I need to get back to Dublin."

He looked at her for a long moment. "We haven't done anything illegal yet, you know."

She felt her cheeks explode into colour beneath the powder. "Of course we haven't! I didn't suggest that for a second! I mean, we only kissed! I don't mean 'only' . . ." She took a breath. "The thing is, kissing is not illegal in this country. It certainly might be in other countries – some cultures aren't that keen on married people having sex with people other than their spouses – but not in Ireland. Morally speaking, that's different; that's where it might get a bit murky. But regarding the law, we're in the clear."

Adam was looking a bit surprised. "I was actually talking about me and Martine and Joey."

"Oh. Oh!"

She felt faint. Imagine! Rabbiting on about them having sex – she had actually said the word sex to him – when all along he had been talking about something else. He must think she was obsessed with him. But he seemed preoccupied with something else – to her relief or chagrin, she wasn't sure which.

"We're just in the planning stages of it," he clarified.

"Of something . . . illegal?" she said. The word was so delicious, so suggestive of danger and excitement that she had her 'motel feeling' again. (She was starting to wonder whether it might be time to seek help.)

"Well, yes, probably," he admitted. "It's the only way to get the message across. I think anyway. As for Martine . . ." His lip curled a bit.

"What message?" Grace whispered.

"You mean you didn't overhear us in the café?"

"No." She thought of his habit of always taking his shoes off. "We're not talking religion here, I hope?"

"God, no." Then he looked worried. "What, do I look like some kind of Jesus freak?"

"No, no." Right now he looked good enough to eat. The walk back from town in the heat had given him a kind of a delicious all-over moistness that on other men would just look sweaty. She thought that she would quite like to lick him like an ice cream.

"Go on," she said.

He moved closer. His breath smelled of coffee and Minnie's apple crumble. "This is highly sensitive information."

Illegal *and* highly sensitive. She started to pant a bit now, like a dog, and hoped he wouldn't notice. "You can trust me," she managed.

He looked over his shoulder; he obviously felt that this conversation was a little surreal to be having outside Mrs Carr's bathroom. He took her hand – she nearly swooned – and led her across the hallway and into his bedroom. He closed the door behind them a touch dramatically, and for a moment she thought that maybe he was going to kiss her again. In fact, she had just raised her face expectantly, praying her lips hadn't gone all nasty and dry in the heat, when he walked off on her and began to roll a cigarette.

"Want one?"

"Ah, no thanks."

"You're right too. Wish I'd never started," he said gloomily.

The situation had lost some of its momentum. Grace began to suspect that she was going to be disappointed at his 'illegal activity'. After all, what could a bunch of backpackers really get up to in terms of badness? Was he going to reveal some kind of a visa scam to her? Or a cunning scheme to defraud Irish Rail?

"Adam, this is nothing to do with . . . banks or anything, is it?" she asked, hopefully. She might be able to give him a few tips; she already had some experience in thieving under her belt, after all.

He gave a short laugh. "Ever the capitalist."

"Shut up," she said, and went to leave.

"Grace. Wait." He seemed surprised. "I'm sorry, okay?"

187

She turned on him. "But you're not. You do it all the time – making me out to be some kind of a meaningless person with a meaningless life!" The final insult was to get her into his bedroom and, instead of trying to ravish her, he was rolling cigarettes instead!

"I never said you were meaningless," he said.

"Selfish, then. Greedy. Just because I don't display my disgust at the world by dropping out of college and bucking the system at every opportunity. Just because I don't go around with a trendy hairstyle sneering at people who sell houses!"

"You sell houses?" From the look on his face you'd think she'd confessed to supplying crack to schoolchildren.

"Yes!" she said, her head high. "Hundreds of them! Thousands! What, did you think I had a rich husband sitting at home bankrolling me while I amused myself by dabbling in B&Bs?" He obviously had. "Like everybody else in this world – well, apart from you – I have a job! I earn money! Most of which goes in taxes to pay for other people's pensions, of course. And unemployment benefit, and hospital beds for old people with foot injuries!"

"It was your choice, Grace."

Was it? She supposed it was. Or, she had no one else to blame at any rate.

"I'm sorry I don't live for my principles, Adam. But I can't afford to."

"You think I can?" he snapped. "Oh, go home, Grace."

"What?"

"Get into that big swanky car out there and go back to your tax-paying life. That's where you were sneaking off to, weren't you? Before I came in and caught you?"

"You didn't 'catch' me. I was going to wait for you."

"Liar. You were probably going to hide over in Frank's house until I'd gone and then you'd have come back and locked up for Mrs Carr."

She flushed. The thought had occurred to her. "I was going to leave you a note!" She had been, too.

"A nice-knowing-you note?"

"Well . . ."

"A fuck-off note, you mean." His customary coolness had evaporated and his tan didn't look as healthy.

"Oh, Adam," she said. "I didn't think there was any point in . . . well, meeting up again. This way things are cleaner."

"Cleaner?"

"I thought – "

"*Cleaner?* What the hell is that supposed to mean?"

"All right, possibly I could have chosen a better word!" She took a breath. "Look, what happened last night was . . ."

"Please don't say it was 'nice'." He took such a long drag of his cigarette that she worried for his lungs.

"We were alone; we'd had wine; it happened. I just think it's better not to complicate matters further."

He exhaled and watched her through a thick cloud of blue smoke. "Don't want to take the risk of things getting messy, yeh? A kiss is safe enough, but we wouldn't want to go rocking the boat, is that it?"

She didn't say anything.

"What's the matter, Grace? Why are you so afraid of letting your hair down? You think somebody's going to come along and slap your wrist for enjoying yourself?"

"You're presuming a lot," she said. "That I would want to let my hair down with you in the first place!"

She had intended that to put him in his box. She didn't like the way he was making her feel; always questioning her, pricking her conscience. It was easy for him. Nothing in the world holding him back except a girlfriend who didn't seem to mind what he got up to.

"Then why are you still here?" he asked.

Silence. Then she heard laughter from the kitchen below. She wondered whether Nick and Charlie could somehow overhear the entire conversation and were chuckling their heads off, much the way Ewan had on the phone the other day: Grace, and a twenty-year-old! Grace, being offered hot sex in a run-down lodging house!

Well, yes, actually, she answered them all rather defiantly. Just because they only saw one side of her didn't mean there wasn't another one! Even if it only had fledging status yet; even if it was some kind of odd mish-mash of amateur grocery thief with career aspirations in either law enforcement or porn film-making. Put like that, she sounded very interesting, she thought. Or she could be.

"Well," he drawled mockingly. "Are you staying or are you going?"

"Staying."

"What?" He was obviously not expected such decisiveness.

"I said I'm staying. I want to let my hair down."

"Uh, right . . ."

"To be corrupted."

"Well, now, let's not take that too literally – "

She pushed him back down on the bed. "I hope you won't disappoint me."

He looked nervous. And so well he should.

In the car on the way home Julia thought about burst pipes. There was no telling how much damage a burst pipe could do, Frank often warned her. He'd told her of at least one case where the water level had risen so high that the family had practically had to escape in an ark. Julia didn't know a damned thing about burst pipes except that you should always turn the water off at some point. The mains – yes, that was it. Then she realised that she didn't even know where the tap for the mains was.

She was being silly. It wasn't even winter yet. There was no need to worry about burst pipes.

Then she thought about birds. Thrushes. One had found its

way into the living-room three summers ago when they'd gone away for the weekend. It had flown demented around the room, leaving a bloody trail across her furniture before dying in a corner under a chair. Julia was absolutely sure now that she had left the front bay window open in the living-room the day of the shotgun. What if a bird had found its way in?

Her mind flooded with other things now, frightening things . . .the attic trap door that was loose, and that might bang tonight if there was a breeze; the backyard sensor light that had been broken for ages now and would not snap on to warn her of intruders. And the uneven floorboards in the living-room that she might trip over in the dark, and she would lose her crutches in the fall and she wouldn't be able to reach the phone –

"She didn't mean those things, you know," said Michael beside her.

Julia gave herself a little shake. "Pardon?"

"Gillian. She just said them in the heat of the moment."

People like Gillian never said anything in the heat of the moment. Everything was carefully thought out beforehand and saved up until the appropriate moment. Cold, that's what she was.

"I don't care whether she did or she didn't. I'll cope just fine on my own," Julia said loudly.

Michael sighed. "How are you going to be fine? You've just had an operation, for heaven's sake! Naturally we're worried."

"I'm sorry that I seem to be such a bother to everybody," she said stiffly.

"Oh, Mammy. It's just that it's time to face the fact that you're not a young woman any more."

A hearse pulled out in front of them. Brilliant. Julia tried to avert her eyes from the coffin inside. That could have been her in there, had she taken those sleeping pills. She had gone as far as imagining her own post-mortem – it had a certain drama about it – but she had never had the nerve to project herself actually into a coffin. There was something a bit creepy about it. The next

191

stage, after all, was a deep pit, and a lot of hungry worms.

Death. It was everywhere. How could she have wanted it so badly?

"Anyway, here's what I think we should do," Michael said.

Again Julia dragged her mind back to the matter at hand – which still appeared to be the fact that she was a problem for everybody. "I'll drop by on the way to work every day, and then again on the way home, okay? And I'll try to get over at lunch-times some days as well – I'll tell them I have a meeting or something."

"I don't want you putting yourself out like that." She started to feel guilty.

"We'll have to hire someone local to come by and do a bit of housework and cooking during the day. I'll sort that out today after I drop you home."

"There's no need. If I do want someone, I can hire them myself."

"But you can't. You're on crutches. How are you even going to get down to the shop to put up a notice? I mean, you don't even drive, Mammy."

She had that horrible sense of foreboding again, and she wanted him to stop outlining all the things she couldn't do any more, all the dangers that lay in wait for injured elderly women living on their own.

She realised that they were driving down Hackettstown main street now. In a minute they would be home.

"I don't want a stranger in my house," she said. She saw the dead bird again, bluebottles swarming over its corpse.

Impatiently, Michael turned down Bridge Road. "You don't want someone to live with you. You don't want to come and live with me and Gillian. So what *do* you want, Mammy? Because we've all tried to please you but it just won't do!"

She saw her house now. It looked decrepit and old and unloved.

192

"I didn't ask for anyone to please me," she said. The broken shutter on the upstairs bedroom seemed a bit menacing somehow and she was afraid she was going to start crying or something.

Michael swung into her driveway and cut the engine. He turned to her. "The whole idea of you coming back here today on a pair of crutches is ridiculous! At least stay with us until your foot is healed. Then you can come home."

"She just wants me to come crawling back, that's all!"

"Stop it, Mammy."

"Well, I won't come crawling back. Because I have my own plans made!" she ended up saying.

"What plans?" Michael said. She was caught now. "That guy Frank across the road, you mean? The one you tried to shoot? He's going to come look after you, is he?"

Julia's fists balled helplessly. "No . . ."

"Who, then?"

She was rescued by a cigarette butt, which landed on the bonnet of the car. It sizzled happily on Michael's paintwork for a moment before dying with a little puff of smoke.

"What the hell?" he said, astonished.

They looked around for the source of this outrage. And they saw that the living-room bay window was wide open.

"Burglars," Michael said, ashen-faced.

But then a loud burst of laughter rolled out from the windows. Burglars with a sense of humour? Julia held her breath. Somehow she didn't feel in the slightest bit afraid.

There was another sound now. Music.

"They're playing your old gramophone, Mammy!" Michael said. "The nerve of them!"

"Elvis," Julia murmured. She was thrown back years, to the parties she and JJ used to hold. 'Heartbreak Hotel'. She hadn't heard it in decades.

Michael said beside her, "You know, it's more likely that they're squatters than burglars."

"Yes, shhh, Michael." She wished they would turn the music up.

Then the front door opened and a rather tarty-looking young blonde woman emerged from Julia's house. She was clutching a flagon of cider in one arm. The other arm was wrapped firmly around a tall, lanky fellow in leather trousers and disgracefully long hair. He had a guitar slung over his shoulder.

"Daddy's guitar!" Michael said in horror. "They've stolen it!"

"I think they're just borrowing it," Julia said, watching as the pair sauntered across her lawn. The man started to strum the guitar. He wasn't bad. The woman carefully laid herself out on the grass to the best possible advantage.

"Don't you worry, Mammy," Michael said grimly. "I'm going to ring the police. They'll get rid of these two in no time."

But someone else was coming out of the house now: a young boy with floppy hair, who was eating a Snickers bar.

"Gavin!" the woman called over, waving to him.

Michael scuttled down lower in his seat. "There could be a whole commune of them in there! Lock your door, Mammy," he ordered. "We're driving down to the police station. There's no sense in confronting them ourselves." But when the leather-clad guy on the lawn lit up a cigarette, Michael couldn't contain himself. He beeped the horn angrily, rolled down his window, and shouted, "You burned my car, you lout!"

The pair on the lawn looked over laconically.

"Sorry, man."

Michael's eyes bulged. He beeped again, very angrily, and reached for the ignition key.

"Wait, Michael," Julia said.

Someone else was coming to the door, obviously alerted by all the commotion. It was a young man, who looked a bit like those rap fellows on MTV with his hair in those dreadlocks, and he was only half-dressed. He looked out at the car.

Then a woman pushed up behind him. She was patting down

her hair, and adjusting her clothing, and she looked a bit bright around the eyes. Possibly they were drunk too.

The woman said something to the young man. Then she came out of the house on her own and walked down the path to the car. She shielded her eyes against the sun and peered in very tentatively through Michael's open window.

"Mrs Gill?" she said rather limply. "I thought you weren't due back until tomorrow."

Michael was further astounded. So was Julia. "Don't tell me you . . . know this woman?" he said to Julia.

"What? I've never seen her before in my . . ."

But she had. As she looked into the woman's eyes she knew exactly where she had seen her before – in her own kitchen, at the other end of a shotgun. Her tormentor! And here she was again, in Julia's house – how had she even got in? – and she was hosting some kind of a wild party behind her back!

It would only take a single word from Julia and the police would descend for a second time in a week on Bridge Road. But the other woman looked back at her, seeming to know Julia's thoughts, and silently begging her not to go through with it. Well, if Julia was going to save Grace Tynan's bacon, then Grace Tynan could bloody well save hers.

"Of course I know her," she amended to Michael. "This is Grace. She's the person I was telling you was going to look after me – isn't that right, Grace?"

There was brief moment in which Grace Tynan and Julia locked eyes and got each other's measure. Then Grace Tynan said to Michael, "That's right."

Michael wasn't stupid. "Are you telling me this was all *arranged*?"

"It was all very last minute," Grace Tynan lied easily to him, and Julia was very impressed. They would get along just fine.

"So you can go on home now, Michael," Julia said, energetically throwing open the passenger door. "And be sure to tell Gillian that I won't be changing my mind."

Grace Tynan was quickly around to take Julia's arm, to position the crutches, to retrieve her overnight bag from the back seat.

But she wasn't going to get off *that* easily. Julia found her balance, and then leaned over and said in a voice that only Grace could hear, "You have a lot of explaining to do."

ELEVEN

"Do you ever think about it, Grace?" Natalie asked three weeks later.

"What?"

"Having another baby."

"Me?"

"I don't know what you find so amusing."

"Sorry. It's just not something on my mind at the moment." She was stirring a pot on Mrs Carr's stove and looking out the kitchen window at Adam on the lawn, and debating whether or not to tap on the window and ask him to pick her a handful of basil. He would uncurl his long, brown, muscular body and come striding across the grass, with his sexy smile –

"You could easily do it, you know," Natalie chattered on. "You're still only thirty-four. And there's Jamie and Neil practically raised – they're no trouble any more. In fact, they could help you with the new baby!"

Suddenly it had become *the* new baby, as though it were already a probability.

"I don't think so."

"Why not? We could meet up in the afternoons and go to the zoo and things – it'd stop me going mad," Natalie begged, rubbing her huge pregnant belly. *"Rosie!'*

Over by the door, two-year-old Rosie was systematically pushing the contents of Natalie's handbag through Mrs Carr's cat flap.

"So I'd be having a baby for you then?" Grace enquired.

"And for Ewan. I bet he'd love another baby," Natalie said.

Ewan had said nothing about babies when he'd rung from Florida last night. In fact, he had complained that he was starved of adult company, so it was pretty certain that he felt little need to procreate any time soon.

Natalie saw that perhaps she had been too optimistic. "You could talk him around," she suggested.

"Why would I want to do that?" (She probably could, too.)

Natalie flopped back in her chair crossly. "You were saying only a few weeks back that you were at a bit of a loss these days! That you were thinking of taking up art classes."

"You suggested that. Not me. I don't want another baby, Natalie."

She had never spoken the words out loud; perhaps she hadn't made up her mind until now. It wasn't any big thing; the decision just hung there for a moment then floated away, leaving her with a pleasant, light feeling. Irresponsibility suited her, she was beginning to think.

"Well!" Natalie shrugged as though Grace were being very selfish. "I mean, what else are you going to do with yourself?"

"Natalie, Rosie's managed to get her head through the cat flap. We don't want her to be garrotted, do we?" Grace said kindly.

"Oh!" Natalie sprang to the rescue. Just in the nick of time too – the back door burst open and Julia hobbled in on one crutch.

"Two more for dinner, Grace."

"Oh, Julia!" The numbers were up to fourteen already – most of them were with Adam on the lawn out there. They were having some kind of a strategy meeting, by the looks of it.

"I'll cook if you want," Julia said airily, and Grace suspected she only offered because she knew full well that it wouldn't be accepted. Judging from her culinary efforts so far, Julia was not a woman who took all that well to a kitchen. Or to any kind of domestication, really.

"Where's your other crutch?" Grace enquired.

Julia shook her head at Natalie. "Nag, nag, nag! That's all she ever does."

"I *am* supposed to be looking after you," Grace pointed out. This included cajoling Julia into keeping her out-patient appointments at the hospital, keeping tabs on her medication, and ordering her into bed for an early night. Looking after two boisterous boys was tame in comparison, and she had told Ewan that when he suggested during one of their phone-calls that she had the lesser of two evils.

"And isn't it time for your exercises?" Grace added.

"Yes, yes, later – Martine is waiting for me. Cheerio!" Julia poked the back door open again with her crutch and was gone.

A lovely cool breeze drifted in from outside, along with the muffled sounds of a radio they were playing on the lawn.

The Government has yet to decide whether to provide naval support for the controversial shipment of MOX nuclear fuel en route from Japan to Wales and due to enter Irish waters at the weekend . . .

"Rosie! Come back here!" Natalie grabbed the child and kicked the back door shut.

"Here, Grace, what really happened with that guy Frank's house?"

"What about it?"

"Well, him ringing up Head Office to make an official complaint about you." Her eyes widened. "You didn't really call his house a dump, did you?"

"Oh, yes," Grace said cheerfully.

She could feel Natalie's eyes on her back for a long moment, assessing. Well, perhaps the kaftan Julia had lent her was a little big. But the material was lovely and light, and it cleverly concealed the fact that she wasn't wearing any bra (so constricting and sweaty in the summer. She didn't know how she'd ever worn one, really. They weren't natural.).

Natalie hadn't noticed yet, which was surprising. She had already commented on Grace's hair, which she'd said could do with a trim. Good thing she wasn't privy to Grace's armpits, or indeed her legs, nestling cosily against each other under the kaftan now, gloriously unshaven.

"Can you stay for dinner?" Grace asked. "It's such a nice evening that we're going to eat outside."

"No," Natalie said quite definitely, with a little look out towards the back lawn. "Are all those people actually living here?"

Grace gave a little laugh. "Lord, no. Just Adam, obviously. And Charlie and young Gavin – they share the third guest room. And Nick stays over quite often, of course, now that he and Charlie have fallen madly in love." She looked out the back window too at the crowd scattered across the lawn. "And you've met Martine – and those are her two French colleagues by the shed – and Joey – but they all live in tents out there. We hardly see them at all. Julia doesn't seem to mind. I don't know who the rest of them are, to be honest. But Adam would know them."

Natalie was giving her That Look again. Well, she'd got a bit of a start when she'd arrived earlier to be confronted by two New Age types squatting on the stairs eating stew, and a skeleton sitting in a wheelchair wearing a mask of Tony Blair. Grace had explained that the wheelchair belonged to Julia, who had never really needed it in the first place, preferring her crutches. Grace wasn't sure who Tony Blair belonged to; most likely they intended to use him in the demonstration. She had neglected to mention that the skeleton was plastic, now that she thought about it.

Possibly Natalie was thinking about it too, because she suddenly burst out, "Grace, I'm worried about you!"

"Are you?" Grace was surprised. She had been expecting something along these lines, of course, but not with such force. Surely a kaftan and unshaven legs weren't that remarkable? "Why?"

"Why? Well, you're not yourself!"

"In what way?" Interested, she looked up from the sauce, which was reducing nicely. Soon it would be time to put on the pasta.

Natalie wasn't going to mince her words. "Look at you – drifting barefoot around someone else's kitchen like Mother Earth, cooking up a big pot of food for a bunch of weirdos!"

"At least they appreciate it," Grace said mildly.

"It's not just the cooking thing!"

"What then? My hair, is it?" Grace said helpfully. "I think it kind of suits me like this. It's softer, don't you think?"

"It's matted. And Grace, you're not even wearing a bra!"

She *had* noticed, of course.

In the garden Adam was picking basil. He had read her mind, bless him. It was quite uncanny sometimes – look at how he had brought her up a cup of tea in bed this morning before she'd even known she wanted one! And just last night, when she'd mentioned after dinner that she had a hankering for something sweet, he had slipped out for half an hour and returned with a big tub of Ben & Jerry's ice cream (double chocolate-chip cookie) from the Spar, and had presented it to her as proudly as a cat laying a dead mouse at her feet.

Nobody had ever tried so hard to woo her. Well, perhaps Ewan had, way back when they were dating – she distinctly remembered him recording a whole tape of love songs off the radio for her, to illustrate how he felt. She wondered now if he had been too mean to buy a compilation album.

She was being unfair, of course. But she found herself doing that a lot – concentrating on all his negative points in order to justify her own behaviour while he was away: the way he made sucking noises though his teeth at mealtimes, for example; his habit of laying his hand on the small of her back, as though he were resting it or something.

And look at the way he had implied for years that she was smothering the boys! All those little sighs, the way he threw his eyes to heaven behind her back whenever she happened to wonder where they were – and they gone five hours! Any responsible parent would worry. But Ewan, with his little looks and throw-away comments, managed to imply that she was a fusspot, one of those over-anxious parents that sometimes featured in his ads on the television, and who always seemed to be the butt of some joke.

Take that ad of his for microwave chips last year! The whole concept had revolved around two children trying to dupe their mother – their hard-working, caring mother – who had made a healthy casserole for tea, but of course they wanted chips. Who walks into the kitchen just then? Dad! He has the brilliant idea of fabricating a phone call to get Mum offside, and the minute her back is turned, the kids and Dad give the casserole to the dog, microwave up three big plates of chips, and snigger amongst themselves as they stuff their faces.

It hadn't occurred to Grace at the time, but it was quite obvious to her now that the whole thing was modelled on her home life. *Their* home life, with Ewan and the boys conspirators against boring, fussy Mum. The woman in the ad even looked like Grace! Oh, she had never felt so betrayed in all her life – by her own family! So used, such an object of ridicule! The three of them were probably in some fast-food joint in Florida right now, gorging themselves on double cheeseburgers and laughing to each other at how they had cunningly managed to escape Mum for a whole month. Well, let them! Let them have fat-induced heart attacks for all she cared! She was through being their minder!

Adam suddenly looked up from the herb garden and smiled at her. And it was a smile so full of respect and warmth and liking that she wanted to curl up into a little ball and start to purr or something. He would never refuse one of her healthy casseroles in favour of chips.

When she turned away from the window, Natalie was lying in wait.

"You see? This is exactly what I mean!"

"What?"

"It's like you've gone into some little world of your own! Look at you – you'd prefer to gaze out the window than talk to me!"

"That's not true." The view was certainly good, though.

"Isn't it? I've told you all about the cutbacks in Head Office. I've asked you about Frank's house – I even told you about Liam shagging the new girl in accounts. And you're acting like you just don't care any more!"

"I'm on my holidays, Natalie – maybe I don't want to talk about work."

Natalie was not appeased in the slightest. "You don't want to talk about babies, either. Or what I should do for Paul's fortieth birthday party."

"I gave some suggestions!"

"Organising a party at Stonehenge?"

"One of the girls out there was saying it's a fabulous experience. And very few overheads either."

Natalie looked at her as though she had lost her marbles. Grace knew that if she didn't put her mind at rest, she would tell the whole office that Grace was having some kind of a breakdown.

"Look, I've just learned how to relax, Natalie, that's all. To reassess things. To take time out for me. It's not a crime – in fact it's a very healthy thing. You should try it."

"Oh stop it!" Natalie cried. "You've done something silly, haven't you!"

"What?"

"Don't look at me like that. You told me on the phone a couple of weeks ago that you were thinking of it!"

"I was only joking you."

Natalie looked at her very suspiciously. "Are you having an affair, Grace?"

Grace gave a little laugh. It was very convincing. "Hardly," she said.

"What, then?" Natalie cried. "Is it that gang out there, then? Have you joined them?"

"Who?"

Natalie jerked a thumb towards the lawn. "The anti-capitalists!"

"They're actually anti-nuclear," Grace clarified. Although a good few of them were anti-capitalist as well. And vegetarian. Mealtimes could be quite tricky sometimes, trying to keep everyone happy.

Natalie pitched forward in her chair, very serious, and began with the inflammatory words, "Grace, please don't take offence here."

"I'll certainly try not to," Grace assured her.

"I know that sometimes you feel that maybe you married too young. That you didn't experience all the things you could have. And I'm sure all this . . ." She waved a hand rather distastefully at Grace's bare, dirty feet, "is some kind of delayed reaction to missing out on your youth, but – are you laughing at me?"

"No, no. Please go on."

"All I'm saying is that there are other ways of rediscovering yourself. Of finding personal fulfilment."

"Such as art classes?"

Natalie ignored this. "You don't have to go to extremes, Grace. I'm sure what they're doing is . . . laudable, but at the same time, it'd be a shame if you looked back on this period in your life and had regrets."

"I certainly intend to regret nothing," Grace declared.

Natalie looked more alarmed. "If you can't think of yourself, at least think of the boys! They're at a very impressionable age – you don't want them to be embarrassed to be seen with you, do you?"

"Bit late for that. They're already embarrassed to be seen with me. Up the revolution!"

Rosie clapped her fat hands enthusiastically and gurgled.

Natalie flopped back in the chair, bemused and defeated, and Grace hid a smile. She'd only said that last bit to rile her.

But it wasn't fair to tease her like that. Natalie was looking out for her, in her own way. It was strange to think that she herself had thought like that until very recently: so rigidly!

"Look, I'm not joining their campaign, Natalie. I don't have much to do with them at all, if you must know, apart from cooking the odd meal. It's too much like hard work." It was far more enjoyable to lie out on the lawn in the afternoon sunshine with a book on gardening, which Julia was encouraging her to take an interest in. She had planted her very first tomatoes yesterday, and they had celebrated with a bottle of white wine. The revolutionaries had traipsed back from town, hot and tired, to find Grace sprawled in a deckchair asleep, her mouth open catching flies. What use are you to the campaign, Adam had said. None at all, Grace had replied, happily.

"How are Ewan and the boys?" Natalie enquired eventually, obviously striving for a normal topic of conversation.

"Having a whale of a time. They fly back on Sunday."

"Right. Good." Then, "Does he know you're not at home?"

"Sorry?"

"Ewan. He must be wondering what's going on. I mean, you've been here three whole weeks, Grace . . .'

"He is fully aware that I have moved in here temporarily to look after Mrs Carr. And Ewan, I would remind you, is not at home either."

"No need to be so defensive," Natalie huffed. "I was just asking."

Adam arrived in with the basil, bare-chested and brown from the sun. He looked like an advertisement for milk, or something equally wholesome.

"Hi there, Natalie." He had remembered her name. But he would, of course.

"Adam," she said, immediately coy. Honestly! It seemed that

good-looking anti-nuclear activists were okay in her book.

"And who's this?" Adam said, bending over Rosie, whose busy fingers immediately tried to grab one of his dreadlocks.

"Rosie," Natalie said, proud as punch. "She's two. Say hello to Adam, Rosie!" But Rosie refused. She refused to speak at all, which caused Natalie no end of worry.

"Excuse me," Grace murmured, taking the basil to the sink. It was better to get out of Adam's vicinity. Especially when she wanted to grab him and crush him to her breasts. That would certainly cause a stir in the office.

She stifled a giggle, and there was Natalie looking at her again.

"I was just saying to Grace that she should think about going home," Natalie said to Adam in a low voice – as though Grace were not there! (She understood now what Julia meant when she said that she had felt invisible since she'd been about sixty.)

"You said nothing of the sort," she said.

"Well, I was thinking it. I just didn't get around to saying it." Natalie turned to Adam again. "Mrs Carr looks absolutely fine to me. Fully recovered."

"Apart from the metal pins in her foot," Grace remarked. "And the crutches."

"Is there really any need for Grace to hang around here any longer?" Natalie asked Adam. "Mrs Carr is one thing, but that anti-nuclear lot out there on the lawn . . ."

"I'm actually one of that 'lot'," Adam said.

"Oh – yes, of course!" To make up for her slip, Natalie smiled brightly at him. "So, tell me, what kind of work do you do anyway? Handing out leaflets, that kind of thing?"

"Leaflets certainly form one part of the campaign," Adam said. His voice was no longer so friendly.

Natalie couldn't take the hint, of course. "I used to be involved in something like that in college. Do you remember I was telling you, Grace? We had such a laugh!"

"You laughed about nuclear disarmament?" Adam enquired.

There was a faint redness on his cheekbones now. Under her breath Grace started to hum 'I'm in the Mood for Dancing'.

"Ours was more trees really. How to stop the multinationals cutting them down to make cornflakes boxes. And paper hand-towels – that was the big one in our day. It took five trees to make a single paper hand-towel or something like that." Then she frowned. "But hang on, that seems like an awful lot. Maybe it was one tree made five towels? And a cornflakes box? Oh, I can't remember. Do you do trees as well as the nuclear stuff?"

Grace had the sensation of watching a bluebottle fly into the path of a rolled-up newspaper. But Natalie was such a prattler sometimes! On the other hand, Adam was so terribly idealistic. Grace's natural tendency was to intervene; she had a great urge now to march over and say, 'I will not stand for any fighting in this house today!' and send the two of them to their bedrooms to cool off.

But she wasn't wearing her mother hat in Mrs Carr's house. She wasn't quite sure what hat she was wearing, but it didn't involve solving other people's difference of opinion, and so she reached for the chopping-board instead.

"No, we don't 'do trees' as well," Adam said behind her. "We're too busy trying to close a nuclear plant less than a hundred miles from your back door. Because if there's an accident or explosion tomorrow morning, and the wind is blowing the wrong way, then there's a significant chance that you'll contract cancer within twenty years, or that little Rosie here will suffer from thyroid problems or leukaemia and will go on to have genetically deformed babies. If she lives that long, that is."

Dead silence. Grace peeked over her shoulder. Natalie was rather white, and clutching Rosie so hard that the child began to whimper.

"Are you sure you won't stay for dinner, Nat?" she said, kindly. "There's plenty."

"I can't," Natalie said, getting to her feet very quickly. "If Rosie

207

gets out of her routine at all she's a terror."

"Okay." Grace followed her to the kitchen door. "You'll let me know, won't you? If you have the baby early or anything?"

Alarmed, Natalie said, "I won't have the baby early – why would you think I'd have the baby early?" Then she looked over her shoulder at Adam, as though suspecting him of putting some kind of hex on her. He smiled back rather nastily.

"I'll see myself out," she told Grace, and almost ran out of the place.

"That wasn't very nice of you," Grace remarked when she and Adam were alone.

"She's an idiot."

"She is not an idiot. She's just not as passionate about nuclear disarmament as you."

"That's an understatement. 'Ooh, I used to dabble in that in college!'" His mimicry was spot-on. "I can't stand people like her. Nothing in their lives except their jobs and their husbands and their precocious kids. Too well-fed and too well-off to care what's happening in the real world."

Grace said nothing.

"I didn't mean you, of course," he added hurriedly.

"Good thing I've got a thick skin."

He was mortified. "But you haven't! She's the one with a thick skin! You're nothing like her!"

"But I'm exactly like her in lots of ways," Grace pointed out reasonably. "In fact, three weeks ago you were very fond of pointing it out."

"Why do you have to keep bringing that up?"

"I'm not. I'm just saying."

"I don't point it out now."

"Why not? I haven't changed. In fact, I'm going back to it all next Sunday."

Perhaps she shouldn't have mentioned that. They were having such a good time pretending it didn't exist. But Adam just regarded her out of his very blue eyes. Sometimes when she stared into them for long enough she started to sway dreamily on her feet.

"That's just window dressing," he said.

She was half insulted. "You're calling my life 'window dressing'?"

"It's not the real you. I know the real you."

"Now that you've stepped in to rescue me. Now that you've corrupted me."

"Yes," he said, smiling as proudly as a teacher with a rather slow student. "You can't fool me, Grace. I've seen your inner core."

"Oh!"

He could be very intense sometimes. In one way, it was incredibly flattering – nobody had ever bothered with her 'inner core' before. Indeed, she herself hadn't been aware that she had one. But now that she did, she felt complicated and interesting and mysterious. Another little gift from Adam.

But sometimes all this made her want to giggle nervously – because surely he couldn't find her all that fantastic? Last week he'd said her brain was the finest instrument he'd encountered in a long time and she actually *had* giggled. All because she had done the *Irish Times* crossword in twelve minutes! He had been very offended and had pointed out that he had met nobody in Ireland who could do it that quickly. That, of course, had made her feel very intelligent indeed, and she had apologised humbly, and started to wonder whether she was wasted as an estate agent. Perhaps she might even go back to college! That would give Ewan a run for his money!

She didn't believe all the things Adam said, of course. But for some reason he believed them, and she loved him for it. It was more than flattery. It was a kind of nourishment and, starved, she drank it up.

"What are you thinking about?" he asked. He always liked to

know what she was thinking and enquired at least ten times a day.

"Sex," she admitted honestly.

"You're always thinking about sex."

"I know. Am I strange?"

"Sometimes I feel like a piece of meat," he complained.

"All right," she said. "I'm thinking about you. Is that better?" And she did think about him quite a lot. Usually in sexual positions. But there was no need to tell him this. He could be overly sensitive, she had discovered.

"Yes," he said, putting his arms around her. She had to suppress the urge to emit a sort of primitive guttural sound, like those tennis players who gave pent-up grunts every time they hit the ball.

"And what exactly do you think of me?" he enquired.

The urge to grunt passed. "I was thinking how good you are to me. How well we get on. How nice you feel without any T-shirt on."

"There you go again. Thinking about sex. I'm trying to have a serious conversation here."

"Let's not be serious," she begged. "I can't be serious about anything any more." It was true. Since Adam, she felt she was floating along on her own little individual cloud of bliss where, like in fairytale land, there were no bad thoughts or ogres or bills or taxes (or husbands). Or else she felt she was in the throes of a perfect holiday romance, all passion and romance and hot August sun. And it would all come to a natural end before either discovered the other's nasty bathroom habits or gambling addiction.

She did not think she had ever felt such uncomplicated happiness in her life.

"Maybe I want to be serious," Adam said.

"Do you?"

He looked like he was about to say something, but then he smiled instead. "There's no need to look so scared, Grace."

"I'm not."

"I know what this is about," he said.

"Yes. You," she replied. "And me."

"You and me," he repeated, burying his nose in her hair – which hadn't been washed in a week, now that she thought about it. But then again neither had Adam's. Until now Grace had almost forgotten what a human body smelled like when it wasn't coated daily in shampoo and shower gel and perfume. It had a kind of musky, yeasty smell, not at all unpleasant – or at least Adam's wasn't, anyway. She hadn't got close enough to Martine to know what hers smelled like, and didn't intend to. Martine had not washed her hair since Christmas, maintaining that once it was left alone, hair was actually self-cleaning. Hers did not seem to bear out this theory, on appearances at any rate.

Then she forgot about Martine.

"Let's go upstairs," she said.

"The pigs are back," Julia hissed.

She was in the garden shed. Through the tiny window she could see a squad car drawing up across the road. Two uniformed police stared out at the crowd of young people sitting on her front lawn.

Martine frowned. "We don't really call them 'pigs', Julia. They don't like it."

They were so politically correct, these anti-nuclear people. Julia pressed up against the window.

"It's two new ones," she said excitedly. Usually it was just Sergeant Daly, and rookie Garda Paul O'Toole. They would park under the shade of the elm tree and after a while Julia would bring them out a cup of tea and a plate of fig rolls. They always protested that they were on duty, but she left the tray just the same.

But two *outside* police officers? And after six o'clock?

"Binoculars!" she cried. "One of them has a pair of binoculars –

he's training them on the house!"

Martine didn't even look up. She was obviously used to police harassment and continued to paint a canvas banner with the word MOX, in big red letters. Julia had already ironed on a transfer of a black skull.

"I don't see why they're bothering," Martine complained. "We are a peaceful organisation."

"Until Saturday anyway," Julia said with relish. She imagined riot police and baton charges and young people chaining themselves to railings singing 'We Shall Overcome'!

"I've told you before," Martine said with a sigh. "We are not going to cause trouble at the festival. We're simply making our views on nuclear reactors clear." She jerked her head contemptuously towards the police car. "Nothing to justify this – this spying! It's outrageous! It's a violation of our right to protest in a peaceful manner in a democratic society!"

"Yes, yes," Julia said. Sometimes Martine could go on a bit about her rights. In fact, a lot of them on the lawn out there seemed very aware of their rights, and what they could and could not lawfully do. Which was wonderful, she thought hastily. She would just have preferred a bit more action herself. Like those demonstrations in the sixties: Free love! Ban the Bomb! They knew how to rock the boat back then all right, and to hell with the law.

Privately, she thought the music festivals had been far superior too. Just look at Woodstock, for heaven's sake! That was a proper music festival, with lots of drink and illegal substances and bad food. Not like now, where they had five-star toilets and glossy programmes, and where the catering trucks served noodles, apparently.

There would be mud, though, Martine had promised her. Lots of it. Fifty thousand people squatting on a hill for two days tended to generate a lot of dirt and mud. But apparently they were bringing plastic sheets for the tents, and double-lined sleeping bags. There would be hot food and books to read if things got too boring. One of them was even bringing a coffee-maker!

Anyhow. The important thing was that they were letting her join in. She was a part of it, an important part – not some useless old biddy with a crocked foot who was a nuisance to everybody.

Martine finished with the paintbrush and held up the banner proudly. "What do you think?"

"Terrific!" Julia said, thinking how much more terrific it would be if they brought along a box of matches and set the thing on fire in the middle of the festival opening act. But apparently there were certain ways of doing things. And any kind of fire was out, she knew without even asking. Apparently so were sharp implements, decaying fruit and hijacking a catering truck. (Back in her day, when an organisation said it was 'peaceful', it didn't actually mean it.)

If she were honest, the banner looked a bit amateurish; not like those wonderful placards Adam had brought over with him. He'd saved them from some previous demonstration, which had obviously been better resourced than this one.

Still, she thought quickly, appearances weren't everything.

There was a knock on the shed door. She pressed herself up against it and hissed, "Who is it?"

"Mammy?"

She suppressed a sigh and opened the door. Michael squeezed in, blinking owlishly as his eyes adjusted to the gloom.

"I wasn't expecting you today," she said.

He was dressed in his work suit. "I thought I'd call in on my way home. And a good thing too! Mammy, I'm going to have to insist that you come indoors this minute."

The implication that she was a child up to no good annoyed her. "I'll come in when we're finished."

"Where's Grace?" Michael demanded. "Because she doesn't seem to be anywhere in the house."

"I have no idea where Grace is. Michael, you're standing on our banner."

"First she shoots you, then she can't be bothered to look after you properly!"

"Grace looks after me extremely well. She's entitled to an hour off every now and again."

Stymied, Michael turned to Martine instead. "She's seventy-three, you know! She's injured! You shouldn't be letting her get involved in all this."

Martine looked him up and down dismissively. "It's her own choice. Now, can you leave? You're taking up too much room."

Michael positively quivered with indignation. "I will not leave without my mother!"

"Michael – "

"No, Mammy, enough is enough. I didn't say anything in the beginning. I let you get on with it; housing these people, and painting banners, and acting like a hippy. But it's gone too far. There are police cars parked outside, for God's sake!"

"We know," she said.

"It's time to terminate your involvement in this whole ridiculous – campaign, if you want to call it that."

Martine curled her lip in a very threatening manner. "And what is that supposed to mean?"

Michael wasn't used to naked aggression and took a step back. He said to Julia, "And I don't know why you're saying 'we' all the time. You're not part of this madness!"

"But I am, Michael," she declared proudly, and was rewarded with a nod of solidarity from Martine.

Michael snorted in disbelief. "You didn't even know what MOX meant before this lot came along! You thought it was something you spread on a bagel!"

"I didn't! That's lox – I know what lox means!" she retaliated. She hoped he wouldn't embarrass her further in front of Martine. But Martine was looking at her watch.

"I'm starving. I'm going to find Grace and see about dinner."

"Oh yes," Michael said grimly. "Nothing like a free dinner. Or a free lunch. Or a free breakfast for that matter!"

Martine took a step forward ominously. But Michael stood his ground.

"I know your game. You think she's a soft touch, do you?" He jerked his head towards Julia. "Think you'll get free bed and board, and in exchange you can let her dabble?"

"Michael!" Julia's voice cut through the air. "That is enough."

With another venomous look, Martine shoved past Michael and out.

"I'll remind you that this is my house, Michael," Julia said. "And you'll treat my guests with respect."

"Guests!"

"Yes, Michael."

"Mammy, you're making a fool of yourself here."

Julia picked up Martine's paintbrush and began to daub at the banner. "What, because I care?"

"About some shipment of nuclear fuel on its way from China?"

"Japan. You don't even know that much."

"Neither did you until now."

"So what?" she said loudly. "Look, why is it so hard for you to believe that I'm doing this because I want to?"

"Because you and Daddy never gave a hoot about environmental issues! Daddy bulldozed that listed building, remember? And you owned a mink coat. I don't ever remember you fretting about the fifty minks that had their necks wrung just so you could look good!"

"In retrospect, it's not something I'm proud of, okay?" Julia said haughtily. "But people change. Can we just leave it at that?"

"No." He sucked in his gut officiously. "I went looking for some information today on Martine and her friends. I got on the Internet, and I rang some of the big anti-nuclear groups, and I combed the telephone directory."

"Slow day at work then?"

"And guess what? Mammy, they're a mickey-mouse outfit who travel from place to place spreading some daft anti-nuclear message, and relying on the generosity of people like you. Officially, they don't exist."

"What, because they're not registered in some niggly companies' office? Because they don't have a policy manifesto printed on nice paper? Well, maybe that's because they're too busy trying to save this island from possible nuclear annihilation!"

"They wouldn't save a fly," Michael said. "With their home-made banners and their painted tents! They're like a crowd of children let loose with crayons!"

"Shut up, Michael. Just shut up."

She didn't want him spoiling everything with his probing and questioning and his cynical insinuations that she was being used. For the first time since JJ died, her house was full of the sounds of life again. She had a reason for getting out of bed in the morning. And maybe she hadn't known what MOX had meant before now but that was hardly the point. At her very lowest point, Grace and Adam and Martine and Joey – total strangers! – had been sent by some angel of fate to rent rooms in her lodging house.

Not that any of them were actually paying her, of course. But they couldn't be expected to; not when they were dedicated full-time to changing the world! She felt a moral duty to help the cause in whatever way she could, and she didn't care that they weren't part of some established group. Martine said those big earth outfits were all administration, anyway. Paperwork. She didn't want to shuffle papers behind a desk; she wanted to get out there and make a difference.

Michael obviously saw that further argument was hopeless because he said, "Actually, Mammy, I have another reason for calling around." He held out a white envelope. "It's from Gillian."

The very mention of her name was like a blast of dry ice.

"What is it?" Julia asked, not taking it.

"You know she does some voluntary work with the local tin-nitus group?"

Julia looked at him blankly.

"Ringing in the ears. She thought she had it once, but it was just that new kettle we'd bought – "

"Oh yes, I remember."

"Anyway, she's having a coffee morning tomorrow to raise some funds. She's sent an invitation for you to come along."

He held out the envelope again.

"She said some very hurtful things to me, Michael."

"I know. I know that. But she'd already done so much work on the conversion – "

"Without consulting with me first."

"Yes. That was wrong. The things she said . . . can we not just put it all behind us?"

Gillian could, maybe. It would be a very long time before Julia would forget that day.

"What did she mean, Michael? When she talked about filling JJ's shoes?"

"I have no idea." His florid face looked uncomfortable.

"Because I don't expect you to, you know – I mean with all this fussing over me, the ringing me up all the time – not that I don't appreciate it," she added quickly. "But it's not necessary."

"Maybe I want to," he said.

"And that's very kind of you. But I don't want you neglecting your own life. The fact is that JJ's gone, and I'm just going to have to learn to live on my own again. Anyway, I have Grace and Martine and the rest to keep me company now."

She had meant this to ease the pressure on him, but he looked at her oddly, and said, "You always know how to make me feel really good, Mammy."

"What?"

But he was making for the door. "Can I tell Gillian you'll be along?"

"I don't think so. Not yet anyway," she added, lest he think she was rejecting the olive branch entirely. Besides, she had her whole day planned tomorrow; they urgently had to come up with a plan to smuggle in the banners and tents to the festival. Security would be on the lookout for them. Adam had suggested hiring a truck and simply driving through the fence with the stuff, which Julia had very much liked. But Martine said things had to be done by the book. How boring!

"She'll take it very badly, you know," he said.

"I'm sure she'll survive," Julia said, and put it out of her mind.

TWELVE

The waiter wore a shiny black quiff and a pair of blue suede shoes. Not that you could call him a *waiter*, of course – in Walt Disney Land all employees were known as 'cast members'. This one supplemented his uniform with a badge saying 'Elvis', just in case you were a bit slow.

"Hiya doing, kids!" Elvis boomed at Jamie and Neil now.

"Okay," they mumbled back. They'd just eaten beefburgers containing the meat of a whole cow, or so it seemed, and a mountain of fries, and were slumped bloated and listless on the fake red leather diner seats.

Ewan couldn't blame them. His own colon had packed up about five days ago under the sustained onslaught of fast food. Still, not long to go now. They were flying home on Sunday. Perhaps Grace would cook something homemade for them. In fact, given everything, it was the very least she could do.

"And you, sir?" Elvis said to him, with another dazzling smile.

The relentless cheer was beginning to impinge upon Ewan's nerves too. But he managed, "Terrific, thank you."

"Dessert?" Elvis fired off.

"Oh, I don't think – "

"Sundae? Apple pie and cream? Double-whammy-white-chocolate Mud Pie with Raisin 'n' Caramel ice cream? Chocolate sauce optional."

There was so much excess in this country. Ewan found himself offended by it. "Not for me," he said. "Boys?"

"Your foot is touching mine," Neil said to Jamie accusingly.

"It's not! Your foot is too far over."

"Tosser!"

"Dad!"

"Now, now, boys," Ewan murmured, feeling his irritation rise. It was time to leave. To Elvis he said, "Just the bill, please."

Not put out in the slightest, Elvis whipped out a docket and put it on the table. "You be sure to have a nice day now!"

"Certainly," Ewan said dutifully. This was The Happiest Place on Earth, after all. Any kind of mediocre or off day wasn't allowed. You might just have lost your job, your children and your wife, but it was still mandatory in this place to have a nice day.

Not that any of those things had happened to *him*, of course, Ewan corrected quickly. The Slimchoc account had last week doubled in size (they'd just green-lighted a range of milkshakes – *No Milk!* – according to Ewan's colleague Mick) and he had seen more of his children in the past three weeks than he might have ordinarily wanted. All right, so his wife might have upped and deserted him on what was supposed to have been the holiday of a lifetime and left him in charge of two demanding boys in a weird cartoon town while she tended to some old dear's foot in the leafy countryside, but he hadn't let that little detail spoil anybody's nice day. No sirree, he had carried on regardless. Nobody would be able to point the finger and say that he hadn't pulled his weight on *this* gig.

"So, guys!" he said to Jamie and Neil, feeling unusually superior and high-minded. "What are we going to do this afternoon?"

Normally he didn't give them any choice. Grace had warned

him several times on the phone – in that irritatingly helpful way of hers as though he were suffering from some kind of disability – never to invite any kind of debate because he would only bring trouble down upon himself. 'Just *tell* them, Ewan.' Thinking about it now, Ewan decided that he didn't agree with this rule of parenting at all. It was practically treating the boys as though they were children! All right, so they *were* children. But how were they ever to grow up if they were denied simple choices? Mollycoddled, he thought, that's what they were. (He would never say this out loud). They never knew what they wanted to do anyway, so there was no harm in giving them a choice.

So it was a bit of a shock when Neil announced, "We want to go to Tarzan's Tree house."

Damn anyway. That wasn't what Ewan had in mind at all, so he blurted, "You can't." Seeing their faces, he gave a little laugh and said lightly, "We went to Tarzan's Tree house last week – you'd be bored stiff!"

"We won't," Neil said, giving him that confrontational look that he'd developed in the last three weeks and which made Ewan slightly nervous. As though Ewan were his enemy or something, the minute he had the temerity to disagree with anything Neil wanted to do! No, it wasn't right, and Ewan would tell Grace about it as soon as they got home.

"Well, you can't go to Tarzan's Tree house because I've got something else planned," he said loudly, determined to reassert his authority.

"So why did you ask us what we wanted to do in the first place?" Neil enquired, and Ewan began to sweat. He should never have offered them a blasted choice. She had been right.

It was just holiday fatigue, he reassured himself. They'd spent three whole weeks in each other's company. Tensions were bound to be a bit high. And Grace's absence was sorely felt. She was great at kind of gelling everyone together. Sometimes when Ewan looked at his sons he didn't know what to say to them. It was in those odd moments back in the hotel room, in the hour before bedtime for example, when he felt his own lack most keenly. There just wasn't the same intimacy between them all as there would have been had Grace been there too.

Still, they would be home in a little less than a week. Every day on the phone Grace would do a countdown to how many days left before they were back. It would be six days from today.

It stuck him now that Grace hadn't done the countdown in ages. Maybe a week or more.

The boys were waiting for him, so he squared his shoulders and said, "Today I've arranged for us to go swimming!"

Jamie bolted upright, and said with such vehemence that Ewan was taken aback, "I don't want to go swimming!"

"But we haven't been swimming at all this holiday."

Jamie looked across the plastic table at him, face rigid and closed. "I said I don't want to go swimming, okay?"

Neil had been the confrontational one this holiday. In fact, Jamie had been even quieter than usual, now that Ewan thought about it. Surely to God he wasn't going to start kicking up now? With only a week to go?

"Why?" Ewan said this very nicely in the hopes of getting things back on track.

But Jamie just threw himself back in his seat silently. It was all very odd.

Ewan tried to think of what Grace would have done in this situation. She would have jollied him along. So he said, with a wink, "Ah, but you haven't been to the guitar-shaped pool!"

"They have a guitar-shaped pool?" At least Neil looked interested now.

"Yes. I've booked diving lessons for you both with Angie-Piranha-Pirelli!"

That impressed them. And so it should. She was costing Ewan twenty-five dollars an hour.

"The piranha bit is her stage name, of course," he added hur-

222

riedly. He added carelessly, "She's an ex-Olympic diver."

Ah-ha! Neil was sitting up straight now, probably already imagining himself on a podium with a gold medal around his neck. Ewan snuck a look at Jamie. Was that the faintest glimmer of interest he saw?

But Jamie just said stubbornly again, "I'm not going."

"Oh, for goodness' sake!" But then Ewan took a breath. He must have patience. So he tried again. "It's all booked and paid for, Jamie."

"Let Neil go. I'll stay here with you." Jamie said.

"No." Ewan would get no time to himself that way. "You both go or not at all."

"Hey – so I can't go because he won't go?" Neil said. "That's not fair!"

Ewan said, "Jamie, what's the problem here?"

"He's a wimp who's afraid of cold water," Neil said.

"I am not!"

"Or heights or something. Oooooh, Angie, I'm too high up, I'm going to shit myself!"

"Fuck off!"

"Stop it, the two of you!" Ewan gave Neil what he hoped was an intimidating look before turning back to Jamie. "Are you scared, is that it?"

He tried to sound sympathetic. But, honestly, Grace had him ruined! All that fussing over him since he'd been a baby, like he was delicate or something. And look at him now – no guts about him, not like Neil.

"No." Jamie slumped down in his seat again, his arms wrapped very tightly over his chest.

Ewan felt his irritation rise again. If he wouldn't even say what was *wrong* . . . "Then finish up your drink, eh? Angie said she'd be at the pool at two."

They shouldn't have eaten all that food before swimming, he belatedly thought. Still, Angie would soon work it off them. She had been frighteningly efficient when he had met her in the hotel lobby last night to arrange a week of lessons. Everything had been 'sure, sir' and 'no problem, sir'. Ewan had liked that; the fact that Angie was prepared to look after any problems.

Neil was on his feet, excited. "Let's go."

Ewan said, "Actually, I'm not coming with you." He felt guilty, even though there was absolutely no reason why. He had looked after the two of them single-handed for the best part of a month, after all. And they would love the diving lessons. This was his holiday too, and he shouldn't feel bad about taking a couple of afternoons for himself.

But for some reason he hadn't told Grace about the lessons. Well, she'd have gone all silent and judgemental, wouldn't she? She, who had organised this protracted holiday in the first place and then jumped ship! She didn't know what it had been like for him over here by himself! He hadn't wanted to go on about it too much, he hadn't wanted her feel bad, and so she didn't know about the night the boys had set the hotel fire alarm off by accident, or the torrential rain that had trapped them in the Haunted Mansion for four hours or the day Jamie had gone missing in a merchandising store. No, he hadn't complained about the crowds or the relentless heat or the peculiar rotting smell in their hotel room or the fact that he hadn't had sex in three weeks! And now he couldn't take a few afternoons off for himself without being accused of being a slack, irresponsible, uncaring parent? It was too much!

His glasses were steaming up. He reminded himself that nobody had actually accused him of anything. It was just his own paranoia, the result of years of being on the receiving end of Grace's 'looks'.

One day he would stand up for himself, he decided. The other option, of course, was to just go on ignoring the looks. That didn't require as much energy.

"I'll see you back here later," he said. Jamie looked at him over the table, resistance coming from his every pore.

"For goodness' sake, Jamie, Angie will look after you," he said, as much to reassure himself as Jamie. "Just try it, okay?"

To stall any further argument he handed over the bag he'd already packed with their swim things. Neil made for the exit without a backwards glance. Jamie eventually slouched after him, his body hunched over a bit. He'd been doing that for a couple of days. Perhaps the child had tummy ache. Ewan wouldn't be surprised, with all the fattening food.

At last he was alone at the plastic-topped table in the vast red diner. He took a breath and, for the first time in days, he felt himself relax. The chrome jukebox was playing 'Stupid Cupid', Elvis was gossiping with Marilyn Monroe at the counter, and Ewan wondered what Grace would have made of it all.

She had been a bit odd on the phone recently, now that he really thought about it. It wasn't just failing to count down the days; that was just a silly thing. No, it was more a detachment on her part. A feeling of distance or something.

Perhaps he was reading too much into it. The boys didn't seem to have noticed anything; or at least they always came off the phone with big happy smiles on their faces. They hardly ever smiled like that for Ewan, unless he bought them something in one of those damned merchandising stores that were waiting to ambush you around every corner.

Elvis was hovering again. "Coffee, please," Ewan said hastily, lest he be pressured again into going for dessert. Everyone around him seemed to be forking in cream-covered concoctions like there was no tomorrow. Almost all of them were obese, or on the way to it.

"One coffee coming up!" Elvis chirped. "Could I interest you in a chocolate-chip cookie or – "

"No."

Blessedly alone again, Ewan reached for one of the white paper napkins that had come with the food. It took him a moment to collect himself, to order his thoughts. Then he searched in his pockets until he found the stub of a pencil, which he licked, and then he bent over the napkin and he wrote a few words and then crossed them out, wrote more, and crossed them out too. He no longer heard the music blaring from the jukebox, or Elvis arriving back with his coffee. Finally he turned over the bedraggled napkin, smoothed it out, and started over again: *Eat Your Way Thin*. No, he thought, been done before. *Eat More Lose More*? Terrible. All the damned sunshine was addling his brain, he thought rather cheerfully.

"Dad?"

It took him a moment to come back to earth and he pushed his grubby glasses up on his nose and looked out of them to see Jamie standing by the table, plucking at his T-shirt, and looking at his feet.

It was an effort to stay calm. "What are you doing back here, Jamie?"

He wouldn't even answer the question properly; just said, in that plaintive voice again, "Can I stay here with you?"

Oh, for heaven's sake! After all the trouble Ewan had gone to! And not just over the diving. He'd given them a great three weeks and now he was to be refused an hour to himself because Jamie had decided, seemingly on a whim, that he didn't fancy diving?

And so he snapped, " No. Go up to the room if you don't want to go diving. That's the choice, okay?"

"I want to talk," Jamie said now.

More procrastination!

"Too late! You had your chance!" Ewan said.

Jamie walked off very quickly. For a moment Ewan considered going after him. Oh, better than they both cooled off, he decided. He would follow him in a minute.

He picked up his pencil and went back to work.

"Do that again," she said.

"What?"

"The tongue thing."

"Grace, I'm getting a bit of a blister here – "

"Five more minutes."

Oh, good lad. Grace buried her cheek in Mrs Carr's pillow, which smelled musty. Not that she cared. Neither did she care that her toenails needed clipping, or that Adam was making little lapping noises with his tongue. Normally noises like that tended to be vaguely embarrassing. Why else did they always play gushing background music during lovemaking scenes in the movies? It was to cover up any unromantic moist noises or shoulder-joints clicking.

But with Adam, she revelled in it. The more noise the better! Apart from lapping, she actively encouraged sucking, licking, chewing (where appropriate) and the little sticky noise that damp skin makes when unpeeled from other damp skin. Heaven! Or the wet snuffle of a neck being kissed all the way down. Or that delicious –

"You're not even paying attention." Adam looked up at her, accusingly.

"I am," she said tenderly.

But now he was unsure. "What, am I not doing it right?"

"You're doing it just perfectly."

"Because if you prefer I can – "

"Adam. Just keep going."

She pushed his head back down. He didn't need any guidance from her in the sex department. They knew it all these days. Some of the things he had proposed, and done, had completely shocked her, and made her own little attempts to spice up her and Ewan's sex life look laughably dull. But honestly, some of them were so rude! Not to mention unnatural. You had to wonder how people discovered them in the first place.

She had tried to appear blasé in the beginning, of course. Bored, even. Except for that time when he had casually suggested that she ask a friend to join them.

"Natalie? For God's sake, she's eight months' pregnant!"

He had been joking. He had laughed at her horror: her, veteran of a thousand porn fantasies (which now seemed as innocent as *The Waltons*). But it was slightly embarrassing that she was so inexperienced compared to him. Surely in this kind of older woman/younger man scenario, she should be teaching him a trick or two? But all she had up her sleeve were a few variations on the missionary position.

Mind you, there were compensations. Men his generation took it completely for granted that her pleasure was as important as his own. Imagine! She thought of the men she'd slept with in the past, and how none of them would dream of putting her before them. Most would only enquire about her satisfaction in the sleepy afterglow of their own, as though remembering their manners. After five minutes' rest, one of them had lifted himself off the pillow with a cheery, 'Now, let's sort you out!'

That had been Ewan, actually. But it had come from good intentions, she'd told herself. It was just that she didn't really know what to tell him. Much less how to show him. Where did you get that kind of confidence at twenty-two?

Ewan had stopped trying to 'sort her out' years ago, and she had stopped asking. Neither of them had noticed her slow metamorphosis from a gauche girl into a fully-fledged, mature, sexually-charged woman. No wonder she thought about sex all the time! She was frustrated, and had been for years!

"More!" she commanded, in a magnificently husky voice

"You bet," Adam said, filled with admiration. (He liked it when she bossed him around a bit. It was a bit predictable given that she was older than him, but if it kept him happy . . .)

Through sluttish half-closed eyes, she watched him. The deep brown tan of his back ended abruptly at his shorts-line. His little high bottom was very white and somehow vulnerable, and she felt so tender that she reached down and stroked his face.

"What?" he said.

"Nothing," she said, not wanting to reveal the depth of her feelings to him. He might feel all pressured and run off on her. And he hadn't even finished down there. "I'm putting on weight," she said instead.

"Are you?"

So sweet of him to pretend he hadn't noticed.

"Look at my tummy."

He did. "Hmm. You might be getting a little Rubenesque."

"*Rubenesque?*"

Embarrassed, she pulled the sheet up. They were in his bed. She had spent only those first two nights in her little single bed across the hall.

"Don't," he said. "It's cute."

She took another peek down. There it was – a solid little white mound of flesh spanning from hip to hip, the kind she hadn't had since she'd been a teenager and had gone on Dr Wright's Revolutionary Combined Foods Diet (he had been wrong).

"I think it suits you," Adam declared, giving it a little pat. "You were too thin anyway. Scrawny."

She felt another big wave of affection. "I'll miss you."

He tickled her tummy. "Ah, but that's assuming that we're going to break up."

She laughed. "What are you suggesting? That we stay together?"

He smiled back. "Why not?"

"I'm too old for you. All my friends would laugh at me if I took up with you."

"So let's move to Tasmania. None of my friends will laugh at us."

"That's because you don't have any friends. Except crusties."

"Crusties are very non-judgemental," he said. "So, what do you say?"

"About moving to *Tasmania*?"

"Stop laughing. I'm very patriotic," he said, wounded.

"What would we live on? Anti-nuclear leaflets?"

"I'd support us."

"You're a college dropout."

"I could get a job! Teaching silly tourists how to surf, that kind of thing. We could live in a little hut by the beach."

"That sounds nice. What would we eat?"

"Fish, of course."

"And some nuts and wild fruits that I would collect in the forest?"

"You're getting the hang of this," he said admiringly.

"And I could make all our own clothes from the pelts of wild animals that I would trap and skin!"

"Steady on, Grace."

She clapped her hands excitedly. "We'd live off the land, with no mobile phones or filofaxes or cars or anything. We'd be hippies! I always wanted to be a hippy."

"Did you?"

"Actually, no." But neither did she want to be the harried hassled thin woman that had first come to Hackettstown. Wasn't it wonderful that people could actually change, she thought sleepily? Heck, she mightn't even be finished changing yet! She might change some more tomorrow! Who knew what she might eventually become? (Although she wouldn't like to get too fat. Curvy was attractive. Obese was not.)

"Grace," Adam said, after a while.

"Hmm?" she said, lost in visions of herself shopping in outsize stores and having to book two seats when she wanted to fly anywhere.

"I want to talk to you about something."

"Oh, Adam. Martine doesn't mean those things she says. The two of you are just different, that's all. You're a radical and she's more conservative – "

"She's a fucking fossil."

"Yes, well, she's running this campaign and there's nothing you can do about that."

"I wouldn't be so sure. Anyway, I don't want to talk about Martine. I – "

"Sorry to cut you off, Adam." Something had caught her eye.

" What's that?"

"What?"

"Out the window. No, no, don't sit up!" she hissed.

"How can I look if I don't sit up?"

"Just look!" She pointed. "There – across the road!"

Being on the first floor, they hadn't bothered to close the curtains. It was still broad daylight outside. And they could quite clearly see the sun glinting off glass in the upstairs bedroom of the house opposite.

Grace squealed and pulled up the sheet to cover her chest. Adam jumped up and shook his fist at the window.

"That little bastard," he said grimly. "I told you, didn't I? I told you!"

"Frank? I know you're in there. So you might as well come out now!"

She rang the doorbell again. But still he didn't come. So eventually she took out the office's set of keys and let herself in.

He was hiding in the living-room watching television, and she startled him.

"What are you doing here?" he blustered.

"What were *you* doing, spying on us?" she returned heatedly.

"I was not! I was searching for the Lesser Spotted Woodpecker, a very rare bird in these isles – "

"Balls!"

"Look it up if you don't believe me!" He tossed a reference book at her. "I was told a pair of them were nesting in Croft's Wood over there. So there I was, going about my legitimate business, and next thing I see two bare bottoms bouncing in front of my nose in broad daylight! Imagine the fright I got!"

231

Grace fought down a hateful blush. But something told her he was telling the truth. Or partially at least.

"You didn't have to keep looking though, did you?"

"Well, I . . ."

"You could have turned away! That would have been the decent thing to do. You know, I had to stop Adam coming over here. He'd like to give you a good thump."

"I'd imagine your husband would like to do the same to Adam. Someone should tell him what his wife's been up to while he's been away."

"And you'd just love to, wouldn't you? That would pay me back nicely for calling your house a dump!"

"My house might have been sold only for that," Frank said piously.

"Tom and Charlie weren't going to buy your house whether I called it a dump or not."

"Sandy says that if that had happened in the States, you'd have been fired. And she's right."

"Yes, well, Sandy is always right. We should know that by now," Grace muttered.

Frank gave her a look. "I'm sorry for spying on you, okay? But there's no need to take it out on Sandy! I was only doing it for her in the first place."

"Sandy told you to go and spy on people making love?" Perhaps there was hope for her after all.

"No, no." He clammed up.

Grace had a suspicion what was worrying him. "Frank, is this to do with what we were talking about a while back?"

"I have no idea what you're referring to."

"Look, every couple is nervous about the first time they make love."

"Would you like a cup of tea?"

"Sandy won't expect you to be some Lothario with all the right moves."

Frank sank back into his chair and threw his head back on the greasy headrest with a groan. "But she's so lovely. Beautiful!"

"Well, yes . . ."

"I'll be too afraid to even touch her. A woman like her, she'll expect perfection, technique, expertise!"

"Maybe not. It sounds like she isn't too active in that department herself. Hasn't she been fighting rakes of them off in the gym?"

"She's had previous boyfriends though. You saw that photo where one of them was chopped out. Greg. *Greg*. I bet he made her happy."

"We don't know that – "

"I bet he was a hunk with a big lunchbox who knew all the tricks!"

"Calm down, Frank. I'm sure you have a few tricks yourself," Grace said, rather queasy at the thought. He should have a few more now, after watching herself and Adam at it. Oh God.

"Not really," he said.

Grace swallowed hard, and battled on. "Come on now! I'm sure if you think back to your previous . . . experiences, you'll find something to draw on."

"Hardly," he said. "I'm a virgin."

"Ah! Um!" She nodded sagely, wishing he hadn't confided this in her. She tried not to look surprised or amused in any way and said, in a very jolly way, "Just think of all the fun you'll have learning!"

Frank looked more miserable. "I thought if I watched you and Adam I might be able to pass myself off as sophisticated."

Grace said, mortified, "Did you see . . . everything?"

"Pretty much."

She hoped that he hadn't taken any notes. Or drawn diagrams. That would be just like him. "You know, maybe you should talk to Sandy about this."

"I can't."

"She won't mind that you're not experienced."

"She kind of thinks I am."

"What do you mean?"

"Well, she was going on and on about Greg! And I just kind of boasted that I'd slept with more women that I actually have."

"How many more?"

"I told her three."

"That's not too bad."

"But then I began to add a couple here and there, and suddenly it was ten, and then twenty, and then it just all got out of control!"

"How many, Frank?"

"Eighty-two." He rubbed his hand over his eyes. "I was afraid she'd go off me if she knew I'd never had a girlfriend before. She might think there was something wrong with me."

"But eighty-two, Frank!"

"I know."

"You need to tell her the truth."

"I can't!"

"Why not?"

"She's got enough worries without me adding to them."

"Her sister?"

"No, no, that's all patched up with the hubby. Do you remember Sandy was feeling tired?"

"Yes."

"She went to the doctor that time. And he took a whole heap of tests. And something has come back that he's not happy with."

"What?"

"They won't tell her until they do a second test. The results should be in today. But she doesn't want me worrying. She says I'm just to concentrate on getting my house sold."

"Does she now."

"She suggested that maybe you should think about dropping the price a bit."

Grace was taken aback. "Sorry?"

"I know it'll affect your commission."

"I wasn't thinking about my commission."

"Sandy says we're not attracting much interest."

"It's August, Frank. Half the country is on holidays."

"She says that if we cut the price by, say, ten per cent, we'll draw in a whole new section of the market."

Her brain was certainly sharp for someone who wasn't well. But she did have a point. Imagine – a woman living thousands of miles away, who communicated only by computer, a woman who had never even seen Frank's house, could sell it for him.

Grace's job had never seemed so meaningless.

"I'll think about it. And Frank?"

"What?"

"This spying business. I won't say anything to anybody if you won't. Okay?"

THIRTEEN

The next day Nick and Charlie arrived back from town, red-cheeked and giggly.

"Have you two been drinking?" Grace asked suspiciously. It wasn't unknown, at two o'clock in the afternoon.

"Why do you always think the worst of us, Grace?" Nick complained.

Charlie burst out, "Oh, I can't keep it to myself a minute longer! Can we tell her, Nick?"

"Go on so."

"We're engaged, Grace!"

"Engaged?"

"Yeh. Like, we're going to get married," Nick elaborated helpfully. "At some point in the future. You know, whenever we can get things organised."

"We're doing it as soon as we can," Charlie said firmly. "Look!"

She held out her hand. A ring with a very small diamond sat on her third finger. "We just picked it in the jewellery shop in Hackettstown – isn't it adorable?"

"It's perfect," Grace said. "Well, ah, what can I say! Congratulations!"

"Now, I know what you're thinking," Charlie told her.

"I don't – "

"I know I said I'd never touch another man with a bargepole. That they were all a crowd of fucking bastards," she said happily. "But Nick is different."

"I am," Nick said vigorously.

"I knew it the very first time I set eyes on him! I've never felt that way before about any man, have I, sweetheart?" Charlie said over her shoulder. Gavin had trailed in after them.

"Apart from Bob," he said.

"Well, maybe Bob."

"And Tony," he added.

"Oh, yes, Tony! I'd nearly forgotten about him. But we were only engaged for two weeks."

"You and Nick have only known each other three weeks," Grace ventured. She didn't want to spoil the moment; but this was Nick they were talking about! Her brother.

"Three weeks, two days, twelve hours and forty-seven minutes!" Charlie said. "Isn't it marvellous? I always believed in love at first sight," she confided in Grace. "Anyway, we'd like you to be matron-of-honour at the wedding – wouldn't we, Nick?"

He nodded. "Absolutely."

"Don't forget, you have to divorce Didi first," Grace said. Now she did really sound like a mean cow.

Charlie gave her a look. "Kind of like you're divorcing Ewan?"

Touché. Grace flushed. "I told you. That was a minor misunderstanding."

"Anyhow, Nick has already been in contact with his solicitor, haven't you, honey? And Gavin's going to be a pageboy, aren't you, darling?"

"I am," he said proudly. "Will I fit into the suit I got for the wedding to Tom?"

"We'll get a new one," Charlie declared. "We'll get a new everything!"

Nick said, "Obviously we'll have to look at our budget – "

Charlie gave him a rather steely look. "This is going to be a proper white wedding, Nick. With printed invitations and a hotel reception and a band playing. I've been engaged six times and this time it's going to work. I'm going to be respectable for the first time in my life!"

"Me too!" Gavin said.

Charlie chucked him under the chin, then said airily to Nick, "And don't worry about the money. I told you – just look at Johnny Logan."

Nick cleared his throat loudly, then said to Grace, "Anyway, keep the news under your hat for the moment. I don't want Didi getting wind of it."

"Not before she hears she's being divorced anyway," Charlie said confidentially. "It wouldn't be fair on her."

"And what about the kids?" Grace asked Nick.

"I won't tell them for the moment either," he said. "Not until things settle a bit."

"And now, of course, you'll be responsible for Gavin as well," Charlie reminded him.

"You will," Gavin said vigorously. "I can be tough going sometimes, can't I, Mum?"

"You can," she said fondly.

Nick began to look a bit pressured, Grace thought.

"Things might be a bit clearer when you finish your computer course," she said diplomatically

"He's dropped out of that," Charlie said casually.

"What?"

"The IT industry's bust anyway." She said to Gavin, "Come on, let's go upstairs and get my wedding magazines out!"

"She's got ones from 1990 – haven't you, Mum?"

"Before you were even a twinkle in my eye!" she said.

They went off upstairs hand in hand, leaving a little silence behind.

"Go on, then," Nick said at last.

"What?"

"Say I'm making a big mistake. You know you're dying to."

"I am not! It's just a surprise, that's all. Especially so soon into things . . ."

"That doesn't matter. I love her."

"I'm sure you do. "

"Even if she's a bit loud and brassy and not up to your standards of perfection."

"Nick!"

"But Charlie says we're going to make a great team. She says that under her management we're going to make a packet."

"Her 'management'?"

"She's my new manager – did I not mention it?"

"No."

"She said you advised her to quit lap dancing and to go into management instead."

"What? I did not!"

"Well, you said something to her. She doesn't want to be the talent any more. So now *I'm* the talent. We're relaunching me as a solo artist. Steel Warriors, crappy computer courses – that's all in the past now. I've got genuine star quality, Charlie says, and we have to tap it."

"I'm glad."

"I don't need your approval, Grace."

"I was just wishing you luck, that's all."

"We don't need luck either. Charlie is going to make us millions!"

Then he bowed his head, and his face was so tortured that for a moment she was frightened.

"What is it, Nick? What's wrong? Is it one of the kids? Are they sick?"

"She wants me to enter the Eurovision," he blurted.

"What?"

"I know. Imagine! From Steel Warriors to Johnny fucking

239

Logan." He rubbed his eyes and for a moment Grace thought he was going to cry. "She wants me to give up rock 'n' roll and write ballads. She says that if I win the Eurovision then Scandinavia is my oyster. A number one in Finland could keep us afloat for a year. Sweden, and you're talking a new house."

Grace didn't really know what to say. To express any kind of enthusiasm would be very false, given that it had been an annual family pastime to mercilessly slag off the Eurovision, from the bad haircuts to the risible lyrics and the naff dance routines. *'Nul point!'* she and Nick would roar derisively at the television. How they despised those people: so desperate for success that they would stand up in spangly pink outfits and make fools of themselves in front of a hundred million people.

"I believe the costumes are more stylish now," she said carefully.

"Yes," said Nick, after a moment. "And Celine Dion did very well out of it, Charlie says."

"Oh, she's right! And Abba! And, um, Buck's Fizz."

There was a little silence. Three weeks ago Grace might have left it at that. Now she couldn't. "It's a ridiculous idea, Nick!"

Nick looked relieved, as though she had proved that he was not in fact going mad. "She's got her heart set on it."

"It's one thing to give up rock music – the thing you love! But to sell your soul?"

A bit of colour was creeping back into his cheeks now. "I know! But try telling her that."

"I will!"

"You will?"

Shit. She hadn't really been serious. So it was a relief when Nick added, "Thanks anyway, Grace, but it would really have to come from me."

"Well, then, say it to her!" she cried, remembering that sweat-filled night in the SFX – and Nick, the most alive she had ever seen him. "You've got to stand up for what you believe in, Nick!

Surely there have to be some things in this life that we can't compromise on? I mean, what's the point in it – in any of it – if we end up only half a person?"

She wasn't sure where this was coming from, but right now she believed it completely. Nick believed her too.

"You know something? You're right! Just because I'm going to marry her doesn't mean I have to sell out! Just because I have an ex-wife and three kids to support – "

"Four now."

"Four – and nowhere to live and no income doesn't mean I should demean myself!" "No, I'm going to tell her straight out that I'll have nothing to do with the Eurovision! I'll tell her right now!"

"Good for you!"

He stopped by the door. "You know, I never thought you were like this."

"Like what?"

"I don't know. Cool."

She gave a little laugh. "I was always cool. You just never bothered with me. You were too busy with your band."

"You were our number one groupie," he said fondly. "Derek and Mick even thought we should ask you to join the group."

"Me?"

"Yeh. They said it would broaden our appeal. You were okay-looking back then. Derek said you reminded him of Susie Quattro. That you both looked a bit . . . what was it he said? Dangerous."

Grace had a flash of déjà vu. Dennis the Menace and Bewleys.

"My black and white striped scarf," she whispered in wonder. "He must have seen me wearing it." It had become an omen now, a thing of great significance in her life.

"No, it was that pair of black leather pants you used to own. Stuck to you like glue. He said they gave him a stiffy every time you wore them." He frowned. "I never liked it when he spoke about you like that. I said to him, she's my kid sister for Chrissake, go and throw your leg over someone else."

"Thank you," Grace said, faintly.

"Anyway, it didn't work out," Nick finished up.

"Why?"

"What?"

"Why didn't you ask me to be in the band?"

Nick laughed. "You? In a band? Didn't figure it'd be part of your life plan. No money, no security. Even at sixteen it wouldn't do!"

"You're probably right," she said, still smiling.

She didn't tell him that she'd actually had a life plan when she was sixteen, carefully written down on a piece of pink notepaper which she had sellotaped to the underside of her sock drawer. On it was a list of top ten careers. Number one was being a famous actress. That had dropped to number two after she had read a book on fearless women explorers. Undercover police work or being an international spy, the old reliables, had featured heavily on the list too, along with circus trapeze work (her thighs had been slimmer then), and an untitled one that involved wearing very few clothes and which was probably a career in the sex industry only she hadn't realised it at the time.

Selling property was not on the list. At sixteen, Grace Tynan had had great hopes and dreams for herself. Back then she could have been anyone she wanted. Maybe she still could.

She picked up the phone.

"I handed in my notice today," she told Adam sleepily in bed that night. She had a satisfied kind of feeling, as though she had finally done something she had meant to do for ages. Well, technically she still had to put it in writing to the partners – singing, 'I'm not coming back, I'm not coming back', on Natalie's office answering machine would probably not count as official notice.

"Good for you," he said. "I finished with my girlfriend today."

Her eyes sprang open in the dark. "What?"

"I broke up with her."

"I'm sorry, Adam."

"I'm not."

"Well, the distance . . . it's hard when you're away from each other . . ."

"It has nothing to do with the distance." She felt him looking at her in the dark. "Grace, do you not think it's time we stopped all the bullshit? I need to know how you feel about me."

She lay very still in the bed. Perhaps he would think she had fallen asleep.

No such luck.

"Grace?"

"Yes, yes," she said.

"We need to talk," he declared. "We've needed to talk for a few days now."

"Have we? It's just that it's a bit late now, and you have lots of, um, campaigning to do tomorrow – "

"Are you putting me off?"

"No. I'm just thinking."

She wasn't. Or, at least, nothing coherent. How could she rationalise and verbalise feelings that she wasn't even sure of herself? How would she translate those light, airy, effervescent feelings she had whenever she was with him into cold, hard words that might be taken down and used against her?

"Because I think I'm in love with you, Grace," he declared. He appeared to have no such problem. But he was like that, Adam. With him everything was straight down the line. No nasty blurred edges, just neat black and white, even when it came to emotions. But that was part of his attraction for her.

"How is she?" she asked eventually.

Adam was suspicious. "Who?"

"Your girlfriend."

"My girlfriend?"

"Yes."

"What has she got to do with anything?"

Grace looked at him indignantly "You've just split up with her! Told her it's over! She's probably nursing a broken heart right now!" Men never thought of these things. The hardest bit for them was the actual act of breaking up. Women knew that the really horrible bit came days, weeks, even months afterwards, when the sight of that special brand of bubble bath in the supermarket was enough to bring you to your knees, sobbing, right there in the middle of the Personal Hygiene section. And as for restaurants! There were certain eateries that some of Grace's friends still refused to go to, for fear of collapsing with the weight of memories. And this was years afterwards! Trying to organise a girls' night out these days required considerable diplomatic skills, and the very latest copy of the Restaurant Guide.

"Imagine not even knowing how she was taking the whole thing!" she added, getting annoyed now. "Poor Babe!"

"Who the hell is 'Babe'?" Adam said.

Grace was embarrassed. "Ah, nobody."

"Look, Amanda will be fine. She has loads of friends and family."

Amanda. Grace tried out the name in her head. A classy name, of course, for a girl like Babe. Nobody would ever dare call her Mandy, or anything common like that. She wondered what her surname was. Something French, possibly. Or with a double barrel. It certainly wouldn't be Tynan.

"Did you love her?" she asked, almost in love with the girl herself.

Adam hoisted himself up onto one elbow. "What is this? Why are we talking about my girlfriend – my ex-girlfriend – when we should be talking about us?"

"I was just wondering!"

"Yes, of course I loved her at some point – I wouldn't have been with her for four years otherwise."

Four years! Babe must have been a childhood sweetheart. Grace

244

could just picture her – a beautiful little girl at the bottom of the street playing with a hula-hoop, her blonde pigtails bouncing, while all the neighbourhood boys looked on longingly from their chopper bikes.

"So what happened?" she asked. This was better than a Mills & Boon.

He looked impatient. "Nothing happened. Look, it was coming for a while. We were too different. It would never have worked out."

"How different?"

"Oh, Grace!"

"Does she not believe in anti-nuclear politics or something?" she said doggedly.

"Of course she does – she's extremely active, that's how we met," he said. "I meant background. Her family, well, they're pretty well off."

Filthy rich too! Babe began to take on mythical status in Grace's head, who now had a firm vision of a Miss World type lounging on a yacht, coordinating Save The Whale campaigns from a pink mobile phone. How could Adam be so foolish as to break up with her? For Grace? (Not that Grace was putting herself down or anything, but honestly, if any sane person were given the choice they'd take Amanda. Grace herself would.)

"Is her money such a problem?"

"Money is not what I'm about!" Adam exploded. "Jesus, if you don't know that much about me!"

She did. The very sight of cold hard cash seemed to greatly offend him. Amanda must have a truly captivating personality if he had been prepared to overlook her millions in the first instance.

"Pretend she doesn't have any. Pretend she's broke!" she suggested brightly.

He gave her a peculiar look. "Grace, I've just told you I've split up with my girlfriend because of you. I've just told you I'm in love with you. And you're trying to get me back with her?"

Was she? Perhaps she just couldn't believe that he had done such a thing for her: Grace Tynan, thirty-four-year-old mother of two, estate agent. She listened to Lite FM, for God's sake.

"I'm just afraid that you've done something rash," she said humbly.

"I am well aware of what I've done." He lifted his head proudly. "It wasn't easy, but there comes a time when you have to decide what is important to you. *Who* is important. And I've made my decision and I'll stick with it." He added, "And now it's up to you."

To do what? Break up with Ewan? "Adam . . . all this, it's obviously a bit of a surprise," she said with admirable understatement.

"I know. But I can't go on like this, Grace. Pretending that we're just having a roll in the hay, a bit of slap and tickle, and that when it's all over we'll go our separate ways as though none of it matters. When it does. To me anyway."

"I never thought of it as a bit of slap and tickle either," she said.

"You do! You're always thinking about sex! We're always *having* sex!"

"But that's what people do at the beginning of a relationship," she protested. Have sex and visit art museums. Didn't he know anything?

"I think we're past the beginning," he said rather ominously. "Don't you?"

"I think – I think – I think . . ." she stuttered, desperately trying to buy time. Oh, she would just ask for it. "I need more time!"

There was little silence.

"That sounds to me like a bit of a cop-out, Grace."

"It's not! Look, Adam, I'm having a wonderful time with you. The best! I've never met anyone like you before. I've never *felt* like this before." She flopped back in the bed. "I just didn't think past the beginning bit, that's all."

"Neither did I," he admitted. "I didn't ask to fall in love, Grace. I didn't want to break up with my girlfriend. But I did fall in love. And I need to know how you feel."

There was a great big expectant pause.

"You want to know whether I'll go and live with you in a mud hut on the beach?" She gave a little laugh.

Her levity was not appreciated.

"You know what I mean, Grace. You're going to have to make up your mind."

It had the horrible feel of an ultimatum, and she looked at him, a bit shocked.

"You mean choose between you and my husband?"

He didn't answer.

"Guess how hot it gets at the centre of a nuclear explosion?"

"A thousand degrees?"

"Wrong! Several million degrees!" Martine said. "You'd be vaporised. Kaput! Nothing left but your shadow."

"I'd take shelter in a bunker," Julia retaliated as she cracked open her second can of cider (she would dispose carefully of the cans and Grace need never know).

"No good. All the oxygen would be sucked out of the atmosphere and you'd suffocate."

"I'd drive off in my car then!"

"Forget it. Radioactive rain can fall up to a thousand miles away. You couldn't drive fast enough!"

Julia threw up a hand in defeat. "We're all sunk then!"

"Exactly!" said Martine, red-faced. "Which is why we've got to stop all nuclear development, Julia."

"Let's kidnap the festival lead act and say we're not giving him back until the MOX shipment is stopped," Julia begged.

"Oh! You've been talking to Adam!"

"He has a point. Maybe we need to be a bit more radical."

"This is my group!" Martine declared. "And we'll do things my way. How can we hope to be taken seriously if we go around breaking the law?"

"I suppose," Julia said, half-heartedly. Martine was far too earnest for her own good sometimes.

"I think he's turning Joey against me too," Martine said darkly.

"Yes, yes – now, tell me again what kind of internal injuries I might suffer if I was within half a mile of a nuclear blast." It was quite fascinating.

But Martine was yawning. "I'm going to bed, Julia. And you should too. I promised Grace I wouldn't keep you up too late."

"Not everything has to go through Grace," Julia protested. Still, she didn't say it too loudly; only for Grace, Julia might very well be in Gillian's less-than-tender care right now. And it wasn't as though Grace suffocated her or anything. No, Grace understood boundaries and the value of free time. They had a kind of an unspoken understanding about this free time; it was theirs alone, and no explanations were required on either part.

In that way it was almost a professional relationship, Julia thought, like that between patient and carer. Which suited her just fine.

"Do you need some help up the stairs?" Martine asked.

"No, no. I can manage." She was still on one crutch, but didn't want Martine to see her as incapacitated; otherwise she might not let her come along on Saturday.

"At least you'll have a bit of peace on Monday," Martine said.

"Why, what's happening Monday?"

"We're leaving, of course."

Julia was shocked, but hadn't the faintest idea why. It wasn't as though she'd thought they would stay in her house forever. She just hadn't expected it to be so soon, that was all.

"You'll be exhausted after the festival. Why don't you stay another couple of days?" she said.

"We can't. We're flying to Wales to meet the MOX shipment when it arrives. All the earth groups are going – there's going to be a massive demonstration." She kissed Julia on the cheek. "Good night, Julia. And thanks for everything."

It was almost like she was already saying goodbye.

Julia sat there in JJ's old red armchair for a long time after Martine had gone out to her tent at the bottom of the garden. The sheen had gone off the day somehow. And she had that chilly feeling again. But she would have to go out to the shed to put on the heating, out into the dark on her own.

The telephone rang. It sounded very loud in the stillness of the house. Who could be ringing at ten past one?

She picked up the receiver. "Hello?"

There was no reply.

"Hello?" she said again.

Then, somebody breathing: heavy breathing, loud and coarse and distorted and which seemed to ooze out of the receiver at her malevolently.

She didn't know what to do. So she slammed the phone down and stood looking at it, dry-mouthed. She had an eerie, creepy feeling, like there was someone in the house with her.

And of course there was. Grace was upstairs asleep in bed. Charlie and young Gavin too, and Adam. Martine was in her tent at the bottom of the garden, for heaven's sake! She had plenty of people around her. Plenty of people to protect her.

But they would be gone on Monday. All of them. Grace too.

There was a peculiar tightness in her throat now that she tried to swallow down but couldn't. The walls seem to close in on her and she wanted to turn around and leave – to run out of the place fast. She took a breath. It was ridiculous: to be so afraid of her own living-room. Of her own home, for heaven's sake! She would be fine. Fine. She had lived on her own for two years. There was no need to think that she couldn't cope again, even with silly phone calls. They were just cowards, that was all.

But the feeling kept rising in her – panic, coming from the pit of her stomach and roaring up through her like some wild thing out of control, crippling her. She hunched over, and said, "Grace . . ."

But Grace, asleep upstairs, wouldn't hear that.

Her throat was so closed that she couldn't breathe properly. She lurched over for the support of a chair, knocking the can of cider to the floor. It splashed on her legs but she didn't feel it. She was going to pass out.

"Julia? Julia!"

She felt hands on her shoulders, half-lifting and half-pulling her across the carpet. Then the support of cushions as she was eased down into a chair.

"Are you all right?" Frank said over her.

"Yes, fine . . . Frank, what are you doing?" His hands were on her head, pushing.

"Your brain needs to be lower than your heart." He was trying to force her head down between her knees. "Deep breaths!"

For the second time that evening Julia almost passed out. She managed, "Frank, you're choking me!"

He let go. And gradually the black dots stopped dancing before her eyes. She felt the tightness in her chest disappear and the strength come back into her legs. She sat up slowly. "I'm fine now."

Frank shook his head in disbelief. "Fine! You're out of your skull on cider."

"I am not out of my skull on cider."

"What's this then?" He picked up the incriminating can of cider. "Wait till I tell Grace!"

"There's no need to tell Grace . . . I only had two cans, I'm not drunk, okay?"

He wasn't convinced. "What then? Your foot?"

"I don't know." She didn't want to tell him it had been a panic attack, pure and simple. It would sound so feeble and weak. "Maybe I had some reaction to those new pills."

"I'll ring Michael."

"No."

"He really should know about this. He might want to call a doctor – "

"I said no, Frank." Her tone stopped him in his tracks. "Thanks anyway, but I can manage."

"Hardly."

To divert him, she said, "What are you doing here anyway?"

"I was on the Internet late with Sandy and I was just going to bed when I saw your kitchen light still on, and thought I'd come over to check whether you were okay. But the next time I won't bother. Good night."

She was taken aback by his over-reaction. "Frank, wait. Are you all right?"

"Yes. No."

"What's wrong?"

He looked a bit pale. "The results of Sandy's tests came back."

"Oh, yes?" Grace had mentioned something.

"They're not good."

"What's wrong with her?"

"The doctors think she has some kind of kidney malfunction."

"What?"

"They're not sure exactly what yet. It might be viral. Anyhow, the thing is, her system is being flooded with impurities and that's why she's been feeling so tired lately."

"I'm sorry to hear that, Frank."

"It's a bit of a shock, all right."

"Which kidney is it?"

"Both."

"Both! At the same time?"

"That's why the doctors think it might be an infection of some sort."

"I'm sure they know what they're doing," Julia said. "She'll be back on her feet in no time, you'll see."

"Yes," Frank said bravely. "That's just what I said to her in an email just now. I told her that everything would be just fine."

The phone rang again. Julia gave a little cry and spun around to look at it.

"Bit late to be ringing anyone," Frank grumbled.

Julia just stared at it.

"Here, I'll answer it if you want," Frank said.

But Julia grabbed his arm. "Don't," she hissed.

"What?"

"It's her again."

Frank was mystified. "Who?"

"I just got a call a minute ago. An obscene call. She's trying to frighten me."

The phone kept ringing.

"Who, for heaven's sake?"

"Gillian!"

Frank was incredulous. "What?"

"I wouldn't go to her silly coffee morning. Michael said she'd take it badly. But I didn't think she'd stoop this low."

"What did she say to you on the phone?"

"Nothing . . . I mean, she didn't *speak*."

"How do you know it's her then?"

"Because she's malevolent and cowardly and she can't bear it when Michael gives me any little bit of attention at all."

The phone kept ringing and ringing.

"I'm going to answer it," Frank declared.

"No! I won't give her the satisfaction – "

"We don't know it's her!"

"I know it's her," Julia said grimly. "I've never been surer of anything in my life."

Frank said, "Even if it is – which I very much doubt – then maybe a man's voice will scare her off."

Without further argument he picked it up. "Hello?"

It was Ewan Tynan, calling from America.

"Oh." Frank looked at Julia, and asked Ewan, "Did you just ring a minute ago?"

Ewan told him no. Then he asked to speak to Grace. It was an emergency.

Jamie had grown breasts.

"Ewan, what on earth are you talking about?"

"Breasts, Grace. Two little lumps of things on his chest. With nipples on top. I'm looking at them now!"

He sounded vaguely hysterical. Grace had to sit down at the kitchen table. Her heart was still thudding unpleasantly from the fact of a phone call in the middle of the night in the first place.

"Okay, Ewan, let's just take this slowly, all right? Are you sure they're not bruises or something?"

"Bruises?"

"Maybe he knocked against something – oh, look, I'm just trying to get a clearer picture here!"

"They are not bruises," he said quite definitely.

"An allergy then? Has he eaten anything peculiar over there that might have made him swell up? Those grits?"

"No. Anyway, there's no other part of him swollen. Just his chest."

It had been a wild hope. "How long did they take to grow?"

"What?"

"His breasts, Ewan! Did they . . . bud over a few days? Or just spring up overnight?"

"I don't know."

"You don't know! Does everything pass you by, Ewan? Do you observe anything that isn't to do with work?"

"For God's sake, Grace! You expect me to go around all day watching his chest? *You* wouldn't!"

"I'd have noticed a pair of breasts if I was there!"

"Well, you're not here, are you! I am! I'm the one who has to deal with this, not you! He's been off for a few days, okay? I thought it might have been a damned tummy ache or something!

He went around hunched over the whole time – how the hell was I supposed to know he was hiding breasts!"

His voice was perilously high again. Grace didn't think she'd ever heard him so uncollected before. The stress of looking after two boys single-handed must be getting to him. That, and the heat.

She went on in a much nicer voice, "Would you be able to tell me how big they are? Just roughly."

There was an uncertain silence. Ewan had never had a great interest in such things. "Not as big as yours," he declared eventually.

"I should hope not." And hers had grown a size too, with all the weight she'd put on.

"They're kind of pert," he elaborated. "The way you see on young girls."

"Ewan!"

"I'm just trying to explain here!" He sounded agonised. She could almost see him forming embarrassed shapes with his hands. "About as big as that bikini top you bought by mistake last year. What size was that?"

"32A?"

"That's it!"

Oh God. Jamie – with size 32A breasts? Her first training bra had only been 28AA.

"Is he upset?" she said, her heart twisting in sympathy.

"Of course he's upset! He's a boy! And overnight he's grown a pair of tits!"

"Ewan!" There was no need to be crude.

He took a shaky breath. "Sorry. It's taken us all by surprise. He never said a thing – just refused to go diving. It makes sense now, of course."

It was the first she'd heard of diving. But then another thought struck her.

"What about Neil?" she asked in dread. "He hasn't . . . ?"

"Oh, no. Flat as a pancake. I just had a look."

Thank God. But it would make it worse on Jamie. "You *are* talking to him about this, aren't you?" she asked.

"What?"

"Supporting him, Ewan." This seemed an unfortunate choice of words, so she added, "Reassuring him."

Ewan said, "No, Grace, I've put him in a corner and totally ignored him."

"I didn't mean – "

"Of course I'm talking to him. But it's kind of hard to explain to a boy why he's suddenly grown a couple of puppies like that."

"Ewan. That is exactly the kind of thing *not* to say."

"Look, there'll be plenty of time for talking later," he said impatiently. "We need action. I'm ringing you to find out what we should do."

Good question. She felt ridiculously helpless, sitting there on a hard wooden chair in Adam's red *Save The World* T-shirt and precious little else. And shaky, too, after the news – well, obviously it wasn't as bad as a phone call saying Jamie was very sick or something, or badly injured. But it was still unexpected to say the least.

"Well?" said Ewan expectantly, irritating her. Couldn't he take charge for once?

"Let me speak to Jamie," she said.

"Great," he said, sounding relieved. "And while you're sorting him out, I suppose I could look up the phone book and call a doctor."

Grace plucked nervously at her T-shirt as she waited for the handover to take place. What on earth was she to say to him? That these things happen? That it was perfectly normal? (She could just imagine gym class at school.) No, none of her usual reassurances or guarantees could be applied in this instance.

A voice came on the phone. "Mum?"

"Jamie?"

255

He burst into tears. "I want to come home!"

"Oh, Jamie." She swallowed back tears of her own. "Look, I know this is hard. Dad has been telling me all about it."

"I'm an embarrassment to him," Jamie said, crying harder.

"You are not!"

"I am. He tries not to look at my chest, and he keeps asking me do I want to have a lie-down, like I'm sick or something! And Neil says they're going to have to cut them off in the hospital."

"Sweetheart! Nobody is cutting them off." She was raging with Ewan for not nipping that one in the bud.

Jamie went on, "Neil says I'll have to get a job in a circus freak show, or on a smutty TV programme – Mum, who's Benny Hill?"

"Nobody, it doesn't matter. Listen, the very next time Neil says something like that, you ring me straightaway, do you hear me? I'll deal with him," she said grimly.

Her heart was all Jamie's at the moment. Jamie – her delicate little boy! Much better had the whole thing happened to Neil really. He would probably have turned them into assets and made a fortune out of the tabloids.

"Mum, what are we going to do? I can't go back to school the week after next with boobs!"

She made her voice very bright and breezy. "Don't be silly now. Whatever this thing is, we're going to sort it out. It's probably something very simple, maybe an allergy or something – " she crossed her fingers behind her back – "which the doctors will know when they examine you. Okay?"

"Okay," he said. He had stopped crying.

"I'll just bet that you're not the first boy in the world this has happened to, and you won't be the last." At last she'd found one of her old reassurances that could apply – surely it must be true, even in the case of renegade breasts?

Jamie appeared to think so. "I suppose."

"Now put Dad back on. I'll talk to you tomorrow, all right?"

"Yeh."

After a long moment Ewan was back on. "Well done," he said, sounding quite chirpy now. "Whatever you said to him really calmed him down."

"Did you find the number of a doctor?"

"I did."

"And it mightn't be a bad idea to order in a pizza and rent a film – take his mind off things."

He must have sensed recrimination in her voice or something, because he said, "Grace, this isn't exactly easy, you know. The last thing you expect on a Disney holiday is to find that your son has grown a pair of breasts."

"I know, Ewan."

They had probably been bouncing merrily under his nose like *Baywatch* extras for days and he hadn't noticed. Although, in fairness, Grace would bet that Jamie had been doing his best to hide them, possibly even strapping them down – all those long sessions in the bathroom! – for how could he confide such a thing to a father and brother whose only thought was the next gung-ho activity? It would be like confessing to periods in a rugby locker room.

"Right, well, ring me in the morning and tell me what the doctor says," she instructed Ewan. "I'll try to find out more this end."

"Okay," he said. "And Grace?"

"What is it, Ewan," she said impatiently, expecting more excuses and apologies.

"Where were you when the phone rang?"

She sat very still. "What?"

"Mrs Carr, it seemed she couldn't find you. I thought it was a bit funny, given that it's the middle of the night over there."

"I was just in the bathroom," she said, amazed that her voice sounded so normal. "Call me tomorrow." She hung up before he could ask anything else.

FOURTEEN

Even in the midst of all the upset, the sleeplessness, the frantic chats with Natalie's sister-in-law who was a doctor, the phone calls back and forth to the States, Grace could not conceal her sense of triumph; of victory. She hated herself for feeling such things, of course, given the seriousness of the situation, but she couldn't help it: they still needed her. Desperately. Right now she was the only person who would do. Oh, how it made her heart sing! In fact, it was difficult to maintain the required level of gravity at all times.

"Boobs – isn't it awful!" she sang happily to Julia.

Julia looked at her rather peculiarly.

"Poor little mite," Grace added guiltily.

Of course it was awful – but wasn't every cloud allowed a little silver lining? And if it benefited Grace in this case, was that so awful either? No longer would she be forced to retell bad jokes or perform incredible tricks with foodstuffs in an effort to get their attention. An unexpected twist of fate had brought her boys back to her (well, Jamie anyway. God only knows what it would take for Neil to need her again. The growth of a second willy, perhaps.) She felt as if her whole world had shifted on its axis and suddenly come right again.

It was hard to hide her feelings from Ewan, even though she did her best – Jamie was in the throes of a crisis, after all, and now wasn't the time to go chortling loudly to her husband that she was top dog again and he was out, buster! But it was there in her tone, which had acquired a new confidence and authority. "Put him on to me, will you?" she would instruct Ewan calmly in the days that followed, as though she were an eminent surgeon about to perform a life-saving operation while he was merely the nurse in the background appointed to wipe her brow.

"Grace," he'd said on the phone yesterday, "with all due respect, I think I know how to put on a Band-aid."

"I'm not saying you don't. I'm just reminding you that you need to make sure the area underneath is dry first, that's all. Sometimes you forget," she said nicely. He did too. (This was nothing to do with Jamie's breasts – Neil had skinned a knee whilst roller-blading. But Grace asserted her new authority in his case too.)

But his protests were token only, and at their end of their conversations he would hand over the phone to Jamie with indecent haste. "You always know what to say to him, Grace."

It was flattering. And she *did* know what to say to him. Ewan would only go upsetting him by pointing out other people who were a bit physically odd, as he had yesterday apparently. "I didn't want him thinking that he was the only one," he had said in his defence.

Grace had let it pass. She was letting a lot of things pass because she didn't want Jamie to get caught in the middle of an argument about shortcomings and inadequacies.

Also, she was a bit afraid that if she pushed Ewan too far, he might bring up again the subject of her exact whereabouts that night. Careful questioning of Julia had revealed a couple of worrying details.

"Well, when you weren't in your room or the bathroom, I

checked the back garden in case you couldn't sleep and had gone for a walk. You often went missing at night, I told him."

Grace had felt as though the air had been sucked out of her chest. "You told . . . Ewan this?"

"Well, it's a cordless phone, Grace. I was just kind of making conversation as I went." She must have seen something in Grace's face. "Did I do something wrong?"

"No, no!"

But Julia had been worried, anxious to clarify. "Remember last week when I lost my crutch in the middle of the night and I couldn't find you anywhere? And the time I woke up and the dressing was too tight and my foot had gone numb . . . I didn't tell Ewan this," she'd added hastily. "I'm just saying."

"Weak bladder. That's always been my problem," Grace had said limply.

"Yes, of course," Julia had replied, but her eyes were alert in a way they hadn't been before.

Grace felt she should come clean. This was Julia's house after all; and Grace was supposed to be looking after her, not having it off with one of her lodgers. And now that Julia was suspicious, it wouldn't be fair to ask her to lie on Grace's behalf should the occasion rise again.

"Julia," she had begun.

"Yes?"

"About Adam."

"Oh, I know. He's a lovely young man, isn't he? Look at all that wood he cut for me yesterday – and winter months and months away yet! I don't know what I'm going to do when he's gone." And she had given Grace one of those toothless smiles, as though she were much older and dafter than she actually was. "Now, I really must go and do my exercises."

"You haven't done your exercises in days."

"I'd quit while I was ahead if I were you," Julia had murmured, and hobbled off on her crutch.

"Testosterone!" Frank pronounced now.

Grace looked up, startled. Frank had got wind of the drama from Julia and was sitting at the kitchen table with a big thick medical book which he had brought over.

"Did you know that boys have eight hundred per cent more testosterone in their systems as teenagers than they have as toddlers?" he demanded.

"Eight hundred per cent!" Grace marvelled. It was along the lines of what the American doctor had mentioned to Ewan.

"It's a fact," Frank said, jabbing a finger at the book. "Your two lads are going around right now bursting with it!"

"But they're not teenagers yet."

"Near enough." He read some more. "My God. This testosterone stuff is responsible for all kinds of things!" he said in horrified fascination, as though he didn't possess any himself. "Aggression! Skin disorders! Poor concentration! Erectile, um, problems."

"Does it say anything about breasts?"

"I don't see anything here . . ." He turned a page, as though half hoping to see a colour illustration of a pair. "Oh, there might be something in this. *'Hormonal Imbalance. Can lead to excessive hair growth . . . sleep disorders . . . breasts!'*" he cried. Then he looked a bit embarrassed at his enthusiasm. Probably because he'd never seen a real, live pair in his life.

"What does it say?" Grace said eagerly.

He scanned the book in silence for a moment, then said, "It's nothing to do with testosterone at all!"

"What? But you just said it was!"

"It's oestrogen that's the culprit. It says here that when the body produces too much testosterone, some of it is converted into the female hormone oestrogen. This can cause swelling of the nipples and breasts!"

She was elated. She would go upstairs and ring Ewan immediately, and tell him about this. He would be very grateful.

"Aren't you marvellous for bringing that book around?" she said.

"Sandy sent it over to me."

Grace looked at the cover: *The Complete Guide to Illnesses and Disease.*

"How thoughtful of her," she said.

"She's just trying to keep me in the picture about her condition. I think she'd prefer me to read about it. She gets a bit embarrassed when she has to answer questions about it and stuff."

"She has a slight kidney problem, Frank. Not an STD."

Frank recoiled. "Look, Sandy is very private that way, okay? She feels very strongly that her body is a temple, and that anything concerning it is a matter for her and her Maker."

Convenient, Grace thought, but then felt bad. The woman had potentially a serious condition. "How is she, anyway?"

Frank busily turned to a dog-eared page in the book. "See all these symptoms? She's marked the ones that she has."

There were at least twenty symptoms marked. They were highlighted in a rather jazzy pink pen.

" '*Dry hair*'," Grace read. " '*Dull skin, fatigue . . .*' We've all experienced those at some point. It's called getting older."

"They're only the minor ones," Frank said grimly. "Read on."

She did. Highlighted in pink were '*extreme thirst*', '*chronic fatigue*', and '*dangerously low blood pressure*'. The accompanying photo was rather alarming: a woman lay prone in a hospital bed hooked up to a battery of machines, and it was arguable from her pallor whether she was alive or dead. It would frighten anyone.

"Frank, is this her way of telling you that it's serious?"

His face crumpled. "She said she didn't have the heart to come right out with it. Not that there's anything wrong with her heart," he added quickly. "But the doctors says she's not responding to standard antibiotic treatment. They've upgraded her condition to serious kidney malfunction."

"Oh, Frank."

"Yes, well, the worst things happen to the best people." It was unclear whether Sandy had said this herself.

"So what's going to happen now?" Grace enquired.

"Well, she's trying some alternative treatments. You know, tea tree oil and stuff."

"Frank, I don't know if tea tree oil would pack much of a punch against serious kidney malfunction."

"Obviously you have to have faith. Sandy prays a lot. And she meditates twice a day using powerful words – she repeats, 'My kidneys are working just fine!' five times, that kind of thing. You have to remain optimistic about these things, she says."

"And the doctors? Are they meditating too, or are they actually doing something about it?"

"Of course they're doing something about it!"

"What then? Different drugs? A corrective operation?"

"They don't know yet. But one thing is for sure – she has to go on dialysis straight away." He looked like he was fighting back tears. "I feel so helpless. She's over there weak and in pain – the most frightening time of her life! And I'm over here!"

"Go to her then," Grace said.

"What?"

"Get on a plane. She's your fiancée, Frank."

"Do you not think I've suggested it? I told her only this morning that she wasn't going to put me off this time! But she said she'd only blame herself if the house sale suffered because I wasn't here to look after it. And anyway, I gather she's in some isolation ward."

"I didn't realise kidney problems were contagious?"

"They're just taking precautions until they know exactly what's wrong."

"I'm sure they'd let you in. You are engaged."

He still dithered. "I don't want her worrying . . ."

Grace said, "Don't tell her then. Say nothing, just go over. And I'll make sure the house sale goes smoothly from this end. I promise."

Frank could hardly contain his excitement now. "If you're sure . . . I'll go and book a flight this minute. Imagine her face when I turn up at her bedside with a big bunch of red roses! Our very first meeting!"

Grace just said, "I hope she'll be everything you expect, Frank."

She was rather preoccupied when she met Adam on the stairs a few minutes later.

"Oh! Hi," she said.

"Hi."

It had all been a little peculiar since the night before last. His break-up with Amanda and the phone call from Ewan had sent things into a bit of a spin. There had been no time to talk. With the festival tomorrow he was out all hours. And she was on the phone all hours. They hadn't even met at meals.

He asked, "How's Jamie?"

"Okay, thanks. We think it might be oestrogen excess."

He nodded furiously. "I see. Ah, is it treatable?"

"Oh, yes. He'll be fine. Absolutely fine!"

There was a long silence.

"Well!" he said at last, his hands digging deep into his shorts pockets. "This is certainly embarrassing, isn't it!"

"Adam, I'm sorry," she began.

"About what?"

"Well, Jamie."

"It's hardly your fault, Grace. Probably something in the American milk."

She tried again. "I meant about me being so . . . distracted."

"Well, I've been pretty busy myself. They're moving the tents and stuff down nearer the festival site this afternoon. In broad daylight! Radical."

She had never heard him sound this bitter before. Relations must have deteriorated with Martine.

"Adam, can we talk properly?"

His eyes snapped up to meet hers, and the defensive jokey thing was gone. "About what?"

"You know what."

"There's no hurry, is there?" he said. "As least there hasn't been so far. You haven't exactly been seeking me out."

"This is an emergency," she pointed out.

"I know," he agreed. "Handy, that."

"Sorry?"

"Well, it's got you out of the whole thing nicely, hasn't it? You don't have to get into all that messy business of trying to let me down gently. Trying to extricate yourself from a little involvement that you had no intention of taking seriously."

He gave her a look that left her cold. Her Adam! With the perma-grin and the cheeky dreadlocks!

"Come on, be honest here, Grace. It's what you're really feeling, isn't it?"

"It is not!" She took a breath. "We haven't even had a chance to discuss any of this properly."

"Because you've been avoiding me."

"I have not."

"Why didn't you come to my room last night so?"

"I was tired!" This was partially true. But the look he gave her, so knowing, so cynical, annoyed her. "Stop sulking. My son is unwell and he needs my attention. I'm sorry if that doesn't suit you. I'm sorry if you feel neglected."

"Neglected?" he exploded. "I finished with my girlfriend because of you!"

"I didn't ask you to."

"You're starting to sound like a defence attorney, Grace."

She found that she was a bit shaky. "You're the one who suddenly decided to change the rules, Adam! And I'm supposed to drop everything and everybody for you? Drop my sons because you decided you were in love?"

"I can't help my feelings, Grace."

"Well I can't help them either!"

There was a horrible little silence.

Grace said, "I didn't mean it like that . . . but we're not living in fairytale land here, Adam. Whether we like it or not, I am married. I have responsibilities that I can't shake off on a whim."

"Not on a whim! I'm not asking you to do anything on a 'whim'! If I were asking you to do it, you'd be doing it for me."

How was she to answer that? Her hesitation must have stung him, because he said, "I don't know why I'm bothering here. You've already made up your mind, haven't you?"

"No, I haven't."

"You're already thinking about the trip back to Dublin, aren't you, and how you have to air the house and water the plants and prepare a big welcome home meal for the boys. Busy, busy, busy."

"Don't be so childish," she snapped.

"I knew you'd say that sooner or later," he said conversationally.

"My son needs me," she said.

"And you just can't bear not to go, Grace, can you? Nothing would stop you swooping in there like superwoman, ready to sort the whole thing out! Get those sleeves rolled up and muck in there until you have your three boys all sorted out to your satisfaction. And if you keep yourself busy enough looking after everybody else, then maybe you'll forget that this ever happened."

She was not going to listen to this . . . this rubbish. "Go take your anger out on someone else, Adam. I'm not staying for it."

"I gathered that much."

She was halfway to her bedroom when he said, "Did you care about me at all? Even a little bit?"

She turned around. "Of course I did. Do."

"Then come away with me, Grace."

"Adam – "

"I know, I know. You're not going to abandon your boys, and I'm not asking you to. Stay here then, and I'll come visit you. Come on, we can work it out! We'll rent a cottage for you and the boys, maybe near the sea, and I'll come at weekends when I'm not campaigning. Or I'll only come once a fortnight, or once a month, if that's what you want. We can make this happen, Grace, if you want to."

She must have looked tempted because he went on, very intense, very low, "Don't go back there, Grace. Don't go back to that. It's killing you, you know it is."

"Adam – "

"I love you more than he ever will."

There was a movement on the stairs and they both turned around. Natalie stood there, red-faced after the hike up the stairs. She had Rosie under one arm and a bag of chocolate doughnuts under the other.

"Hi there!" she tried brightly. "Say hello to Grace and Adam, Rosie!"

Rosie just stared mutely at them. And Natalie knew there was little point in pretending that she didn't realise what was going on. "Listen, this is none of my business. I just dropped around for a cup of coffee to try and take your mind off the breast thing. But obviously you're busy. Must go – say goodbye, Rosie!"

Rosie maintained her customary silence.

"Cheerio!" Natalie said, and she puffed off down the stairs, careful to take the doughnuts with her.

Grace and Adam looked at each other.

"That was unfortunate," Adam said. "But maybe it's for the best."

"What?"

"It's make or break time, Grace."

She was cross at his presumption. "I'll decide that."

She left him there and ran down the stairs after Natalie.

"I knew it! I knew you were up to something!"

"Natalie – "

"But with a *boy*, Grace!"

"He's twenty."

"He's hardly out of short pants." A thought struck Natalie, and she squealed, "In fact, he was *wearing* short pants!"

"He was wearing khaki cut-offs." This sounded vaguely ridiculous even to herself. "Look, what's bothering you, Natalie – the fact that he's younger or the fact that I'm having an affair?" Had an affair? She didn't know any more.

"My God . . . an affair!" Natalie moaned, mercifully diverted in another direction.

From the back seat of the car, Rosie said clearly, *"Jack and Jill went up the hill."*

"Oh, good girl!" Natalie said, clapping her hands. "Did you hear that, Grace? Anyway, listen, have you lost your bloody marbles?"

"I know this is a bit of a surprise to you."

"I'll say!"

"But really, it's none of your business."

"What?"

"It's not your concern. Thanks anyway."

"So I should just butt out and let you make a total mess of your life?"

"I have no intention of making a mess of my life."

"Grace, you're having an affair. You've given up your job, for God's sake! I don't suppose Ewan knows about that either, does he?"

"No – oh, and listen, about Frank's house."

"Relax. I sold it."

Grace was dismayed. "What?"

"I was just over with Frank to get the okay. He was so excited that he upgraded some airline ticket he was buying to business class. Now stop trying to change the subject. We were talking about Adam!"

"What about him?"

"What are you doing with him, Grace? Experimenting? Enjoying all that 'youthful energy'?"

"For heaven's sake, Natalie."

"What? Well, it's true, isn't it? They have loads of go in them at that age, I hear. You couldn't stop them – at it morning, noon and night!"

"Now you're just being crude."

Natalie was making it all out to be so cheap and lurid: the older woman desperate for sex, and the young, lithe man only too happy to oblige. Grace could perfectly understand why some women hid their relationships with younger men.

At the same time, it would be very false of her to claim that she wasn't having sex – and enjoying every minute of it.

"It's not just the sex!"

Natalie scoffed. "What, you're after him for his personality?"

"I think I might be in love with him."

"You . . .?" Natalie was aghast. "Please tell me you're joking."

"Jack and Jill went up the hill!" Rosie shouted.

"Yes, lovely, darling." Natalie twisted in the driver's seat to look at Grace straight on.

"And is he in love with you?"

The way she said it was so doubtful, so insultingly doubtful, that Grace felt compelled to boast, "Madly. You heard him yourself."

"Yes, yes. Look, Grace, I don't mean to take the gloss off things, but men that age . . . well, they can say things they don't necessarily mean."

"Adam does not say things he doesn't mean," Grace said coldly. Damn her anyway.

"But, Grace, they can get carried away."

"Does this have a point, Natalie?"

"Look, do you really know what you're doing? I mean, how

could this have happened?"

Good question. In retrospect she should have weighed up the pros and the cons a bit better before rushing right on in there. She, who could juggle a household budget with one hand tied behind her back! (And do the washing-up.)

"I don't know," she said honestly. "I guess it was just one of those impulsive things. I gave in to the heat of the moment."

"The heat of the moment!" Natalie looked like she would pass out at this point.

And suddenly Grace was sick of it. "Yes, such things do exist still, you know! Passion, romance, lust – remember those? Just sheer possibilities, Natalie? Or did you leave them behind in the mad rush, just like me?"

Natalie's mouth puckered; how come she was suddenly under attack? "Don't be excusing your actions, Grace."

"And don't you be hiding behind your outrage when you'd take it too if it were offered to you on a plate."

Now Natalie really did look outraged. "I would not!"

"You'd be crazy not to."

"Well . . . well . . . supposing Paul found out!"

"Supposing there was no chance that he ever would?"

"Jack and Jill – "

"Shut up, darling! I would never have an affair on Paul!"

"Not even if some gorgeous, charismatic man came along and plucked you from the ironing and the washing-up and told you how beautiful and desirable you were?"

"The ironing?" There was a slight catch in her throat. Rosie's stuff alone was a full-time job.

"Who made you feel special and strong, and like you were the only woman in the whole world?"

"There's no such man!" Natalie shouted jealously.

"There is!" Grace shouted back. "There is, and I bloody had him, and he makes me feel the best I've ever felt in my whole life, and I'm not a bit sorry!"

This outburst shocked them both, and they flopped back in their respective seats and fanned themselves furiously with road maps and spare nappies. The heat was cruel. Grace took a breath and suddenly she felt like laughing out loud: at the ridiculousness of the situation; at the choice she was facing. As Natalie said, how could she of all people get herself into this mess? And, oh, wasn't it invigorating?

Beside her, Natalie said, "Where could I find one?"

"What?"

"A boy."

"You want a boy?"

"Yes. Does Adam have any friends that might be interested in me, do you think?"

"Natalie – "

"After I have the baby, of course. And drop some of this weight – nobody could fancy me the way I am now. Rosie! Eat that banana or put it down."

Grace said, "Natalie, you don't want a boy."

But Natalie pitched forward in her seat, her swollen belly almost crushing the steering wheel, and her face red and upset. "I do! I bloody do. Why should you have all the fun? You think I don't deserve a boy or something?"

"No, I'm not saying that at all."

Natalie blurted, "Paul forgot our wedding anniversary."

"Oh."

"I know. Married seven years and he forgets our wedding anniversary. *Two children*, and he forgets our wedding anniversary!" She gave a little high-pitched sob. "I know it's just a small thing. But it's the sum of the small things, Grace. That's what's so upsetting! That's what wears you down in the end!"

Rosie threw a lump of banana. It hit Natalie squarely on the back of the head before sliding stickily away. She didn't seem to care. "Sometimes I look at him, Grace, and I know him so well that I can't stand him. The shape of his ears and the way he

271

answers the phone and the smell of his breath in the morning. Here I am, having another baby with him, and only this morning I wanted to smash his head in with the frying pan."

Rosie stopped chucking banana and listened with interest.

"Maybe I should have an affair!" Natalie went on. "Maybe then he might look at me as someone . . . well, as someone! Not just the eejit who cooks the dinner and holds down a full-time job and does the crèche run and gives birth to his children. Maybe I *should* start fucking someone else!"

"Fucking!" Rosie said.

Grace didn't quite know what to say. She hadn't meant to go encouraging Natalie. "I'm not sure you can look on it as a solution to marriage problems . . ."

"Why the hell not? It'd be like taking a course of vitamin pills! Or having colonic irrigation or something. I mean, look at you, Grace! It's done wonders for you!"

"Apart from my matted hair and lack of underwear?" she couldn't resist saying.

"Yes, well," Natalie said. "What I meant was that it's softened you up. Changed you for the better. You were always such a control freak."

A beat, then Grace said, "A control freak?"

Natalie prattled on, oblivious as usual to any offence she might cause. "We're always saying it in the office. Look at your desk, for heaven's sake! Never a paperclip out of place. And you do up a work plan for the week, like management tell us to do, and you actually stick to it. To be honest, you make some of us puke," she confided.

Grace tried to give a little laugh. But she was hurt. Natalie made her sound like such a goody-two shoes. Just because she was conscientious! Just because she was organised.

A working woman with two children *had* to be organised! If she didn't do the organising, then nobody else would bother and then, well, then . . . She tried to think of some dire consequences.

Then it just wouldn't get done she supposed, rather lamely. The world wouldn't actually stop turning or anything, now that she thought about it.

Natalie finally twigged that she might have put her foot in it. "Some of us envy you too, of course," she added hurriedly. "And I'm sure the boys appreciate you."

"Ewan is not a boy," she said sharply. "Why does everyone persist in calling him a boy? He's not a boy! He's a grown man, and it's about time everyone started realising that!"

Natalie was rather taken aback. "I wasn't referring to Ewan. I meant Jamie and Neil."

Grace was embarrassed now. But she said, "I knew that! I was just making the point. And what about Jamie and Neil?"

"Nothing," Natalie said.

"Are you saying I control them too?" Grace said loudly.

Natalie blanched. This had all gone horribly wrong. "I didn't suggest that for a second! All I meant was that you do so much for them – all the dental appointments you make for them and those healthy packed lunches and the way you drive them practically everywhere in case they get snatched by a man with a big bag hiding in a rhododendron – "

"Oh!" said Grace. She had once said this to Jamie, purely as an illustration of the dangers that might lurk should he wander off on his own. She hadn't meant for him to go around repeating it.

"The thing is, you . . . you care!" Natalie finished up, damningly. Then, in a spectacularly bold change of subject, she said sunnily, "So! Do you think he sees you as a mother figure?"

"Who?"

"Adam."

"I'm going to thump you, Natalie."

"What? Do you know if he even has a mother?"

"I've never asked." She added spitefully, "We're too busy having sex."

"Oh!" Natalie said.

Grace opened the car door.

"Hang on!" Natalie said. "You haven't said what you're going to do!"

"About what?"

"About Adam. Do pay attention," Natalie said crossly.

"I think he wants me to run away with him."

"What? Where?" Natalie screeched, and Grace thought that surely all this excitement couldn't be good for someone in her condition.

"I don't know. Tasmania, maybe."

"Tasmania? But what about Ewan? And the twins?"

"I know," Grace agreed.

"You couldn't leave him, Grace. Not for a boy." When no denial was immediately forthcoming, Natalie's jaw dropped another inch. "Grace!"

"Look, I don't know what I'm going to do about anything." She stepped out onto the drive and slammed the passenger door.

"But Grace . . .!"

"Bye. Safe home."

Raging, Natalie was left to manoeuvre her lumpy four-wheel drive with a hungry toddler out into the traffic while Grace drifted off across the lawn, her red kaftan swaying in the breeze.

FIFTEEN

"I don't believe this!" Gillian exploded. "She's saying that I've been ringing up and asking her the colour of her knickers?"

"Please don't talk about me like I'm not here," Julia said calmly.

"Answer the question then!"

"It wasn't about underwear."

"What then? Maybe I was shouting the word 'willy' at you, was that it?"

Michael blanched. "There's no need for that."

"Willy, willy, willy!" Gillian chanted.

"Ladies," Sergeant Daly said sharply. "There are children present."

Over by the door, Susan threw her eyes to heaven in despair. "I know what a willy is. I've seen loads of them."

"Go outside and wait in the car," Michael said sharply.

"But Dad – "

"Now."

She flounced out. Sergeant Daly said, "Right – let's take this from the beginning, will we?"

Gillian said, "If I'm going to be accused of making obscene phone calls, then I should at least be told what she allegedly heard!"

"She has a point," Sergeant Daly said.

"You were doing a breathing thing," Julia said.

"A breathing thing?"

"Don't pretend you don't know what I'm talking about."

"I don't."

"You do! You were doing a kind of heavy muffled breathing." This sounded a bit lame so she went on, "It was very threatening. Very intimidating! Frank was there." She turned to Sergeant Daly. "Have you asked him?"

"Not yet," he said.

Gillian, meanwhile, was doing a very good impression of being completely innocent. "She's bonkers," she said to Michael. "She's gone completely bonkers this time."

Michael, to his credit, didn't entertain her. He just looked anguished that all this had come to pass.

"Let's not bandy around insults here," Sergeant Daly murmured. Why didn't he just arrest Gillian and be done with it? Instead of standing around talking it over? The law had gone very soft these days, Julia thought darkly. "Look," he went on, "I asked us all to meet here in Julia's house today so that we might try and sort this thing out between us before it all got . . . official."

"I still want to lodge a complaint," Julia said defiantly.

"So do I," Gillian chimed in.

Julia looked at her. "Sorry?"

"You're not the only one who's upset by this, you know. My name has been blackened by these vicious, hurtful and – and untrue rumours!"

"Try telling that to a court," Julia said grandly. She wondered whether there would be a jury.

Still Michael said nothing. His eyes must surely be opened now, to what he had married: a spiteful, vengeful woman who had resorted to terrorising a pensioner. Julia was surprised that he hadn't left her.

Sergeant Daly consulted his notebook. "Have there been any

calls since, Julia?"

"No."

"Just that one?"

"Well, yes." But one call was all it took to wreck a person's confidence. Especially if you knew they were vulnerable to begin with.

"Right . . ." he said, in a very doubtful voice. Did he think she was making it up or something?

"Why aren't you bringing charges against her?" she demanded. "She has a motive!"

"And what might that be?" Gillian enquired.

"I didn't come to your coffee morning for deaf old farts!"

Gillian was furious. "They are not deaf! They have tinnitus."

"I have a touch of tinnitus," Sergeant Daly said. "Damned annoying."

"I'll give you the number of our support group afterwards," Gillian offered.

Buttering him up! Oh, she knew how to bend the law all right.

"I thought we were here to talk about obscene phone calls?" Julia said loudly.

"We are." Sergeant Daly closed his notebook with an impatient snap. "I was hoping this would resolve itself with the minimum of embarrassment, Julia. But I have to tell you – I went to the trouble of checking some phone records. And the call did not come from your daughter-in-law's home phone number on Wednesday night."

"Are you sure?"

"One hundred per cent."

There was a horrible little silence. "Could it have been a mobile number?" Julia enquired tentatively.

Michael finally said, "Gillian was in bed beside me that entire night. Unless she snuck under the duvet to do some heavy breathing at you, you've got the wrong person, Mammy."

He looked at her very coldly. Like she was the malevolent one here! After all the hurtful things Gillian had said about her tripping and falling down and dying alone! Was it any wonder she had made such a mistake?

"I'm sorry for accusing you in the wrong," she said to Gillian stiffly. "I can see that it must have been very . . . hurtful for you. I'm sorry," she repeated.

Sergeant Daly gave a heavy sigh. "Right, well, I think we've sorted that out." Then, completely ignoring Julia, he turned to Gillian and Michael and said, "I'm very sorry you had to be put through this. I know it's been upsetting for you, but obviously I had to investigate."

"Of course," Michael and Gillian murmured.

"And do bear in mind what I was telling you. There are obviously . . . outside influences at work here."

"We know," Michael and Gillian said grimly. And then they all shook hands!

Julia stood there smarting. There was no mention of her upset. No concern at the fact that she was now terrified of her own phone.

But Sergeant Daly said, "There was a problem at the central exchange that night. Quite a few people complained of buzzing noises from their phones."

"I know a buzzing noise from a breathing noise," Julia said, but she knew she just sounded even more foolish. Worse still, she sounded mistaken. Were her ears playing tricks on her?

"And how do you know the phone call wasn't for you at all?" Sergeant Daly went on. "It could have been for one of your lodgers! Of which you have quite a few, I hear. Did you ask any of them whether they were expecting a call?"

"No," Julia whispered, the bottom having just fallen entirely out of her case. It had never occurred to her, so convinced had she been that it was Gillian wreaking retribution.

"No!" Sergeant Daly skewered her with a very long look. "Consider all investigations into this matter suspended," he bit out. "I'll see myself out."

Julia was left to face Michael and Gillian over the kitchen table.

"I'm sorry," she said again. And she was. She let her head droop a little to convey this. "Truly sorry," she added for good measure.

"So you should be," Gillian said coldly. She was dressed all in white today. She was obviously going for the pure, innocent look.

"Yes, well, Mammy's apologised, I think we can leave it at that," Michael said.

"Maybe I could make everybody a cup of tea?" Julia said. She was anxious now to made amends.

"We don't want to put you to any trouble," Gillian said stiffly. The last time she'd had tea in Julia's house she had kept looking into the milk jug as though she suspected there was something growing inside it. And actually, there had been.

"Beer then?" Julia offered. "Or Scrumpy Jack – we have plenty of that. And I think there's a bottle of ouzo lying around somewhere as well that wasn't finished."

Michael looked worried. "Mammy, we've been talking to Sergeant Daly. And in the light of that discussion, and what I've seen with my own eyes in recent weeks, we'd like you to reconsider our offer to come and live with us." He added, "Despite the phone . . . mix-up."

"It was hardly a mix-up," Gillian snapped.

Michael said impatiently, "Gillian, can we just let this go?"

This was too much for Gillian. "She falsely accused me, Michael! And now we're begging her to come and live with us again?"

"Gillian, please," Michael hissed, casting an anxious look at Julia.

"No, really, Michael! It's too much!"

It was only fair that Julia put them out of their misery once and for all. "If I could just say something." She faced them over the kitchen table; her pudgy, unimaginative son and her fractious daughter-in-law (who was covered in little pink blobs of calamine lotion, she saw now. Was it mosquito season or what?) "Look," she said to them, "It's not that I don't appreciate your offer. It's very kind and . . . generous of you, given that I'm probably not the easiest person in the world to live with." She thought she heard Gillian give a bit of a snort, and acknowledged it with a bow of her head. "But this is my home. I don't want to leave it. I'm sorry if you've gone to all this trouble converting the garage, but I'm doing quite nicely by myself."

"Nicely?" Michael said, exploding finally. "Your lawn out there is overrun by crusties!"

As if to underline his point, there was a high-pitched roar from the garden outside.

Gillian tensed like a startled deer.

"Don't mind that. They're just warming up their vocal chords for the festival tomorrow," Julia explained kindly.

Michael and Gillian were looking at her with saucer eyes. "We're worried for your safety," Michael announced.

"My safety is not in question," she said.

"Sergeant Daly said there are plans to disrupt that music festival."

"There are no such plans. We are simply going to make our protest in a peaceful and non-confrontational manner."

Michael said to Gillian, "She's talking like a zombie. I told you – they've brainwashed her."

Julia said impatiently, "I haven't been brainwashed. I'm going along tomorrow of my own free will."

"To the . . . festival?"

"Yes. I quite like a bit of a sing-song."

"This is not funny, Mammy."

"I know it's not. A shipment of spent nuclear fuel is deadly serious for us all."

"Well, supposing . . . supposing it rains!"

"I'll be in a tent."

"A tent!" Michael was quivering in indignation now. "No, Mammy – I'm sorry, but I simply can't allow you to go. It's totally irresponsible in your condition!"

"You're not responsible for my condition," Julia said. Why did they persist in treating her like a wayward child?

"Daddy wouldn't have let you go!" Michael blurted.

A little shock of guilt ran through her. It wasn't that JJ would have objected – the notion!

It was more that this was the first time she had thought about him the whole day. She felt like she had betrayed him or something.

"Are there any tickets left?" Michael was saying now.

"I've already got my ticket," Julia told him.

"For us, I mean."

Julia wasn't sure she'd heard him correctly. "You . . . want to come to the festival?"

"You don't seriously think we can let you go on your own?"

"I won't be on my own. Grace is coming." She had no idea whether this was true or not, but it was the only ammunition she had left.

"Grace!" Michael snorted. "That woman never seems to be around when she's needed."

Suddenly Julia couldn't bear any more of them, so she said, "Where did Susan get to?"

"I sent her to the car."

"Well, she didn't stay there. Isn't that her out on the lawn there with Martine and young Gavin, getting love beads put into her hair?"

"What?" Gillian clattered over to the kitchen window. She moaned, "Oh, my God! Our little girl . . ."

"They're not permanent or anything."

But Gillian and Michael were elbowing each other out of the way in their haste to rescue their daughter from the vile influences of zealots. The back door slammed shut after them. The kitchen felt cool and airy again, and Julia inhaled deeply.

Grace's tomato plants were not doing well. For starters, there was no sign of any tomatoes. And the leaves were starting to turn black at the edges, like the lungs of a chain smoker.

She consulted Julia about them after her visitors had gone. "What can I give them? More plant food?"

"A decent burial," Julia muttered. "And for heaven's sake don't give them any more water." Grace immediately lowered the watering can. "The roots are rotting – look," Julia said. "And that goes for the basil too. Just leave things alone, Grace. Sometimes they do better."

Grace smarted – how was she supposed to know? She was only a learner when it came to gardening. And was there no end to the accusations of smothering today?

She picked up the trowel in a bit of a temper. What the hell did Natalie know anyway, about being a mother? Toddlers were so easy! Nothing on their minds except food and sleep and the occasional poo. Just wait till Rosie turned ten and wanted to buy records by bands called Suck. Or until she decided that her left buttock wasn't complete without a tattoo. Then Natalie could turn around and dish out advice. She seemed to think that you could just point them in the right direction and let them off, whilst congratulating yourself for having the courage to 'let them go'! Next thing you knew, you were on the receiving end of irate phone calls from the neighbour two doors up about broken windows and intimidation, or the school checking the truancy records. Or worse again, the hospital emergency room checking whether you had any dental records handy (all right, so this was a bit far-fetched, but not outside the realms of possibility).

No, there was a very fine line between glorious freedom and criminal irresponsibility, and often it was a parent's whole life's work to negotiate it. People didn't realise how difficult parenting was! On the one hand, you didn't want to be so liberal that you ended up with fourteen-year-olds sleeping with each other under your own roof – take Shane O'Leary's mother, who brought up Coco Pops for him and his naked girlfriend every morning before driving the pair of them to school. But on the other hand, you couldn't lock them up (although some of Grace's friends had tried, with moderate success). The thing, of course, was to find the right balance; which was wonderful in concept but usually completely unworkable in practice and you ended up veering towards one or the other end of the spectrum.

Grace was not a Coco Pop Parent and never had been. It wasn't because she didn't want to be; wouldn't every parent love to teach their pre-teen five simple recipes, give them a set of house keys and a packet of condoms, before swanning off into the sunset to pick up the threads of their own lives again? Lord knows it must be easier to let the little buggers run wild and free. Wouldn't she just love to do it, and go on the piss for an entire weekend or something!

She dug the trowel hard into the ground again, triumphantly unearthing a lump of rotting basil. "Take that!" she cried, and hurled it into the hedge. The action felt very symbolic somehow, very right in the light of her soul-searching, and she gleefully attacked the basil again, a little disappointed that it didn't offer more resistance. Perhaps the tomato plants might put up more of a fight.

"Excuse me?"

Grace looked up, red-faced and clutching the head of a severed plant. A girl was standing a cautious distance away, watching her warily.

"Hello there!" Grace said. "Just doing a little weeding!"

The girl was in her early twenties maybe, with long hair that was neither blonde nor brown but some unremarkable colour in between. She was thin and boyishly flat and wore the standard activist uniform of faded denims and some kind of loose multicoloured shirt. A rucksack was slung over her shoulder.

"If you're looking for Martine, she's out the front, I think," Grace told her, turning back to the basil.

"I'm not looking for Martine."

Grace tried to place the accent. South African? It wouldn't surprise Grace. Two activists from Cuba had arrived yesterday.

The girl said, "Is this where Adam is staying?"

Grace immediately placed the accent now: Tasmanian. She noted the airline luggage ticket on the girl's rucksack, and then she put down her trowel and stood up, heart beating a little fast.

"Amanda, isn't it? I'm Grace. Pleased to meet you."

She held out her hand. The girl hesitated, obviously confused.

"Adam has told me all about you," Grace assured her.

"Has he?" Amanda's thin, open face looked painfully hopeful, and all Grace's preconceptions of Babe were banished forever. This girl had never owned a pink mobile phone in her life! (She had money, though. Those runners on her feet cost more than Grace's weekly food bill. Grace had learned designer prices from the boys if nothing else.)

"I shouldn't really have come here, you see," Amanda said, looking over her shoulder a bit nervously. "We broke up the day before yesterday."

Grace had to bite back a sympathetic 'I know', and ended up saying, "Gosh!" instead, despite the fact that she couldn't ever remember saying the word in her life before.

"He says it's for the best," Amanda added miserably.

Grace nodded compassionately. The treachery! "Maybe he spoke in the heat of the moment," she murmured.

"I don't think so," Amanda said.

She looked so woebegone and downtrodden that Grace blurted, "Oh now, come along! You haven't flown all the way to Ireland to show him a face like that!"

Amanda looked slightly startled. But, really, Grace had expected Adam's girlfriend to have a little more bottle.

"Do you think he might want me back?" she asked meekly.

"I don't know, do I?" Grace said a little impatiently. "I mean, you've hardly talked to him yet! Nothing gets sorted in a quick phone conversation!" She saw from Amanda's face that perhaps she had said too much. "I mean, I presume all this was in a phone call . . .?"

"It was," Amanda said, looking a little more alive. "Not even face to face! A five-minute phone call where he had his little speech all prepared and I didn't get a chance to say hardly anything at all!"

"They're the worst kind of conversations!" Grace cried. "Especially long distance."

"Tell me about it!" Amanda agreed.

She really was quite pretty, Grace thought – lovely brown eyes when they looked directly at you, and yet another set of those glorious white even teeth. If you were to describe her in beauty terms, it would have to be 'natural'. A description of Grace right now would probably be 'has let herself go disgracefully'. Oh well.

Amanda said, "He's got someone else."

Grace felt a little sick. "He told you that?"

"Of course he didn't. Gave me all this stuff about how we weren't suited. But you always know these things, don't you?"

Grace thought of Ewan. "Do you?"

"Oh yes," Amanda said grimly. "It's probably one of the girls on the campaign. Some gorgeous girl with long blonde hair and a cute French accent." She gave a small bitter laugh. "You probably know her."

It was with great relief that Grace could state categorically, "There's only one girl here with a French accent and that's Martine. And I can assure you that Adam is not seeing Martine." Before she was forced down the road of ticking off the females in the house one by one, until it left only her, she said, "Are you sure you're not mistaken?"

"I know him," Amanda said definitely.

"Even if . . . even if he was seeing someone else, how do you know it's serious?"

"Well, I don't, I guess," Amanda said.

She looked less sure now and Grace moved quickly to press home her advantage. "You know what it's like being away from home! From your family, your friends – all the things that usually keep you grounded. Suddenly you meet someone attractive, they seem to be the answer to all your prayers, and bam! You get involved! And you might like them, you might even genuinely love them, but they're just in your life at a particular time, and they're absolutely right for that time in your life, but then suddenly everything shifts again, and . . ."

"And it's over?" Amanda said hopefully.

"Well, it might be."

"Thank God."

"But it might not. Oh, you just don't know what the future holds, do you!" Grace cried, agonised.

Amanda was watching her with a peculiar expression. Dear God, had she let too much slip?

But then Amanda said, "I wish you'd talk to him."

"Me?"

"Everything you've just said – it makes perfect sense!"

"Does it?"

"Absolutely! If you knew Adam – he's so passionate and intense, he never does anything in half-measures. And he probably met this girl while she was all needy and insecure – that's how I met him – and he looked on it as a challenge and got involved and now he thinks he's head over heels in love!" She was smiling indulgently now. "You know, he probably thinks he's going to take this girl home to Tasmania and set up home in a hut on the beach or something – that's his dream, teach tourists how to surf, you know? – but she's probably just a flash in the pan who means nothing to him at all if only he could see it!"

"Hmm," Grace said.

"That thing you were saying about the future?" Amanda said. "And what it might hold? Well, you see, I know what it holds for me and Adam!"

A job on the board of one of Daddy's multinationals, Grace thought rather maliciously.

Amanda looked radiant now. "I just need to tell him."

So much for lacking in confidence! And really, she wasn't that pretty after all. Flat as a washboard.

"Wouldn't you have to patch up the relationship before you start planning the future?" Grace couldn't help enquiring.

Amanda immediately looked lost and broken again, and Grace felt as though she had deliberately burst a toddler's balloon.

"Say you'll talk to him," Amanda begged. "You seem to know him quite well."

"You could say that," Grace murmured. "But really, it's not my place to interfere."

As if she were going to find Adam with the express purpose of putting herself down! Of talking him into getting back with Amanda! She didn't know whether she wanted him for herself yet or not.

Anyway, she didn't think she could look at him – all that stuff about him liking 'challenges'! Hadn't he said from the start that he wanted to corrupt her? It was almost as though he had looked upon her as some kind of project, much like his anti-nuclear work. He might have ended up falling in love with her, but somehow it took the gloss off things. It took the gloss off him.

Amanda was chewing contemplatively on her lower lip. (What was it with young people, Grace thought? Why couldn't they ever be still? Always worrying at some bit of themselves; poking and prodding and chewing).

"Maybe you're right," Amanda declared at last. "Maybe I should talk to him myself. I might be able to change his mind."

"Good luck to you," Grace said, with just the right hint of doubt. Well, she was allowed! "Here's Julia out now. I'm sure she'll let you have the living-room for a bit, if you want some privacy." She waved over. "Julia! Amanda here is looking for Adam."

She would stay out in the garden with the basil, she decided. She didn't know what she hoped the outcome would be; a passionate reconciliation, or else Adam might identify Grace as the new love of his life. Which obviously had a certain gratification value. But where would that leave poor Amanda?

Immediately Grace berated herself for harbouring such sympathies; surely femmes fatales weren't supposed to worry about the other woman? Perhaps because the other woman in this case was only a girl, and stealing her man on her rather made Grace feel like a big fat bully.

"Adam?" Julia said. "Oh, he's gone."

Grace said, "Sorry?"

"Yes, they needed someone to go on ahead of the main group tomorrow. To set up and things. He left in a bit of a hurry with Joey."

"What am I going to do now?" Amanda burst into tears.

Grace felt like doing the same. It had been a very emotional day. And, what with Ewan and the boys not arriving home until Sunday, she had half-expected another night with Adam.

But her upset wasn't noticed, of course; not with Amanda spluttering and choking like a walrus beside her. Then Julia – Grace's friend! – rushed forward to put an arm around the girl, rudely elbowing Grace and her pain aside.

"Now, now," she murmured to Amanda, before turning to Grace. "Put on the kettle for a cup of tea, would you?"

Tea!

"I have to see him! I have to talk to him!" Amanda sobbed pitifully.

Julia looked at Grace as if to ask what all the hysteria was about. Grace shrugged – *she* didn't know.

"This might call for something stronger than tea," Julia

decided. She led Amanda off across the lawn, and Grace heard her murmuring, "Everything's going to be all right. I have two litres of Strongbow in the kitchen press."

Grace was left alone with a handful of rotting basil and a stomach that felt as though it had just stepped off a roller-coaster. Oh, why did everything have to become so complicated? She had been having such a perfectly lovely time, and now it was all tough questions and hard decisions and soul-searching! She got a headache just thinking about it.

In fact, she might just sit down and have a rest. She threw the basil onto the lawn and flopped down into a deckchair. The fierce sun was adding to her light-headedness; for a moment there, she thought a young boy on the road out there was Jamie. The boy wore an Arsenal T-shirt, just like Jamie's, and had the same knock-kneed stance – imagine! It was probably because Jamie was on her mind so much, with the whole boob thing.

Then she sat up a bit in the deckchair. Surely that boy on the road couldn't have the exact same rucksack as Jamie too? With the same football stickers?

But it couldn't be – Jamie was in America, and would be until Sunday. Was she hallucinating in the heat? Worse, was she having some kind of near-death experience? Had all that blasted bending done her heart in?

But it was no hallucination. She saw Ewan now, stepping out of a taxi into the road, and dragging suitcases after him. Then Neil, brown as a berry and wearing a baseball cap backwards.

She was on her feet now, the deckchair knocked backwards, and her fist pressed hard to her chest. She couldn't believe it. They were here. Her children were home.

"*Jamie! Jamie! Neil!*" For some reason she didn't call out Ewan's name.

Then she was galloping across the lawn towards them, her arms outstretched, her heart hungry for them. And they were turning towards her in the road as if in slow motion, and then

. . . they were backing away from her. What was going on? Why was Jamie clutching Ewan, like he didn't recognise her or something? Her baby!

She stopped in the middle of the road, hot and cross now. "For heaven's sake, it's me. Your mother!"

"Mum?" Neil said doubtfully, his eyes wide as he took in this plump, hairy woman in a dirty red kaftan.

"Grace!" Ewan managed. "You look . . . different."

"What are you doing here?" she said, still a bit put out that such a glorious reunion had been spoiled by a case of mistaken identity.

"The airline phoned with a cancellation," Ewan said. "I asked Nick for the address of this place. We wanted to surprise you."

"And we did, didn't we!" Jamie said triumphantly, automatically plucking at his T-shirt to hide his breasts.

"Oh, Jamie! Come here!" she said, holding out her arms, and he ran into them, and she hugged him as though she would never let go. She whispered in his ear so that the others wouldn't hear. "How's your chest?"

"They've gone down a bit," he whispered back.

"Thank heaven." Her poor baby! She planted a big kiss on his forehead, and he let her.

She became aware of Ewan hovering.

"You don't mind, do you?" he said, half-joking. "I mean, maybe I should have rung first or something . . ." It kind of hung in the air.

She thought about Adam and Amanda and Julia and the antinuclear demonstration at the festival tomorrow, and gave her biggest, sunniest smile. "Don't be ridiculous! Come on in, everybody!"

SIXTEEN

"Who brought egg sandwiches?" Frank demanded. "They're stinking the whole bus out!"

He looked around, very accusatory.

"We didn't. We have tuna and sweetcorn, haven't we, Neil?" Jamie said timidly. He was afraid of Frank. But everyone had to be very nice to him today, apparently.

"Uh-huh," Neil replied. After the month in Florida, he had acquired a strong American accent.

Julia enquired, "What did you bring, Charlie?"

"Crisp bread with cottage cheese." Charlie pulled a face. "I'm on a diet."

"You don't need to go on a diet," Julia protested.

"I do! Here I am, planning a wedding, and I have thighs on me like a turkey, don't I, Nick?"

"Hm? Oh, yeh," said Nick, who seemed to have acquired an ability to tune out every time he heard the word 'wedding'.

Gavin piped up defensively, "Well, I think you're gorgeous, Mum."

"Thank you!" She said to Julia, "I've worked it out: I only need to lose a pound every six months and I'll be down to my target weight in time."

"Oh, that's very do-able," Julia said encouragingly.

"It is." Charlie smiled very bravely, given that it would be at least four years before Nick's divorce from Didi came through, under Irish law. None of her engagements had lasted beyond eighteen months. But she remained very optimistic, everybody thought.

Young Gavin gave a little look over at Neil and Jamie. They had runners with lights in the soles of them, and didn't have to talk about weddings with their mother.

"Does anybody want a toilet stop before we get on the motorway?" Martine called from the driver's seat.

"No, no!" everyone called, even though several of them actually did. But nobody wanted to upset Frank further by confessing to a perfectly functioning set of kidneys. Not when his fiancée was in a New York hospital at that very moment and listed as 'serious'.

"We'll soon have you there," Julia said to him encouragingly.

"You're very kind. Everybody has been very kind," he said.

They were driving him to the airport, as an act of solidarity, before turning back for the festival. He was flying to London, and then on to New York.

"How is she holding up?" Charlie enquired, leaning over to pat his hand.

"All right, under the circumstances. The doctors are still trying to figure out why her right kidney crashed like that."

It had been a terrible shock. And so sudden! One minute, she had been happily getting dialysis – well, not happily, obviously – and the next, her right kidney had packed up. That was the term written on her chart, she'd said, when she'd spoken to him last night.

Not that they'd actually spoken, of course, because they didn't allow mobile phones in the hospital. But she'd managed to sneakily use hers long enough to get on the Internet, surf some sites on kidney transplants, check the state of her medical insurance, and then compose a long e-mail to him, Frank had said.

"So now she has only the one kidney left?" Charlie said.

"For as long as it holds up. It's getting weaker too."

Everybody clucked and shook their heads. Of all the bad luck.

"But they're hoping that it'll keep her going long enough so that they can operate. She's top of the list, you know. They're just waiting for a suitable donor."

"I knew a woman once who had a kidney transplant," Nick offered. "It was a terrific success."

"Obviously not for the poor bugger who owned the kidney in the first place," Charlie said, after a moment.

They all reflected on this.

"Sandy won't know whose kidney she's getting," Frank offered, as though this made any difference.

"I'm sure she'll love it anyway," Julia said.

Charlie patted his hand again. "It'll be okay, you know." Then she shouted, "Martine! Can you get a move on? This poor man has a flight to catch!"

Martine threw a black look over her shoulder. "I'm going as fast as I can."

This was perfectly true. The sheer weight of tents, banners, food supplies for two days, rucksacks and people almost threatened to defeat the ancient minibus entirely. But every other vehicle had already been hired, and nobody had a car big enough to fit everybody. Several others had bagged places in other people's cars, including Amanda and Martine's two French colleagues.

It was becoming increasingly apparent that Martine's little band of activists weren't terribly efficient. But their hearts were in the right places, everybody agreed.

"I say that we all have a minute's silence," Charlie declared. "For Sandy!"

"For Sandy!" everyone cried, before lapsing into silence.

At the very back of the bus, Grace gave a loud snort.

Beside her, Ewan gave her a look. "What's wrong?"

"Do you not think it's all a bit coincidental? This whole Sandy business?"

"Not particularly. I'm sure she didn't ask to get sick."

"And I'm sure it's more than a coincidence that she suddenly needs a double-kidney transplant the very day Frank agrees the sale of his house!"

Charlie looked around disapprovingly. "Ssssh!"

After a moment, Ewan said, "This is not like you."

"What?"

"To be so cynical. Do you not believe in love any more?"

She looked out the window and gave a little laugh. "Of course I do." She didn't want to pursue this line of conversation so she said, brightly, "So! You picked up a great tan!"

And he was wearing his contact lenses for a change, which gave him an unusually alert look. Mostly he preferred to peer vaguely through his rimless glasses. That way people would hand him things, like cups of freshly made coffee, and not bother him with nasty stuff like electricity bills or the fact of his emotional irresponsibility.

"Thanks."

She said, "Go on. You can say it."

"What?"

"That I've got very fat."

"I wasn't going to say that at all. I mean, look at me." He patted his own gut, which really hadn't got all that much bigger.

"I'm not going to be offended," she said.

"In that case, perhaps I can offer you a Slimchoc bar?"

She laughed. But he'd always been able to make her laugh. "And a packet of razors?"

"I haven't been privy to your underarm hair yet."

It was the wrong thing to have said, given that she had failed to invite him into her single bed last night. Instead he had slept with the boys on the floor of Adam's vacated room. After the shock of finding his sleek city wife barefoot and hairy in a red kaftan, it was probably his second strong indication that Something Was Wrong.

She felt him looking at her now.

"I hope you don't mind us tagging along today," he said.

"Gosh, no!" She had said the word 'gosh' again. It was as if her nose had grown five inches.

"Because we don't want to cramp your style or anything," he added.

Her head whipped around warily. "What's that supposed to mean?"

He hadn't found a pair of her knickers under Adam's bed last night, had he? But no. Ewan would never recognise a single item of her underwear – even the things he had bought her himself.

"Just, you know, if you're trying to 'find' yourself."

Oooh! How had he known she was even looking? The very same man who had once passed her in the street without recognising her (never mind her underwear)?

She said, slowly, "I just had this opportunity, Ewan. To do something different. To have experiences I never had before. Maybe you felt the same in Florida."

"Well, now that you mention it . . ." he said.

She waited, wildly hopeful. Would he confess to watching hours of gay adult TV in the hotel room while the boys were asleep? Or perhaps to snorting a kilo of cocaine? Had he groped Snow White in Disneyland? Could he too have changed?

"Actually, no, I didn't really do anything that different," he concluded, and she deflated. "But it's hard when you have to look after children," he added rather piously. "You don't get the same opportunities."

"I know that, Ewan. Believe me."

"They did miss you, you know, Grace."

"I missed them too."

"And what with the whole breast thing . . ."

295

"Yes."

"He really needs you, Grace. That's why I kept bugging the airline office for cancellations. I thought, Jamie's in trouble, and the best place for him right now is with his mother," he declared.

"For God's sake, let's stop this once and for all," she said sharply, and Ewan looked at her, hurt and surprised. "This . . . this competition."

Now he was really was confused. "What? I'm not in any competition!"

"No, you just sit on the sidelines like always. Just admit it, Ewan. It was easier for you to come home early because you knew I would deal with the problem and you wouldn't have to."

He was cross. "I did deal with it! Who phoned up doctors and hospitals and health insurers? Who got him started on hormone treatment?"

She sighed. This was pointless. "You did, Ewan."

"No, no, hang on here. Apparently I can't cope because I'm hopeless, but the few times I do cope on my own, that won't do either, will it?"

"Don't be ridiculous."

"You *want* me to make a balls of things, don't you? You'd love it if we'd arrived home from America half-starved and wearing rags! Nothing would make you feel more superior! Well, I'm sick of it. Sick of always being in the wrong."

"Then do something about it!" she hissed. "You've managed to sit in the back seat for ten years now. And I'm sick of that!"

She realised that the chatter in the bus had given way to complete silence. In fact, the bus itself had stopped dead in the middle of the road. Oh Lord. Had Martine decided to eject them? Were the boys crying hysterically at the sight of their parents about to tear the stuffing out of each other?

But nobody was paying them a blind bit of attention. All eyes were riveted to the front of the bus: Julia's son Michael was huffing up the steps, laden with bags, rucksacks, tent equipment and a huge cooler box. He was followed by Gillian, dressed in dazzling white and carrying what appeared to be a fly swat, and, finally, Susan, with an expression of utter boredom on her face. They had obviously got tickets after all. Julia had confided in Grace last night that she hoped they wouldn't.

"Mammy!" he cried now, and they all descended on Julia.

It took them an age to settle themselves, between finding seats, stuffing things into the overhead storage space, taking it all down again because they'd forgotten something, and then pursuing a bluebottle with the fly swat.

"Get it, Michael! They can carry up to fifty different bacteria on their horrible little legs!"

Finally the bluebottle was eliminated and the bus started up again. It passed streams and unremarkable hills and green fields, and Grace looked out the window enviously at the herds of tranquil-looking cows and placid sheep. None of them with a care in the world! Whereas in a few miles she would be at the festival grounds, and Adam would be there, and he would not expect her to turn up with a husband and two kids in tow, and all hell would probably break loose.

Perhaps Ewan sensed something of her inner thoughts, because he said, "Grace, obviously we have a few things to sort out."

"Yes," she said.

"You never know – maybe the month apart was a good thing," he said optimistically.

"Do you think so?"

"Yes, if it puts things in perspective. Gives us things to work on. I don't suppose there's any harm in giving a marriage a good spring-clean every now and again."

"Ewan, that's from one of your ads."

His brow crinkled. "Is it?"

"The one for lemon-zest floor fluid," she said dully.

"Oh, yes!" He was delighted at the resonance; pleased that she had remembered. Then he reached over and squeezed her hand.

"The important thing is that we're home now, Grace. Things will get back to normal, you'll see."

"Maybe," she said, trying to sound positive.

But too much had happened that summer for her to doff her kaftan and pick up the threads of her old life just like that, even with a few minor improvements. She knew she couldn't go back to being that efficient, oatmeal-suited woman with a good career and a well-turned-out family, because that woman didn't exist any more. She had mutated into a person who was still very fuzzy around the edges: a plumpish woman who was confused and flawed and whose hair needed a good trim.

But she liked her better.

They dropped Frank at Departures.

"You're not coming with me," he said, alarmed, when Grace got out of the bus too.

"I know that. I just wanted to say goodbye, that's all."

He was all dressed up in a jacket and tie, like he was going to an interview, and he had a little nick on his chin from shaving. He looked like a country hick on his way to the big city, and her heart constricted.

"Am I all right?" he asked, worried.

"Yes. I just hope that Sandy appreciates how much trouble you've gone to on her behalf."

"I'm not the one lying in a hospital bed," he said stoically. "I'm the lucky one, not her."

"You know what hospital she's in and all that? And the ward number and everything?" Grace said, hating the doubt in her voice.

"Room 229, Floor Two, Memorial Hospital, New York," he rattled off. "She mailed it to me last night."

"Good," said Grace. Perhaps this thing might work out after all.

"Mind you, she said that might change at very short notice," he added.

298

"And why's that?"

"Medical insurance or something. She may have to downgrade to a different hospital."

Grace felt a great big sigh work its way up from her toes. "I see."

"It's different in America. You have to have insurance or the hospitals won't do a thing for you. Everyone has insurance."

"Except for Sandy?"

Frank was suddenly very busy checking the tags on his bag. "You see, she thought her employers were paying it at the nursery school. It was in her employment contract, in black and white. She got a terrible shock when she found out they actually weren't. She'll sue them, of course, once this thing is over."

"So the only way she'll get those kidneys now is to find the money somewhere?"

"Well, you can't put a price on health, can you? That's what I tell her. You can have all the money in the world but it doesn't matter a damn if you're not well. And you only understand that – "

"What is going to cost? About a hundred thousand?"

He went right on as if he hadn't heard her. "You only understand that when someone close to you is sick. When they're near death. That's when you see your priorities in life."

"Or do you get a discount for two?"

Frank clamped his hands over his ears as though he was a small child. "Stop it. Stop it. She's my fiancée and I'm not going to have you say things against her. Always niggling away, spoiling things! She would never say anything against you, you know, because she's too kind!"

"Frank, sometimes people are not what they seem."

"How do you know? How do you know *anything*? What gives you the right to go poking your nose into other people's lives and pull apart the people they love? You think you're somehow better than the rest of us? And you sitting on that bus with your husband and your children, and all the time you're sleeping with another man! If I were you I'd get my own life in order before I go commenting on anybody else's."

"Frank. It's just because I care."

"You don't care. You pity me. Well, I don't want your pity. Because I've found someone who loves me, all right? And I thought I never would." He picked up his bags and said to her, "And she's going to have her operation. Because I'll make sure she has it. I'm going to get on that plane, and I'm going to be by her bedside, and then I'm going to nurse her back to health, and we're going to be happy, okay? We're going to be happy ever after."

And he turned and walked off into the airport. She watched him until she could see him no longer, and then she went to get back on the bus, hoping that she was wrong.

"Grace! Thank God you're here!" Amanda cried.

Grace didn't know why. Last night at dinner she had been positively rude to the girl – well, they were love rivals after all. But that was before Amanda had started to sob quietly into her soup and Grace had ended up fishing her hair out of it and sending her to bed with a hot-water bottle. And comforting her in the middle of the night when she'd awoken from a horrible dream about Adam bonking another woman – 'A fat woman, Grace!' – and then this morning coaxing her to eat just a little bit of porridge before making her two ham sandwiches and sending her off to the festival in someone's car.

She might as well just face it: she was Amanda's new best friend.

"What is it, Amanda?" she asked, lifting a lump hammer. She was attempting to put up a tent. On the side of a hill. With a stiff wind at her back.

"He's here!" Amanda announced, bursting with the news.

Grace narrowly missed her foot with the lump hammer.

"Who?" she asked, very vague.

"Adam. There was a sighting of him!" Amanda squealed triumphantly.

"Really?" Now Grace narrowly missed Amanda's head with the lump hammer. She put it down altogether. Probably safer.

"Martine's colleague François met John from the UK who said that Gunther had been speaking to Ivan who had just seen Adam!"

"Where?"

"Where what?"

"Where exactly did they see him?"

Amanda looked blank. "They just said he was here, nothing specific . . ."

"Think, Amanda, think!" Grace rasped, then, at Amanda's rather startled look, said, "Just, um, curious."

"You're right! I should have asked!" Amanda was anguished now. "There are fifty thousand people here, Grace – I'll never find him."

"Nonsense," Grace said, looking desperately around at the crowds of young people. Worse still, everybody looked more or less the same: jeans and T-shirt, jeans and cropped top, jeans and . . . well, just jeans. So much for youth being largely a quest for individuality. "Maybe he's wearing his khaki shorts today," she said, standing on tiptoe. "And his red *Save The World* T-shirt."

Amanda looked at her a bit oddly. "You seem to know his clothes very well."

"Me? Yes, well . . ." She felt her face flame guiltily. She must cover. "I'm a clothes designer."

"Wow!" Amanda smiled radiantly. "Do you know any of the Guccis?"

"All of them," Grace murmured.

"Mummy has dinner with them all the time. Wait till they hear I met you!"

"I try to keep a low profile."

She was delighted to see Martine marching up the hill to join them.

"Well?" Martine demanded. "Where is that filthy piece of shit?"

"Sorry?" Amanda said, startled.

"Adam. He and Joey were supposed to have come on ahead to get a good pitch! Instead we end up on the side of a rocky hill, totally away from the action, while he skives off to enjoy the music. After all his radical talk too! The guy is nothing more than an armchair activist."

Amanda's lip quivered in outrage. "He is not!"

"Oh? How come he's down by the stage then? Instead of up here with the rest of us?"

"He's down by the stage?" Amanda's head whipped around. (Admirably, Grace resisted).

"Yeh, like some fucking groupie," Martine snarled. "If he shows his face up here, you can tell him from me to get lost, okay?"

Off she went, back down to her colleagues who were busily putting up their MOX-painted tents and unfurling banners. Someone else opened a box of leaflets. Security would be over in a minute, of course. And maybe even the police. Surely Sergeant Daly would have alerted them to the possible presence of a band of fifty anti-nuclear protestors?

Amanda gave a kind of a half-sob now. "I'll never find him down by the stage! What am I going to do? I have to see him, Grace! I have to talk to him!"

Her knees buckled rather tragically, and Grace felt a bit impatient. "Amanda, we're only talking about a man here."

A very lovely young man, granted, with plenty going for him. Including a good line in making women fall in love with him.

Was she in love with him? She didn't know any more.

"You don't understand a thing!" Amanda cried, which Grace found a trifle irritating, given that she had a good ten years' experience on the unfortunate Amanda. Not that she seemed to have benefited all that much. Well, look at her! Everything solid and respectable and dependable in her life turned on its head, while she toyed with the idea of relocating to a hut in Tasmania.

The whole thing sounded so crazy that she laughed out loud.

"I thought you were nice!" Amanda said, bursting into fresh sobs. "Instead you're laughing at me!"

"Amanda, I wasn't . . ." Grace looked at her. The girl had flown halfway around the world to find Adam. Now *that* was love. "Stop all that blubbering and let's find him, will we?"

Amanda was so surprised that her upset shifted down a gear to a kind of a wet snuffle.

"How are we supposed to find him in the middle of fifty thousand people?"

Good question. Grace looked around, her eye coming to rest on a tall metal pole about fifty yards away. Two enormous concert speakers were attached to the top of the pole.

"Follow me," she ordered Amanda.

Amanda trailed after her, protesting. "Where are we going?"

"Excuse me . . . thank you . . ." Grace made her way through the crowd. "If I could just get in there . . ." She shushed away a couple of teenagers who had taken up residence at the bottom of the pole. "Maintenance," she told them.

The pole was very tall and slippery-looking, but thankfully there were metal footholds to aid her ascent. She just needed to get onto the first one, which was at shoulder level to deter any would-be climbers.

She turned to Amanda. "Lend me your shoulder."

"What?"

"Just do it."

Amanda's shoulder looked like it wouldn't support a fly, never mind the width and girth of Grace, but it felt surprisingly strong under Grace's hand. Then she put one foot firmly on a rucksack that one of the teenagers has carelessly left behind. Something in the rucksack collapsed with a squishy sound as she applied her full weight to it – it felt like banana sandwiches – but she didn't stop; she hoisted herself up onto the pole and clung to it like a monkey. Now it was simply a question of reaching that first metal foothold. Easy peasy.

"What a marvellous idea!" Amanda squealed. There was a little pause. "Are you stuck, Grace?"

"No, no! Not at all. Just . . . catching my breath. Ouch! I think I just tore my kaftan."

Amanda peered up at her. "Will I give you a push from down here?"

"That won't be necessary." The pole was too slippery to get any kind of grip on. But people were turning to watch now, and pride and willpower lent her a surge of strength. She managed to pull herself up far enough to get her knee onto the first metal foothold.

"Grace? I'm not sure you should be doing this," Amanda called. "Apart from it not being very safe, you might get arrested or something."

"It wouldn't be the first time I've done something illegal!" Grace shouted back, for the benefit of the onlookers. Someone clapped, and Grace's confidence grew. By now she had both feet firmly on the footholds, and she began to climb. It was much harder than it looked, and she was panting and ready to give up halfway. But she couldn't give up, not with everybody watching. At last she reached the speakers at the top, and grabbed onto the nearest one, praying that it was attached securely. It seemed to be, and now she had a little platform to rest on, and there was a smattering of applause from the crowd below, and she gave them a little wave.

"Grace? Are you all right?" Amanda called.

"Yes, yes."

She felt very high up, and she could see for miles and miles around; acres of fields, and distant towns, and the thousands and thousands of people below her, milling around like ants. Well, they were more the size of dogs really – she wasn't that far up. And there were wonderful sounds and smells and colours, and the wind was snapping at her hair, and it was as if the whole world was laid out at her feet, just waiting for her, and she laughed out loud again.

"Grace, what on earth are you doing up there?"

She glanced down. Ewan stood beside Amanda, his arms folded over his chest a bit crossly. Neil and Jamie were down there too, looking up at her with interest. They were carrying four cartons of chips.

"She's looking for my boyfriend," Amanda earnestly explained to them.

"What?"

"Adam. Well, *I'm* looking for him really. But he doesn't know I'm here. He knows Grace very well, though."

Ewan looked up at her. "You haven't mentioned any Adam," he called.

"Haven't I?" The smell of chips wafted up to her. Hmm, delicious. "It's a very long story, Ewan."

He squinted up at her in that vague, myopic way of his that always made her feel tender. "Come down and tell me about it."

"I don't think you want to hear it," she said back.

He said something else, but the wind carried it away.

"Speak up, Ewan, I can't hear you," she said.

"I said I do want to hear it!" he shouted. More people turned to look at them with interest, and he looked embarrassed, but he went on anyway. "I want to hear it, Grace. Everything."

It was a kind of an invitation and she shifted a bit on the speaker.

"Dad, can I climb up too?" Neil wanted to know.

"No. You'd fall and break your neck."

"Mum hasn't fallen and broken her neck."

"She might yet. Sorry, Grace. I mean, obviously we hope you won't . . ."

"No, Neil. You can't come up," Grace said. "But maybe you could send up the chips?"

Ewan planted his hands on his hips and glared up at her. "There you go again!"

"What?"

"Butting in!" He saw the boys were looking, sensitive to marital argument. "Go on over to Nick," he ordered them.

They did. Amanda shifted from foot to foot, agonised, seeming to sense that this had veered into the personal, but obviously desperately wanting news of Adam.

"Could we have a little privacy here?" Ewan said to her shortly, surprising Grace with his decisiveness.

Amanda reluctantly turned and followed the boys.

Ewan looked up the pole again at Grace belligerently. "You butted in on my authority with my sons! You're always doing it!"

Grace gave a snort, but the speaker rocked dangerously with the motion and she stopped.

"What authority?" she shouted down. "You don't have any authority because you don't want to have any! Because that would mean making tough decisions and taking responsibility and just . . . being there!"

"I spend a lot of time with them! I've just spent the last month with them, for God's sake!"

"Yeh – but you only want the good times, Ewan! The fun times! Where were you when they had chicken pox and bruised egos and when Mr Guppy died?"

"Who the hell is Mr Guppy?"

"Neil's secret friend. The one who held his hand when he felt too shy to leave the house."

"Neil? Shy?"

"Yes. I'd swear he has panic attacks sometimes. But he never lets on."

306

"What happened to Mr Guppy?"

"I think he got pulverised in a giant food-processor – look, it doesn't matter. The fact is that you didn't even know about him! Face up to it, Ewan! You've been copping out all their lives."

A few people in the watching crowd clapped.

"You go, girl!" someone shouted.

Ewan glared around at them.

"Oh, shut up!" he said. "My wife hasn't been home in a month! She's running around with a bunch of teenagers, she's got dragged into some political cause, and now she's halfway up a pole in the middle of a rock concert! I ask you, who's the mature one here?"

More clapping now, but a louder smattering of boos.

"You would have to belittle it, Ewan!" she shouted down, furious. "Make it all sound so silly. Well, I'm not the one making up stupid advertising slogans for a living! I'm not the one who invests more of myself in fucking chocolate products than in my own family!"

Silence. Sensing that this had gone beyond mere entertainment, the spectators muttered to themselves and turned away. And after all the shouting up and down the pole, neither Grace nor Ewan seemed to have anything left to say.

"Will you come down, Grace?" he asked at last, quietly.

"I don't think I want to," she said.

"I know, but the music will start up at any moment and you're sitting on a speaker. You might get a terrible fright and fall."

"I'll risk it."

He peered up at her, his hand shielding his eyes from the sun. "I'm sorry that I seem to have let you down so badly with the boys."

She gave a sigh. "It's not just the boys, Ewan. You know that."

He gave a little nervous laugh. "Let's not get too dramatic here."

"Maybe I want a bit of drama," she announced. "Maybe I

haven't had enough drama! You're in the cut and thrust of the advertising world, Ewan. I show duplexes and the odd semi-detached." She corrected herself. "Well, used to. I handed in my notice."

If he was appalled he didn't show it. "Did you?"

"I just couldn't bear it any more."

"So . . . what will you do now, do you think?" He must have thought this was a very loaded question, because he added, "Work-wise, I mean."

"I don't know. I can do anything. Or nothing at all." She thought of Natalie's suggestions of art classes, and she gave a little laugh. "I might become an artist, maybe."

He looked confused. "No offence, but you can't draw a straight line."

She had meant it as a joke, of course, but had forgotten that Ewan wasn't in on it. A lot had happened to her in the last month – big, important things – that Ewan wasn't in on. Perhaps he would catch up. But she couldn't say it with certainty. That was the problem.

"Are you going to come down?" he asked again.

"In a minute," she said, hedging. "Maybe you'd go and make sure that the boys aren't eating my chips." Even in the midst of a marital crisis, she couldn't stop thinking about food.

"Okay," he said. He looked up at her for a very long moment, rocking back and forth on his heels, then he gave a kind of jerky little salute and walked off up the hill.

From the top of the pole, Grace could see Julia and Michael and Gillian. Nick and Charlie were going down to queue at one of the catering trucks. There was no sign of Gavin, but Neil and Jamie were stretched out on the grass with their chips, enjoying the sun. Below them, Martine and Amanda and the other anti-nuclear activists had nearly finished setting up their gear, and there was a small sea of tents, banners and flags all bearing one word: MOX.

When she tried to see Ewan in the crowd again, she couldn't.

Instead a red T-shirt caught her eye. She knew it was him even before she saw the T-shirt slogan. Adam. She had forgotten entirely that she had been looking for him.

But she hadn't been, of course. She realised now that Adam was never what she had been looking for. She had just been a bit blinded by the summer sun.

She would have to tell him. Anguished, she wondered how you went about breaking the news to someone that you were not going to live with them in a shack on a beach in a strange country with no income and only fruit and berries for food and abandoning your ten-year-old children to fend for themselves – it was impossible!

But he deserved the benefit of her new insight as soon as possible. It was only fair.

"Adam! Adam!" she shouted, waving her arms hard over her head like someone trying to guide in an out-of-control aircraft.

He looked around suspiciously for a moment.

"Adam! Up here!"

He saw her then, and his expression turned to disbelief. Perhaps he would think that she had flipped over the edge. Perhaps he might decide that, really, she wasn't the one for him at all and that he should extend his search immediately for a suitable candidate to join him in that beach hut.

But he shouted ecstatically, "Grace! You're here!" and gave such a huge, beatific, loving smile, that her heart sank. Telling him it was over might be harder than she had anticipated. Then he started to push his way through the crowd towards her, the way you would see lovers do in the movies, and she should be swooning at the cinematic turn her life had taken – hadn't she yearned for it? All that was needed was a bit of swelling music in the background and the fantasy would be complete.

But that particular fantasy had gone. She had new fantasies now, fantasies that didn't involve Clarice Starling or small handguns or making videos with titles like *Rita Rides Again*. They didn't involve Adam, either.

She took a deep breath, and then she began to climb back down the pole.

SEVENTEEN

"My God, Michael – did you see that? A cowpat!"

"Brace yourself. There's another one over there."

"You don't think the cows are . . . still here, do you?"

"Gillian, cows won't hurt you."

"They can carry TB! And I'm just over a mouth ulcer – my defences are probably down."

Julia threw her eyes to heaven, and called over, "Everything all right?"

"Oh, terrific!" Michael called back hastily.

"Couldn't be better!" Gillian chimed in. They were wrestling with a huge red striped tent that stood out like a beacon in the midst of all the other small green ones dotted on the hillside. Already two people had mistaken it for a catering tent and tried to order burgers from Gillian. Someone else had thought it was a public toilet judging by the wet patch on the back of it.

"You don't think it's going to rain, do you?" Gillian asked Julia, plucking at her white trousers doubtfully. She had already acquired a grass stain and two ant bites.

"I don't think so," Julia said regretfully. A good thunderstorm might send them home quickly enough. Although knowing them, they had brought umbrellas and waterproof gear: God knows they had brought everything else, including a barbeque, an extensive medical kit, and two folding deckchairs. And they hadn't even opened that third rucksack yet.

Susan emerged from the tent. "I'm going to the toilet."

"You can't!" Gillian blurted.

"What?"

"It's just . . ." She looked off down to the bottom of the mucky hill where white prefabs were lined up. Already queues of young people were forming. "They're probably not that clean."

"I don't care. I'm bursting."

"Well, you might get lost!" She looked around nervously. "There must be at least thirty thousand people here – mustn't there, Julia?"

"More like fifty," she said.

"Fifty!"

"Stop fussing. I'm going on my own." Susan flounced off.

"Well . . . well . . . don't touch anything!" Gillian called after her.

Julia gave a little sigh and looked down the hill at Martine and Joey and the rest. They were erecting the MOX tents and some of them were already settling down with banners. There was a great air of excitement and purpose and comradeship. Oh, it wasn't fair that Julia was stuck up here with the lay people, so to speak, away from all the action!

"I hope this isn't going to be too loud for you, Julia," Gillian said. She nodded towards the vast stage. "The first band must be due out soon."

"Group," Julia corrected her.

Michael hitched up the band of his Hawaiian shorts over his gut, and adjusted his Red Sox baseball cap. In the midst of the sea of faded denim all around them he looked like something from a cartoon.

"Well!" he said to Julia. "Here's to a great weekend!"

"You really didn't have to come," Julia said. "Grace is here. She would have looked after me."

"Really. I just saw her up that pole over there," Gillian said.

"Probably just a . . . temporary aberration," Michael said. He had never been a fan of Grace's but he was obviously anxious to avoid a renewal of tensions between Julia and Gillian. To her credit, Gillian hadn't mentioned the phone thing once, although there was an odd-looking tightness around her lower face, as though her jaws were wired together. Which they might very well be – she had once contemplated a weight-loss diet that was based on such a thing. But that had been before the discovery of all her allergies and thankfully a diet hadn't been necessary since.

"It's not that we don't trust Grace, Mammy, it's just . . ." He looked around doubtfully at the crowds, the cowpats and the anti-nuclear demonstrators, before rallying. "Heck, we wanted to come! Didn't we, Gillian? We thought, we've never been to an outdoor concert before – let's live dangerously!"

"Actually, we went to the RTE concert orchestra in the park that time," Gillian reminded him.

"That's right. And UB40."

"Oh, yes, they were terrific!" Gillian clapped her hands enthusiastically. 'Red Red Wine!'" Then her face clouded over. "Do you remember we drank some that night? And I came out all in bumps?"

A chant went up from below: *No Mox! No Mox! No Mox!*

Gillian cast a little look down. "Do you think they'll keep that up all afternoon?"

"I hope so," Julia said evenly. "That's why we're here, after all."

"Of course," Michael said soothingly. He gave Gillian a look that said, *humour her.*

Julia looked out over the crowd. Pretty soon security would be over to see how they had slipped through the net. But there were no television cameras in evidence. It wouldn't be much of a campaign if it only got reported in the music press. Why didn't someone do something to attract a bit more attention?

She was surprised by the strength of her feeling on the subject. Perhaps some of Martine's zealousness had rubbed off on her.

"Now!" trilled Gillian. "Who's for a glass of Chardonnay?"

"You came," Adam kept repeating. "I didn't think you would, you know. But you came."

"I did. Adam, we need to talk. There have been some developments – "

"You're here," he marvelled.

"Yes, I think we've established that much. Is there somewhere we can go to talk?"

Preferably out of the vicinity of her husband. "Adam?"

He was staring at her. "Sorry. It's just, I've missed you."

"You saw me only yesterday." She tried a little laugh. But he didn't laugh back. His blue eyes were kind of starey. Possibly he had been skimping on his sleep.

"I know. But a lot has happened in the last twenty-four hours," he said, rather hoarsely. He leaned in and said, "I have a plan."

"Adam, please, I don't want to talk about the beach hut any more – "

"I meant the campaign."

"Oh! Well, Martine would be interested in hearing it, I'm sure. She thinks you're not pulling your weight."

"Pah!" he spat. "Amateurs, the lot of them. Doing things by the book. Prissy, fussy little civil servants, that's what they are. No passion! Now, you and me – we understand passion, don't we, Grace?"

"Ah . . . yes! Certainly we do!" she said, humouring him.

"And Julia," he added. "She has passion too."

His eyes were definitely on the burning side. Combined with the dreadlocks and the beginnings of a beard, he had a vague look about him of a young Jesus Christ.

"In fact," he said, "I have to go. If the plan is going to work."

314

"In a minute," she said. "I have something to tell you, Adam."

"I know," he said.

"You know?" She'd only just made up her mind herself.

"The very fact that you're here says it all."

It took her a moment to realise the implications of this.

"No, no, no, I'm not here! Well, of course I'm *here* . . . Adam, I don't know how to say this."

"Spit it out, Grace. Joey is waiting for me."

"Right, um . . ."

Over her shoulder she saw Ewan stand up and look around the crowd for her. She ducked.

Adam said, "Grace, what are you doing?"

"Nothing!" Peering up through cracks in the crowd, she saw Ewan turn to look in the other direction. "Found it!" She straightened again, holding a muddy size-ten shoe. Possibly the wearer hadn't missed it yet.

Adam moved in on her. "I know that you feel the same way as me, Grace. You were just in denial. And that's okay. The important thing is that you realised it in the end. The important thing is that we'll be together."

She clutched the shoe tighter to her chest, like a kind of barrier between them. She looked him straight in the eye. "Adam. There's no easy way to say this."

He must have guessed what was on the way, because he started to talk very quickly. "Then don't say it. Don't speak, don't rationalise, just go with your feelings, Grace. I have, and I know that we're meant to be together."

It was like he had borrowed the lines from somewhere. A book, maybe. They weren't his words, and she suddenly wondered whether he had borrowed the emotion as well. Because there was something very . . . not false, but unreal about all this. It was as if he believed they were both caught up in some big romantic intrigue, and her eschewing her husband and family in favour of him at a crowded rock festival was the natural passionate conclusion to it all. All that was missing was for his T-shirt to be torn strategically at one tanned shoulder, and for her to ditch the smelly shoe.

She saw for the first time how very alike they were, her and Adam: for them both, real life had proved to be disappointing.

"I'm not coming with you to Tasmania, Adam," she said. "Neither am I going to sit and wait in a cottage somewhere in Ireland for you to come back when you can manage it."

He must have realised how unreasonable the request had been in the first place, because he said nothing.

"This summer with you, well, it was perfect. Magical. I'll never forget it."

"You don't have to forget it," he said, but it lacked fire.

"Oh, Adam. You must see that it can't go on. Not for either of us, no matter what we might hope or dream might happen. I have two children. You have a cause. Sometimes the two are incompatible, do you not see? Please, let's just leave it like this. Here, now, today. Let's not spoil it at the very end."

Perhaps he was beginning to see the sense in her words; perhaps they might have had a last hug, and a tear or two, and slipped off their separate ways into the crowd with their store of memories. Perhaps this might have happened had Martine not spotted Adam, and bellowed out across the crowd, "You lazy pig!"

Adam whirled around belligerently. Grace immediately knew that she had a 'situation' on her hands and that she had better act fast.

"She doesn't mean you!" she said. Ewan and the boys were looking down at the stage, oblivious, she saw. "No, it's me she's shouting at, and I *am* lazy sometimes, I'll freely admit it – "

But Adam had given Martine the two fingers. This inflamed her further.

"Fuck you!" she shouted, and began to march down towards them.

Then – oh, horror – Amanda turned around to see what all the fuss was about.

"Grace!" she said, waving over.

"Yes, *sssh*!" Grace waved back feebly, still hoping to contain things. But then Amanda spotted Adam beside Grace.

"Adam!" she squealed.

The name 'Adam' seemed to register very strongly with Ewan because he suddenly looked over too, alert to something in the air. "Grace?" he called.

Grace pretended she didn't hear him, and anyway, there was Martine upon them, poking a finger into Adam's chest.

"You get your ass up there right now!" she ordered, pointing up the hill.

"Shut up, Martine," he said, his attention riveted to the hill, and the sight of Amanda joyously skipping down the grass towards him, her ponytail bouncing, just like in the closing sequence of *Little House on the Prairie*. She skilfully dodged tents and festival revellers and catering vans whilst never once taking her eyes off him.

"Adam! Oh, Adam!"

He looked at her like he was seeing a ghost. "What the hell is she doing here?" he asked nobody in particular.

"She just came." Grace began to see a way of salvaging all this. "Imagine! All the way from Tasmania. Just to see you!"

But Adam just looked cross. "She's a fool then. I told her it was over."

"At least hear her out!" Grace said desperately. Up on the hill, Ewan was watching them intently. She decided there was no point in pretending she hadn't seen him, so she waved up happily. "Be up in a minute!" she mouthed.

Martine, ignored, was getting increasingly frustrated. "I'm giving you one last chance to participate in the campaign, Adam!"

"Who was that?" he asked Grace.

"Who?"

"That man."

"What man?"

"The man you were waving at."

"Oh, I have no idea," she said.

"I'm going to count to three!" Martine warned.

"Count to a hundred if you want." Adam stared up the hill. "And those boys, Grace."

"Boys?"

"Up on the hill. Waving at you."

"I don't think it's me they're waving at . . . Look! Here's Amanda!"

And she was, puffing and wet-eyed at the sight of Adam. But she must have seen something very uninviting in his face because she came to a stop at the bottom of the hill and looked over at him pleadingly.

"Three!" Martine announced. "Right. That's it. You've had your chance!"

"So?" Adam enquired.

"So I'm officially expelling you from the group."

"Ooh, you're frightening me now."

"And you can tell Joey the same too. We can do without your 'help'."

"Yeh, I can see you're really shaking the place to its foundations, Martine." He looked up contemptuously at the small band of protestors.

"We're doing more than you!"

"Don't bet on it."

She gave him one last look before stomping off back up the hill, almost knocking over the unfortunate Amanda.

"You two should really talk," Grace said brightly.

But Adam didn't even look at Amanda. His eyes were on Grace, and they weren't particularly warm.

"You should have said in the first place that you'd brought the whole family along."

"What?"

"Stop it, Grace. The man and the two kids. It would have saved us both a lot of empty words."

"They weren't empty words . . . look, they just came, Adam. They arrived last night as a surprise."

"Not too much of a surprise, thankfully," he said sarcastically. "We wouldn't want to have been caught in the act, would we?"

Now Ewan was making his way down the hill. Grace had a sick feeling in her stomach.

"Adam, I would have made the same decision whether they had come back or not. It doesn't make any difference that they're here."

Except for the fact of his wounded pride, of course. Which was not to be underestimated, as she was about to find out.

"Maybe you're getting some kind of a kick out of all this. Me and him here today while you run from one to the other." He had that rather starey look back in his eyes again, and his hands were jumpy and nervous. She wondered what this plan was that he and Joey had hatched.

"Don't be stupid."

"Maybe someone should explain to him that his wife was having a little fling while he was away in America."

Ewan was almost upon them now, his face very watchful.

"Maybe someone should explain to Amanda. But that would just be spiteful, Adam."

"You're trying to dig yourself out of a hole now, Grace. I have nothing to lose compared to you."

"It's not about losing. It's about hurting people unnecessarily."

Ewan must have had the same feeling of impending doom as Amanda, because he stopped beside her at the bottom of the hill, and they watched the drama they didn't quite understand unfold before them, even if they couldn't hear it.

"As far as I'm concerned *I've* been hurt unnecessarily," Adam

319

told her. "You used me, Grace. Why should you get away with it?"

"Please don't," Grace said quietly. "Not here. Not now."

Adam turned to Amanda and Ewan and gave a funny sort of a smile.

"Talk to you later," he told them rather cryptically. It sounded like a warning.

Then he turned and walked off fast into the crowd.

Come on, Libby, give it up!
Stop teasing, Libby, get it on
Come on, Libby, give it up!
Let's get it on till the crack of DAWN!

The deafening din from the stage rolled out over the heads of fifty thousand people and hit them full blast.

Gillian swayed slightly, as though she had been attacked. She said something but nobody could hear her. Michael held on to the armrests of his padded deckchair as though he were in the midst of a particularly turbulent take-off. When the lead singer went on to extol Libby to join in what sounded like group sex – or else rude sex, it was difficult to know – Julia thought Gillian and Michael would pack up their bags and leave altogether. She certainly felt like it – not that she would admit it, of course.

But, to their credit, they stayed put. And, finally, the song was over.

"Not bad!" Michael shouted bravely, as the last strains died down. "I wonder who's on next?"

Gillian consulted her concert programme. "Mutilation," she said, faintly.

"They'll be starting up on the second stage in a minute," Julia informed them cheerfully.

"They have a second stage?" Michael faltered.

"That way we can move around depending on what acts we'd like to see," she explained. "Apparently the hottest gig to catch this year is Plutonium Miss."

Down the hill, the anti-nuclear protestors began their chant. They did it during every interval between acts.

No Mox! No Mox! No Mox!

"Where's Susan?" Gillian said suddenly.

"The toilet."

"Michael, that was half an hour ago!"

Immediately it was panic stations all around.

"There are fifty thousand people here!" Michael began to look helplessly around the crowds.

"There's a Meeting Point near the entrance," Julia suggested. "Maybe we should try that?"

But Gillian was looking down at the anti-nuclear protestors. "I'll just bet she's down there. I warned her, you know. I said to her, don't you dare go near any of those smelly people today!"

Unfortunately, just at that moment, there was a lull in the chanting below, and several of the 'smelly' people overheard and looked up at her belligerently.

"Give my daughter back!" Gillian called down, bravely taking a step forward. "Right now this minute!"

"Who?" Martine asked.

"Susan!" No response. "Thirteen? Pink top, denim jacket – "

"Oh. Her. We haven't seen her," Martine tossed back.

Gillian was more determined. "I saw you yesterday, you know! Putting beads and stuff in her hair. Grooming her, that's what you were doing! You lot, you're worse than those weird religious sects!"

The whole group turned to look at her now, rather startled.

"Found her!" Michael sang into the silence. "She's in the tent." Then his face fell. "Susan!"

Susan was indeed in the tent. Her pink top was unbuttoned and young Gavin was rolling around on her – doing unspeakable things, Gillian would recount later to anyone who would listen. Depraved things. But what would you expect, with a mother like Charlie?

"Sorry about that!" Julia called down to Martine, embarrassed. "A slight mistake!"

"Ah, yes. Sorry!" Gillian chimed, her normally ashen face bright red. Meanwhile, Michael had pulled young Gavin out of the tent and was shaking him like a terrier with a rat. "You little shit. That's my daughter you were licking."

Susan was leisurely buttoning up her top. "Chill *out*, Daddy."

"And as for you, miss . . ."

She faced up to him. "What? Are you going to ground me? Suspend my pocket money? Take away the scooter you never bought me?"

The anti-nuclear protestors attempted to start up their chant again, but half of them were watching the drama up the hill. The chant petered out altogether as Charlie stormed past now, holding three fish suppers and a carton of noodles. Nick trailed after her with three cokes.

"What the hell are you doing to my son?" she demanded of Michael.

Gavin said, embarrassed, "Mum, leave it."

"Your darling son was trying to shag my daughter," Michael informed her. Neil and Jamie, Grace's sons, perked up and listened with interest.

"Michael!" Gillian moaned.

Charlie was outraged. "Yes, well, if she dressed a little less like a tart . . ."

"Well!" said Gillian. "If that isn't the kettle calling the pot black!"

"Let him go right now," Charlie commanded Michael.

"Mum, I said I can handle this," Gavin protested strongly.

"My pet!" she said. Then she elbowed Nick viciously in the ribs. "For God's sake, do something."

"Uh . . ." Nick began reluctantly.

"You are totally ineffectual, do you know that?" she said to him.

"Why is it that I have to do everything around here?"

This was too much for Nick. "Because I'm only the fucking talent! I just have to look good and entertain the punters, isn't that right? You have no idea how I feel sometimes!"

And he turned on his heel and walked off on her. Just like that!

Red-cheeked, Charlie grabbed Gavin from Michael. "Come on, baby. Let's go watch the concert from somewhere else." She marched off with Gavin firmly in the crook of her arm.

"And where do you think you're going?" Michael said to Susan, who was pulling on her denim jacket. "To get more sex?"

Several nearby males looked over hopefully.

"Michael," Gillian moaned.

"I'm going because I can't stand it any more," Susan announced. "No wonder Granny doesn't want to come and live with us!"

She stalked off, leaving an appalled silence.

Julia said, at last, "That isn't the reason why I don't want to come and live with you."

"What reason?" Michael said.

"I don't know," she admitted. "Whatever reason Susan meant."

"Oh. Yes. We know that, don't we, Gillian?"

"Yes, yes," she said, looking no wiser than the rest of them.

Michael cleared his throat, and rallied. "Let's fire up the barbecue!"

Julia suppressed a sigh. They just never learned. It was relentless.

Gillian reached for the picnic hamper. "We brought some jumbo sausages and all. Would any of your . . . friends like to join in?" She nodded towards Martine and the rest.

"Actually, Gillian, I really think we should leave them alone," Julia said. Martine had just managed to get everyone going again, and the shouts of *No Mox!* were gradually gathering momentum.

"I want to make it up to them," Gillian insisted. "For accusing them in the wrong."

"I'm sure they've forgotten about it already . . . Gillian, please . . ."

But Gillian was already on her way down to them. She shouted gaily over the chants of *No Mox!*, "Anybody down there for a spare rib? Or a burger? Home-made this morning!"

Fifty hardened environmentalists stopped their chanting for a second time, lowered their banners and flags yet again, and turned to look up at her in incredulous silence. Well, Julia had tried to warn her . . .

"You brought a *barbecue*?" Martine said at last.

"Just a disposable one."

"We're in the middle of a political protest here! You can't go lighting up barbecues!"

Gillian swallowed rather nervously. "Why not?"

"Who is going to take us seriously? Stuffing our faces with burgers?" She spat this last word and Gillian recoiled. "You stupid woman! Go home!"

"Go home," someone else echoed.

It was taken up now as a mantra amongst the others, low and pointed. "*Go home – go home – go home!*"

Without another word, Gillian walked back up the hill. She put the jumbo sausages back into the cooler box, and the burgers. Julia felt sorry for her.

"This protest is important to them," she said to her, kindly. "They take it very seriously."

Gillian looked at her. "Whereas I am an embarrassment to them. A joke. To everyone."

Julia was taken aback. "Gillian . . ."

"But especially to you, Julia. We always have been, haven't we, Michael and me? With our boring jobs, and our little illnesses and our stroppy daughter and our attempts to get you to live with us. Oh, please don't protest – you don't hide your feelings very well. But then again, you never intend to, do you? Because that

324

wouldn't be as much fun." And she started hurling more things into the cooler box with fast, jerky movements.

Michael began, "Gillian . . ."

But Gillian just flung a hand in the direction of the protestors. "Go on down to your crusty friends, Julia! They're welcome to you."

She hurled a tube of sunblock into the cooler box, and the coal for the barbecue, and a couple of glossy magazines she'd brought along to pass the time.

Julia was stricken. She begged Michael, "Say something – stop her."

Michael said, "Gillian, will you calm down – "

But she turned on him, two little red spots of colour high on her cheeks. "Don't, Michael. *Don't*. I swear to God if you take her side one more time . . ." She hurled her handbag into the cooler and grabbed it up. She ignored Julia entirely and said to Michael, "I'm going to find Susan and then hire a taxi or something to take me home. And if you have any sense you'll do the same. Because first she had JJ – Saint JJ, who could do no wrong – and now she has some daft political cause and when that passes, she'll find some-thing else to lavish her attention on. And it won't be you, Michael. It never has been and it never will be, so will you just stop trying! Just . . . stop it."

Then she turned, the cooler box banging against her legs, and walked off, straight into a cowpat. She didn't even notice.

Julia and Michael looked after her, and it was like everything was frozen for a moment, then Julia tried a breathy little laugh, and began, "Michael."

But he wouldn't look at her. All those times he had demanded her full attention, and now he was getting it, and he didn't want it. Julia felt cold under the afternoon sun.

He said, "You might like to keep the tent for tonight. I'll send someone to collect it tomorrow."

And he turned and walked off after Gillian.

Nobody had seen Adam.

"What would he be doing up here?" Martine said. "I kicked him out of the group."

She looked a bit disheartened. Apart from the unseemly scenes of family drama disrupting the protest, the noise from the stage was so tremendous that their chanting was totally ineffectual. To add insult to injury, security hadn't even bothered to come over to kick them out!

"Thanks," Grace said. She began to make her way down towards the stage. More people were arriving on the hill by the minute. She might as well forget it. She would never find him in this.

"Oh, Nick! Nick, have you seen Adam?"

Nick was sitting on the grass on his own with his lanky arms wrapped around his knees, staring at the stage.

"Huh? No."

"Are you sure? He must have come this way." She had a kind of a sick, nervous feeling in her stomach. There had been something very odd about Adam; something reckless. She couldn't think what he might do, but she was sure he was going to do something.

"I haven't seen him, okay?" Nick said.

His voice sounded muffled.

"Are you okay?" she asked.

"Fine." Then he broke down in long, loud sobs. "Oh, fuck!"

Grace forgot about Adam and hunched down beside her brother. "Nick, what's the matter?"

"Listen to it!" he sobbed, poking a finger at the stage. "Listen to that music!"

Grace did. There were no lyrics. Instead, the base guitarist's instrument seemed to be possessed, and all she could hear was a relentless *woarr-woarr-woarrrr-neh-neh-neeeeeh*.

"It's so beautiful!" Nick blubbered. He wiped his sleeve

roughly over his face. "That could have been us up there, Grace. Steel Warriors. Me and the lads giving it welly! Derek out of his skull on something. Vinnie strutting around in his string vest. And the noise and the sweat and young girls hurling their underwear at us!"

"That never happened," Grace reminded him.

"Oh, yeh," he said. "We just lived in hope."

She squeezed his arm. "You could start again, Nick."

"No," he said.

"Come on. Now that you're not entering the Eurovision, you can still follow your dreams."

"Um," he muttered.

Grace looked at him suspiciously. "You haven't told her, have you?"

He pretended ignorance. "What?"

"About the Eurovision, Nick."

He flung himself back onto the grass a bit petulantly. "Charlie can really set her heart on something, you know? I'm starting to realise that much about her."

"Tell her then. It's not fair to let her get her hopes up."

"I know, okay?"

"I mean, how far has this thing gone? You haven't entered yet, or anything?"

Nick gave a snort of laughter. "God no! No, no, I've just jotted down a few lyrics. And Charlie's tinkering about with the overall look, you know? And we've talked to a few backing singers – nothing serious."

She always knew when he was lying. He was lying now. "Nick."

"All right! The song is called 'Kissing The Blarney', I'm wearing green and black and my first TV heat is in November, okay? Please don't tell anyone," he begged.

"Jesus." Charlie certainly had been busy this past week.

"Not even Ewan. And promise me you won't watch it."

"But . . ."

"Promise!"

"I promise, okay?"

Now that he'd got it off his chest, he looked a bit more chipper. "*EastEnders* will be on the other channel anyway," he confided. "So probably nobody at all will know I've done it."

"But you'll know."

"What?"

"It's obvious you don't want to do it, Nick. Look at you, for heaven's sake! You're dying to be up on that stage playing heavy rock!"

"Sometimes we have to do things we don't want to do," he said bravely. "And the costume isn't so bad. She decided against the spangles in the end. Says they're too old-fashioned. And I agree with her on that one."

"Nick – "

"She has a good business head, you know," he said rather defiantly. "No matter what else you say about her."

Grace couldn't recall saying anything at all about her.

"Anyway, it's all your fault," he added in a breathtaking about-turn.

"Sorry?"

"For advising her to go into management in the first place! I have all this pressure on me now to perform!"

"You hardly wanted her to go back dancing in those clubs, did you?"

"No. She still dances sometimes, though." And he went off dreamily into some private place. Grace didn't particularly want to follow.

"Grace!"

Ewan was hurrying down the hill towards her now, his arm protectively around Amanda. She was in a terrible state. Her face was all blotched from crying, and her nose swollen.

"G-G-Grace," she began.

"Don't start me off again," Nick said, sniffing a bit.

Ewan gave Grace a look. "Thanks a lot. You ran off on us back there!"

"Yes, sorry about that. I had something to do."

"What exactly did you have to do?"

Amanda was racked with fresh sobs, and Grace ignored Ewan and put her arms around the girl. "Now, now."

"He wouldn't even speak to me!"

"I know, I know."

"What am I supposed to do now?"

Grace tried to push her down on the grass beside Nick. "Why don't you have a rest, maybe take a few deep breaths?"

Amanda snapped, "Stop patronising me."

She shrugged off Grace's hand and stalked off.

Ewan looked after her sympathetically. "Poor girl. She's had a terrible shock."

"But she hasn't. I don't mean to sound cruel, but she knew before she ever came here that it was over with him!"

Ewan regarded her. "You seem to know a lot about their relationship."

"Not really."

"How come you're so interested?"

"Me? I'm not. I couldn't give a hoot!"

"You seem to know Adam very well too."

"We lived in the same house for a month, Ewan. You can't live with someone without getting to know them well."

Although that was debatable. She and Ewan had lived in the same house together for over a decade and he had no idea of most of the things that went on in her head.

"You know something? Adam isn't important to this discussion at all."

It wasn't that she was trying to wriggle out of the consequences of her own actions. But it would just complicate matters further.

"And what are we discussing here? Because I haven't a clue!"

"Us," she said.

It had been coming all day, of course. All month, really. Actually, thinking about it, she realised it had been coming for a couple of years now.

He was looking at her peculiarly. "I don't think the middle of a rock festival is the place to be discussing this."

"Fine. We can go home and discuss it if that's what you want. My position isn't going to change."

He was angry now. "Your *position*? And what might that be? That our marriage doesn't suit you any more?"

"We're not the same people we were when we met fifteen years ago, Ewan."

"You're absolutely right there. Now we're a married couple who have made a commitment to each other. We're parents of ten-year-old twins."

It was true. It was also emotional blackmail, and she was angry with him for stooping so low.

"Yes, Ewan. Two boys who have a right to expect more than they're getting right now! And we've a right to expect more of each other."

"Gee!" he cried. "I had no idea you were doing it for us as a *family*! You should have said!"

She gave a little sigh. "Stop it. I know it's not going to be easy. I know people are going to be hurt. And if there was any way at all that . . . but there isn't. Not for me."

The words were like a cold gust of wind blowing through the very foundations of their marriage. The surrounding crowd gave a little surge forward – a new act had probably come on stage – but Grace and Ewan were frozen, two people standing too far apart to be mistaken for a couple, but with some invisible ties keeping them together.

Then Ewan said, "Grace, I'm not accusing you here, but if . . . if something had happened while I was away – " He took a breath. "If all this was to do with another person, then I wouldn't be angry. Well, I'd try to understand. It can happen to anyone – you think there's something better out there when really it's just short-lived. A flash in the pan, and then you come to your senses and go home to your family where you belong. I could understand that, Grace, if that's what's happened. I could forgive it."

If she said yes, if she told the truth about her and Adam, then he wouldn't believe a word she'd said about not being happy in their marriage. He would think a young buck had turned her head, and that it was merely a question of turning it back.

He was waiting. She didn't know what to do. Tell him and be honest? Endure his 'forgiveness?' Or shut her mouth and run while she still had the chance?

There was a growing whisper around her that she could no longer ignore.

"Look! Look!"

Everyone was pointing. Grace turned to look too, and at that moment all the lights went out on the stage. The music screeched to a halt. It was as if somebody had pulled the plug on the whole thing.

The rock group on stage looked around, bemused, holding instruments that no longer worked. The lead singer turned to the wings, and said something, obviously along the lines of, "What the hell is going on?"

Then someone ran on from the wings, and grabbed the microphone from the startled singer's hand, and shoved him away. It was difficult at first to see who it was, because he was wrapped from head to toe in a huge MOX banner.

"Adam!" Martine roared from the top of the hill, startled.

Grace stood on her tiptoes, straining to see. It was Adam all right.

"What's he doing?" Ewan asked

"I don't know," she said. 'Talk to you later', he had said rather ominously. Was he going to announce to Ewan, to her friends, her *children*, that they'd been having an affair? Surely he wouldn't be so cruel as to hurt them like that just to get back at her?

Suddenly all the lights on the stage came back on. The mike sprang to life. Joey was obviously playing his part

"Sorry about the interruption, everybody!" Adam roared into the mike. "But I have something very important to say!"

Then he turned to look directly at her, it seemed. In the midst of thousands of people, was it possible that he had found her? She stood there, mesmerised, as he leaned forward to the mike . . .

"There's a shipment of nuclear fuel on its way from Japan! And we've got to stop it! We've got to take whatever action is necessary – all of us!"

Hoots of approval erupted from some of Martine's gang.

"Stop it! Stop it!" Martine shouted at them, furious. "He's not engaged in a peaceful protest! We must distance ourselves from this!"

But she was drowned out as the chant went up again: *No Mox! No Mox!*

It spread out across the crowd until hundreds were clapping and chanting, then thousands.

"No Mox! No Mox!" Adam roared into the mike, getting everyone even more stirred up. Look at him – he was loving it! It was like he had been born to lead some kind of revolution. Grace found herself clapping along with everybody else.

But then he motioned for quiet, and shouted, "There's just one more thing!"

Grace swallowed nervously. She cast a little look at Ewan. He was watching the stage very intently too. Looking at him now, knowing it was over between them, she didn't know what she felt: bereft, certainly. But it was a release too.

On stage, Adam said, "I'd just like to say – "

Here came security at last: four big bruisers of guys bounding onto the stage. The crowd roundly booed them as they set upon Adam. But they couldn't wrestle the mike from him. He managed to get it to his mouth again. "I'd just like to say – "

"For God's sake! Take him down! Take him down!" Martine roared.

But she was in a minority, and the crowd were really behind him now, screaming NO MOX, NO MOX, and – would you believe it – he managed to get to the mike again, kicking over two amps in the struggle.

"I'd just like to – " he rasped again.

The mike was finally snatched from him, but not by the inept security guys. There was Amanda on the stage, tiny and determined, and she shouted into the mike for whole crowd to hear – for the rock group and for Ewan and for Grace and for Adam to hear: *"I'm pregnant!"*

EIGHTEEN

Nick had put on ten pounds, and wouldn't fit into his costume.

"Try holding your breath," Charlie instructed.

"I can't sing if I'm holding my breath."

Charlie sighed as though he were being very unreasonable.

"I'm going to let out one of the darts at the waist. That might work," Grace said, her mouth full of pins.

"He's been comfort-eating like mad," Charlie confided in her. "I found him in the fridge at four o'clock this morning making a beetroot-and-peanut-butter sandwich. Maybe I should put a lock on it."

There was a knock on the door, and one of the television people popped their heads in. "Ten minutes, Nick."

He moaned. Charlie said, "Hurry, Grace!"

"I'm going as quick as I can. It's hard to see with all these ruffles . . ."

The fussy shirt was tucked into a pair of narrow-legged black pants, finished off with a pair of ankle boots. Privately, Grace thought that Nick looked like something from Spandau Ballet. But she couldn't say that, of course – not when Charlie had hand-picked the outfit after looking at nine videotapes of previous Eurovisions. All of them seemed to have been from the 1980s.

"Nick, your nose has gone all shiny again," Charlie said crossly. She took a big powder brush and swiped at it. "Try to stop sweating, okay?"

Nick didn't answer. He stood still as a statue in the midst of the flurry, his face white and his pupils dilated and fixed on some distant point.

"Nick? Nick, are you all right?" Charlie said. No reply again. "Nick, stop it. This is not funny!" She turned to Grace, worried. "What the hell is wrong with him?"

"Oh, he's always like this before a gig," Grace said.

"What?"

"It's called stage fright. Usually it passes."

"*Usually?*"

"Once he escaped through a fire exit, didn't you, Nick?"

"Jesus," said Charlie.

"But that was in the very early days," Grace added hurriedly. "The best thing to do is leave him alone."

But Charlie said, "He just needs a little pep talk." She stepped forward and rapped Nick sharply on the chest with her knuckles. "Now listen here, buster! You are going to be stepping on that studio stage out there in ten minutes. There are two hundred thousand people tuning in their TVs right at this moment! Our whole *future* depends on your performance tonight!"

Nick gave a kind of a low, animal moan, then gagged as though he were going to projectile vomit. Charlie took a hasty step back, and obviously decided to change tack.

"How about a cup of tea, sweetie? No? Oh, I know – hash! A little spliff would loosen you up. Tell you what – you wait right here and I'll go score some drugs, okay?"

She hurried out of the dressing-room, waving frantically at a passing member of the television crew.

"Nearly finished," Grace assured him, deftly sewing up a new dart. They had learned all about darts in class last week: how they were vital in the shape of a garment, but more importantly, in its fall. Of course, they had measured and marked them out properly on the big cutting table, and sewn them up on shiny new Brother sewing machines. Still, this was an emergency.

Nick burst out, "I can't remember the words to the song! I can't even remember the first line!"

"Of course you can," Grace said soothingly. "You won't even have to think about it. The minute you hear the music, you'll be away."

"Not this time. I can't go out there, Grace."

He did seem more terrified than usual.

"Nick, it's just the same as all those gigs you used to play with Steel Warriors."

He looked at her. "What, in the SFX to an audience of two hundred? Tuam town hall, to fifty people? You heard Charlie – there are going to be two hundred thousand people watching tonight! All hoping and praying that I make a balls of it. It's sick, that's what it is. Sick!"

Each week viewers would telephone in their votes on the candidates, and each week the one with the lowest number of votes would get eliminated, until eventually a winner was declared and sent forward as the Irish entry to the Eurovision. It was, Nick contended hotly, a particularly tortuous selection procedure, designed solely to appeal to bloodthirsty reality-show junkies. And the beneficiaries of the premium-line telephone charge, of course.

"Have you seen the rest of them?" He jerked a thumb towards the other dressing-rooms. "They're all about twenty, Grace." The same age as Adam. "They're wearing leather, and bra-tops, and fucking Bermuda tans. They've all got their own *hair*." He looked at himself in the dressing-room mirror. "And look at me. An ageing rocker dressed in a frilly shirt and singing about blarney stones."

"You're not. The song is good. Whatever else you say, don't put the song down."

336

The song had undergone a radical rewrite. He had insisted; had faced Charlie down over it and threatened to walk out if he didn't get his way. Any mention of blarney stones had gone. There was still a strong Dana feel about it but, as Nick had pointed out, people had certain expectations of an Irish Eurovision entry, and he didn't want to disappoint them.

"They'll be watching, you know," he muttered now.

"Who?"

"Derek and Vinnie." The other two members of Steel Warriors. "Vinnie rang me to wish me luck. He could hardly stop laughing."

"I'm sure that's not true." She added, "And even if it were, he's just jealous!"

"They're going to watch it in his house. Derek's bringing pop-corn and beer. He mentioned 'popcorn' twice, Grace!"

"There are other people watching as well – people who support you," Grace said. "There's Didi and the kids out in the studio audience – they're rooting for you!"

"Didi says she wants a fifty per cent cut of any earnings from this," Nick said. "Charlie is going mad. And Dusty says she'll be too embarrassed to go to school any more. She says it's the final insult."

Grace cried valiantly, "Well . . . well, I'm rooting for you! And Ewan and the kids, and Gavin, and Frank."

"Frank hasn't even turned up." Nick was indignant. "And I after getting him a studio ticket and everything! They're in quite big demand, you know," he added a bit importantly.

"Yes, well, he's a bit down over the whole Sandy business at the moment, Nick."

Even more so since he'd arrived back from the States, confused and empty-handed, so to speak, only to discover that she had bought sixty-four DVDs on the Internet with his credit card, including *The Greatest Love Songs Ever*. That, he said, had hurt more than anything.

Grace had hoped he would turn up tonight. He was spending too much time brooding by himself, and waiting for the police to ring. Sergeant Daly had tried to tell him that Internet fraud was so endemic that it could take months. Frank had said he didn't care: he couldn't get on with his life until he knew who Sandy really was.

"Where's Charlie?" Nick said nervously now.

"She'll be back in a minute." Unless she was stoned in a corner somewhere.

"You know the way you hate her?"

"I do not hate her! I never say a word against the woman. Why do you always think I hate her?"

"The thing is, no one's ever believed in me the way she does, Grace. And I know it's only the Eurovision, but I'm terrified of letting her down. If I get eliminated tonight, I won't give a damn for *me*. Well, I might – I've put a good bit of work into this, after all. But it's for Charlie really. Tell me honestly: do you think I'll get through to the next round?"

Grace looked at her long, lanky brother in the Gary Kemp shirt and the drainpipe trousers tucked into cowboy boots and she said, without missing a beat, "Absolutely! But, you know, I always thought red was more your colour than white . . ."

"I know! I said that to Charlie. White makes my skin look jaundiced."

"Doesn't Ewan have a red shirt on tonight?"

"Dunno."

"And you wore your nice new leather trousers in tonight, didn't you?"

Finally the penny began to drop with him. He looked at her, half elated and half terrified. "She'd murder us."

"If we're quick enough you'll be on stage before she even knows. Hurry, Nick!"

338

Julia was watching it on the telly at home in Hackettstown.

"Good lad!" she shouted, as Nick sang the last note of his song, and then bowed to rapturous applause; well, not as rapturous as it had been for the contestant before him, but she had been wearing a tiny miniskirt, and had simpered and flirted shamelessly with the studio audience. She hadn't had any real talent, not like Nick.

Duncan was on next, the contestant with the stringy beard and unfortunate nose, and Julia turned the volume down.

"Mammy? Do you fancy something to drink?" Michael called from the kitchen.

She perked up. "Yes, please." Maybe he had brought some wine, or perhaps even a malt whiskey.

"Tea or cocoa?"

"Oh. Cocoa, I suppose."

"Coming up. Where do you keep the . . . Ow! Found it. Shit. Spilled it!"

Julia had to suppress a little sigh. No matter how hard she tried, there was something about Michael that would always irritate her.

"Here we go!" He eventually swept in bearing a tray of cocoa and bourbon creams, which he put down on the crowded table top with much huffing and puffing.

"Michael, please don't move the telephone."

"Sorry . . ."

"I'm expecting a call from Bono."

Since she'd got shot, she liked to have things within reach. Her foot tended to ache a bit, especially at night, and the doctors said there was a bit of arthritis setting in.

And she was getting old. There was no denying that.

"Mammy," Michael began heavily, and she braced herself. Although recently she had begun to suspect that he liked giving her little lectures. She played her part by letting herself be lectured. "I wonder whether you're up to all this."

"I'm just lending a hand, that's all."

"Stop downplaying it. Bono is ringing you up, for heaven's sake!"

"And Sinead O'Connor," Julia said proudly. "She's really very nice, you know. Are you going to come along, Michael?"

He was caught with his mouth full of bourbon cream. "Me?"

"It's going to be great. Thousands of people marching simultaneously in Dublin and London! And we've got rock stars and actors and politicians marching, and two boy bands – we'll have to separate them, we think – and a couple of game show winners. And Sinead and Bono, of course, if we can persuade them."

It was going to be the biggest anti-nuclear protest in years. Martine, disillusioned with her solo efforts, had been seduced by one of the big environmental groups in London. She had asked Julia whether she wanted to work from home as a volunteer – "Stuffing envelopes, that kind of thing."

Within a week Julia had stuffed as many envelopes as she was going to stuff. She started to mutter about age discrimination and, sure enough, her job was swiftly upgraded to PR assistant for the forthcoming march.

She was surprised by her passion for it. She woke every morning eager to get going for the day, to start phoning Dublin and London and Edinburgh, and winning converts to the cause.

She didn't know what JJ would have made of it all: another of her fads, probably, like the rockery and the rose garden and making home-brew down in the shed. But he'd had a career; that part of him had always been amply fulfilled. He had travelled the world.

She had been left at home on her own with a small child whom she didn't understand half the time. A child who would look at her blankly when she impulsively suggested that they paint his room the colour of a sunset with a moon rising just over his bed.

He had asked if it would fall on him.

What?

The moon.

It's just a painting, Michael, a fantastical painting.

Oh – can I have something to eat?

She should have had a career too. But it wasn't done in those days. She'd had to wait until now.

She thought now of how close she'd come to missing out on this chapter of her life. She hardly ever thought about her ham-fisted suicide attempt – it was far too embarrassing – except to wonder where her mind had been. With JJ, she supposed – JJ, her most enduring and passionate fad. Well, it was difficult, in the throes of grief, to believe that there might be a new beginning.

"Could you get me their autographs?" Michael asked now.

"Sorry?" She could never be able tell him – Michael – about that most private and desperate episode of her life. But then that wasn't the sort of thing you told your children.

"The boy bands," he clarified. "For Susan. She's into all that."

"How is she settling into the flat?" Julia enquired. It was no longer referred to as the 'granny flat'.

"Very well. Except that she doesn't want me or Gillian having a set of keys to it. She says it invades her privacy. Gillian says over her dead body."

Julia was indignant. "She's absolutely right. Susan is only thirteen. I think you're very brave letting her live in the flat in the first place."

"It's not as though we had any choice," Michael said gloomily. "She threatened to run away with young Gavin if we didn't."

"They're still an item then?"

"Charlie is coming over for dinner at the weekend. Says she wants to meet us formally." Michael rolled his eyes. "Her and Gillian . . . you can imagine."

Julia cleared her throat. "How is Gillian anyway?"

"Okay. She's got the hang of the injections now; at least, she doesn't faint any more."

By a cruel twist of irony, Gillian had snagged herself on barbed wire as she had left the festival grounds that day. A routine blood test had revealed certain abnormalities, nothing to do with the barbed wire. More tests were carried out. And after fifteen years of unfounded concern about her health, of rogue symptoms and false diagnoses, Gillian had succumbed to chronic diabetes.

"They still can't understand it," Michael said, shaking his head. "It's usually linked to obesity and sugar consumption in someone her age. But she never ate anything."

"I suppose she has to have regular meals now?"

"Every three hours, to keep her insulin levels up. She carries an alarm clock, you know, just in case she forgets and falls into a coma."

"Would it be that sudden?"

"Who knows? And she carries two Mars bars in her bag at all times in case she gets stranded in her car during a flood or a hurricane, or there's an extra long queue at the dry-cleaners." He thought for a moment, then said, "You know, I haven't seen her this happy in years."

Julia took a sip of her cocoa and said, "She doesn't know you're here, does she?"

"Well . . ."

"Michael, I don't want to cause any aggravation between you and Gillian." Any more than she had already caused, that was.

"You're not."

"It's not fair to be coming here behind her back."

He had stayed away for a whole month after the festival. She had wondered whether she would ever see him again when she'd spotted his Jeep parked down the road half-hidden behind the big elm tree. It had been empty. She had thought perhaps she had been mistaken when she'd seen him sneaking across her back garden. On tiptoes. Bemused, she had watched as he had climbed up onto her oil tank, looked in, and then stealthily driven off in his Jeep again.

The following week he was sneaking across her lawn again, this time with a toolbox. She had gone out to confront him and had found him halfway down one of her manholes.

"Michael, what are you doing?"

"Checking your drains," he had confessed sheepishly. "And you need an oil fill too before the winter sets in."

He had come once a week after that. She didn't know what stories he made up for Gillian. Golf, maybe.

"What do you want me to do, stop coming?" he said stubbornly. "You're seventy-three, for heaven's sake. You're my mother."

"That doesn't really matter, Michael."

"What?"

She said, "I wouldn't want you to do anything out of obligation. Because obligation is a funny thing. It can tie you down, stop you doing things you want to do. It can make you resentful and neglectful to the very people you should love the most."

"You're not stopping me doing anything," he said.

She looked at his round, uncomplicated face and searched for the right words. God, it was hard. Theirs wasn't the kind of relationship where they talked. Or at least about the same things.

"Am I not? Here you are, sitting with an old crock because you feel you have to, when you should be at home with your wife and daughter."

"Susan's gone with Gavin and Charlie to that telly thing tonight to watch Nick." He added, "You should have seen what she went out wearing."

She tried again. "Gillian then."

"It's her diabetic support group tonight. It's the same night as her tinnitus group – isn't that bad luck?"

"Michael, what I'm trying to say is that maybe Gillian was right. Maybe I wasn't the best mother in the world."

He looked at her. "Maybe I wasn't the son you wanted either."

"That is not true."

"I never could think of anything very interesting to say," he said, with a little laugh. "And then when I *did*, Daddy would get in there before me. He had a knack of doing that." He looked into his cocoa. "I miss him, you know."

"Me too."

"But when he was gone, I thought, you'd need someone. I saw this chance, Mammy. Gillian thinks I'm pathetic," he added.

"Yes, well, she thinks I'm a cow." She had to say something smart, because she felt too warm and her eyes were smarting.

"She doesn't. She thinks you're insecure."

"*Insecure?* I'm seventy-three years of age. I'm as secure as I'll ever be."

There was a little silence, then Michael said, "Will we have another cup of cocoa?"

"And then will you promise me you'll go home?"

"Yes," he said. "Then I'll go home."

She watched him pick up the tray, and she said, "What about Gillian?"

"What about her?"

"She'll hate me even more if you don't tell her you're coming here."

"She doesn't hate you. She thinks you have a problem with aggression."

"How can I be aggressive as well as insecure? It doesn't make sense!"

"Apparently it does if you're a passive/aggressive personality."

"Just get the damned cocoa, Michael."

"Can we have chocolate?" Neil enquired.

"Have they had chocolate already today?" Grace asked Ewan. It was always best to check. In the beginning, when everybody had grappled to get used to the new living arrangements of weekdays with Grace and weekends with Ewan, some very grave liberties had been taken by Neil when it came to the truth, almost always involving chocolate,

McDonalds, and the amount of television watched.

"No," Ewan confirmed.

Grace reached for her purse.

"If you're sure we can afford it," Neil added under his breath.

"Poverty is good for the soul," Grace informed him.

"I'd rather have loads of money than a good soul," Jamie said gloomily.

"Can you not make her go back to work?" Neil asked Ewan.

"Neil!"

"No, it's okay, Ewan." She faced the boys. "You know that I'm studying at the moment. And when I get my qualification, I'll go back to work, okay?"

"No offence, Ma, but you're not going to rake it in making *dresses*."

"It's not just dresses. It's fashion as a whole. Which includes footwear, hats, ready-to-wear garments, underwear. Look at all the revolutionary brassieres that have been designed recently, for example!"

The boys looked alarmed. "We'll be a laughing stock," Neil told Jamie.

Secretly, Grace wanted nothing to do with underwear. This wasn't just because she never wore it any more. It was the texture of the fabric – if you could call it fabric – that put her off. They even had bras with plastic straps now, for heaven's sake! And most modern underwear completely ignored the body's natural shape – how could any normal bottom hope to look good in a G-string? And most padded bras were nothing more than shelves for tired bosoms that deserved a little more comfort.

But, oh, *fabric*. Proper fabric, and the way it could be transformed into a flowing skirt or a beautiful blouse for the fuller woman. And the wonder and versatility of cotton, for example! At night Grace dreamed of bales of the stuff, and linen, and warm vibrant wool, and she would wake up to find herself licking the bedclothes ecstatically.

And to think that she never would have found fabric had it not been for Amanda! That little white lie had stuck in her head, and matured and blossomed into a concrete idea, and finally into a postgraduate course at The Design Institute.

Natalie was taking all the credit for Grace's new path in life, of course. All because she had gone out and bought a book on further education and presented it to her. "You'll have to do *something* now that you're an unemployed separated woman, Grace."

"He's sweating over it. Nick is sweating all over my shirt!" Ewan said, looking up at the television screen in the corner of the room. Grace had hastily engineered a clothes swap between the two men, and Ewan now wore Nick's Gary Kemp ruffled affair – under duress, it should be pointed out. On the television screen, Nick looked splendid in Ewan's red shirt and his own black leather pants.

"Sssh! Here we go!" Grace said.

The presenter sombrely informed them that the telephone votes had been counted, collated, distributed, re-counted, tallied and verified by an independent adjudicator. And he could now confirm that the contestant in the white miniskirt and the flirty smile was the recipient of loads of them.

"Twenty-five thousand votes!" Grace groaned. "Nick will never beat that!"

"He doesn't have to beat it. So long as he doesn't come last, that's what matters," Neil said.

"Stop sweating on my shirt," Ewan told Nick, quietly.

The votes for the beardy guy were now read out – twenty-nine – and he was being roundly rubbished by the presenter – "You were pretty crap out there, weren't you, Duncan?" – and Grace was on her feet and clapping.

"He was crap! Oh, thank God!"

"Nick won't do worse than twenty-nine," Neil declared. "He's through." And without further ado he and Jamie went off in search of a chocolate-vending machine. Grace still kept on eye on the television. "Isn't it marvellous?" she said.

Ewan plucked at Nick's white ruffled shirt unhappily. "Supposing somebody sees me?"

"Nobody's going to see you in here," she said.

It wasn't like him to be so concerned with his appearance. Especially now that he was slowly but surely morphing into Bob Geldof.

Grace had been right – after a mere three months, Ewan was starting to show all the signs of a scatty genius who lived on his own. His hair stopped artistically just above his shoulder, and he had taken to wearing stubble and a selection of faded denims. Even his speech was more laid-back, and he said 'yah' a lot. All in all, he seemed about ten years younger. Wasn't it sickening?

Grace, of course, had filled out quite a bit more. She now took a fourteen in clothes, a size she found both comfortable and right. She didn't wear kaftans as much any more – very chilly on the legs in winter – and her wardrobe was now full of beautiful silky shirts and loose pants. Her hair had grown longer too, and it was lovely now, and so easy to manage – all she had to do was wash it and leave it alone. For Natalie's sake she got it trimmed every two months but that was about it.

On the television, the twin sisters from the midlands who had sung a cover of 'The Power Of Love' were declared the recipients of over eighteen thousand votes.

"Pah," Grace said rudely. And then the programme went to commercial break! "I don't believe this!"

"It's all part of the plan to build tension," Ewan, the advertising man, said. He reached up, turned down the volume, and looked at her.

"So!" he said, overly casually.

She wondered whether he was going to ask whether they might try again. He had every day for weeks on end in the beginning. He hadn't asked recently, though.

"Is there something on your mind, Ewan?" she prompted.

"Actually, there is."

For all his newfound grunge sophistication, his glasses were held together with sellotape at the bridge, she saw. He had probably sat on them again. A feeling of such fondness came over her that she almost changed her mind.

It would be so easy to get back together. And so wrong. Because one of the first things she would probably end up doing was taking his glasses down to the optician's.

"No!" she blurted. "I must have said no a hundred times! Honestly, Ewan, I thought we had moved on from this!"

He looked a bit startled. "I was just going to ask whether I could take the boys on Wednesdays evenings."

"Oh!"

"In addition to the weekends. Look, I can get my solicitor to run it past your solicitor if that's what you'd prefer."

"No, no. Obviously we'll have to discuss it with the boys, but I don't have a problem with it . . . Ewan, I thought you were too busy to take them during the week? That you only wanted them at weekends?"

"I never said 'only', Grace. You make me sound so heartless!"

"Sorry. It's just with your work and everything . . ."

"Yes, well, I won't be so busy any more. We lost the Slimchoc account."

"What?"

"Word came through last week."

"Was it the slogan?" She couldn't really blame them. She hadn't liked it herself.

"The company's gone bust, Grace. I thought you might have seen it in the papers."

She didn't really buy newspapers much any more. (She had started reading books again, and was in her science fiction phase at the moment, and her fantasies now involved her being captured by a couple of three-fingered Zulites with very large penises.)

"They did some new laboratory research in America," Ewan went on. "And they discovered that the fat substitutes in Slimchoc not only did nothing to aid weight loss, but caused abnormal hair growth and stomach distension in male rats. What it does to female rats isn't clear yet, but it's not going to be pretty."

"Oh, Ewan."

"They've pulled everything – the chocolate bars, the milk-shakes, the Wicked Slimchoc Cake. They were going to trial-run the chewing-gum anyway, but decided against it on legal advice."

"Probably wise."

"Yes. So it's over. Finished." He sounded very final and she felt sorry for him.

"Come on. You'll bounce back," she told him encouragingly.

"You don't understand. I'm glad Slimchoc is gone. I'm delighted!"

"Oh!"

He flicked back a shirt ruffle from his neck and said, "We've both had a lot to think about in the last three months, Grace. Me especially. And you were right about me not giving the boys a hundred per cent. I wasn't even giving them eighty. So I've decided to cut down on my work. Spend more time with them." Then he added, very modestly: "If that's okay with everyone."

"The boys would love it, I'm sure." She added, "Mind you, that means there will be even less money."

"They'll just have to make do," Ewan said emphatically. "I don't want money worries to distract you from your course, Grace."

"Thank you." She was touched. He had never been so supportive of her career before. "Imagine! We're both in creative careers now!"

"What? Oh, yes." He was looking at his watch. Possibly he had left his car on a meter. "So this Wednesday thing – have we it sorted?"

"Absolutely. I'll tell the boys tonight."

"It means we'll be seeing each other a bit more too. I don't know how you feel about that."

It was another loaded question, she felt.

She kept it jokey. "I'm sure we'll manage. We haven't killed each other so far, have we?"

"Not at all." He looked out at her from his sellotaped glasses meaningfully. "In fact, I don't think we've ever got on better."

"So we're the classic case of a couple who split up only to discover that we're falling in love all over again? How boring!" she said lightly.

"I never said anything about falling in love."

She felt a bit foolish now. "I didn't mean . . . of course we're not . . . "

"Grace, I'm seeing somebody. Obviously I wanted to tell you before anybody else."

She smiled and nodded enthusiastically. She had no idea why. They had scarcely been separated a wet weekend and there was her husband telling her he was seeing somebody!

"It's not serious," he added as though by way of compensation. "I mean, we've only just started going out."

She kept smiling as she wondered what he expected her to say. That she was glad for him? At the same time, it seemed a bit rich to feel so hurt, given that she had been seeing somebody *during* their marriage. But still, three months seemed a bit, well, indecent.

"What's her name?" she asked. Not that it mattered. Anyhow, she already knew that she would be called Sophie or Clio, and that she would work in advertising, and that she and Ewan had been out twice, probably three times, for sushi, and that they had probably slept together. (Had he initiated things by licking her neck the way he always had with Grace, or had Sophie said crossly, 'Oh stop it!', as Grace had wanted to many times, and made him put on a leather collar and bark like a dog?) She tittered.

"Anna," he said, looking a bit hurt. "She's a hairdresser. She does films and stuff." He added, a bit bashfully, "She says she won't rest until she gives mine a good trim."

Poor, poor Anna. Grace felt a flash of sympathy for the woman who would gradually, without even realising it, start to organise Ewan's life for him. Eventually she would be making his medical appointments and getting him two pairs of glasses for the price of one.

"I wish you and Anna the very best of luck," Grace said, with the fervent sincerity of one who had narrowly escaped.

"Thanks, Grace!" He was delighted with himself now – at least there would be no unpleasantness with the ex-wife. He even went so far as to enquire jokily, "And how about yourself? Any sign of a bit of romance on the horizon at all?"

It was like Adam had never happened; like he had never had a suspicion in the world that his wife was cheating on him with a twenty-year-old.

"Oh, no," she said, smiling nicely. "What with the boys and the course and everything, I don't have time."

"I'm sure," he said, nodding sagely. "Still, you never know what's around the corner!"

He obviously harboured no mixed feelings at all about his wife starting to date again. Grace saw again, very clearly, how little of him had ever really belonged to her, and to their marriage. And for the first time in three months, she was completely sure that she had done the right thing.

For herself, in any case, and very probably Ewan, who had that unmistakable excitement about him of being back on the market again. It was Neil and Jamie she worried about.

Sometimes she thought it would have been better had they been very young, and had no memories of being part of a conventional family. Or older, in their teens maybe, with a better grasp of the difficulties of relationships. Ten seemed to be the very worst age, halfway between childhood and adolescence, and she didn't know how to make it easier on them.

"Night nappies," Natalie had declared.

"What?"

"They've probably started wetting the bed again, have they? Lots of children going through a separation do."

"Not at ten, Natalie."

They seemed okay, at least on the surface. But it must affect them, how could it not? It was so hard to know. And if there was one thing she had learned out of this whole experience, it was that she knew absolutely nothing at all.

Except that Ewan had a date tonight. He was wearing the after-shave she had given him for his birthday last year. The idiot.

"Are you meeting her tonight? Anna?"

He tried to be casual. "As a matter of fact, I am." But he was fidgeting, looking at his watch, then at the TV screen. "It's just . . . my shirt. I've got a table booked for nine. Anna's not keen on eating too late."

It wasn't like him to be so sensitive.

"You'd better run then," Grace said.

"Yes . . ." He plucked at the Spandau Ballet shirt, agonised.

Grace said, rather spitefully, "I suppose it'll be a kind of a test. If she really likes you, she'll overlook it."

Now he was even more worried, and he hardly said goodbye as he left.

He was back within ten seconds, looking sheepish. "Hi, I think I might have . . . "

"Yes. Your car keys," Grace said crisply, handing them over and roundly closing the door on him. She might still pick up after him occasionally but, by God, she didn't have to pretend any more that it was love.

When the door burst open a minute or so later she thought it was him back again, to look for change for the parking meter perhaps. But it was Nick, fresh off the stage, and jerky with adrenalin.

"Well?" he demanded. "What did you think?"

Grace stared back guiltily. Imagine – she had been so engrossed in Ewan's revelations that she didn't even know how many votes he had scored! And she couldn't tell anything from his face; that peculiar stare could mean it had gone either way.

"I saw your performance," she said, hedging her bets. She added strongly, just in case he had been eliminated, "And you were great. You have absolutely nothing to be ashamed of."

He exploded, "Ashamed? I was fan-fucking-tastic, man! They loved me! They wanted me! I would have won only for your woman flashing her legs at the cameras. The lighting guy said a girl at the back fainted during my encore – chew on that, Vinnie!"

And he ripped off Ewan's sodden red shirt and flung it to the floor, then spat on it for good measure.

Charlie danced into the dressing room, hooting and whooping. "Second place! What do you think of that, Grace?"

"Brilliant!" Grace said, just glad that she knew.

"Hey," Nick said to Charlie. "Maybe tonight. But there are no second places. *There are no second places.* We're going all the way to the Eurovision, baby!"

And he grabbed her, swung her around, and gave her a long hot kiss. Grace studied the ceiling.

"Nick!" Charlie said, when she eventually broke free. "Are you serious?"

"Course I am! What do you think I was doing out there? Scratching my balls?"

"Well, no, it's just, I felt I was pushing you . . ."

"I need to be pushed. No kidding. Sometimes I need to be pushed, don't I, Grace?"

"I – "

"But sometimes I feel I'm pushing you too hard."

"Push me harder. Push me all the way. Oh, baby, you smell good."

"Listen to me. I want you to be happy too. I don't want to make you do something you don't want to do – "

"They loved me out there, didn't they?"

"They adored you. But are you sure you won't miss rock music too much? Will he, Grace?"

"I – "

"Rock music? What the hell is that? A load of old noise! I never thought I'd say it about the Eurovision, but I got *respect* out there tonight, man. I got artistic gratification. I've never played to a sober audience before – the hairs stood up on the back of my neck," he said fervently. "In fact, they're still standing. Mmmm, come here, baby."

"Nick . . ."

"I love your bottom."

At that point Grace gave up and left.

NINETEEN

Her full name was Sandy Elizabeth Roth. Aka Jennifer O'Carroll. Aka Pavlova Martinez. Aka Marie Trudeau. The search had finally led to a semi-detached on the outskirts of Ballybunion.

"She was in Kerry all the time?" Grace said, eyes wide. She had only just recovered from the Eurovision last week.

Frank said nothing. He sat on the edge of his sofa, hunched over, his eyes fixed on the brown carpet.

Julia answered for him. "In a manner of speaking."

"And have they arrested her?"

"Yes, this morning, Sergeant Daly said," Julia told her confidentially. "I thought I'd better ring you to come over."

She was loving all the excitement, Grace could see; not to mention the fact that she had all the inside information, and Grace didn't. Look at the way she was patting Frank's arm!

"So what's her real name?" Grace asked.

He looked harder at the floor, his cheek muscles bunching furiously.

"Frank," she said. "There's nothing to be embarrassed about."

"Isn't there?"

"Of course not!" Grace reiterated strongly. "You have done absolutely nothing wrong here. Except perhaps trust too much.

She's the one who's taken advantage of you! Exploited your love and stolen your money!"

"Steady on," Julia murmured.

Grace tempered herself. "I'm just saying that if anyone should feel bad, it's her."

"Him," Frank whispered.

"Pardon?"

"Mr Liam Hughes. Sandy is a man."

There was a moment of dead air, and then Grace finally said, "Well . . . well . . . I might have known!"

Julia looked at her askance, eyebrows arched. Oh shut up, Grace mouthed back at her.

"Imagine," Frank moaned. "All this time, I was engaged to a man!"

Julia stood. "I think this calls for a drink," she declared, and set off for the kitchen.

Alone with Frank, Grace put her arm around him. "Oh, Frank!"

"What's worse," he said, "is that he was cheating on me!"

She eventually coaxed it out of him. At the time of his arrest, Liam Hughes was conducting at least eleven Internet romances through his various aliases. He selected his targets carefully, and his modus operandi was the same: after a number of months of grooming, he would encourage and agree to a marriage proposal, get the victim to put his house on the market with a view to moving to the States, and then at the point of sale a serious illness would suddenly strike which almost always required an expensive transplant. The double-kidney transplant was his favourite, but in the past he'd gone for a heart transplant, heart-and-lung, lung only, and once a complete brain transplant.

"But the police believe that may have been a cry for help," Frank said. "They said nobody could have been so stupid as to buy that one."

"Well . . ."

"But we were. The lot of us."

"You're not stupid. We all want to believe in people, Frank."

"Everybody could see it a mile off except for me! You saw it! Well, didn't you?"

"Yes, but I'm naturally cynical, it doesn't mean – "

"The fact that she never seemed to be able to come to the phone. Her sister having a bust-up with her husband the very week I was due to go over . . . God, when I think of the lies she wrote! *He* wrote, *he* – I can't seem to get that into my head. The stuff about disabled kids, and singing at church, and wanting to be a stay-at-home mom. All that shit about fate and destiny and how we were so lucky to have found each other." He took a breath. "And all the time he was laughing his head off at me in Kerry!"

"I'm sure he wasn't."

"Thinking how hilarious it was to wind up some sad old fart at the other end of the country! Cracking up every time he opened one of my emails to him!"

"Frank, stop."

"You know, I think the police are wrong. I don't think he was in it for the money at all. I think he just got a kick out of making middle-aged men fall in love with a Perry's hot-dog girl!"

"What?"

"Oh – I didn't show you, did I?" From his pocket he took a folded A4 sheet. He spread it out, handed it to her and looked away.

It was a copy of the photo Sandy had sent to him of her on the beach, supposedly on her day-trip for paraplegic children. Only in this copy there was no tea towel covering her hand, which quite clearly held a nine-inch hot dog. There was a caption underneath: *I love Perry's Hot Dogs!*

"Oh, Sandy," Grace said with a sigh, looking at the hot dog. Still, it could have been worse.

"That's actually an obscure model called Carole Wall. Liam Hughes just lifted the ads from American magazines, knowing full well the chances of me spotting them were slim. And he was right." He gave a bitter laugh.

"So what happens now?" she ventured.

"Nothing."

"But the money she's – he's – stolen from you, the DVDs . . ."

"Gone."

"Surely that can't be it? What are the police going to do?"

"They can't do a thing unless I want to prosecute."

"And do you?"

"What, stand up in some court and have the intimate details of my emails read out to a crowd of strangers? Try to explain how I could possibly believe that a woman like Sandy – had she existed – could have fallen in love with a man like me? No thanks. I've made enough of a fool of myself."

He tore up the photo of Sandy on the beach and threw it into the bin. There was a very long silence.

Grace ventured, "At least you still have your house."

"At least I still have my house," he repeated bravely. "At least nothing was signed before I found out."

"And your car."

"He was never after my car."

"I know, but I'm just saying. And your friends. Me, and Julia, and Nick." She had meant this to be reassuring, but the little roll call just sounded short and sad. She thought of something else. "And your health!"

"Oh, shut up, Grace."

"Yes, sorry."

He sighed and said, "Deep down I knew it. Knew it couldn't be true. Grace, don't even say it, okay? Let's just be honest for a minute: I'm a middle-aged man with a strange job and no friends, and who hasn't had a date since – oh, it doesn't matter. The Sandys of this world don't go for men like me unless there's something in it for them. In her case a couple of kidneys."

"And I think it says a lot about you that you were prepared to give them to her!" Grace said strongly.

"They're fictional. The kidneys."

"It doesn't matter. She didn't pick just anybody, you know. She only went for generous guys."

"Is that supposed to be a compliment? And she is a he."

"And guys that were easy to talk to. Well, she had to, if she was writing up to eleven emails a day!"

"Guys that were gullible, you mean."

"Frank, if she was only trying to rip you off then she could have done it in less than eleven emails a day."

"She had nothing better to do."

"That's a lot of stuff to say to someone you despite or pity or just want to make fun of. A lot of personal stuff, *beautiful* stuff – do you remember the moth? And how she turned off all her lights so that it wouldn't burn itself? And she described what its wings looked like and you took out your books and looked up what it was?"

"She also described how her kidneys had shrivelled up like a couple of old prunes," he said, but she could see he was affected. "And she is a he."

"So what, Frank. So what! Maybe you were both pretending to be things you weren't."

"I never pretended!"

"So how come she thought you'd slept with eighty-two women?"

"Oh. Yes."

"But it doesn't mean you didn't get on. It doesn't mean she didn't like you. Love you even, in her own way."

Was this pushing it a bit far? She held her breath.

"She is a he," Frank eventually said. He sounded a bit more robust. "How many times do I have to keep telling you?"

Julia came in with a tray of drinks then, and her timing was so perfect that Grace knew she had been waiting inside the kitchen door. And she was glad that they had each other, Frank and Julia, their houses just right across the road. Because Lord knows nobody could *live* with either of them.

"I made them doubles," Julia announced.

"I'll just go and clean up." Frank gave a bit of a sniff and set off for the bathroom.

"Your limp seems to have improved," Grace couldn't resist saying to Julia, as she deftly handed out drinks, pulled up the coffee table, and settled the bottle within top-up reach.

Julia gave her a look. "Well, it's a while since you've seen me. But I know that you're busy with your own life . . ." She gave a little sigh, ever the drama queen.

"So are you," Grace retaliated. "Any time I ring, your phone is engaged!"

"That's because of the march. You are coming, aren't you?"

"Of course I am."

"So is Michael. And maybe Gillian." Julia lowered her voice. "We're in the middle of peace negotiations. Michael is the broker."

"That's great, Julia."

"I have a list of things to apologise for, apparently. Don't hold your breath." She took a big swig of her whiskey, and then said, "I was talking to Martine today. Adam's case is in court next week. He's flying back for it."

At the mention of his name, Grace tensed, her eyes flying to Julia's. "Is he?"

But Julia was studying her glass. "Martine wanted to come over for it – she says she feels half-responsible, seeing as he was part of her group – but the people she works for now have said no. They don't want to be associated with a lawless element, they said."

"I suppose." Grace didn't know how she felt.

"He should be given a medal in my opinion. Not many people stand up for what they believe in, and to hell with the consequences!" Then Julia reined herself in. "Still. We must do things by the book these days."

"Yes."

Julia added, "Anyway, I just thought you'd like to know. Seeing as we all shared a house together for a month."

"Yes. Thank you, Julia."

A week later Grace was driving back through County Meath.

She hadn't been meaning to go at all. She'd had no intention of
it. She'd been sitting over a leisurely breakfast that morning, with
her day all planned out. She'd had a lunch date arranged with
Natalie, for goodness' sake. And she had suddenly wondered
whether she would regret not going. She already had so many
regrets in her life that she couldn't bear another one, so on the
spur of the moment she had cancelled all her plans and jumped
into the car.

Natalie hadn't been a bit impressed, of course.

"But why?"

"I don't know. Maybe I want to say goodbye to him."

"So send him a postcard. You don't have to go and see him."

"Nat, I can't explain it, okay? It's just been going around in my
head like some kind of . . . oh, I don't know what."

"A festering sore?" Natalie had jumped in.

"Well, no, it's not as big as that . . ."

"A nagging toothache then."

"It's not really anything painful – "

"A niggling itch?"

"That's it exactly." Anything for the sake of peace.

"If you want my opinion, I think you're making a big mistake,"
Natalie had declared.

"Everything I've done recently has been a mistake according to
you."

"That's not true. Although I think that house-swap idea with
those people in Spain *is* a big mistake."

"It's not decided yet, it was just something Frank saw on the
Internet . . ."

"And we all know his track record with the Internet."

"I'm just toying with it, okay?"

"Grace, there are some things you don't toy with. And going to see Adam is one of them."

"I'd like to know how he is."

"What makes you think he would want to see you, anyway? You dumped him, his girlfriend is pregnant, and as far as he's concerned you're history!"

A big stung, Grace had said, "You don't know that – maybe it's a festering sore with him as well!"

"Maybe he has the sense to leave things alone. Oh – you said it was only a niggling itch!" She had said, very sternly, "Are you still in love with him?"

"Oh, Natalie."

"Not even a little bit?"

"No! I wasn't ever in love with him in the first place. Not properly in love anyway."

"Really."

Natalie would never understand, and Grace had long ago given up trying to explain it to her.

Natalie had finished off with, "You're not going to start running after young lads now, are you, Grace? Now that you and Ewan have split up?"

"I don't know what I might run after. I'll have to see what takes my fancy."

"Because you won't be popular, you know. A lot of our friends have teenage boys."

"Adam was not a teenager. And you wanted a boy too, if I remember correctly."

"Oh! I was pregnant! That was my hormones speaking! And I don't ever want you to mention that to Paul, okay?" And she had rung off quickly with some excuse about having to give Paul Jnr his bottle.

Grace saw a signpost for Trim now, and she had an odd kind of feeling: anticipation or something. Which was ridiculous! She had a whole new life now. Well, it wasn't quite there yet, it was still in the making – which was probably the fun part, like assembling a complicated toy which, when finished, didn't seem all that great given the amount of work that had gone into it. But it was still hers, and she was enjoying it.

And she began to wonder whether Natalie was right – what sense was there in stirring everything up again? Getting everyone all agitated and worked up over something that was all in the past anyhow?

But that was the thing: it wasn't.

It began to rain just as she reached the outskirts of Trim. By the time she had found the courthouse and parked, it was pouring. She pulled on her raincoat, hunted for her rather decrepit black umbrella and got out.

She felt nervous as she approached the courthouse entrance. A woman about the same age was going in too.

Grace nodded to her. "Filthy day!"

"Mine's up for handling stolen goods," the woman said, without being asked. "What about yours?"

"Well, he's not actually my . . . we *were* . . . disturbing the peace and damage to property."

"What, like a pub? A shop front?"

"A microphone and two amps."

The woman gave this some consideration and then declared, "He'll get off with a fine."

Grace was delighted. "Do you think?"

"And maybe some community service."

"That might be difficult. He's from Tasmania."

"Well, that's even better!"

"Is it?"

"Justice Murphy, he generally doesn't go too hard on foreigners. You'll be fine, love." She patted Grace's arm and disappeared into the building.

Grace huddled outside for a moment under her umbrella, reconsidering her entrance. What if he were standing in the dock, for instance, when she barged in? (Would he have to stand in the dock for damaging a couple of amps? She didn't even know that.) What if the sight of her threw him so much that he blurted 'Guilty!' when really he'd meant the opposite? What if, at the sight of *him*, she was so overcome with sudden emotion – or worst still, lust – that she jumped on him and started to drag his clothes off? Or her own? Mind you, she didn't think she would; she was confident that she had sufficiently detached herself from that period in her life – from him – to do anything silly.

Still, better to wait outside, she decided. That would make it more casual. She would catch him on his way out, and they could exchange a few civilised words on the pavement, like two acquaintances pausing for a brief, concluding chat, before continuing on their respective journeys. Yes, that was the effect she wanted exactly.

The problem was, it was lashing rain. And it was coming in at an angle too, and Grace was getting wet from mid-thigh down. Her hair was blowing into rats' tails as well, which was certainly *not* the effect she wanted.

"Shoot!" Now the umbrella refused to stay up, and kept collapsing on her head ('shoot' didn't express her feelings adequately at all, but she'd picked it up from Neil, who still spoke in an American dialect, and it was better than cursing and swearing on the step of a courthouse).

The pub across the road was rather aptly called The Crooked Penny, and Grace waited for a break in the rain and ran for it. She struggled in the door, ignoring the curious stares of the few mid-morning male drinkers, and shook herself like a wet hen. Hoping her mascara wasn't dripping, she went to the bar.

The barman was already reaching for the jug of filter coffee in anticipation. The presumption annoyed Grace, and she plonked herself down on a bar stool, and said, loudly, "A gin and tonic, please." Less loudly, she added, "And a packet of those bacon fries."

She was munching and sipping away and hoping the rain would soon let up when, out of the corner of her eye, she saw a man in a suit approach her. Honestly – a young mother couldn't have a couple of drinks in peace on a Tuesday morning in a tavern without some man thinking she was fair game! There was no real equality yet, she thought darkly.

She stared haughtily ahead, trying to think of some scathing put-down. She could say that she'd seen better-looking specimens crawling out of a sewer on a Saturday night. Or she could comment loudly on the bad smell (Natalie's favourite – old-fashioned but effective, she maintained – not that she'd had cause to use it in recent years). Some of the younger girls in work had had some really nasty ones involving genital size and odour and Grace tried to remember them now. Oh, yes –

"Grace?"

The man in the suit was Adam. Any scathing put-downs about his manhood died in her throat.

"Adam?" she said, uncertainly.

No wonder she hadn't immediately recognised him: apart from the ill-fitting grey suit, which he wore over a white shirt that was too big around the neck, he was close-shaven and rather pale. Instead of his familiar big walking boots, he wore a pair of black leather shoes scrubbed so shiny that Grace could see her own startled expression in them.

"And your hair!" she cried indignantly. "What have they done to it?"

It was gelled and combed and darker than she remembered. It was *short*.

"I had no choice," he said, and Grace thought he sounded very tortured. What on earth could have happened to him? Instead of a free spirit, he looked like a double-glazing salesman!

Suddenly, it all came together in Grace's head with perfect clarity – of course! Amanda's pregnancy! Her family had shunned her, cast her heartlessly out into the world, and he had been forced to trade in his ideals for a nine-to-five job to support them both. It was very likely that he *was* a double-glazing salesman!

"Oh, Adam!" Her heart swelled with pity. She half expected him to whip out a glossy brochure.

He looked at her rather oddly. "It'll grow back, Grace."

"Sorry?"

"My hair. I did it for Judge Murphy. I haven't been in yet, but apparently he doesn't like long-haired louts."

Grace felt presumptuous, at best. "All this . . . it's for the court?"

"Of course. The suit, the shirt, the tie – it's all borrowed."

"Really, there's no need to – "

"The shoes belong to my brother." He gave her another look. "You didn't think I was going to show up in court wearing shorts and a T-shirt?"

"Of course not," she murmured, unwilling to offer her theory about PVC windows and sliding patio doors (he would hardly have been trying to flog them in Ireland, anyhow. Mind you, everything was gone global these days, in her defence. They sold fresh fish from the Mediterranean by post now). Still, anxious to make up for her speculation, she said, "He likes foreigners, though. Judge Murphy."

He looked a bit more cheerful. "Do you reckon?"

"I have it on very good authority," she said. "I was over at the courthouse just now. That's why I came. To . . . wish you well."

"Thanks, Grace." He half-smiled, then drummed his fingers nervously on the counter. "I just hope I don't get a prison sentence. I can't go to prison – not with . . . well, not with everything."

"I know," she said, even though she didn't. Did he mean Amanda and the baby? Or the next big anti-nuclear demonstration? She felt she couldn't ask – things weren't like that between them any more. In fact, it was all a bit more awkward than she'd anticipated. She found herself searching for a neutral topic of conversation – dear God, what did you say to a young man you'd spent a month bonking? – and was about to make some clumsy excuse and leave when Adam said, "Do you mind if I sit down?"

"Um, not at all."

He joined her on a bar stool. "It's just that these shoes are a size too small and, to be honest, they hurt like hell."

Both of them looked down at the shoes. Along with being mean in size, the leather looked particularly tough and unyielding.

"I suppose you could take them off," Grace suggested eventually, veteran of hundreds of pairs of uncomfortable shoes.

"In a pub?"

"Why not? Nobody's looking."

And indeed they weren't. The other male drinkers in the pub had lost all interest now that someone else had apparently got in ahead of them with Grace. And a slip of a lad too!

Adam slipped off the shoes surreptitiously. And almost immediately he seemed to relax, to become more himself, as though deep down he were a creature of nature that would resist any attempt by fashion, or the courts system, to rein him in.

Some of the tension in the air had gone with the shoes, and she was glad. They looked at each other for a little moment, and Adam said, "Thanks for coming today. It's good to see you."

"You too."

"How are the boys?"

"Great."

"And Jamie's . . . you know?"

"Nearly gone, thank God. He still won't go anywhere without wearing a baggy jumper though." She looked at him. "And how are you?"

He gave a jumpy grin. "Apart from a court appearance in half an hour?"

"It'll go okay," Grace assured him. "You're still in touch with Martine, I gather?"

He gave a bit of a snort. "She rings me occasionally – she gets bored sitting on her ass at a swanky desk all day long. Selling out to the establishment didn't turn out to be everything she'd thought."

Still as radical as ever. And he hadn't mentioned Amanda yet. Another theory began to form in Grace's head, and not a particularly attractive one: was it possible that Adam had decided that early fatherhood didn't suit him? Had he told the hapless Amanda to sling her hook, that he was off to save the world?

"Why are you looking at me like that?" Adam asked.

"Oh, I wasn't – "

"You were!" He was indignant. "Like I did something rotten on you!" He shot her a glance. "You were the one who dumped me, if I remember correctly."

There. It was out in the open. But he said it without any great heat, and she didn't know whether she was relieved or miffed. Then she was amused by her own vanity.

"I suppose I did," she agreed.

Adam played with a beer mat. "And how's Ewan?"

"Pretty good. I think."

He stopped playing with the beer mat and looked up.

"Ewan and I have split up, Adam."

"What?"

"Amicably, I think is the term. We're sorting out the conditions of the separation at the moment. I initiated it, by the way." She drew herself up on her bar stool, tossed back her hair over the ankle-length wool cardigan she'd knitted herself (she'd got a bit carried away) and went on, "And I've gone back to college – I'm doing design. I was top of the class at the end of the first term. And I'm writing a science fiction book. Well, I just started it on Friday, but I've got five pages written already, and Natalie thinks it's really good. And I'm probably going to be summering in Spain, if a time-share thing works out." She was going to mention too that she had collected more Computers For Schools tokens than any other mother, but that would just sound like boasting.

Adam said nothing for a moment, just watched her with that old expression of affection mixed in with mockery.

"Are you laughing at me?" she said. She decided that she didn't care anyway.

"Not at all. I'm just thinking that I can't top that."

"It's an age thing," she said sweetly. "You'll get there eventually."

Any further banter was cut short when the door of the ladies' toilet opened, and Amanda emerged.

"Grace!" she squealed joyously. She hurried up and swatted Adam on the arm. "You never said she was coming today!"

"I didn't know," Adam said.

"I didn't know myself, really," Grace confirmed.

Any further speculation as to Amanda's position in Adam's life was laid to rest when she put her arm around him tenderly and patted her belly.

"I spend most of my time in the loo," she said confidentially to Grace. "It's the baby. It's on my bladder, you see."

Grace dutifully had a look. Underneath a multi-coloured hippy smock-top, Amanda's pregnancy was a small, hard, neat bump, no bigger than a honeydew melon – in fact, Grace was half convinced it *was* a honeydew melon until Amanda took her hand without invitation and placed it on her belly.

"There! That's you two introduced!" she giggled, and Grace had that old familiar urge to slap her very hard.

"Congratulations," she said instead, retrieving her hand. "I'm delighted for you."

"We are too," Adam said evenly.

"Well, *eventually*," Amanda said tartly, giving Adam a little look. "It's taken a little while to get used to it," she told Grace.

"Of course it has," Grace said. "I remember when I was pregnant with the twins. I didn't know what to expect. Suddenly everything is different, *you're* different, you're going to become a parent, and you start worrying to yourself that you haven't the first clue about anything!"

"That's it exactly!" Amanda cried. "I knew you'd understand, Grace."

"We've got books and stuff," Adam interjected strongly. "We're not going to make a complete mess of it."

"Of course not," Amanda said. "It's just probably not a good idea for us to go on that campaign in Chile next month. Supposing my waters break?" She added to Grace, "He thinks I can just squat down and give birth in some bush hospital."

"As opposed to a private suite in the hospital your father is on the board of?" Adam shot back.

Amanda sighed. "He just *offered*. We don't have to take him up on it."

"And we won't." Adam looked steely. "No child of mine will be born with a silver spoon in its mouth!"

Amanda looked to Grace again in despair. "We're not talking about silver spoons. It's just that Daddy feels offended that we won't accept any help."

Grace made a diplomatic 'um' kind of sound, and watched the squabbling from some detached place in her head. And she suddenly saw how right they were for each other, Adam and Amanda. Adam needed someone to bring him down to earth every now and again, and Amanda was just the woman for the job. But she had spirit too, in her own way.

Grace finished up her gin and tonic and snuck a glance at her watch. If she hurried, she could still make her lunch date with Natalie. And there was a lecture this afternoon in college on period costumes that she would really love to catch.

She suddenly felt a great urge to leave the pub now, to get on with things. That feeling of anticipation that she'd had all morning wasn't anything to do with Adam at all, she realised. Or anybody else, for that matter. It was entirely to do with her.

Amanda and Adam were still arguing. "Daddy does kind of have a point, Adam, about us not having any jobs, or anywhere to live, or even a nappy to put on the baby when it's born."

"Ellsworth will have a nappy," Adam declared.

There was a little silence. "Ellsworth?" Amanda ventured.

Adam shrugged, a bit embarrassed. "I thought that's what we might call the baby. It means 'lover of the land'."

Amanda's bossiness dissolved into dreamy adoration. "Oh, Adam. I think it's beautiful."

"Yeh?" Then he looked at Grace. "What do you think?"

Grace thought that the child wouldn't thank either of them when it got to school age – look at poor Dusty – but that was something they would have to learn. Grace had finished giving out advice a while ago.

"I think that it's none of my business," she said lightly. She slid off her bar stool and reached for her umbrella.

"You can't go yet!" Amanda said. "We haven't caught up properly at all!"

"I know. But I'm in a rush." She leaned over and sort of patted Amanda (a hug would be going too far). "Good luck with the baby."

"Thanks, Grace. We'll let you know any news, won't we, Adam?"

"Just tell Martine," Grace said. "She'll pass it on."

Adam walked her to the door. "Are you sure you won't stay for a drink?"

"No. I'd better be getting back."

"All right," he said. "I'm glad you came, Grace."

"Me too."

She turned to face him at the door. He seemed awkward and inexperienced in a way that she had never seen before.

"Maybe we can meet up again sometime?" he said. "You know, when I'm back in Ireland . . ."

"Adam." She smiled at him affectionately. "Let's just say

371

goodbye, will we?"

"I suppose." He put out his hand to shake hers. "Goodbye, Grace."

"Oh, Adam." She brushed his hand aside and leaned in and kissed him on the cheek warmly. Then she turned and left the pub.

It was still pouring outside. She lifted her umbrella.

"Blast!"

It refused to yield to persuasion. She tried again. This time it went up halfway before two spokes snapped and reared malevolently through the black plastic. She huddled under it and made a dash across the road to her car, trying to dodge puddles on the way. Eventually she stopped trying to dodge them, and she began to jump from one to the other. She lifted the broken umbrella high over her head, and she did a little pirouette.

THE END